Francis Henry Underwood

John Greenleaf Whittier

A Biography

Francis Henry Underwood

John Greenleaf Whittier
A Biography

ISBN/EAN: 9783743305915

Manufactured in Europe, USA, Canada, Australia, Japa

Cover: Foto ©Raphael Reischuk / pixelio.de

Manufactured and distributed by brebook publishing software
(www.brebook.com)

Francis Henry Underwood

John Greenleaf Whittier

JOHN GREENLEAF WHITTIER

A Biography

BY

FRANCIS H. UNDERWOOD

AUTHOR OF "HENRY WADSWORTH LONGFELLOW, A BIOGRAPHICAL SKETCH,"
"JAMES RUSSELL LOWELL, A BIOGRAPHICAL SKETCH," ETC.

BOSTON
JAMES R. OSGOOD AND COMPANY
1884

UNIVERSITY PRESS:
JOHN WILSON AND SON, CAMBRIDGE.

One Ash, Rochdale, Sept. 9, 1883.

Dear Sir, — . . . I have had great pleasure in reading what my friend Mr. Whittier has written. He has done much to elevate the tone of public sentiment with you, and his services in your great struggle to free the colored portion of your population cannot be overestimated.

It is a great gift to mankind when Providence sends us a true Poet whose genius is distinguished by the purity which is visible in, and indeed is inseparable from, the writings of Mr. Whittier.

I think it a great compliment you pay me in proposing in any way to associate my name with the record of the life of a man for whom I feel no small degree of affection and of reverence. . . . Believe me

Very sincerely yours,

JOHN BRIGHT.

Francis H. Underwood, Esq.,
Boston, U. S. A.

PUBLISHERS' NOTICE.

This work was undertaken with the approval of Mr. Whittier, and in its preparation the author has received valuable assistance from relatives and friends of the poet. It is not intended as a critical study, but as a friendly guide and interpreter. The subject of the memoir is presented as a man as well as poet, and his public services and character are set forth with as much detail as is deemed proper. The letters now for the first time printed, and the early poems reproduced, have Mr. Whittier's sanction.

CONTENTS.

CHAPTER IV.

EARLY YEARS.

CHAPTER V.

YOUTH AND EARLY MANHOOD.

CHAPTER VI.

WRITING FOR THE PRESS.

CHAPTER VII.

SEEING SERVICE.

CHAPTER VIII.

POLITICAL MOVEMENT AGAINST SLAVERY.

CHAPTER IX.

TRIED BY FIRE.

CHAPTER X.

VOICES OF FREEDOM.

CHAPTER XI.

FOUNDATIONS OF FAME.

CHAPTER XII.

PROGRESS.

CHAPTER XIII.

PERSONAL MATTERS AND CURRENT COMMENT.

CHAPTER XIV.

LITERATURE AND REFORM UNITED.

CHAPTER XV.

IN WAR TIME.

CHAPTER XVI.

POEMS IN TIME OF PEACE.

CHAPTER XVII.

"AMONG THE HILLS."

CHAPTER XVIII.

FRIENDSHIPS.

CHAPTER XIX.

"HAZEL BLOSSOMS."

CHAPTER XX.

SEVENTIETH BIRTHDAY.

CHAPTER XXI.

"THE VISION OF ECHARD." — "THE KING'S MISSIVE."

CHAPTER XXII.

CHARACTERISTICS OF WHITTIER'S VERSE.

CHAPTER XXIII.

CONCLUSION.

———

APPENDIX.

———

LIST OF ILLUSTRATIONS.

INTRODUCTORY.

THAT all the world loves a poet is true chiefly of the poet whose songs are in the hearts of mankind. His birthplace becomes classic ground. His features, manners, traits, and habits are subjects of natural curiosity and lasting interest. The hills and streams he was familiar with are beautiful, if only because his eyes dwelt upon them; his haunts in the woods or shaded vales, his outlooks from the heights, are charming because he enjoyed them. If visible Nature filled his forming mind with the sources of poetic images, he in return impregnated the same scenes with his own spirit, and left, as it were, an immortal benediction upon them; so that the grandeur and beauty which first broke upon the poet is reflected back by the splendor of his genius, and his admirers in later days see all things in the newer lustre he gave them. The chair he sat in, the school-bench whereon he carved his name, the brook he followed for trout or in search of strange flowers, the secluded retreats he loved, the silent pool into which he looked for the fairy, — all these are pervaded as by an unseen presence. A thrill comes with every thought of contact transmitted from the beloved hand; the latch falters; the threshold throbs under foot; the fireplace glows and yearns; the wind croons in the chimney. Without, the elm-tree waves a welcome with its pendent arms; birds sing as if they had traditions of him who loved their race; the flocks gather in sympathetic groups; and the great barn, filled with the shorn beauty of the meadows, and with lines of patient cattle, opens its weather-beaten doors in invitation. All things lead the poet's disciples in his loved ways to the sources of his loved thoughts.

It is only poets that are thus universally loved and honored, because theirs are the distillations of thought made portable for the ages.

The subject of this sketch is a spontaneous, natural singer, to whom the Muse came in early youth unsought. Among eminent modern poets he is the one who has had fewest advantages of culture and travel, and has made the least show of scholarship. He was brought up under an austere rule, with a total denial of pleasure as the world esteems it;

and an unquestioning obedience to duty early took and maintained the place of boyish impulse.

From his birthplace no house or chimney-smoke was visible; it was a valley shut in by forests,— only hills, trees, and heaven in sight. He had few companions and fewer books; and he had known no more of the actual world than could be seen at a small seaport a dozen miles away. Yet while he was a boy of sixteen, toiling daily in the fields or tending sheep and cattle, he was already living a twofold existence; and, though untaught in literary art, he wrote poems for the county newspaper which educated men stopped to read and admire.

In observing the development of a poet and the growth of his fame, it is common to consider it a miraculous rise from obscurity; but Whittier was never obscure, even in the seclusion of his father's farm; the promise of genius was manifest in the first lines he wrote; and the delay of recognition on the part of the world,— was it an unusual circumstance?

We shall see, further, that his struggles and sufferings for conscience' sake have been no less remarkable than his purely intellectual efforts; that his services to humanity would have been memorable even if he had never penned a stanza; that the story of his life would have been a noble lesson even if the world had never felt its influence; and that he would have been loved and revered if his name had never gone beyond the limits of his native county.

The outward facts of a human life may be carefully recorded, and yet that life as it truly is may be quite beyond the biographer's grasp. The truth concerning a man (varying the celebrated formula of Holmes) may depend upon the point of view. It is the difference between what he thinks of himself, what others think of him, and what is the estimate by the Judge that never errs.

If it were not for an inborn shyness, the restraint of modesty, or for the religious desire of leading a purely inward life, the poet himself would best tell his own story. He alone could reveal the progress of his silent thoughts, and portray for us his hopes and fears at the time when he meditated his flight into the region of song.

Whoever has felt the power of Whittier's mind and heart in conversation must have been conscious of two strong forces in equipoise. His emotion is all-absorbing, yet his intellect is clear and just; and the Will (the only Ego we know) is seen balancing the promptings of feeling and the deductions of reason. We cannot doubt that in early days, before he was led to the almost sublime self-control which is the distinction of the Friends, he must have been often carried away by new-found conceptions, and impatient at the limits set for him by the Divine Providence. But an auto-biography or any trustworthy view of his interior life is not to be looked for.

Moreover, our poet has not been even ordinarily careful to preserve letters and memoranda to serve a biographer's turn. There are authors of less note whose intellectual luggage is assorted, inventoried, neatly done up and addressed to the care of posterity, ready to be delivered at the supreme moment. Unfortunately, much of it remains uncalled for on the hither bank of the Styx.

In Whittier's case the published poems are well known, and those which his later judgment rejected are not likely to appear for the gratification of the curious. His part in the great revolution in thought and morals which has distinguished our century is familiar to his contemporaries, and is to be read in the anti-slavery journals which it was the fashion to contemn. It is only necessary to make a faithful study of his works, and of the scenes and events he has illustrated, in order to interpret the poet, the philanthropist, and the man. It is a task full of pleasure, but not without difficulty.

A recital of the inevitable experiences of life is necessary, however old-fashioned or obsolete such a course may be considered by reviewers. Poets, like other human beings, have an earthly origin and often commonplace surroundings. When all the necessary details are gone over, perhaps the reader may be able to create for himself a picture of the man.

The experience of the author while making studies for this work leads him to believe that the most attentive and appreciative reader of poetry needs at times an interpreter. Many an allusion is passed over by those who are not familiar with the natural scenery, the legends and traditions of the poet's neighborhood, or with the events of his life, and the friends of his youth and his age. When fully illustrated, the poems of Whittier become his own life and experience. We trace his character in every line. We see the abounding sympathy and the love of beauty which were his inheritance. We mark, not unmoved, his simple content with poverty while he was toiling for the oppressed. We see also that the various poems form a charming itinerary of the Merrimac valley, the mountain and lake region of New Hampshire, and the coast of Maine. A stranger to those scenes has but vague impressions when he reads of

" The Laurels," " Artichoke **River**," " **Powow** Hill," " Deer Island," and " Hawkswood : " names remain only names.

Instead **of** assuming **a** purely critical office, it will be the aim of the author to show the character and work **of Whittier** as man and poet, **by** means of authentic personal narrations, **and by** references to the poems which **so** eloquently depict his inner life, and **to** those which have **given an undying** interest to some **of the most** beautiful scenes **in** New England.

JOHN GREENLEAF WHITTIER.

CHAPTER I.

ANCESTORS.

Thomas Whittier settles in Salisbury ; removes to Newbury, and afterwards to Haverhill. — His Son marries the Daughter of Joseph Peasley, a Quaker. — Intermarriage with Family of Greenleaf, also of Hussey. — Tradition of the Bachelor Eyes.

THOMAS WHITTIER, the first of the family in this country, was born in the year 1620, and sailed from Southampton, England, for Boston, Mass., in the ship "Confidence," of London, John Jobson, master, April 24, 1638. John Rolfe, his wife, Anne, and their daughter, Hester, were Whittier's companions on the voyage. Thomas subsequently married Ruth Green, who was Rolfe's sister, and settled in Salisbury, on the north shore of the Merrimac River, not far from its mouth. His land lay on the Powow River, a tributary of the Merrimac, and included a beautiful hill, which bears his name. His marriage probably took place in 1645 or 1646, as the birth of his first child, Mary, is recorded in August, 1647. He was deputy to the General Court from Salisbury, and was one of the commissioners who laid out the road from Salisbury to Haverhill. He afterwards lived for a time in Newbury, and in 1648 he removed to Haverhill, — both towns being situate on the same river. The town records of Haverhill mention that he brought with him a hive of bees, probably the first in the new settlement. His estate was rated at £80.

"Freemen," or voters, were admitted by the General Court, and not by the towns; and Whittier was not made a freeman until May 23, 1666. As various circumstances show that he was a capable man and a good citizen, we shall not err, probably, in supposing that the long delay in his admission to the body politic was owing to the fact that his opinions in regard to religious liberty did not accord with those of the ruling power. It is said that John Rolfe, his brother-in-law, was from the first an open opponent of the laws framed to secure uniformity of faith and practice in the churches of the Colony.

Thomas Whittier was certainly a man of blameless conduct; and various minutes in the town records attest the esteem in which he was held

during his **long and** tranquil life.[1] He remained
in fellowship with the church **in** Haverhill, while
it is certain **that he** inclined **in** heart to **the
Quakers, and held to many of** their **tenets. It is**
mentioned that during **the** Indian wars, in which
so many **of the** settlers were murdered, it was the
custom for neighbors to sleep together in fortified
houses ; but Whittier constantly refused such shel-
ter. Relying **on** the weapons of his faith alone,
he left his house unguarded, and unprotected **with**
palisades or arms. **The Indians** frequently **visited**
him ; and in the stillness of evening **the** family
often heard **them** whispering beneath **the** windows,
and sometimes saw their **grim faces** peering in
upon the defenceless group. But the Indians were

[1] **In** 1651 Thomas Whittier was one **of** a committee to **lay** out
the **bounds of** the plantation. In 1652 he was one of a large number of petitioners in Haverhill and other towns in the **Merrimac
valley for** the pardon **of** Lieutenant Robert Pike. The General
Court had passed an order prohibiting Joseph Peasley and Thomas
Macy, who were afterwards avowed Quakers, from exhorting on the
Lord's Day ; and Pike, having inveighed against the order as unchristian, was subjected to a heavy fine. The court made a show
of punishing some of the petitioners, also, but did **not** trouble those
in Haverhill. In 1669 Thomas Whittier was chosen constable and
compelled **to serve,** much against **his** will. The **constable was an**
important person in those days. **In** 1680 he **was one of the church**
committee **to look out for an** associate minister. In 1686 he was
appointed **to run** disputed and uncertain bounds among the settlers. (Chase's History of Haverhill.)

always treated civilly and even hospitably by him, and neither he nor any of his family or descendants was ever molested by them. Yet for many years houses were burned, and men, women, and children were tomahawked and scalped in all the river towns.

He settled upon a tract of land in the eastern part of the town, about three miles from the centre, and built for his family a log-house, in which he lived for a great many years; after which he erected the large and solidly framed house, half a mile northwest from the first, which has ever since been the home of a line of his descendants, and in which the poet was born.[1] The house was of two stories in front, while in the rear the roof sloped back to a single story. The rear part of the roof was raised, and the house otherwise improved, in 1801, by the poet's father.

Thomas Whittier died November 28, 1696. His wife survived him, dying in 1710. There were ten children, and all were living at the time of their mother's death, except the eldest, Mary. The

[1] The date of the erection of the house is not known. Mr. Whittier thinks it was not many years before the death of his ancestor. In a sketch written some years ago, he stated that the house was built "about the time of the overthrow of the Stuarts" (1688).

eldest son, John, administered upon the estate.
The line of descent to the poet **is** through Joseph,
the youngest child, who was born **May 8,** 1669,
and **was** married May 24, 1694, to Mary, daughter
of Joseph Peasley, whose residence was near Rocks
Bridge, and is standing to-day.[1]   **In** this alliance
with the family of a well-known Quaker we recognize one **of the** influences which led the Whittiers
to the new communion.

Joseph Whittier died December **25, 1739,** leaving nine children, **of** whom **the** youngest, also
named Joseph, born March **31, 1716, was the**
grandfather of the poet.   Joseph the younger was
married **to** Sarah Greenleaf, of Newbury,[2] and
died October 10, 1796.   Eleven children were the
fruit of this marriage.   John, the tenth child, was
born November 22, **1760, and was married Octo-**
ber 3, 1804, to Abigail, daughter of Joseph Hussey,
of Somersworth (now Rollinsford), **N. II., and**
died in June, **1832.**   Abigail, his wife, was born **in**
1781, and died December 27, 1857.   **The** children
of this marriage were four in number: (1) Mary,

---

[1] The house **was built of brick** brought over from England.

[2]   "**The name** the Gallic exile bore,
 St. Malo, from thy ancient mart,
 Became upon our Western shore
 Greenleaf for Feuillevert."
 WHITTIER's **poem** *to his grand-nephew,* "*A Name.*"

born September 3, 1806; (2) JOHN GREENLEAF, born December 17, 1807; (3) Matthew Franklin, born July 18, 1812, died January 7, 1883; (4) Elizabeth Hussey, born December 7, 1815, died September 3, 1864.

The line of descent, it will be seen, was almost continuously through younger sons; so that there were only four lives from 1620 to 1807, — a very remarkable fact. It is generally believed that the elder children of a family are likely to inherit more bodily vigor, and the younger more intellectual power. A descent derived through successive generations of younger sons might be expected to leave a peculiar impress upon the vital stamina and mental character of the last in the line; and it is perhaps not wholly accidental that our poet has been remarkable for an extreme sensitiveness coupled with nervous force, while all his life he has been in delicate health and has suffered from nervous headache.

Abigail Hussey, the poet's mother, was descended from Christopher Hussey, a fellow townsman with Thomas Whittier in Haverhill, who afterwards removed to Hampton, N. H., where he married the daughter of the Rev. Stephen Bachelor (sometimes written Batchelder), the first minister of that town. The Husseys came from Boston, England, and were **people of** distinction **both** in the old country and the new.[1]

The tradition is that Mr. Bachelor **was a man** of remarkable personal presence, and was particularly noticeable on account **of his** wonderful **eyes.** They were dark and deep-set under broad arches, and could throw lightning glances upon occasion. For more than a century the " Bachelor eye " has been proverbial **in** New Hampshire and in **Essex** County, Massachusetts, and **the** striking **feature has** been steadily perpetuated.

The resemblances **between** Whittier **and Webster** were long **ago** observed by those **who were** unaware of any relationship. Though unlike in many respects, there appeared to be a marked similarity in their broad and massive brows, **swarthy** complexions, and expressive **eyes. The** common characteristics of the eyes were **in looks of inscrutable** depth, the habit **of** shooting **out** sudden gleams, and the power **of** tender **and** soul-full expression as well. It is now known that not only Whittier and Webster, but William Pitt Fessenden, Caleb Cushing, **William B.** Greene, and other prominent men, inherited **their** fine features, penetrating eyes, and gravity **of** manner from the same

[1] Rev. A. P. Peabody, D.D., in a memoir written for the North American Review, January, 1859.

ancestor. The majestic bearing and presence of Webster were everywhere known. The keen glances of Cushing, the eminent scholar and diplomatist, and the deeper, haughtier looks of Colonel Greene are well remembered in Massachusetts.[1]

[1] Greene was educated at West Point, but he resigned from the army, married a famous beauty and heiress, daughter of Robert G. Shaw of Boston, and was for some years a Unitarian preacher. In the war of the Rebellion he commanded the 14th Massachusetts Regiment of Heavy Artillery. He was an able writer and an original thinker.

In the "Genealogy of the Whittier Family" there is a letter to the editor, D. B. Whittier, upon this subject, not without interest.

JAMAICA PLAIN, MASS., Sept. 24, 1873.

DEAR SIR, — Yours of September 20th is just received, and I reply to it at once. My grandfather, on my mother's side, was the Rev. William Batchelder, of Haverhill, Mass. In the year 1838 I had a conversation, on a matter of military business, with the Hon. Daniel Webster; and, to my astonishment, Mr. Webster treated me as a kinsman. My mother afterwards explained his conduct by telling me that one of Mr. Webster's female ancestors was a Batchelder. In 1838 or 1839, or thereabouts, I met Schoolmaster Coffin on a Mississippi steamboat near Baton Rouge. The captain of the boat told me, confidentially, that Coffin was engaged in a dangerous mission respecting some slaves, and inquired whether my aid and countenance could be counted on, in favor of Coffin, in case violence should be offered him. This he did because I was on the boat as a military man, and in uniform. When Coffin found he could count on me, he came and talked with me, and finally told me he had been hired by Daniel Webster *to go to Ipswich*, and there look up Mr. Webster's ancestry. He spoke of the Rev. Stephen Batchelder of New Hampshire, and said that Daniel Webster, John G. Whittier, and myself were related by Batchelder blood. I did not feel at all ashamed of my relatives. In 1841 or 1842 Mrs. Crosby, of Hallo-

well, Me., who had the charge of my grandfather when he **was a**
boy, and knew all about the family, told me that Daniel Webster
was a Batchelder, that she had known his father intimately, and
knew Daniel when he was a **boy.** At the time of my conversation
with her, Aunt Crosby might **have been** anywhere **from seventy-**
five to eighty-five years of **age.**

When I was a boy, at (say) about the year 1827 **or** 1828, I used
to go often to the house of J. G. Whittier's father, a little out of
the village (now city) of Haverhill, Mass. There was a Mrs.
Hussey in the family, who baked the best squash-pies I ever ate,
and **knew how** to make the pine **floors shine** like looking-glass.

This is, I think, all the information, **in answer to** your **request,**
that I am competent to **give you.**

Yours respectfully,
WILLIAM BATCHELDER GREENE.

CHAPTER II.

PURITANS AND QUAKERS.

Fox's Preaching a Protest against Formalism. — Puritans Intolerant because not Enlightened. — Splendor of Modern Worship unapostolical. — Quakerism an Inward Life. — Stripes, Imprisonment, and Death. — Quaker Influences in the Whittier Family.

WHEN Thomas Whittier settled in Haverhill, George Fox had just begun his career as iconoclast and apostle, but the advocates of the new doctrine did not appear in New England until a few years later. The body and form of Quakerism came from Fox, but the soul of the movement was not evolved from the thought of any one man. The religious portion of the English people, excluding the adherents of the despicable Charles II., as well as the church which was basely subservient to such an impious head, had long been in a state of ferment in regard both to doctrines and observances, and many, like Fox, had been seeking for a purely spiritual worship. The student of the life and times of Milton will remember with what fierce zeal religious disputes were conducted, **and** that dogmas which in our time are attacked and defended without a flutter **of the** pulse on either side **were** then bound as **with the** heart-strings **of** believers.

While a facile courtier like **Dryden** might one day elegize the great Cromwell, then welcome the restoration of the licentious Charles and the Established Church, and afterwards defend **the** doctrines **of** Rome in order **to please the** gloomy tyrant, James **II.,** the fervid zealots of **conventicles and** the preachers **of the** highways **and hedges were,** all of them, ready to die **for any** iota of **" the faith** once delivered to the saints,"* as they held it.*[1]

An exact classification of **the** dissenters of the seventeenth century would be impossible; but so far as concerns **New** England, they might **be** approximately divided **into** Independents **or** Puritans, disciples of Fox, and **the** followers of Roger Williams. The Quakers and **the** Baptists were insignificant

---

[1] " While Christianity was struggling against innumerable opponents, it displayed a life and an energy which diminished in proportion as the opposition was withdrawn. . . . Every religion, after being established, loses much of its vitality. . . . What was formerly a living truth dwindles into **a** dead dogma. . . . **Of** all evils, torpor is the most deadly. Give us paradox, give us error, give us what you will, so that you save us from stagnation. It is the cold spirit of routine which is the nightshade of our nature." — Buckle, *in his **review of** Mill on Liberty.*

minorities, and both were hunted out of the Colony like enemies of the human race.

The reader may like to renew his acquaintance with Carlyle's vigorous sketch of George Fox, copied from "Sartor Resartus:" —

"'Perhaps the most remarkable incident in Modern History,' says Teufelsdröckh, 'is not the Diet of Worms, still less the Battle of Austerlitz, Waterloo, Peterloo, or any other battle; but an incident passed carelessly over by most historians, and treated with some degree of ridicule by others: namely, George Fox's making to himself a suit of Leather. This man, the first of the Quakers, and by trade a Shoemaker, was one of those, to whom, under ruder or purer form, the Divine Idea of the Universe is pleased to manifest itself; and, across all the hulls of Ignorance and earthly Degradation, shine through, in unspeakable Awfulness, unspeakable Beauty, on their souls: who therefore are rightly accounted Prophets, God-possessed; or even Gods, as in some periods it has chanced. Sitting in his stall; working on tanned hides, amid pincers, paste-horns, rosin, swine-bristles, and a nameless flood of rubbish, this youth had, nevertheless, a Living Spirit belonging to him; also an antique Inspired Volume, through which, as through a window, it could look upwards, and discern its celestial Home. The task of a daily pair of shoes, coupled even with some prospect of victuals, and an honourable Mastership in Cordwainery, and perhaps the post of Thirdborough in his hundred, as the crown of long faithful sewing, — was nowise satisfaction enough to such a mind; but ever amid the boring and hammering came tones from that far country, came Splendours and Terrors; **for** this **poor** Cordwainer, as we said, was a Man; **and** the **Temple** of Immensity, wherein **as Man** he had been **sent to minister,** was full of holy mystery to him.

"'The clergy of the neighbourhood, the ordained Watchers and Interpreters of that same holy mystery, listened with unaffected tedium to his consultations, and advised him, as the solution of such doubts, **to "drink beer** and dance **with** the girls." Blind leaders of the blind! For **what** end were their tithes levied and eaten; **for what were** their shovel-hats scooped out, and their surplices **and cassock-aprons girt on; and** such a church-repairing, **and** chaffering, and organing, and other racketing, held **over** that spot of God's earth,—if **Man** were but a Patent **Digester,** and the Belly with its adjuncts the grand Reality? Fox turned from them, with tears and a sacred scorn, back to his leather-parings and his Bible. Mountains of encumbrance, higher than Ætna, had been **heaped over that** spirit: but **it was a** spirit, and would not lie buried there. Through long days **and nights** of silent agony, it struggled and wrestled, with a man's **force, to be free: how its** prison-mountains heaved and swayed tumultuously, as the giant spirit shook them to this hand and that, and emerged into the light of heaven! That Leicester shoe-shop, had men known **it,** was a holier place than any Vatican or Loretto shrine.—**"So** bandaged, and hampered, and hemmed in," groaned he, "with thousand requisitions, obligations, straps, tatters, and tagrags, I **can** neither see nor move: not my **own am I,** but **the** World's; and Time flies fast, and **Heaven** is high, and Hell is deep: Man!

bethink thee if thou hast power of Thought! Why not; what binds me here? Want, want!—Ha, of what? Will all the shoe-wages under the Moon ferry me across into that far Land of Light? Only Meditation can, and devout Prayer to God. I will to the woods: the hollow of a tree will lodge me, wild-berries feed me; and for clothes, cannot I stitch myself one perennial suit of Leather!"

" ' Let some living Angelo or Rosa, with seeing eye and understanding heart, picture George Fox on that morning when he spreads-out his cutting-board for the last time, and cuts cowhides by unwonted patterns, and stitches them together into one continuous all-including Case, the farewell service of his awl! Stitch away, thou noble Fox: every prick of that little instrument is pricking into the heart of slavery, and World-worship, and the Mammon-god. Thy elbows jerk, as in strong swimmer-strokes, and every stroke is bearing thee across the Prison-ditch, within which Vanity holds her Workhouse and Ragfair, into lands of true Liberty; were the work done, there is in broad Europe one Free Man, and thou art he!' "

Now, at the distance of two centuries, the question between a symbolic baptism and the actual immersion of a convert appears a very small matter. We cannot see how for the one form or the other Christian men should doom their fellows to death, or to a banishment which then meant delivering them over to the clubs and knives of savages. But year by year the Christian liberty for which Roger Williams contended has become a higher and nobler doctrine in the minds of men, and there is no son of the persecuting Puritans who does not hold the founder of Rhode Island in reverence.

In like manner the opinions of men have changed in regard to the once despised Quakers. What is to be the future development of Christianity no one can say. If its energies and resources are to be expended in building gorgeous temples, furnished with luxury and adorned with *chefs-d'œuvre* of art, wherein professional singers and musicians are employed to display their accomplishments, and great men give scholarly lectures to people of the highest fashion, that will be one thing. But if Christianity reverts to its primitive type, its home will be once more in " upper chambers," among humble and sincere believers who are alive with the Divine love, and from whose hearts worship arises as naturally as fragrance from flowers, — whose songs and ascriptions of praise are not echoes from either the opera or the mass, — who are not " conformed " to the world but are " unspotted " from it, and who live (in Milton's austere phrase)

> " As ever in their great Taskmaster's eye."

If primitive Christianity shall ever have a revival,

it will be as great a surprise and shock to the affluent and comfortable as were the simple truths of Jesus to the great and learned of his day. And though we are far from believing that all truth was revealed to Fox, or that the gentle and excellent Friends have the exclusive possession of all indisputable doctrines, or that they are wise in banning so many of the innocent enjoyments which are proper to the social nature of man, yet we shall probably find that in their teachings, and especially in their lives, they exemplify the spirit of the Evangelists and Apostles more fully than any sect of professing Christians.

The dominant class were just as sincere, God-fearing, and enthusiastic as the Quakers whom they persecuted. But they had, many of them, been trained to the use of arms in the civil wars, and their minds had taken on a military habit. In seeking for the Divine guidance in their many desperate straits, they had dwelt largely on the lessons and parallels of Jewish history. The bush that burned and was not consumed was perhaps more frequently in mind than the emblem of man's redemption. They thought habitually more of conquering Joshua than of the Man of Sorrows,— of triumphant Jael with her nail and hammer, rather than the *Mater dolorosa.* Cotton Mather

in his "Magnalia," Ward, in his "Simple Cobler
of Aggawam," and indeed all the writers of the
century, completely show the Hebraistic temper of
the Puritan church. They were uncompromising
because tolerance of error was crime; for them
there was no "dividual essence in truth." And
though we must in justice decide for them as
against the corrupt or worldly body they had left,
still we cannot but allow the force of Butler's en-
venomed satire: —

> " That stubborn crew
> Of errant saints whom all men grant
> To be the true Church Militant;
> Such as do build their faith upon
> The holy text of pike and gun;
> Decide all controversies by
> Infallible artillery;
> And prove their doctrine orthodox
> By apostolic blows and knocks."

The persecution of the Quakers has been considered in elaborate articles, on the one side and
the other, by our poet and the Rev. George E.
Ellis of Boston, upon the historical basis of "The
King's Missive." It is not within the province
of this work to renew that discussion. It is only
necessary to show in an adequate light the position
of Quakers in the Colony so far as may serve to
illustrate the poems of Whittier. And as he is

not a sentimentalist, but a man of deep and abiding convictions, stern in allegiance to duty and unbending to worldly courtesy, it is necessary for the reader to try to fix in mind the sincerity, spiritual-mindedness, and utter self-abnegation of the early Quakers, in order to appreciate the surging tides of feeling and the noble earnestness of these poetical tributes.

We are not to pass judgment upon the Puritans as statesmen. As has been observed, they had a difficult part to play. To keep terms with a hostile and jealous home government, to repel murderous savages and French Canadian guerillas, to maintain amity with the other Colonies, to curb the immorality of alien residents, and to keep heresy out of the churches, required an ubiquitous and sleepless vigilance. Toleration in their minds was no less a crime than heresy.[1]

The disciples of Fox came as missionaries, with full hearts and new-born zeal. The core and sub-

---

[1] "These absolute religions, like Islamism and Judaism, allow no participation : if they do not **reign,** they call themselves persecuted. If they feel themselves protected, they become exacting, and seek to render life impossible to other worships about them." — RENAN, *English Conferences : Rome and Christianity.*

"I dare averre that God doth no where in his word tolerate Christian States to give Tolerations to such adversaries of his Truth, if they have power in their hands to suppresse them." — REV. NATHANIEL WARD, *The Simple Cobler of Aggawam,* 1645–47.

stance of Christianity **was all in** all for them; **the** traditions that enveloped it and the forms that had been set up around **it** were naught. Steeples, pulpits and pews, clerical manners and dress, titles of reverend **or** rabbi, salaried expounders **of the** Word, outward rites of baptism and communion, formal service **of song,** pagan names of months and days, degrees and ranks **among men, orna-ments** in dress, **specious flowers of speech,**—all but the simple, central doctrine of faith **in** the **all-**Father, the Saviour **and** Mediator, and **the Holy** Spirit, the Comforter, they **put aside as** profane or useless.

The Puritans had rejected **the** stately service of the English Church, its gradations **of** priesthood, **its** organs and responses, the distinctive dress **of** its public servants, and the pathetic symbol **of the** cross. They had banished **the** festivities of Christmas, the penitence **of Lent, the** rejoicings **of** Easter, and had put **the** whole zodiac of saints' days in lasting eclipse. But still they **had** forms. The phrase " decently and in order" meant much; just as the word " formally " **in the** constitution **of** our State has stood in the way of reform **in** criminal procedure. Their " Sabbath " — quite different from Sunday — was celebrated according **to** unalterable rules. Worshippers were assigned places according to social rank.   A scholar or a gentleman was " Mr. "; the farmer or laborer was merely " Goodman."   This, after the magistrates and other dignitaries were provided for, was the main criterion in " seating the meeting."   Pastors were elevated in pulpits; and though at first the people were summoned to worship by blast of horn or beating of drum, yet as soon as wealth increased, the primitive log house gave way for a more imposing edifice, provided with a steeple and bell.   But the one striking fact was that the minister, or servant, upheld by the local magistrate, was as absolute as the Pope himself throughout the limits of the town.

Against all this the Quakers protested, and declaimed as Paul might have done.   They inveighed against all forms as fetters of the free soul.   The kingdom of heaven *is within you.*   The spirit of God dwells *in your hearts,* and not in temples made with hands.   The life of the Christian is *inward.* Nothing should come between the soul and the Divine Visitant.   To pray, teach, or prophesy, one needs only the prompting from within.   There is no class of Levites, to be fed by the brethren, for vicarious prayer and praise.   Tithes and first-fruits were abolished, with bloody sacrifices.   Give your cheek to the smiter, and when reviled revile not again. Cannon and gunpowder came from the bottomless pit. Shed no blood even in defence of your life. Conform not to the changing fashions of the vain and ungodly. Ruffles, chains, bands, and rings are badges of servitude to the prince of this world. Neither shall you swear, whether in anger, or at the command of a judge. Hath not the Judge of all said, " Swear not at all " ? Call no man master, or its mutilated diminutive, " Mr."

But, truly, to give a faithful copy of a Quaker's profession of faith and duty is so much like repeating the New Testament, that readers perhaps may choose to read it there for themselves.

We can readily see that such a harangue as is intimated above, filled out with good scriptural objurgation, might affect ministers and magistrates very unpleasantly. Though the very soul of early Christianity might pervade it, it would tend to frustrate the hopes and plans of the leaders for such a state as they had in mind. A strong, self-protecting, compact government was needed, not a loose aggregation of visionaries, without subordination and without a head.

The outward form of the Puritan commonwealth was simple enough. One house at first, afterwards two, — mostly composed of local magistrates, — formed the General Court. Then there was a governor and military officers, constables, and the like. But these temporal magnates had only the semblance of power; they were only the body-guard of the church, whose elders and ministers held unquestioned sway over the people, their liberties and laws. So omnipotent a theocracy has not been seen for ages. Woe to offenders, especially against doctrine or discipline! If the colonial statutes and orders of the court, or the laws of England, furnished no adequate penalty, the Pentateuch was an exhaustless armory. This secret prompting from within gave to Puritan jurisprudence a terrible edge. There might be instances where a tender-hearted magistrate would have relented; but the unseen clerical chancellor was inaccessible and pitiless.

In no other way can we account for such inhumanity as drove Ann Hutchinson into the wilderness to die. She had violated no law, unless, indeed, we allow the force of a criminal statute to an *obiter dictum* of St. Paul: "Let your women keep silence in the churches; for it is not permitted unto them to speak." Few people think Paul infallible on this point. As to doctrine, it would be difficult for any but a casuist to make clear the difference, if any there was, between this able woman's expositions and those of her clerical critics. The examination has been preserved, and its subtleties are as perplexing as the demonstration of "the identity of subject and object."

Well or ill founded, the decisions of the clergy were both law and fate for Quakers and other dissidents. Logic might be at fault, but the visible judge was a rock. Constables were "not to make reply," but lay on the lash when bid. A protest, or even a muttered complaint, might, as in the case of Lieutenant Robert Pike, be rewarded by a fine or the stocks.

It is not easy to overestimate the influence upon the sufferers of proscription for opinion's sake — for Christ's sake, we should say — when it has extended over the lives of generations. Each firm and faithful Friend came under the same hard conditions. True, the sun shone for him, flowers bloomed, and fertile fields rejoiced him; the hills imaged his steadfast faith; the solemn heavens drew his soul in adoration; God, brotherhood, and duty were his joys. But the world swept by with something of pity and more of disdain. The minister, the doctor, and the 'squire, the old-fashioned village trinity, wrapped themselves in importance, and regarded him as partly fanatic and always dangerous. At the beginning, the public preaching of a known Quaker was a sure course to martyrdom. It sometimes comes up to us as a novel and startling fact that for preaching according to conscience men and women were flogged with knotted whips, chained in loathsome dungeons, half starved, and banished under pain of death,—nay more, that men of blameless lives and of the very spirit of the Lord Jesus were actually hanged as malefactors on Boston Common! Do the trees remember the burden they bore? Are the relics of the martyrs now dust among their roots? If the world of nature ever sorrowed for the woes and crimes of man, what sounds should we hear on the winds? If the Divine Vengeance moved in wrath and storm, should we not wonder that tempests have not overthrown the accursed trees?

When by the efforts of a reluctant will these terrible scenes are reproduced in imagination, we can only wonder at the calm and unrevengeful spirit which has characterized the Quakers. And can we wonder that our poet's voice at times has the lofty tone of an ancient prophet?

In time the penal statutes against heresy were permitted to slumber. But meanwhile the fiery zeal of Quaker and other innovators had cooled. Neither reformers nor volcanoes continue in eruption beyond a certain period. For many reasons the Quakers made few proselytes. They made too many demands upon self-indulgent **human** nature, and their worship **was** so entirely spiritual that **there** was nothing for common minds **to** take hold **of.** They gave less and less effort to the thankless task of turning Puritans from the errors of their ways, and bestowed their labors more among their own communities. They were no less sincere than was Fox, and **if** persecuted would **go** to judgment and execution as courageously **as** did the martyrs **in** Boston; **but there was no** longer occasion, **as** opposition was dying **out on** both sides. Still, **the** old prejudice lingered, **and the** severe costume of a Quaker, like the beard **of** a Jew, continued to be the badge of an alien race. Time softened the hearts of bigots, and wore off the sharp edges of dogmas; but this was not until Church and State had been divorced, and **not** until the Quaker's memory **of the days of** bitterness **had** become **as** unchanging as his sad-colored garments. He could say, and he can still say, in no unchristian spirit, —

> " Good by, proud world! I 'm going home;
> Thou 'rt not my friend, and I 'm not thine."

To return to Thomas Whittier after this long digression. Although **he** appears **to** have inclined to the new doctrine, and may have received it in his heart, **he did** not, **so far as is** known, openly **break** with the church. But his sympathies were no secret among his neighbors. His children, probably, belonged to the Society of Friends. His son, Joseph, ancestor of our poet, married the daughter of Joseph Peasley, the Quaker already mentioned. Peasley and Macy had been exhorting openly or secretly from 1652 to 1659. In the latter year four Quaker missionaries from Salem visited the river towns, including Haverhill, and there is little doubt that Thomas Whittier and his family " heard them gladly." The names of three are known : Edward Wharton, William Robinson, and Marmaduke Stevenson. The two latter were hanged shortly after on Boston Common.

Thomas Macy was at that time a resident of Salisbury, and these travelling Quakers called at his house for rest and refreshment. He was prosecuted, under the law of 1657, for entertaining them, and appeared to answer. His plaintive letter to the General Court has been preserved.[1] He was ordered to pay a fine of thirty shillings, but he managed to escape after sentence without payment, and put out to sea in an open boat. He sailed past the capes and arrived in safety at the island of Nantucket, where he took up his abode. This incident forms the basis of one of Whittier's early and best known ballads, " The Exiles."

[1] Coffin's History of Newbury, p. 63.

It is not likely that all the members of the Whittier family were Quakers. In the History of Haverhill we find mention of Whittiers with military titles. Particular mention is made of a Colonel Whittier who was offered command of a regiment to go against Ticonderoga during the French War. But from the earliest time to the present most of the name have been known as Quakers.

CHAPTER III.

A QUAKER HOME.

THE Whittier house is more open to view from
the main road than it was sixty years ago.
The woods that hemmed it in have been mostly
cleared, enlarging greatly the fields of pasture and
meadow. The house faces southward, and in
front is a grass-plat sloping towards a small but
faithful brook. Here on this sunny slope it was
that " once a garden smiled; " and at its western
corner rose the tall well-sweep, since displaced by
the prosaic pump. The little brook comes from
a marshy tract on a higher level, and gurgles
pleasantly through a narrow rocky ravine, in which
are the rude remains of a dam; although one must
needs wonder that such a prattling rivulet could
ever have mustered the force to turn a mill-wheel.
The brook with its natural fringe of bushes, and

the abrupt bank of trees behind, forms a charming scene in the still valley. Whittier says that in his youth the little brook used to be very noisy; " it foamed, rippled, and laughed." Little Brook runs into Country Brook. " On its banks we could always find the earliest and latest wild-flowers, from the pale blue three-lobed hepatica, and small, delicate wood-anemone, to the yellow bloom of the witch-hazel, burning in the leafless October woods." The brook afforded fine fishing, to which Uncle Moses was much devoted. Whittier says that one of the great pleasures of his brother and himself was to accompany the good uncle on his expeditions. Looking beyond the brook and the strip of forest, we see the indications of a travelled road running east and west ; and rising abruptly from its farther side is Job's Hill, a smooth, round grassy knoll, perhaps three hundred feet in height. From this eminence there is a beautiful view of the country around. The foliage is rich and varied in the immediate vicinity, and the country is seen to consist of softly rounded elevations, — broad and flattened domes, — lovely in color, and relieved by charming groups of trees. Westward lies Lake Kenoza, half obscured, half revealed, among clumps and thickets. Toward the north is a narrow but distant opening into the mountain region, through which the Saddleback of Deerfield, N. H., is seen on the far horizon. On fine days, looking to the northeast, the pyramidal form of Agamenticus can be traced against the sky. It is in the autumn that this landscape is seen at its best. The varieties of trees are numerous, furnishing a wealth of contrasts and complements of color. Prominent are the oaks with masses of deep foliage, ranging from russet to maroon and purple red; the walnuts show brilliant yellows, and the maples are party-colored,— orange, green, and spotty red; the pines are deep green, and the firs and spruces still darker. In the lower grounds are masses of scarlet interspersed with sedgy greens and soft tufts of brown. There is no region known to the writer in which there is such a gorgeous autumnal display.

Returning to the house, we observe southeasterly a tract of black bog, civilized into a fair field of wet grass; and this is screened from the road by a line of pollard willows, so grotesque that they may have looked to a young poet's eyes like dwarfed and bristly monsters. Westward is a high ridge, with trees towering here and there. Behind the house is the ancient orchard, and near it in a sheltered spot was the barn. Beyond the orchard rises a clump of oaks, near which the generations of Whittiers were laid to rest.[1] The neighborhood road, crossing **the main road** at right angles near the brook, leads northward, passing the house **on the** east side. The modern barn **and** other farm buildings are opposite the house, **across** the road. A short distance northward, on this road, is the Whittier elm, a tree of great size and **antiquity.** Not far from it stood the old garrison house, a place of refuge from the Indians long **ago,** which the poet well remembers.[2]

[1] Within a few years the remains of the dead have been removed to the burying-ground in Amesbury.

[2] "In 1690 six garrisons were established in different parts of the town, with a small company of soldiers attached to each. Two of these houses are still standing. They were built of brick, two stories, with a single outside door, so small and narrow that but one person could enter at a time ; the windows were few, and only about **two feet** and a half long by eighteen inches wide, with thick diamond glass **secured** with lead, and **crossed** inside with bars of iron. The basement had but two rooms, and the chamber was entered by a ladder instead of stairs ; so that **the** inmates, if driven thither, could cut off communication with the rooms **below.** Many private houses were strengthened and fortified. We remember **one** familiar to our boyhood, — a venerable old building of wood, with brick **be-**tween the weather-boards and ceiling, with a massive balustrade over the door, constructed of oak timber and plank, with holes through the latter for firing upon assailants. The door opened upon a stone-paved hall, or entry, leading into **the** huge single room of the basement, which was lighted by **two** small windows, **the** ceiling black with the **smoke of a century and a half: a huge** fireplace, calculated for eight-feet **wood,** occupying **one** entire side ; while overhead, suspended from the timbers, or on shelves fastened to

The house, as has been stated, was built before the year 1694, and probably about the year 1688. In externals it has been somewhat changed of late years, but within it remains substantially as it was in the period in which " Snow Bound " was located. New clapboards and window caps, as well as new outer doors and sashes, all in fresh paint, have given the old home a spruce, modern look. But some of the ancient carpentry remains ; and there are still in use quaint iron door handles, latches, and hinges, which Puritan smiths hammered out two centuries ago. Some of the original doors, too dilapidated for service, are stored in an outbuilding. The glass in the windows is modern, except a few panes in the kitchen and chambers. The sturdy chimney has been newly topped, but its antiquity is evident when its huge mass is seen in the open space of the large back chamber. One sees that the chimney was the central idea of a new settler's home. The kitchen fireplace, once broad enough

them, were household stores, farming utensils, fishing-rods, guns, bunches of herbs gathered perhaps a century ago, strings of dried apples and pumpkins, links of mottled sausages, spareribs, and flitches of bacon ; the firelight of an evening dimly revealing the checked woollen coverlet of the bed in one far-off corner, while in another

> ' The pewter plates on the dresser
> Caught and reflected the flame, as shields of armies the sunshine.' "

J. G. WHITTIER, *Literary Recreations : The Boy Captives.*

to admit benches on either side, has now been narrowed by rows of bricks, thereby closing a curious cave of an oven, buried in the recess.

The square front rooms are unchanged. The marks of their century are upon every part of the work: strength and simplicity. The oaken beams, which a man of fair height can touch with an upraised hand, are fifteen inches square, and as firm as when laid. The wainscots and floors are well preserved.

At one end of the kitchen was a bedroom known as the mother's room; but it was in the west front room that our poet saw the light. The small chamber overhead is the one he occupied when a boy. A flight of well-worn steps leads up to it from the kitchen. Above are the time-stained rafters and the boards pierced with nail-points which used to glisten like powdered stars on frosty mornings. Here it was, as the poet has told us, where, on stormy nights, —

> " We heard the loosened clapboards tost,
> The board-nails snapping in the frost ;
> And on us, through the unplastered wall,
> Felt the light sifted snow-flakes fall."

If readers can recall the parts of this description, and look upon this old farm-house from a proper point without, it will be seen that if there were once more a garden in front, a tall well-sweep at the left, the barn and sheds in the rear, and if the oaks on every side were renewed, — sturdier, thicker, nearer, — the place would be once more as it was when Whittier was a boy.

The silent valley produces an impression of remoteness. Owing to the variety of surface and soil, the trees, shrubs, grasses, and wild flowers include a wide range of species; and the birds and squirrels, as well as woodchucks, water-snakes, and other aquatic animals, and all the bright-eyed skulkers in lonely haunts, have long found in this spot a home.

If one should desire to indulge in the effusively picturesque style, there are materials; but, truth to say, the scene is not remarkably beautiful as compared with many in that most lovely part of Massachusetts. On a drive from Newburyport to Haverhill, on either bank of the river, one can find views far more noble and impressive, — grander forms of hills, with coils and stretches of blue river, leafy arches over silent canals, glimpses of silvery lakes, and undulating pastures.

No; the Whittier homestead is not beautiful, as artists consider beauty; but sweet and tender memories render our eyes misty as we look upon it; and with such associations there comes a feeling which the artist of mere beauty can never create. The scene is quiet, unmodernized, **near to** aboriginal nature, and suggestive of **a** calm simplicity that **asks for no** admiration,—**as** if a segment of another century had survived the changes of time.

It is a scene in which we should naturally expect to see the steeple-hatted farmer, **in** woollen hose and doublet, following his team afield; **the matron in** her coif, **with a** kerchief "over **her decent** shoulders drawn," sitting by the **door at her** spinning-wheel; the comely daughters hanging festoons of sliced apples **to dry; the** boys tending cattle in the lush meadows; while groups of deer, fearless of hounds, were cropping grass and twigs on the heights.

The land **is only** moderately **fertile, and could** never have **been the source** of wealth **to the most** laborious cultivator. **In** the **town assessment for** 1798, the farm stands **as** the joint property **of** Joseph, John, and Moses, and is rated at $200, much below **its** probable value. At all events, when **in 1806** Joseph married and removed **to** Maine, his share was bought by John, father **of** our poet, for **$600. This** sum was borrowed, and **the** interest, even, **was** felt **as a** burden. **The** debt remained during the **father's** life, and was **at** last cleared **by** the exertions of the son.

It will not do to infer from such details that the
family was actually poor, although money must
have been generally scarce. In those days the
wants of men and women were fewer, or the spirit
of self-denial and personal independence was more
common. Each household had its plentiful supply
of food from the crops and herds and the river;
the field of flax and the annual fleeces, spun and
woven at home, furnished most of the necessary
clothing; neighborhood exchanges distributed com-
forts; and surplus wood, nuts, grain, and other
farm produce helped to balance the account of the
country store. The present generation, accustomed to a totally different life, cannot understand
the content of their ancestors with their plain fare,
coarse clothes, an unvarying round of duties, and a
succession of rustic pleasures. Every natural want
was supplied, and, little as they had to spend, poverty was unfelt, or rather unknown.

We know further, by the testimony of neighbors,
that the Whittiers were esteemed as comfortable,
well-to-do people, and they counted among their
friends the best of the town. A cousin,[1] whose
notes will frequently aid us, writes : —

" The social privileges of the family were among
the best which Haverhill and its neighborhood afforded.

[1] Mrs. Gertrude W. Cartland, of Newburyport, Mass.

The father was frequently in the public service of the town, and was intimate with such prominent men as the late Judge Minot, Colonel J. II. Duncan, a Member of Congress, Moses Wingate, State Senator, and Sheriff Bartlett, grandfather of General Bartlett, one of the most noble of the heroes of the late war. Parson Tompkins, also, was as frequent a guest at the Whittier fireside as in the homes of his own parishioners.

" The visits of travelling Friends were also an important element in the social and religious life of the family. The Friends of New England were widely scattered, and the attendance upon their annual meeting, held at Newport, R. I., before the days of railroads, often involved a journey of several days, which they generally performed in their own carriages, receiving hospitable entertainment on the way at the houses of their fellowmembers. And it is remembered that on one occasion no fewer than sixteen were entertained one night at the Whittier mansion.

" Ministers from England also were frequently in this country, making visits to the meetings and families of friends. Among the eminent men of this class was William Forster, father of Hon. William Edward Forster, late member of the Gladstone cabinet. The poet has commemorated the visit in a poem beginning : —

> ' The years are many since his hand
> Was laid upon my head.' " [1]

[1] He died in East Tennessee, January, 1854, while engaged in presenting to the governors of the States of this Union the address of his religious society on the evils of slavery. See Note 61, in Whittier's Poems.

Those whose memory reaches back fifty years, and especially those who were reared in places remote from large towns, will find in "Snow Bound" perfect pictures of the old times. The poet himself calls them Flemish pictures; and it is true they have much of the homely fidelity of Teniers, but they are far more than literal representations. The scenes glow with ideal beauty,— all the more for their bucolic tone. The works and ways of the honest people are almost photographically revealed; and we have afterwards nothing but recollections of cheerful piety, modest and steadfast truth, and heart-felt love. There is but one counterpart in the language: the "Cotter's Saturday Night" of Burns; and that is comparatively limited in scope and less poetical in treatment. An exposition of "Snow Bound" such as could be given by a man of sympathy and knowledge would be a typical history of a New England family half a century ago.

While referring to this poem it is probably best to notice the family portraits. They are exquisite, both in tone and in details.

Readers will remember the one beginning:—

> "Our uncle, innocent of books,
>   Was rich in lore of fields and brooks.
>
>   .   .   .   .   .

> Himself to Nature's heart **so near**
> That all her voices in his ear
> Of beast or bird had meanings clear.
>
> .   .   .   .   .
>
> A simple, guileless, childlike man,
> Content to live where life began."

This **was** Uncle Moses, who lived with the poet's father, and was remarkable for **the** blamelessness and simplicity of his life.

Mr. C. C. Chase, a neighbor of the Whittiers years ago, writes : —

"**He was a man** for **the little folks to love.** . . . I well remember the **shock** which the neighborhood felt when the news spread that Uncle Moses had been killed. [This was in 1824.] **He** had felled a tree in the woods which had lodged against another tree. **To** bring the first to the ground, he felled **the second tree.** The two dropped **at** the same time, and, taking **unexpected** directions, he was caught and killed by one of them. **On a** bitterly cold **day** the good old man was carried **to** his grave, beside those of his relatives, **in the** corner **of a** field **a few rods in the rear of the** house. He comes to my mind **as a tall,** plain, sober man, far less stout and stirring than his brother John."

We are also indebted **to Mr.** Chase for pleasant recollections of **the poet's mother and** aunt : —

"Whittier's **mother was a** woman of natural refinement **of** manners. Being **a** friend **of my** mother, she never failed, when she saw me, politely to inquire for her. Her language was always the same. '*How do thee do, Charles? — and how is thy mother?*' Her face was full and very fair. Her bearing was dignified rather than lively. The word 'benign' best comprehends the expression of her features. She was loved and honored in the neighborhood.

"Her sister, Aunt Mercy Hussey, was for many years an honored member of the family. She, as I remember her, though a person of less dignity of bearing, had a face which revealed a singular sweetness of temper. She was a devout member of the Society of Friends.

"The dress of the two ladies I well remember. The plain Quaker caps, so comely and so spotless, and the neatness and fitness of their whole attire attracted my youthful fancy. They seemed to me to combine all that was sweet, lovable, and excellent in woman."

There is a portrait of the mother, by Lawson, in the Amesbury home of the poet. It is full of calm sense, goodness, and benevolence. In "Snow Bound" there is a brief reference to her: —

> "Our mother, while she turned her wheel,
>   Or run the new-knit stocking-heel,
>   Told how the Indian hordes came down
>   At midnight on Cochecho town.
>   .   .   .   .   .
>   Then, haply, with a look more grave,
>   And soberer tone, some tale she gave
>   From painful Sewall's ancient tome,
>   Beloved in every Quaker home,
>   Of faith fire-winged by martyrdom."

The tender description of the aunt should be
referred to : —

> " **Next,** the dear aunt, **whose** smile **of cheer**
> And voice in dreams I see and **hear,** —
> **The** sweetest woman ever Fate
> Perverse denied a household mate.
> .   .   .   .   .
>
> For well she kept her genial mood
> And simple faith of maidenhood ;
> Before her still **a** cloud-land lay,
> The mirage loomed across her **way ;**
> .   .   .   .   .
>
> Through years **of toil and soil and care,**
> From glossy tress to thin gray **hair,**
> All unprofaned she held apart
> **The** virgin **fancies of the heart."**

The father **of the** household **is a** more silent
force, **and is** not **so** strongly limned.   **But the**
lines in which he **is** mentioned are interesting **as**
showing his adventures in early life, when one
vast **forest stretched** from Southern **New Hamp-**
shire to Canada.   **We see** him skirting **the north-**
ern **lakes,** camping with Indians and trappers, and
enjoying a hunter's **fare ;** then among the *habi-*
tans of St. Francis, **where for** him

> " The moonlight shone
> **On** Norman cap **and** bodiced zone ; "

and where

> " **He heard the** violin play
> Which led the village dance away."

Then come reminiscences of the early residence of his ancestor, —

> "Where Salisbury's level marshes spread,"

with all the sights and sounds of the sea.

Then the poet's elder sister, Mary, is recalled : —

> "A full, rich nature, free to trust,
> Truthful and almost sternly just,
>
> .   .   .   .   .
>
> Keeping with many a light disguise
> The secret of self-sacrifice."

Next we see where

> "Upon the motley-braided mat
> Our youngest and our dearest sat,
> Lifting her large, sweet, asking eyes."

This was Elizabeth, a noble woman, whose crayon portrait is also preserved in the Amesbury house.

In another place the remaining child of the family group is apostrophized : —

> "Ah, brother ! only I and thou
> Are left of all that circle now."

This was Matthew Franklin, a resident of Boston, who died January 7, 1883.

One of the most memorable passages in " Snow Bound " is that beginning : —

> "Another guest that winter night
> Flashed back from lustrous eyes the light."

The picture of the woman, as well as the analysis of her puzzling character, is done with exceeding care. It is evidently founded on observation, and not a creation of the fancy ; and how powerful was the impression made upon the susceptible boy, is shown by the wonderful reproduction of all its force and all its delicacy after so many years. It is not to be supposed that a picture like this is to be taken as a likeness in every respect. There is, however, little doubt that, aside from allowable poetic license, this is a portrait of a brilliant and eccentric lady named Harriet Livermore, a native of Newburyport, who used to visit the Whittier family. One paragraph will recall her wayward mode of life : —

> " Since then what old cathedral town
> Has missed her pilgrim staff and gown, —
> What convent-gate has held its lock
> Against the challenge of her knock !
> Through Smyrna's plague-hushed thoroughfares,
> Up sea-set Malta's rocky stairs,
> Gray olive slopes of hills that hem
> Thy tombs and shrines, Jerusalem,
> Or startling on her desert throne
> The crazy Queen of Lebanon
> With claims fantastic as her own,
> Her tireless feet have held their way ;
> And still, unrestful, bowed, and gray,
> She watches under Eastern skies,
> With hope each day renewed and fresh,
> The Lord's quick coming in the flesh,
> Whereof she dreams and prophesies !

> " Where'er her troubled path may be,
>   The Lord's sweet pity with her go !
> The outward, wayward life we see,
>   The hidden springs we may not know."

She had a certain exaltation of mind that bordered on insanity, and children were heartily afraid of her, for she was very sharp towards them, as well as towards such older persons as she did not incline to. In the course of her travels in Syria she met Lady Hester Stanhope, a woman, if possible, more fantastic and strained in mind than herself. She lived with this " crazy Queen of Lebanon " for some time, but at length quarrelled with her concerning the propriety of keeping two white mares saddled in her stable on which to ride into Jerusalem in company with the Lord at his second coming !

With this interpretation Whittier's lines have a singular subtilty, — resembling, in effect, certain airy shadows that hover (and seem even to waver while you look) between the shoulders of the fruit-seller in Murillo's picture. We have in one masterly picture the fascinating yet uncanny exterior, and the complexity of caprices, whims, and jealousies, and of mutually repelling mental traits.

What a character for Hawthorne !

Every line in this delightful poem has its meaning. It is not difficult to return in imagination to that modest, cheerful home, and to behold the members of the family and the two guests around the great blazing fire. We should miss modern elegance in that kitchen, but we should see faces of intelligence, lighted by tranquil affection, and hear the delightful accents in which heart speaks to heart, — the soft *thee* and *thou*, for which the speech of the great world has no equivalent.

In such a home only the purest and noblest natures are bred.

Nearly all the persons that composed that group around the kitchen fire have since died, and their bodies rest together in the old burying-ground in Amesbury. In a lot enclosed by a hedge of arbor vitæ are six head-stones of white marble, bearing the following inscriptions : —

John Whittier, d. 11th of 6th mo., 1831, ag. 70.
Abigail Whittier, d. 27th, 12th mo., 1857, aged 77.
Moses Whittier, d. 23d, 1st mo., 1824, aged 61.
Mercy E. Hussey, died 4th mo., 14th, 1846.
Mary W. Caldwell, daughter of John and Abigail Whittier, d. 1st mo. 7, 1861, aged 64.
Elizabeth H. Whittier, d. 3d, 9th mo., 1864, aged 48.

Matthew Franklin Whittier has since been buried in the same lot.

CHAPTER IV.

EARLY YEARS.

The Poet's Childhood. — His Schooling, Books, and Religious
Training. — The Barefoot Boy hears Scotch Songs. — Joshua
Coffin brings a Volume of Burns. — Air-castles and Verses. —
Garrison's " Free Press." — Preparation for the Academy.

IN the spot we have endeavored to sketch, John
Greenleaf Whittier was born, December 17,
1807. His father had married at a later age than
common, and was then forty-seven. He was kind
and just, but a man of few words. The uncle,
Moses, was an inmate of the house, and remained
with the family until his death, which occurred
when the poet was seventeen years of age. Though
an elderly man, he was a beloved companion of
children, and was like an elder brother to his
nephews. Most of the pleasant associations of boyhood are connected with wood-craft and the rural
amusements in which the good uncle was such an
adept; and we may add that the brilliant points of
description and the natural images which abound

in Whittier's poems have their origin in the thorough familiarity with nature gained unconsciously in early years.

He went to school at seven years of age, and his first teacher was Joshua Coffin, who was also his lifelong friend. The school was kept in a private house, as the school-house was undergoing repairs. Coffin was afterwards the author of an excellent History of Newbury, a model of its kind. He was an able though apparently eccentric man, and in various ways he was of the greatest service to the future poet. But the schoolmaster who has a prominent place in "Snow Bound" was not Coffin, but an unnamed student from Dartmouth College. The passage referring to him is too long to be inserted here, although readers will be pleased to recall the opening lines : —

> " Brisk wielder of the birch and rule,
> The master of the district school
> Held at the fire his favored place ;
> Its warm glow lit a laughing face
> Fresh-hued and fair, where scarce appeared
> The uncertain prophecy of beard."

There was a private school the following summer, kept by Madam Chadbourne, of Newburyport. Usually, however, there was but one term of school in the year, lasting three months. The school-house was half a mile distant, on the north road.[1] There was usually a new master every winter, and on the whole the facilities for education appear to have been very scanty. A pupil at this day in a first-class school would probably have more opportunities in two years of forty weeks each than were afforded to Whittier in the whole period of his youth. We have no information as to his rank or acquirements, but we shall see by the results, farther on, that *somehow* he had managed to amass a store of information, and to acquire an unusual mastery over his mother tongue.

If his school training was confined to narrow limits, his opportunities for reading were even less gratifying. There were about twenty volumes in the house, mostly journals and memoirs of pioneers in the religious society. One of the books was a poem by Ellwood, the English Quaker and the friend of Milton, entitled "The Davideis." We infer that the boy found it dreary. It has disappeared from view in our times.[2] In a brief autobiographic leaflet Mr. Whittier tells us that he was

---

[1] It was in a tolerable state of preservation until a few years ago, when it was proposed to move it into the centre of Haverhill; but after it had been transported for some distance on the road it was burned by thoughtless boys for sport.

[2] Whittier still has the ancient volume. A more dull and tasteless production can hardly be imagined.

fond of reading at an early age, and that when he heard, now and then, of a book of biography or travel, he would walk miles to borrow it. But in those early years the bulk of his reading was in the Bible. Mrs. Cartland writes : —

"In the Whittier family the reading of the Holy Scriptures was a constant practice. On First-day afternoons especially the mother would read them with the children, endeavoring to impress their truths by familiar conversation ; and to this early and habitual instruction we may attribute in great measure the full and accurate knowledge of Bible history which the poems of J. G. Whittier indicate, as well as the strong bias in favor of moral reforms which was so early manifested. It is a tradition in the family that when J. G. Whittier was very young he often sought from his father and others a solution of his doubts respecting the morality of certain acts of the patriarchs and other holy men of old ; and at one time he declared that King David could not have been a member of the Society of Friends, because he was a man of war."

In a simple, uneventful way his years were passed. He was constantly employed, as he tells us in the leaflet, when not at school. "At an early age I was set at work on the farm and doing errands for my mother, who, in addition to her ordinary house duties, was busy in spinning and weaving the linen and woollen cloth needed for the family." There was no time to be " killed," and *ennui* had not then been invented. The service was unremitting, but a cheerful temper kept it from being irksome; and in a family of which every member practised thrift of time and the concentration of thought and purpose, the steady round of duties was as natural as the rotation of the earth.

The Friends' meeting-house was in Amesbury, eight miles eastward, and thither on First-day mornings the father and mother, and sometimes one of the children, were accustomed to ride. The poet says in reference to this: "I think I rather enjoyed staying at home, wandering in the woods, or climbing Job's Hill."

If he preferred Sunday rambles in pleasant weather, he must have been still more reluctant in winter to encounter the cold in the long drives to meeting. The early settlers came with traditions of England into a climate like that of Russia. It has taken two centuries to get it fixed in the minds of people that against our arctic cold there should be an abundant provision of furs, wraps, and blankets. In Whittier's youth buffalo robes were unknown; so were the huge warm overcoats now so common; few people even wore any heavy flannel underclothing. The cloth woven by farmers' wives, though firm and serviceable, was comparatively thin, — not at all like "beaver" and other felt-like or fuzzy fabrics which are now in use. The suffering from cold was intense in those days, and Mr. Whittier has a most keen recollection of it.[1]

There are continual glimpses of Whittier's early life to be seen by the intelligent observer in going through the works. "The Barefoot Boy" is clearly autobiographical, and between its simple lines we look as through magic lenses into the very heart of his childhood.

> "I was rich in flowers and trees,
> Humming-birds and honey-bees;
> For my sport the squirrel played,
> Plied the snouted mole his spade;
> For my taste the blackberry cone
> Purpled over hedge and stone;
> Laughed the brook for my delight
> Through the day and through the night,
> Whispering at the garden wall,
> Talked with me from fall to fall;
> Mine the sand-rimmed pickerel pond,
> Mine the walnut slopes beyond,
> Mine, on bending orchard trees,
> Apples of Hesperides.
>
> . . . . . .
>
> O for festal dainties spread,
> Like my bowl of milk and bread, —
> Pewter spoon and bowl of wood,
> On the door-stone, gray and rude!

[1] S. T. Pickard, Esq., in Portland Transcript.

> O'er me, like a regal tent,
> Cloudy-ribbed, the sunset bent,
> Purple-curtained, fringed with gold,
> Looped in many a wind-swung fold."

A slight incident appears to have given a new direction to his thoughts, as well as new views of nature and life. He tells us[1] that wanderers frequently made their appearance at the house and were entertained ; and in this way he came to know many queer and eccentric characters. Wanderers, or tramps, are possibly plenty nowadays, but they get small encouragement at most farm-houses. It is not generally believed, in regard to this class, that among them many angels are entertained unawares. He mentions one in particular to whom he was indebted for a new sensation.

"One day we had a call from a ' pawky auld carle ' of a wandering Scotchman. To him I owe my first introduction to the songs of Burns. After eating his bread and cheese and drinking his mug of cider, he gave us Bonnie Doon, Highland Mary, and Auld Lang Syne. He had a full, rich voice, and entered heartily into the spirit of his lyrics. I have since listened to the same melodies from the lips of Dempster (than whom the Scottish bard has had no sweeter or truer interpreter) ; but the skilful performance of the artist lacked the novel charm of the gaberlunzie's singing in the old farm-house kitchen."

[1] " Yankee Gypsies," in Literary Recreations, p. 355.

In the same lively essay he tells us of another wanderer, named Jonathan Plummer, that appeared to have a regular orbit. His description of this odd genius is too amusing to be merely summarized, and we give it as it stands.

"Twice a year, usually in the spring and autumn, we were honored with a call from Jonathan Plummer, maker of verses, peddler and poet, physician and parson, — a Yankee troubadour, — first and last minstrel of the valley of the Merrimac, encircled, to my wondering young eyes, with the very nimbus of immortality. He brought with him pins, needles, tape, and cotton thread for my mother; jackknives, razors, and soap for my father; and verses of his own composing, coarsely printed and illustrated with rude woodcuts, for the delectation of the younger branches of the family. No love-sick youth could drown himself, no deserted maiden bewail the moon, no rogue mount the gallows, without fitting memorial in Plummer's verses. Earthquakes, fires, fevers, and shipwrecks he regarded as personal favors from Providence, furnishing the raw material of song and ballad. Welcome to us in our country seclusion as Autolycus to the clown in Winter's Tale, we listened with infinite satisfaction to his readings of his own verses, or to his ready improvisation upon some domestic incident or topic suggested by his auditors. When once fairly over the difficulties at the outset of a new subject, his rhymes flowed freely 'as if he had eaten ballads and all men's ears grew to his tunes.' His productions answered, as nearly as I can remember, to Shakespeare's description of a proper ballad — 'doleful matter merrily set down, or a very pleasant theme sung lamentably.' He was scrupulously conscientious, devout, inclined to theological disquisitions, and withal mighty in Scripture. He was thoroughly independent; flattered nobody, cared for nobody, trusted nobody. When invited to sit down at our dinner-table, he invariably took the precaution to place his basket of valuables between his legs for safe keeping. 'Never mind thy basket, Jonathan,' said my father; 'we shan't steal thy verses.' 'I'm not sure of that,' returned the suspicious guest. 'It is written, "Trust ye not in any brother."'"

As a part of the same series of events we quote from the leaflet another paragraph.

"When I was fourteen years old my first schoolmaster, Joshua Coffin . . . brought with him to our house a volume of Burns's poems, from which he read, greatly to my delight. I begged him to leave the book with me, and set myself at once to the task of mastering the glossary of the Scottish dialect at its close. This was about the first poetry I had ever read (with the exception of that of the Bible, of which I had been a close student), and it had a lasting influence upon me. I began to make rhymes myself, and to imagine stories and adventures."

His earliest attempts in rhyme were in the manner of Burns; but it is not known that any of them have been preserved.

The Quakers, it will be remembered, did not approve of music. It was a pleasure they had agreed to abandon. In a life seemingly made up of self-abnegations perhaps one more or less did not matter. But it is something difficult for others to imagine, — the entire disuse of a natural expression of feeling. Among those who have been brought up in musical families this repression of song seems hard and cruel; for music suits itself to all moods, and bears an intimate relation equally to the gayest, tenderest, and most solemn events of life. From the mother's holy lullaby, the moving ballad, and the lover's serenade, to the impassioned utterances of the dramatic singer and the sublimity of the oratorio, the scope is almost infinite; and throughout all there is a sense of something "in tune with the nature of man."

Waiving for a moment the question whether an unexpurgated volume of Burns was precisely the most judicious reading for a boy of fourteen, we can see that in this instance it served to awaken feelings and perceptions which were to develop and to react upon his susceptible nature until in time he should behold a new heaven and a new earth, and should himself become their voice. Both the poetry and the music, it seems to us, were necessary influences. The verses touched sources of feeling and aroused ideas before unknown and unsuspected. With what thrills he must have read those clear-cut lines, with their terse, proverbial force, their tingling wit or home-like tenderness! For it is certain that in the essentials of poetry the songs of Burns, such as the Banks of Doon and Highland Mary, for instance, are absolutely unparalleled. The passionate poet insists that all Nature shall sympathize in his sorrows and his joys; and, familiar as the lines may be, they always strike the heart with a new force.

> " Ye banks and braes o' bonny Doon,
>   How *can* ye bloom sae fresh and fair;
>   How can ye chant, ye little birds,
>   And I sae weary fu' o' care !
>   Thou 'lt break my heart, thou warbling bird,
>   That wantons through the flowering thorn ;
>   Thou minds me o' departed joys,
>   Departed — never to return ! "

And when the same beauty of thought and genuine pathos was borne on the wings of song, the soul that *for the first time* heard, comprehended, and felt all this power must have risen into an ecstasy for which there are no symbols.

It was a " barefoot boy " just from the fields with his hoe, or fresh from a ramble in the woods, with only the songs of bobolinks and thrushes in his ears. What new and intenser meaning were the melodies of nature to have for him henceforth !

The next few years were to bring a great change.

The poetry of **Burns** and the Scottish **music had** enthralled him, and **his** own feelings began **to** shape themselves in rhyme. **He** was encouraged by his elder **sister**, though **we may** suppose **his** parents were not at first let into the secret. How with his poor outfit he learned the mastery of verse is one of the mysteries of genius. The time he **had** given to study was so brief,—**yet** he seemed **to have got** at the core of knowledge; his acquaintance with **poetry** (not counting Ellwood's) **was** limited to the songs of **one man written in an ob-**scure dialect,—yet **that one** guide had led **him** into the land of immortal day-dreams.

The firstlings of his muse Mr. Whittier has **not** chosen to place among his maturer productions; **and** there seems **to be no** propriety now, **in the** height of his fame, in displaying all the **work of** his 'prentice hand. **But** reference must be made from time to time to certain **poems that no longer** appear in the " complete edition," because **they** form parts **of his** life, and mark different stages **of** progress.

That rhythmic thoughts were in automatic **ac-**tion in his mind, like warp and woof knitted by the flying shuttle **in** his mother's loom, **there can be no** doubt. The Orient had **come into the** secluded **valley** ; nothing **in** Nature **was** remote ; nothing in the world of imagination was strange; nothing in the spiritual realm was hidden. The creative faculty, having been once awakened, will not sleep until the brain ceases to throb.

It was about this time that William Lloyd Garrison was writing for the "Newburyport Herald." He was but three years older than Whittier, and being an indentured apprentice, and not sure of his ground with his employer, the printer, he carefully preserved his incognito as contributor. He was destined to exert a powerful influence upon the character and career of Whittier. In 1826 he established in Newburyport the "Free Press," and we learn that the Whittier family, having subscribed for it, were greatly pleased with the humanitarian tone of its articles.

Whittier remembers with singular pleasure the first sight of his poem printed in the "Poet's Corner" of the county newspaper. He was employed with one of the elders mending fences when the news-carrier came along on horseback, and, taking the paper from his saddle-bags, threw it over to them. Whittier took it, and was overjoyed to see his lines. He stood rooted to the spot, and had to be called several times before he could return to sublunary affairs. This poem was probably "The Deity," which is referred to elsewhere.

One day when he was hoeing in the cornfield in the summer of 1826 word came that a carriage had driven up to the house, and that the visitor had inquired for one John Greenleaf Whittier. The youth hastened towards the house in great astonishment, and entered the back door because he was not presentable, having on neither coat, waistcoat, nor shoes,—only a shirt, pantaloons, and straw hat. Who could have driven out to see *him?* After being shod and apparelled, his heart still in a flutter, he appeared before the stranger, who proved to be Garrison. The good sister Mary, it appeared, had revealed the secret of the authorship of the poems, and the generous young editor had come from Newburyport on a friendly visit. We can imagine how the praise affected the poet; for the manner and tones of Garrison were always hearty, and often very tender, and conveyed an impression of absolute sincerity. His position as editor gave weight also to his words. To be sure, the "Free Press" was a local newspaper, and in one sense obscure; but it was conducted with ability and conscience, and it reached the best readers in the county. For a young man who had never left his father's farm this was a recognition unexpected and overwhelming. It was a glimpse of fame.

The father was called in, and the prospects of the son were discussed, — the father remonstrating against " putting notions in his son's head." With warm words Garrison set forth the capabilities which the early verses indicated, and urged that the youth be sent to some public institution for such a training as his talents demanded. His clear and intelligent counsel made a deep impression, although at first the obstacles seemed insuperable. The father had not the money for the purpose; the farm did not produce more than enough for the necessary expenses of the family. But the son pondered upon the matter and determined to make every effort to secure a higher and more complete education. A way was opened for him that very year, — not by charity or loan, but by the labor of his own hands. A young man, who worked for the elder Whittier on the farm in summer, used to make ladies' slippers and shoes during the winter. Seeing the desire of young Whittier to earn money for his schooling, he offered to instruct him in the " mystery." The youth eagerly accepted the offer, and during the following season he earned enough to pay for a suit of clothes and for his board and tuition for six months.

It may appear to some a trivial incident to mention, but trifles often show the firmness and self-control attained by those who have contended with adversity. Whittier, after making " an appropriation bill " for the approaching term at the Academy, found himself " square," but without a surplus. At the end of three months, he still had a single Mexican quarter of a dollar which he had at the outset, not having spent a penny except as previously arranged for board, tuition, and books.

The departure of a youth from home is generally far from depressing *to him,* however sad it may be for the family. It is towards the future that his face is turned, scanning its promise with eyes of hope. It appears a light matter to attend a school three miles distant, returning home every week to spend Sunday. But the result in the end is a separation — happily unforeseen. The tree once taken from native soil can never be replaced as it was. It does not appear that Whittier had rebelled against the lot of labor, or of seclusion in an out-of-the-way place ; nor that he had been other than a faithful, honest helper of his hard-working parents ; so that his escape into the great world was not prompted by indolence or vanity. But ideas had been planted in his mind which must needs germinate and expand, and he must at any cost do what in him lay to increase his knowledge and develop his powers. The district school and the scanty home library had done for him the little to be expected. Of the aspects of nature as seen in his native valley and the beautiful surrounding country his soul was full. Schoolmasters like Coffin had given him aids to thought. Ridiculous Jonathan Plummers and " auld carles" of wandering Scotchmen could not longer feed his mental hunger. The valley and its associations were to be left behind. The father and mother were to continue their lives of contented toil, with even closer economy for his sake. Mary and Matthew and the little Elizabeth were to see the elder brother leaving them, while their pride in his coming fame struggled with their natural tears.

The valley was to be left behind, but not forgotten. There is no instance in literary history of a love of home and family more conspicuous, more intense and lasting. It is not the case of a placid and proper affection, but of an all-absorbing feeling which has animated and shaped the poet's whole life. The scenes he was familiar with have reappeared in his verse, and the family are painted in those tender colors over which Time has no power.

The poem which was the turning-point in Whittier's career may be found in the Appendix. It is a versification of the sublime passage of Scripture

(1 Kings xix. 11, 12) in which the prophet relates the appearance of the Lord.

" And, behold, the Lord passed by, and a great and strong wind rent the mountains, and brake in pieces the rocks before the Lord ; but the Lord was not in the wind : and after the wind an earthquake ; but the Lord was not in the earthquake : and after the earthquake a fire ; but the Lord was not in the fire : and after the fire a still small voice."

The poem is mainly an amplification, really adding nothing to the severe grandeur of the text. When a poetic thought is first thrown off it may be likened to the formless mass hurled from the central body, which must be turned patiently before it assumes its roundness, and still more before the development of its possibilities of beauty. There is a season of struggle while the plastic faculty is first giving form to the thought, whether vivid or vague. That struggle is obvious in the poem in question. The prognostication of Garrison was based less upon the success of the effort than upon the promise which the teeming lines seemed to indicate. That this was not his first attempt is certain ; but it is not possible now to find copies of the early productions.

CHAPTER V.

YOUTH AND EARLY MANHOOD.

IN April, 1827, in his twentieth year, Whittier
went to the Academy in Haverhill. It was a
new institution in a new building, then occupied for
the first time. There was a formal dedication, and
Whittier wrote the ode that was sung on the occasion. The master was Oliver Carlton, who died
during the last year (1882) at Salem, having
attained to great age. Whittier pursued the ordinary English studies, and took lessons in French
also. He remained six months at the Academy,
during which time it was his custom to return
each Friday evening and spend the Sunday at
home. The fact that a townsman had written an

ode for a public ceremony, as well as verses which had attained the honor of print, was known in the little village, and he was naturally a youth of distinction. It is said that when he handed in his first composition in prose, — an exercise required of all mature pupils, — the master asked, " Do you mean to say that this is your composition ? " " Yes," was the answer. " Do you say you wrote it without copying either language or thoughts ? " " Yes." " Had you no assistance or prompting from any one ? " " No." The master was nonplussed ; but when, week after week, there came other themes equally original and striking, incredulity gave way to admiration, and from that time he gave him counsel as a friend as well as pupil. His position was established in the school and in the village.

He boarded in the family of Mr. Abijah Wyman Thayer, then the editor and publisher of the Haverhill " Gazette." Mrs. Thayer is still living (1883), at an advanced age, in Northampton, Mass., and takes great pleasure in recalling her impressions of the poet in his youth. She remembers his handsome face and figure, and the appearance of extreme neatness which he always bore ; but she has more to say of the liveliness of his temper, his ready wit, his perfect courtesy and infallible sense of truth and justice. On account of his abilities and his exemplary conduct, no less than on account of his reputation as a rising poet, his society was much sought after. The gatherings of young people, she says, were never thought complete without Whittier; and the young ladies of the school and village were never quite so happy as when they were from time to time invited to her house to tea. He was on a footing of intimacy with the family of Mr. Thayer, and, whenever he came to Haverhill, made their house his home. Long after, when he went to Philadelphia, he became once more an inmate of their house, — Mr. Thayer having set up a newspaper in that city.

Whittier wrote poems for the " Gazette " as early as the year 1828, and perhaps earlier; and his contributions were continued at intervals for nearly forty years.[1]

---

[1] The writer has made diligent search for a complete file of this newspaper, thus far without success. There are a few annual volumes, but no extended sequence of them. The volumes that contain Whittier's first poems, as well as those which he afterwards edited, are wholly wanting. He wrote one poem entitled " The Grecian Woman," and sent it to Mr. Thayer with a note dated March 3, 1828. This note, preserved by a relative of Whittier, is in substance as follows : —

" I am very busy now [preparing to return to the Academy], and can only snatch a moment now and then from the fag-end of a day to read or write. In Morse's ' Historical Collections ' . . .

Among the letters received by the author is one from Mrs. Harriet M. Pitman, of Somerville, Mass., who was a native of Haverhill, and daughter of Judge Minot. The letter is as follows : —

"I am glad that Mr. Whittier's life is to be written whilst he is in this world, and able to correct errors. . . . I can tell you nothing of him as a boy. I wish I could, but he is older than I, lived three miles from the village of Haverhill (where my father's home was), and was nearly nineteen years old when I first saw him. He was a very handsome, distinguished-looking young man. His eyes were remarkably beautiful. He was tall, slight, and very erect ; a bashful youth, but *never awkward*, my mother said, who was a better judge than I of such matters.

"He went to school awhile at Haverhill Academy. There were pupils of all ages, from ten to twenty-five. My brother, George Minot, then about ten years old, used to say that Whittier was the best of all the big fellows, and he was in the habit of calling him 'Uncle Toby.' Whittier was always kind to children, and under

you will find the interesting story which I have endeavored to versify. You will place the note at the bottom . . .

"Thine in haste,

"J. G. WHITTIER."

The manuscript of this poem, "The Grecian Woman," came into the possession of S. T. Pickard, of the "Portland Transcript," who published it in his paper years afterwards. It was copied by the "Anti-slavery Standard" in the same year (1858), with a brief note signed "J. G. W."

a very grave and quiet exterior there was a real love of fun, and a keen sense of the ludicrous. In society he was embarrassed, and his manners were, in consequence, sometimes brusque and cold. With intimate friends he talked a great deal, and in a wonderfully interesting manner; usually earnest, often analytical, and frequently playful. He had a great deal of wit. It was a family characteristic. The study of human nature was very interesting to him, and his insight was keen. He liked to draw out his young friends, and to suggest puzzling doubts and queries.

"When a wrong was to be righted, or an evil to be remedied, he was readier to act than any young man I ever knew, and was very wise in his action, — shrewd, sensible, practical. The influence of his Quaker bringing-up was manifest. I think it was always his endeavor

' To render less
The sum of human wretchedness.'

This, I say, was his steadfast endeavor, in spite of an inborn love of teasing. He was very modest, never conceited, never egotistic.

"One could never flatter him. I never tried, but I have seen people attempt it, and it was a signal failure. He did not flatter, but told very wholesome and unpalatable truths, yet in a way to spare one's self-love by admitting a doubt whether he was in earnest or in jest.

"The great questions of Calvinism were subjects of which he often talked in those early days. He was exceedingly conscientious. He cared for people — quite as much for the plainest and most uncultivated, if they were original and had something in them, as for the most polished.

"He was much interested in politics, and thoroughly posted. I remember, in one of his first calls at our house, being surprised at his conversation with my father upon Governor Gerry and the Gerry-mandering of the State, or the attempt to do it, of which I had until then been wholly ignorant.

"He had a retentive memory and a marvellous store of information on many subjects. I once saw a little commonplace book of his, — full of quaint things, and as interesting as Southey's.

"His home was one of the most delightful that I ever knew, situated in a green valley, where was a laughing brook, fine old trees, hills near by, and no end of wild flowers. What did they want of the music and pictures which man makes, when they had eyes to see the beauties of nature, ears to hear its harmonies, and imaginations to reproduce them? It makes me impatient to hear people talk of the dulness and sordidness of young life in New England fifty years ago! There was nature with its infinite variety; there were books, the best ever written, and not too many of them; there were young men and maidens with their eager enthusiasm; there were great problems to be solved, boundless fields of knowledge to explore, a heaven to believe in, and neighbors to do good to. Life was very full.

"Whittier's home was exceptionally charming on account of the character of its inmates. His father, a sensible and estimable man, died before I knew the home. His mother was serene, dignified, benevolent, — a woman of good judgment, fond of reading the best books, — a woman to honor and revere.   His aunt, Mercy Hussey, who lived with them, was an incarnation of gracefulness and graciousness, of refinement and playfulness, — an ideal lady.   His sister Elizabeth, 'the youngest and the dearest,' shared his poetic gifts, and was a sweet, rare person, devoted to her family and friends, kind to every one, full of love for all beautiful things, and so merry when in good health, that her companionship was always exhilarating. I cannot imagine her doing a wrong thing, or having an unworthy thought.   She was deeply religious, and so were they all.

"I have said nothing of Whittier in his relations to women.   There was never a particle of coxcombry about him.   He was delicate and chivalrous, but paid few of the little attentions common in society.   If a girl dropped her glove or handkerchief in his presence, she had to pick it up again, especially if she did it on purpose.

"I was about to speak of his thrift and frugality, and of his independence, — of which I knew striking instances, — and of his early taking upon himself the care of the family. . . . I have not mentioned the anti-slavery cause, the subject nearest his heart after the year 1833, the subject about which he talked most, for which he labored most, and to which he was most devoted.   All his friends became abolitionists.   I was deeply in sympathy with him on this question; but this is a matter of history, and he should recount his own experience."

This vivid, intelligent, contemporaneous view of Whittier in his youth, by an observer so evidently competent, is worth pages of supposition or vague eulogy.

At the close of this term, which was in the autumn of 1827, Whittier had his first and only experience as a teacher. He taught the district school for the following winter at West Amesbury, now Merrimac. In the spring he returned to the Academy, and passed another six months in study.

Meantime, as the "Free Press" had been unsuccessful, Garrison had gone to Boston and established the "National Philanthropist." It was through his friendly interposition that a place was found for Whittier, in the autumn of 1828, as a writer for the "American Manufacturer." This paper was an advocate of protection to home industry, and was friendly to Henry Clay, the great champion of that policy. Whittier really edited the paper, though not named or paid as editor. He boarded for a short time with Garrison in the family of the Rev. William Collier. His contributions to that sheet are comparatively unimportant, and the topics are now out of date. As his salary was meagre and inadequate, — nine dollars a week, — and as his help was needed on the farm, he returned home in June, 1829, and there remained until July, 1830.

During this period, from 1828 to 1830, Whittier

wrote much, both in prose and verse. John Neal, of Portland, Me., a brilliant but eccentric man, who had achieved a temporary reputation in England, and who was long supposed to be on the eve of writing something great, edited and published, in 1828, a magazine entitled "The Yankee," which at the end of the year was "merged" in a Boston monthly. Four or more poems by Whittier appeared in this periodical, some of them several pages in length. The subjects were either romantic or scriptural, and the treatment was meant to be in the heroic vein. None of them have great merit, and they will not be disturbed in their repose by any true friend of the poet. In one of them ("The Minstrel Girl") there is a passage full of promise, — quoted in a succeeding page.

There cannot be any doubt that this intellectual discipline was of the utmost service reflexively. Whittier was at an age when more fortunate young men in college were wrestling with mathematics, Greek, and philosophy. This training was denied him; and in place of it came the constant and laborious practice, both in prose and verse, by which his faculties were made the ready instruments of his creative soul. No; the juvenile poems are not to be wholly despised! They are the sunken piles that stand under the slowly reared edifice of his fame.

During the first six months of 1830 he was employed as editor of the " Gazette " of Haverhill,[1] doing his work at his father's house. He was also writing articles in prose and verse for the " New England Weekly Review," of Hartford, Conn., as we shall see more fully hereafter.

The quick instinct of contemporary editors had perceived something original and promising in the writings of Whittier, even at that early age ; and the frequent literary notices of the time show that among the fraternity he was already widely known. His early poems had obtained considerable popularity, and though nearly all have been suppressed, several of them are interesting and valuable as indications of his experience and progress.

The extracts that follow, copied from the " New England Review," December, 1829, will show the estimation in which he was held in his twenty-second year.

" J. G. WHITTIER.

" ' The culmination of that man's fame will be a proud period in the history of our literature.' This generous tribute to the abilities of our friend Whittier was contained in a letter which we recently received from one of the most distinguished men in the country. The

---

[1] The files of this paper in the Haverhill Public Library are imperfect ; this period, 1830, also 1836, being wanting.

tribute was merited. Whittier is a poet and a Christian. . . .

"There is a poem by Whittier in the last number of the 'Yankee,' which but for its length we should be pleased to quote entire. 'T is less powerful and sublime than many of his other performances, but almost every part of it is surprisingly beautiful.

> ' The sun went down, and, broad and red,
>   One moment on the burning wave
>   Rested his front of fire to shed
>   A glory round his ocean grave :
>   And sunset, — far and gorgeous hung
>   A banner from the wall of Heaven,
>   A wave of living glory, flung
>   Along the shadowy verge of even.
>   The trees were leaning on the west,
>   Like watchers of the golden sky,
>   Trembling as if the sunset's breast
>   In that warm light were beating high.
>   And Agnes watched the glory.   Slow
>   But beautiful the stars came down,
>   And on the sky's unrivalled brow
>   The bended moon sat like a crown.' "

How far this passage is inferior to the work of his maturer years need not be said. But we observe a sense of color and a glow of feeling that belong to bards by native right.

A survey of his career as a whole shows that he is not — as it is the fashion to say — the product of his age. That much of his poetry has been devoted to great moral and humanitarian topics, is due to the fact that he lived when those topics were paramount in the minds of men. Circumstances made him a reformer, but God only made him a poet.

The influences which moulded the character and affected the poems of Longfellow, Bryant, Emerson, Holmes, and Lowell, were almost wholly foreign to the narrow circle that enclosed Whittier. As a member of the Friends, the current literature of the great world was unknown to him. The culture and learning of Cambridge and Boston had not penetrated the East Parish of Haverhill, nor moulded the tastes of the group depicted in " Snow Bound." There is no probability that there was any correspondence between Whittier and the leading poets until many years later. His first impulses were inborn, not imitative.

Generations of God-fearing ancestors were behind him, and the sympathy of a noble household had sustained and animated him. Every faculty of his being was pervaded by the desire to put himself at the service of God in the affairs of his day. This devotion and singleness of aim were to characterize him and his works throughout his long and fruitful life.

Whittier's youth and brief apprenticeship were

over, and he was about to begin the work of his life. He had made the best of scanty opportunities, and, considering his imperfect training and his naturally impetuous temper, he had made few failures. His sincere and just mind and character, aided by unfailing tact, supplied the place of what are termed cultivated manners, so that the ploughboy manifested the simple dignity and courtesy of a gentleman. His religious training had led to more than a conformity to moral rules; it had developed in him the sublime sense of duty as something to be followed at any cost. Ideas, institutions, and laws, as well as social usages, were to be tried by the standard of right. Literature was useful as it elevated mankind, or as it tended to lessen human suffering; and the poet's art was to be devoted unswervingly to the same service.

CHAPTER VI.

IN the author's sketches of Longfellow and
Lowell there are paragraphs concerning the
poets of the United States who were living and
popular in 1830. None of them survive, and few
of their productions enjoy great favor to-day.
Besides Longfellow, the most eminent were Dana,
Bryant, John Neal, Drake, Halleck, Sprague, Grenville Mellen, Mrs. Sigourney, Percival, and Pierpont. Emerson was known only as an essayist, if
known at all; and Willis was born in the same
year with Whittier. No one of these could have
influenced Whittier in the least. He was wholly
outside the current of theological discussion that
affected so many; out of hearing, also, of the

conflict between " schools" of poetry which followed the ascendency of Wordsworth and his disciples. Whittier was of no school, except as the thought and impulse of the hour might shape his verse. In his early poems we observe the influence of Burns, — a congenial nature, — and in some of them, more strongly, the rhythm and kindling energy of Scott. It was at a later day that he turned to the elder masters, and could write

> " I love the old melodious lays
> Which softly melt the ages through,
> The songs of Spenser's golden days,
> Arcadian Sidney's silver phrase,
> Sprinkling our noon of time with freshest morning dew."

But it should be added that the poems of his maturity have not the least echo; they are wholly without suggestion of influences from masters or predecessors.

For a sensitive, shy, reserved, self-respecting young man, with high ideals and perfect courtesy, there could be few trials more annoying than those which beset the editor of a political and literary newspaper in the year 1830. Usually an editor was forced into the position of an Ishmaelite; and, as there were blows to take as well as blows to give, the literary arena (metaphorically) was something like its ancient namesake. Or shall we say more truly that it was a playground for " tag " by grown-up boys? Editors appeared to pride themselves chiefly on their ability to make rivals ridiculous. Justice, good manners, and even decency were lost sight of. As the most eminent incurred the most envy, they were naturally the marks for all the arrows. Willis was by far the most sprightly, versatile, and original of the younger writers, as was shown by the persistent attacks upon him by foes of all arms. Such paragraphs as were written, read, and chuckled over! It would give the most audacious editor to-day a cold sweat to think of printing such familiar blackguardism. It was as if, in some crowded assembly of best people, a man should break out with the gibes of a Rabelais.

Here are a few paragraphs culled from a literary paper in 1829. It will be seen that journalism rightly called *personal* was in its glory. We may add that in this " literary " warfare the personal journalist is seen at his best. His diatribes against rivals in politics would now need translation ; and being translated, one would wish them covered up again and put out of sight.

" American periodicals are perhaps improving in their character, but they are yet the double-distilled essence of all the available dulness in the universe."

An inspection of a great many files of that time has led us to think this sweeping statement is mainly true.

"If Mr. Willis continues, after this, to indulge in the puerilities that have characterized his writings, he must be pronounced incorrigible. . . . Mrs. Hale in the last number of her magazine takes the pretty fellow upon her knee, and after patting him kindly on the head, fairly laughs him in the face for writing *muling* sonnets about girls, kisses, and blossoms. Mr. W. has come to this pass by obstinately refusing to follow our advice. We have labored to make a man of him, but the ungrateful urchin has perked up his smart little nose," &c.

Alluding to some quarrel between Willis and Mr. W. Gaylord Clarke of the "Knickerbocker," the editor says : —

"Be quiet, young man! If you are as much inferior to Clarke in physical as in mental strength, he would with one hand toss you out of the circle of the earth's attraction, and with the other take a spy-glass and see you move through space."

"JOHN NEAL. We were never so long employed in any single job as in killing this man's Monthly. We announced our intention of doing the work for it almost as soon as it made its appearance, and yet it lived six months in spite of us. The thing had more breath in it than we imagined. John has now united himself with Mrs. Hale in writing for the 'Lady's Magazine.' This is a cowardly deed. We never thought him a fellow of much courage, but we did suppose that he had too much manhood to run and hide himself behind a lady in order to escape our castigation. He is, however, safe," &c.

" EDITOR'S TABLE. Nothing before us this time but sour bread, cold codfish, and an impudent host."

" We wish it were fashionable for ladies to have Poet-Laureats [*sic*]; we would endeavor to get permission for —— to attach himself in that capacity to some soft little miss of fifteen, who should repay him for his services by ordering for him a piece of bread-and-butter for every sonnet. Her canaries, poet-laureat, and lap-dog might eat from the same dish."

Threatening to publish the biography of a rival, the editor says : —

" We have been at work upon it for a year with a pen made of the horn of a rhinoceros, sharpened with a broad-axe and nibbed with a guillotine. He is afraid of us," &c.

" His attempts at poetical criticism are the awkward caperings of an overgrown mule mistaking himself for a pet fawn, and lifting his great muddy hoofs into the laps of the Muses."

These pleasant interchanges of courtesy appear to have seldom led to violence, although personal conflicts were more common then than now. A newspaper paragraph (1831) relates that a leading New York editor had been carrying on one of these duels on paper with the poet Bryant, who was also an editor, in the same city, and that the latter, coming upon his antagonist in Broadway, gave him a rousing cut across the face with a cowhide; whereupon the first named retorted with a cane, "developing upon the poetical cranium of his assailant more organs than a phrenologist ever dreamed of."

Whittier was editor for a year and a half of a paper in Hartford, Conn., styled the "New England Weekly Review." He succeeded George D. Prentice, a native of Connecticut, but who was better known in after years as an editor in Kentucky. We are considering Prentice as he is autotyped in the first newspaper he published. He was a man of ready wit, of almost boyish liveliness, and the discretion appertaining thereto,—with unusual command of language and facility in verse, and was thought to be on the road to eminence as a poet. This might have been the case, if he had continued in a literary career, and had concentrated his evident powers upon study; but his energies were subsequently given to politics, and he has left little more than a widely known name, and a great regret. There was a charming geniality in his speech and manner, and at times in his writing; and he strongly attracted ambitious youths of the period. He was as generous in praise of *protégés* as he was sarcastic towards rivals. Whittier had sent him some of his compositions, both in poetry and prose, which were printed and praised in the " Review," and a correspondence ensued. We have already seen Prentice's estimate of him. As a prelude to the approaching presidential campaign of 1832, Prentice undertook to write the life of Henry Clay, and for that purpose eventually went to Lexington, Ky. Perhaps he did not seriously intend to return to the East. Hartford was not a very important place at that time, and it is believed that the income of an editor was too narrow for a man of his expensive tastes. Be that as it may, after finishing his book in Lexington he went to Louisville, where he founded the " Journal," a newspaper since well known throughout the country. For years his witty sayings were quoted with zest by his contemporaries, and he continued to write and to encourage the poetry of sentiment, — such lightly weighted sentiment as delights young and unsophisticated readers. He and Mrs. Amelia Welby, who wrote for his paper, may almost be said to have founded a southwestern school, of which melody and beautiful adjectives are the chief characteristics. It was almost prophetic that Pope so long ago had written in his Imitations of Horace : —

> "Lull with Amelia's liquid name the Nine,
>   And sweetly flow through all the royal line."

We are not to follow the career of Prentice, and we can say in a few words that he was a man of great natural force, and with a capacity (were he duly ballasted) for doing great things; and that his renown as an influential editor is a small compensation for the loss which our literature sustained by his abandoning the more laborious and self-denying career he had first chosen.

When Prentice was about to leave, the publishers of the "Review" at his suggestion sent for Whittier to take the place of editor. Whittier has stated that he felt himself hardly equal to the position, but accepted it because he was unwilling to lose the chance of doing something in accordance with his growing tastes. A sure instinct was leading him by ways not known towards the pursuit of pure literature. Prentice in his Farewell (July 5, 1830) says : —

"Mr. J. G. Whittier, an old favorite with the public, will probably have charge of the 'Review' in my absence, and I cannot do less than congratulate my readers on the prospect of their more familiar acquaintance with a gentleman of such powerful energies and such exalted purity and sweetness of character. I have made some enemies among those whose good opinion I value, but no rational man can ever be the enemy of Mr. Whittier."

The succeeding numbers of the paper show Whittier's hand, and in that for July 19 his Salutatory is printed. Evidently he considered himself a *locum tenens,* and it was not until September 20 that Prentice's retirement was announced as final.

The industry and the versatility of Whittier as shown in this service are remarkable : at least forty-two poems were published during his connection with the paper, besides a great number of prose sketches and tales, in addition to the regular editorials and current comment.

The poems from this periodical, preserved in the complete edition, are " The Frost Spirit," " The Cities of the Plain," and " The Vaudois Teacher." [1] The poems " Isabella of Austria " and " Bolivar " are to be seen in the Appendix. The reader will probably regret that such really fine verse has been so long neglected. " The Vaudois Teacher " was translated into French many years ago, and has long been read and treasured among the primitive Protestants of the valleys of the lower Alps. For more than a generation these people supposed that it was the original production of some French poet ; but at length it became known that the poem so dear

---

[1] The author's file of the " New England Review " is not complete. " The Star of Bethlehem " was written in 1830, but for what periodical is not certain.

to their hearts was the work of an American ; and at a general assembly of their churches not long ago an affectionate address was adopted and forwarded to Whittier.

In the number for October, 1830, is a noble apostrophe to New England, beginning : —

> " Land of the forest and the rock, —
> Of dark blue lake and mighty river, —
> Of mountains reared aloft to mock
> The storm's career, the lightning's shock, —
> My own green land forever."

Parts of this poem were afterwards incorporated with another poem, " Moll Pitcher," which, like many others, has been suppressed. One passage, we think, should be quoted as a part of the poet's inner life. His judgment in suppressing it was correct — *at the time ;* but now that years have passed, and the prophetic intimation has been more than realized, it will give a heart-felt pleasure to his admirers to know what high thoughts were in the brain of a youth of two-and-twenty.

> " Land of my fathers ! if the name,
> Now humble and unwed to fame,
> Hereafter burn upon the lip
> As one of those which may not die,
> Linked in eternal fellowship
> With visions pure and strong and high, —
> If the wild dreams which quicken now
> The throbbing pulse of heart and brow,

> Hereafter **take a real** form,
> Like spectres changed to beings warm,
> **And over** temples **worn and gray**
> The star-like **crown** of glory **shine,**
> **Thine** be the bard's undying **lay,**
> The murmur of his praise be **thine !** "

There is a modesty affected and false ; **and there** is a self-esteem which is unconsciously simple and noble. As Whittier's conceptions grew definite, and his power to clothe **them** in enduring **verse** increased, such thoughts **as** breathe **in** this **memorable passage** were natural, **and they naturally sought** expression. The *exegi monumentum* **of** Horace we remember, and we read without **shock the prediction** of Shakespeare : —

> " Not marble, nor the gilded monuments
> Of princes, shall outlive this powerful rhyme."

And now that **the** crown **rests** without question upon the " temples worn and gray," we can **enter into the** feeling which inspired Whittier's early verse.

The reader will look through **the file in vain to** find **the** virulence of temper or the offensive personality which constituted then so large an element **of** journalism ; **though** perhaps **his** references **to** the editor of the " Hartford Times " were not quite what an older head would have indited. Whittier **was** just and sagacious. **He** was ready **to** recognize

merit, and he had the tact and taste to avoid controversy. He ardently supported Henry Clay and
the " American System." He was a firm advocate
of Temperance, of Freedom, and of Religion ; but
he never let fly at individuals the pestilent darts
which his predecessor knew so well how to use.
When rival newspapers attacked Prentice after his
departure, they found the Quaker editor a stout
friend of the absent. For a professed peace-man,
Whittier was one of the most resolute and uncompromising.

Not much is remembered of his life in Hartford.
It was not a large city, but was relatively busier
than now ; because in those days before railroads
it was accessible to schooners and brigs by the
river, and it had a respectable coastwise and West
Indian trade. The newspaper from which we have
quoted is full of curious advertisements, — " W. I.
Goods " — the " Victory " steamboat, fare to New
York one dollar, meals extra — runaway appren-
tices — lucky lottery offices — fashionable cloths,
with names now obsolete, — " Souvenirs," and other
forgotten annuals — new books, now out of print —
more lottery schemes — wine from Lisbon and
Cadiz — daily stages to Boston and other remote
regions — flannels, for which beans and dried
apples are received in payment, — forgotten nos-

trums. Verily these old advertisements are full of topics for meditation. It is odd, too, to read of the contemporary efforts of Daniel Webster, such as the " Reply to Hayne " and the argument against the murderers of Judge White. To follow the news week by week is to live over the time when Calhoun, Randolph, Clay, Jackson, Adams, and McDuffie played their parts on the stage.

Whittier appears to have boarded at the Exchange Coffee House, which stood on the northwest side of the State House. His manner of life was nearly as grave and solitary as now. His health was generally delicate, although by constant care he was able to accomplish much. He made some trips into the country, notably to what is now known as Talcott Mountain, and to the groups of hills between Hartford and New Haven, and he faithfully described them in prose.

In March, 1831, he made a visit to Haverhill and spent some time at the old homestead. Two pleasant letters record his impressions of the long and fatiguing journey and of his hearty welcome by the family and friends. A few sentences are quoted.

" I have had a shocking time of it, and ever since have dreamed of stages upset, of ten-feet snow-drifts, and mud immeasurable and interminable. Every bone in my body aches at the bare idea of my journey. I would

as soon ride bare-backed the Rozinante of Don Quixote.
. . . A conveyance in that rascally French diligence
which Sterne complains of would be a luxury to it; and
I can easily imagine how poor Sancho Panza must have
suffered while tossed in the blanket by the muleteers at
the enchanted inn. When I left Hartford I was neither
more nor less than a disciple of Penn and Ellwood;
but before I reached the end of my journey I was to all
intents and purposes a Shaking Quaker."

He passes a night in pretty and rural Worcester,
and admires by moonlight its green spaces and
abundant elms. He stops a few hours in Boston,
and naturally panegyrizes. He reaches Haverhill
with unutterable feelings. "There is no place like
home," and much more of the same honest sort.

"And where, you will ask, are my sentimentalisms
and love adventures? Alas, my dear fellow, these are
not the days of romance. . . . But I *can* say that I have
clasped more than one fair hand, and read my welcome
in more than one bright eye since my arrival."

Then he mentions his little sister, "a girl of
fifteen summers," and sends a poem of hers which
he has surreptitiously obtained. Here is the first
stanza : —

"AUTUMN SUNSET.

"O, there is beauty in the sky, — a widening of gold
　Upon each light and breezy cloud, and on each vapory fold!
　The autumn wind has died away, and the air has not a sound,
　Save the sighing of the withered leaves as they fall upon the
　　ground."

The second letter is mainly political, and exhibits our Quaker editor sparring with Gideon Welles of the "Hartford Times," then and since a famous Democratic leader. It closes with a legendary poem. Succeeding numbers of the paper for three months or more show the work of Whittier's hand, but his articles were doubtless sent by mail from Haverhill. The cause of his journey was evidently the failing health of his father. Whittier remained at home, and ministered to his father's comfort with tender assiduity to the end, which came in June. In July he returned to his duty, reluctantly leaving his mother and sisters. In October he made a brief apology for editorial shortcomings; he had been ill and weary. His heart was drawing him homewards.

As for his intellectual progress, who shall say what was best? But so far as we can determine by subsequent results, we should say he had exhausted the newspaper as a means of discipline, especially in poetic art. The steady recurrence of unchanging and mechanical duties was never favorable to the production of poetry, or of the higher qualities of prose. The fable of Pegasus in harness still has its substantial lesson; not to be cited, however, by indolent, conceited youths, for whom steady employment of any sort is a blessing.

On the 2d of January, 1832, Whittier gave up his position on account of his continued ill health. He had long been unequal to the drudgery inseparable from the conduct of a paper managed in the old single-handed way.

We have mentioned the variety and number of his contributions, and the general reputation he had acquired. His sketches were so much admired that the publishers issued a small volume in February, 1831, entitled " New England Legends in Prose and Verse." Only a portion of the contents had been printed in the " Review." He had also edited the poems of J. G. C. Brainard, and prepared a sketch of his life, and this was published just about the time of his resignation.

In leaving so many of his early poems to rest in obscurity, Whittier was doubtless guided by sound literary judgment. They are referred to as a part of the poet's history, and are useful, if for no other purpose than to serve to mark the expansion of his mind, and the steadily growing mastery over his art. Several of these neglected pieces are devoted to phases of love, — a passion without which poet never existed. As time went by, this feeling became less manifest; and as the care of the household rested upon him, and as great causes appealed to him, demanding all his energies, it has happened generally that love has been treated by Whittier with less of the intensity shown in the other poems of his mature years, although there is one conspicuous exception in "The Henchman," to be referred to later. It is of the pure poetry of love we are speaking, — those throbbing lyrics which the whole world remembers and sings.

An English writer has said, "If Whittier, who is unmarried, ever had a love-story, he has not sung about it in the ears of the world; yet love finds in him a fitting laureate, — one of the loftiest, noblest, most ideal type."

In a certain sense the opinion above quoted is most just. Whittier has written of love in pure and noble strains, showing the possession of a poet's feeling. But a love-song in which the poet puts his own personality, and makes the words burn with the fire of his own deathless passion, is quite another thing. There are few of such in the literature of any modern language, and scarcely any in the western world.

There is a parallel development of intellect and feeling, mind and heart, that belongs to the fully rounded character, and especially to the ideal poet. This duality is conspicuous in Whittier, and is the chief source of his power over men. Perhaps a love-song, alive with passion, is the offspring of a less symmetrical and self-poised nature. The feeling that should prompt it might endure, but the inner song would be a Silent Melody.

It may be added that Whittier has always shown a true and manly reverence for woman, and a chivalric championship of her cause whenever it was needed. He has all his life enjoyed the confidence and friendship of the best and worthiest of the sex.

One word more with regard to the neglected and suppressed poems, which Whittier now so heartily and perhaps justly detests. They had a wide circulation, for the standard of American poetry at that time was not a high one. We have seen that at twenty-two he was becoming somewhat famous, and we know that his reputation up to that time rested almost entirely upon the poems that he would now never hear mentioned.

We are endeavoring to study the development of a poet ;— a wonderful process, differing always in different instances, and not to be seen many times in the course of a century. For a poet is not only supreme in inborn genius, but highest in the results of all knowledge, and in the expression of thought and feeling by words never before so grouped together. The poet's thoughts, it is a truism to say, must be his own ; but it is equally true that their vesture must be original and characteristic. A poem may contain pregnant thought, and be pervaded by deep feeling, and yet if it falls into customary ruts of expression, and is adorned with epithets which custom has staled, it cannot become classic. Each poem that lives has its own soul and body ; the poem that borrows *either* has no immortality. And therefore it would appear that, if the vital power has been given, and the thinking has been done, the matter that most concerns the poet is to create or seek out forms that are new in design, color, and effect. We know that at first every poetic soul is imitative as regards expression ; we also know that if it does not soon escape from the thraldom of imitation, its career will be short.

We have to consider Whittier as a learner, and we can see that as he went on he made use of each opportunity for self-culture. Behind all was the resolute, just, aspiring, beauty-loving, ideal nature ; there was also the holy nurture, the ready sympathy, and the fraternal spirit of a Christian family ; there was the meagre outfit of a scholar, for whom all the treasures of printed thought were not too much ; there was a brief apprenticeship in teaching, followed by labors (necessary but irksome) on the tread-mill of weekly newspapers. So far this was the sum. Do we know,— did he himself know at each juncture what was best? If he did not, a wise instinct decided him.

Fortunately, he did not remain a schoolmaster; his abilities were never of the vocal or didactic kind. He would not have been a Horace Mann, still less a Dr. Arnold.

Equally fortunate that he did not remain for life a working editor. In a certain sense it may be said that the *best* writing is thrown away in columns which are important only for an hour. And whoever has toiled over sentences that are to appear next morning in print well knows, if he has the feeling of an artist, that just at the point when he has rounded them and adjusted their phrases to connect smoothly, he has utterly vulgarized his thought. The smoothness means the employment of familiar turns that seem to be automatic; the antithesis is a mere specimen of see-saw; the phrases that fit so accurately are those which have been used by the " able editor " for generations. If the writer has an artist's feeling, when he finds his sentences going without jolt, he will know that what he has done, though it may serve a present purpose, is wholly ephemeral, because conventional. If he would have it live he must go back ; disrupt the glib connections ; smite the specious epithets ; banish the smug adjectives ; and try to put his thought in proper clothing, by studying the primal meanings as well as customary associations of words, and so gain a sincere, strong, and fresh expression.

Therefore it seems that Whittier had had enough practice of this perfunctory nature, and was in the true path to higher development when he returned to the farm. It is true we shall see him an editor again, but only at the call of duty,— a call he never disregarded.

CHAPTER VII.

SEEING SERVICE.

The Anti-slavery Movement begun. — Garrison establishes the
"Liberator." — His Career in Boston. — Persecution of Abo-
litionists. — Whittier's Great Essay. — He attends the National .
Anti-slavery Meeting at Philadelphia. — Mobs in Haverhill,
Concord (N. H.), and Boston. — Escape of Whittier and George
Thompson. — Anti-slavery Lyrics.

WE find Whittier at home during the year
1832, and we know he was busy, as he
always was. His principal literary work at this
time was done for Buckingham's "New England
Magazine," of Boston. It appears best, however,
now to give some account of his anti-slavery labors,
deferring mention of his contributions to magazines
and reviews until such time as they can be considered together. For Whittier's life and labors
have been devoted chiefly to the cause of freedom
and the brotherhood of man. The great events in
which he has been interested will year by year rise
in importance, while the prejudiced and inhuman

utterances of all Carlyles will be forgotten, or will be remembered in pity or in scorn.[1]

The indefatigable Garrison had established still another newspaper devoted to philanthropic subjects, this time at Brattleborough, Vt. Slavery, war, and intemperance were the three great evils to be attacked. The good wishes of Whittier followed his friend, sent him in a warm and prophetic letter. But within a short time the great agitator was convinced that a village in Vermont was not the place in which to exert his powers to the best advantage upon the nation at large, — being (dynamically) too far from the centres of resistance, and (otherwise) too far from the centre of gravity which some people think can only be Boston. He had made an attempt in Baltimore, where he was imprisoned on account of his inability to pay fifty dollars damages and costs, awarded against him at

[1] Carlyle, a defender of the divine right of Might, said : " Essentially the Nigger Question was one of the smallest ; and in itself did not much concern mankind in a time of struggles and hurries. . . . The Almighty Maker has appointed him [the Nigger] to be a servant," (Essays, vol. vii., — "Shooting Niagara : and After ?") — and much more of the same blasphemous sort. One could believe that the sense of justice was dead in this man. In reading his open and shocking contempt for principles which are the basis of Christianity no less than of free government, we wonder how liberty-loving and religious Scotland could have nurtured him. The American abolitionists were as far above him in moral elevation as he was above the Quashee whom he ridicules.

the suit of a Massachusetts shipmaster for a libel
in calling him a pirate; the fact being that the
vessel had carried a cargo of slaves. While he
was in prison, Whittier made an appeal by letter
to Henry Clay to furnish the needed sum; and
Clay stated subsequently that he was about to com-
ply, when he found that Garrison was already at
liberty, the money having been paid by Arthur
Tappan. After "prospecting" in different parts
of the country, notably in Washington, he finally
decided, and in 1831, having burned his ships, —
the few he had, — he issued the first number of
the "Liberator." His only associate was Isaac
Knapp, a fellow-townsman from Newburyport.
They, with the aid of a negro boy, did the whole
work, the editor using the composing-stick and
the pen with equal mastery. The central doctrine announced was a simple statement, — a truism now, but full of tragic menaces and terror
then: "Unconditional emancipation is the immediate duty of the master and the immediate right
of the slave." For this the editor proclaimed, "I
will be as harsh as truth, and as uncompromising
as justice. I am in earnest; I will not equivocate;
I will not excuse; I will not retreat a single inch;
and I WILL BE HEARD." He stood like Luther when
he had nailed *his* theses to the church door in

Wittenberg. From the sublime courage of the one act came Protestantism and whatever it has done or may do for mankind; from the no less lofty spirit of the other came the final liberation of four millions of slaves. So Garrison began his career in the city which derided, vilified, and mobbed him, — whose preachers, lawyers, and civic officers vied in defaming him, and rendering, as far as men could, his life miserable, — but which at length accepted gratefully the grand result of the toils and sufferings of himself, his friends and disciples, and of the agencies he put in motion, and which now holds him in honor among the noblest of her sons.

The influence of Garrison was to bear still more strongly upon Whittier, respecting his place and his share in the world's work. The farmer's boy had become a man with high ideals and a resolute will. Literary renown, with the prospect of ease and leisure, the companionship of writers and scholars, and the approval of the cultivated and refined classes were on one side; and these tempting advantages were not on the side of Garrison, working in his "obscure hole," with a negro assistant; fame and profit were to be sought, if anywhere, among quietists and conservatives. But Whittier had been trained in a school wherein God and duty are the moving influences. After his return from Hartford, in the seclusion of his home, he meditated long upon the question of slavery, and its incompatibility with Christian doctrine and free institutions. Having mastered the facts in its history, and having studied its relations to social life, political economy, public morals, democracy, and the church, he wrote an elaborate pamphlet, consisting of twenty-three pages octavo in small type, entitled "Justice and Expediency; or, Slavery considered with a view to its Rightful and Effectual Remedy, Abolition." On the titlepage, under his name as author, is the well-known fiery sentence from a speech of Lord Brougham respecting "the wild and guilty fantasy that *man can hold property in man.*" This was printed at Haverhill, in 1833, and the expense was wholly borne by the author at a time when the edition must have cost him a considerable part of his yearly earnings.

This able and well-reasoned treatise touches upon every point then in controversy, and is fortified with abundant references to documents and statistics. It disposes of the plans of "amelioration" as by a re-establishment of manorial villanage, and the like. The hypocrisy of the promoters of colonization and the futility of the scheme itself are shown with unanswerable force and unsparing logic. **It** proves **the** superior productiveness **of** free labor, and argues from experience **elsewhere that** the dangers of emancipation **are** only imaginary. **It is** especially strong on moral and religious grounds, and its startling quotations from Scripture, with which Whittier's home schooling had made him so familiar, hold the mind of the reader with a vise-like grip. It is not the least discredit to the **great leader,** Garrison, **to say that though in** the " Liberator " he touched every **note of the** theme, first **and** last, **yet no** single effort of **his** appears now **to be so full, so** thoroughly **stated,** reasoned, and **enforced as this. It covers the** ground completely, **and its** positions were never met in argument, — only by evasions, misstatements, or more commonly by **abuse or** personal violence. This **is the** concluding paragraph : —

" And when the stain on our own escutcheon shall **be** seen no more ; when the Declaration of Independence and the practice of our people shall agree ; when Truth shall be exalted among us ; when Love shall take the place of Wrong ; when all the baneful pride and prejudice of caste and color shall fall forever ; when under one common sun of political Liberty the slaveholding portions of **our** Republic shall **no** longer **sit like** Egyptians of old, themselves mantled **in** thick **darkness** while **all** around **them is** glowing with the **blessed** light **of** freedom and **equality,** — then, and not till then, shall it GO WELL FOR AMERICA."

The concluding words have reference to a sentence written by William Penn: "Let us not betake us to the common arts and stratagems of nations; let us . . . trust not in man, but in the living God; *and it shall go well for England.*"

Whittier, as stated, bore the burden of this issue; but not long after an edition of 10,000 was printed for gratuitous distribution by Lewis Tappan of New York.

In July, 1833, Whittier addressed a letter to the Providence (R. I.) "Journal" which occupies five closely printed columns of that paper. It is not identical with the pamphlet, but it covers much of the same ground, and is more condensed and in some respects more effective. In the same year he wrote an elaborate letter upon the same topic in the "Essex Transcript." Upon no subject since the formation of our government has there been expended so much labor, ability, and eloquence as upon the question of slavery.

Upon the return of Garrison from England, in 1833, it was determined to hold a National Anti-slavery Convention at Philadelphia, December 4th, 5th, and 6th. Whittier was a delegate and one of the secretaries, and signed the memorable Declaration of Sentiments He has now in his house a copy of this Declaration, framed with wood from the timber of Pennsylvania Hall, an edifice destroyed a few years later by a pro-slavery mob.

We are unable to follow Whittier in all his efforts; his pen was never idle, and his energy in the cause was never relaxed. He wrote for newspapers whenever there was opportunity, and most of his poems at this period were in fact, if not in name, "Voices of Freedom."

He was elected a member of the State legislature for the year 1835, the only public office he ever held, except that of presidential elector. He had never the gifts of an orator, as he was lacking in confidence, and averse to display; but he was an able, well-informed, and useful legislator.

As we look back upon the history of that time, we are struck by the accounts of outrages continually perpetrated by the opponents of the anti-slavery cause. An abolitionist was not only "fanatic named and fool," but was pelted by way of rejoinder to his argument. The criminal statutes were ransacked to find precedents for his being laid by the heels. Grand juries were urged to indict him. The sworn conservators of the peace found the care of him a trouble; for he was outside the pale of humanity, and there was then no society for the prevention of cruelty to animals. Governors of States founded in despotism offered rewards for his

head.   His appearance on the platform was the
signal for horse-play and brutal insult.   Not one of
the twelve Apostles had been more sure of provok-
ing riots.   And these disturbances were not solely
in large cities nor among " lewd fellows of the baser
sort."   The spirit was manifested with equal virulence in such towns as Salem, Haverhill, and Concord, and seemed to have the approval of the
wealthy, learned, and fashionable classes.

An anti-slavery society was established in Haverhill, April 3, 1834, of which Whittier was corresponding secretary.   There was strong opposition,
and in due course of time the usual result, namely,
a mob.   In August, 1835, the Rev. Samuel J. May,
having preached on a Sunday morning, proposed to
deliver an anti-slavery lecture in the evening.

" The evening meeting was entirely broken up by a
mob outside, who threw sand and gravel and small stones
against the windows, breaking the glass, and by their hoot-
ings frightened the female portion of the audience, and
led to the fear on the part of all that more serious assaults
would follow if the meeting was continued.   It was therefore summarily dissolved.   It was perhaps fortunate that
this course was adopted, as a loaded cannon was then
being drawn to the spot to add its thunderings to the
already disgraceful tumults of that otherwise quiet Sabbath evening." [1]

[1] Chase's History of Haverhill, p. 505.

Elizabeth Whittier, the poet's youngest sister, and another young lady, Harriet **Minot,** grasped the hands **of May,** and, pushing their way through **the** crowd of their misguided townsmen, escaped without injury, except that they were rudely hustled.

Some time before this, George Thompson, M. P., having been invited by Garrison, came to this country to address the public upon the great **question of the day.** He had been the leading advocate of the abolition of slavery **in the** British **colonies, and was renowned as an orator.** But the immitigable hate felt towards **an** abolitionist was **intensified** in his case by **a** fierce and unreasoning resentment against interference in a domestic question on **the part of** a foreigner. Thompson, **it** was said, **was** a minion of the English cabinet; England was **our** old enemy and our detested rival in commerce; and Thompson had come over **to** foster dissension between North and South, and so destroy our great and glorious Union. Many people doubtless sincerely believed this. But the abolitionists, **who,** with Garrison, considered the world to be their country, and all mankind their countrymen, **welcomed the generous aid from one of the first of orators and most disinterested **of** men.

Whittier was **not** present **at the** meeting in his **native** town so summarily broken up. He was absent at the time in the State of New Hampshire, where he had the honor of a mob got up partly on his own account.

George Thompson, who could say with Paul that he was "in perils oft," had narrowly escaped from a mob in Salem, and was secreted by Whittier in East Haverhill for two weeks. Thinking themselves secure because personally unknown, the two friends drove to Plymouth, N. H., to visit Nathaniel P. Rogers, a prominent abolitionist. On their way they stopped for the night in Concord at the house of George Kent, who was a brother-in-law of Rogers. After they had gone on their way, Kent attempted to make preparations for an anti-slavery meeting to be held when they should return. There was a furious excitement, and neither church, chapel, nor hall could be hired for the purpose. On their arrival Whittier walked out with a friend in the twilight, leaving Thompson in the house, and soon found himself and friend surrounded by a mob of several hundred persons, who assailed them with stones and bruised them somewhat severely. They took refuge in the house of Colonel Kent, who, though not an abolitionist, protected them and baffled the mob. From thence Whittier made his way with some difficulty to George Kent's, where Thompson was. The mob

soon surrounded the house and demanded that
Thompson and "the Quaker" should be given up.
Through a clever stratagem the mob was decoyed
away for a while, but, soon discovering the trick,
it returned, reinforced with muskets and a cannon,
and threatened to blow up the house if the abolitionists were not surrendered.

A small company of anti-slavery men and women
had met that evening at George Kent's, among
whom were two nieces of Daniel Webster, daughters of his brother Ezekiel. All agreed that the
lives of Whittier and Thompson were in danger,
and advised that an effort should be made to
escape. The mob filled the street, a short distance
below the gate leading to Kent's house. A horse
was quietly harnessed in the stable, and was led
out with the vehicle under the shadow of the
house, where Whittier and Thompson stood ready.
It was bright moonlight, and they could see the
gun-barrels gleaming in the street below them.
The gate was suddenly opened, the horse was
started at a furious gallop, and the two friends
drove off amidst the yells and shots of the infuriated crowd. They left the city by way of Hookset
Bridge, the other avenues being guarded, and hurried in the direction of Haverhill. In the morning
they stopped to refresh themselves and their tired

horse. While at breakfast they found that "ill news travels fast," and gets worse as it goes; for the landlord told them that there had been an abolition meeting at Haverhill the night before, and that George Thompson, the Englishman, and a young Quaker named Whittier, who had brought him, were both so roughly handled that they would never wish to talk abolition again. When the guests were about to leave, Whittier, just as he was stepping into the carriage, said to the land-lord, " My name is Whittier, and this is George Thompson." The man opened his eyes and mouth with wonder as they drove away.

When they arrived at Haverhill they learned of the doings of the mob there, and the fortunate escape of their friend May.[1]

The attempt to mob Thompson in Boston is vividly described by Lydia Maria Child.[2]

" My most vivid recollection of George Thompson is of his speaking at Julian Hall [3] on a memorable occasion. Mr. Stetson, then keeper of the Tremont House, was present, with a large number of his slaveholding guests, who had come to Boston to make their annual purchases of the merchants. Their presence seemed to inspire

---

[1] From a letter written by Mrs. Cartland.

[2] Letters, p. 248 *et seq.*

[3] Julian Hall was on the corner of Milk and Congress Streets, Boston.

Mr. Thompson. **Never, even from his eloquent lips,** did I hear such scathing denunciations of **slavery.** The exasperated Southerners could not contain their wrath. **Their** lips were tightly compressed, their hands clenched; and now and then a muttered curse was audible. Finally, one of them shouted, 'If we had **you down South, we 'd** cut off your ears.' Mr. Thompson folded his arms in his characteristic manner, looked calmly at the speaker, and replied, 'Well, sir, if you did cut off my ears, I should still cry aloud, **" He that** *hath* **ears to** hear, let him hear." '

" Meanwhile **my heart was thumping like a sledge-** hammer; for, before the speaking began, Samuel J. **May** had come to me and said in a **very low** tone, ' Do **you see** how the walls **are** lined by stout truckmen, bran- dishing their whips? They are part of a large mob around the entrance in Federal Street, employed by the Southerners to seize George Thompson **and carry** him to **a** South Carolina vessel **in** waiting **at** Long Wharf. **A** carriage with swift horses is at the door, and these South- erners are now exulting **in** the anticipation of lynching him. But behind that large green curtain **at** the back of the platform there is **a** door leading **to** the chamber of **a warehouse. We have the key to** that **door,** which leads **to a** rear entrance of the building on Milk Street. There **the** abolitionists have stationed **a carriage with** swift horses **and a** colored driver, who **of** course will **do** his best **for George** Thompson. Now, as soon as **Mr.** Thompson ceases **speaking, we want** the anti-slavery women to gather **round** him **and** appear **to** detain him in **eager** conversation. **He** will listen and reply, but keep imperceptibly moving backward toward the green curtain. You will all follow him, and when he vanishes behind the curtain you will continue to stand close together, and appear to be still talking with him.'

"At the close of the meeting twenty-five or thirty of us women clustered around Mr. Thompson and obeyed the instructions we had received. When he had disappeared from our midst there was quiet for two or three minutes, interrupted only by our busy talking. But the Southerners soon began to stand on tiptoe and survey the platform anxiously. Soon a loud oath was heard, accompanied by the exclamation, 'He's gone!' Then such a thundering stampede as there was down the front stairs I have never heard. We remained in the hall, and presently Samuel J. May came to us, so agitated that he was pale to the very lips. 'Thank God, he is saved!' he exclaimed; and we wrung his hand with hearts too full for speech.

"The Boston newspaper press, as usual, presented a united front in sympathy with the slaveholders. . . . But they were all in the dark concerning the manner of his escape; for as the door behind the curtain was known to very few, it remained a mystery to all except the abolitionists."

Not long after these events Whittier went to Boston to attend an extra session of the legislature called for the purpose of revising the laws of the Commonwealth. He had been a frequent visitor at the office of the " Liberator," and the early friends of the editor still love to recall " his flashing eyes and intrepid mien," and to acknowledge his services and devotion to the cause. He witnessed the doings of the mob on Washington Street, for his sister was in attendance upon that meeting of the Female Anti-slavery Society, and, hearing of the disturbance, he had hastened to the spot, and ascertained that the women had escaped. He saw Garrison in the clutches of the mob, with a rope around his neck, and saw his rescue by the police and their hurried drive, followed by the howling mob, to Leverett Street jail, whither they took him for safety. He and the Rev. Samuel J. May went to the jail, and conversed with Garrison in his cell. That day, having been warned that the house at which they were stopping might be attacked by the mob, Whittier managed to remove his sister to a place of safety without her being aware of the danger, while he and May watched during the night.

The Boston mob, led by "men of property and standing," has been frequently described. It was an outbreak with far-reaching consequences, and, with the exception of the Boston Massacre of 1770, will be considered the most important event in the history of the city. It furnishes a striking view of the relations between morals and majorities, and shows that the voice of the people is not yet the voice of God. As it happened, Garrison was the victim of this infamous outrage, but the person aimed at was George Thompson. It was against him mainly that the inflammatory articles in the newspapers, and the seditious handbills and placards throughout the city, were directed. For the leading men had said that Thompson, the foreign interloper, should not be allowed to speak. It is well known that he was not announced, and was not present at the little meeting of women which the mayor courageously ordered to disperse; and after the triumph of the mob he withdrew from the city.

There is an interesting reminiscence of this period of Whittier's life in the form of a small volume entitled "Poems written during the Progress of the Abolition Question in the United States, between the years 1830 and 1838, by John G. Whittier." It bears the imprint of Isaac Knapp, the publisher of the "Liberator," and is dated 1837. The introductory remarks are evidently by Garrison. This is a characteristic paragraph : —

"Those who have read 'Mogg Megone' will see in them the same easy strength of versification, the same thrilling correspondence of sound to sense, the same electrifying *estro*[1] joined to high and powerful conceptions of moral beauty and sublimity, which have become thus strong and exalted because (in Emerson's phrase) the writer 'lives as a life what he apprehends as a truth.'"

[1] Poetic fire or genius.

There is a reference to Körner, "of• the lyre and sword,"—not so inapt, for Whittier has been a very aggressive patriot—for a Quaker. The contents of this little volume are all in the collected edition, excepting a notable poem addressed to Governor McDuffie. The impression made by this brilliant satire (read forty years ago) is not faded to-day. This surely should be replaced among the acknowledged poems.

A few stanzas are quoted. Governor McDuffie had used the phrase, "The patriarchal institution of Slavery."

> " King of Carolina, hail !
>   Last champion of Oppression's battle ;
> Lord of rice-tierce and cotton-bale,
>   Of sugar-box and human cattle.
> Around thy temples, green and dark,
>   Thy own tobacco wreath reposes, —
> Thyself a brother Patriarch
>   Of Isaac, Abraham, and Moses !
>
> .   .   .   .
>
> " Ho, fishermen of Marblehead ! —
>   Ho, Lynn cordwainers, leave your leather,
> And wear the yoke in kindness made,
>   And clank your needful chains together !
> Let Lowell mills their thousands yield,
>   Down let the rough Vermonter hasten,
> Down from the workshop and the field,
>   And thank us for each chain we fasten.

"SLAVES in the rugged Yankee land?
    I tell thee, Carolinian, never !
Our rocky hills and iron strand
    Are free, and shall be free forever.
The surf shall wear that strand away,
    Our granite hills in dust shall moulde
Ere Slavery's hateful yoke shall lay,
    Unbroken, on a Yankee's shoulder."

CHAPTER VIII.

POLITICAL MOVEMENT AGAINST SLAVERY.

Garrison assails the Church for its Conservatism and Silence. —
He deprecates Political Action. — A Division takes Place. —
Whittier sides with the Workers in Politics. — The " Emanci-
pator." — " Reminiscences " of Samuel J. May.

THERE has been dissension in every camp,
under every leader from Achilles to Grant.
In voluntary associations formed for the advance-
ment of moral causes, differences of opinion and
divisions in action are inevitable. When Garrison
found the church indifferent to the claims of human
brotherhood, and willing to temporize with a gigan-
tic crime rather than hazard the unity of General
Councils, he turned upon the clergy with the bold-
est invective, tipping his phrases with flinty points
from their own scriptural armory. Then he was
thought to be " going too far ; " and before long in
many minds the abolitionist and the infidel were
joined in equal reprobation. As he persisted in
plain speech to the " dumb dogs " in charge of the

spiritual flocks, some of his followers seceded. It was in vain that he protested he was not hammering at Christianity, but at the organizations which were denying the spirit of Christ in consenting to the bondage of those for whom Christ died. The conservative clergy made strong points against him, however, as being a man who was willing to destroy what he could not hastily reform. They likened him to a man who would burn his house to be rid of a wasp's nest. His work was undoubtedly hindered by this and other complications, and the number of his open followers did not greatly increase. At the meetings of the anti-slavery societies the same familiar faces were seen from year to year. The avowed friends of the slave were known, almost as a distinct sect is known, and were separated from the religious bodies which form "the Church" by more rigid lines than were ever drawn against Christian men, except in the case of the early Quakers. But treatment of this kind, whether called persecution or isolation, did not trouble Whittier. He was naturally and by inheritance a come-outer. His poems entitled "Clerical Oppressors," "The Pastoral Letter," and "A Sabbath Scene," show that, so far from being intimidated by the action of the church and the clergy, he was ready to use his great powers in sharp aggressive warfare; and **if** we ever **pity** grave and well-meaning men in false **and** ridiculous positions, we might actually feel **some** compunction as we read the terrible though deserved **sarcasms** in those glowing lines. The pillory would have been merciful in comparison; and there was none to reply; the poets were all inspired by the same feelings; there was no orthodox prophet to be led forth against the Abolition-Israel.

Though **the number of** professing abolitionists was small, their influence **was pervasive. Before** long, men of practical experience in politics began to say, Why agitate forever? **Why not make a** beginning, vote as we believe, and let ideas crystallize in laws? Garrison opposed this view, on the ground that a moral cause could not be carried on to success without ignoble means. **He was for** the diffusion **of** light **and truth** through **all** educational, moral, and religious agencies, and **he** hoped the desired result would be brought about through the action of conscientious men in both of the old parties. **A** small but faithful band adhered to him in this course, but the anti-slavery sentiment of the North, especially in Massachusetts, was generally in favor **of** political **action.** Those who thought they should sustain their religious convictions and church polity in harmony with their anti-slavery doctrines and with political action were supporters of the "Emancipator,"[1] a newspaper conducted with eminent ability by Joshua Leavitt.

There is not space in a volume like this to notice the various attempts at combining voters for the cause; it is sufficient to mention succinctly the leading incidents.

In 1840 there was a Liberty party convention at Albany, N. Y., at which James G. Birney was nominated for President. In 1844 Birney was again nominated, and received over 60,000 votes. In 1846 there was a vehement discussion upon a question of national importance, known as the Wilmot Proviso. This arose upon a resolution offered by David Wilmot, M. C., from Pennsylvania, declaring that slavery should not be permitted in the territory that had been acquired from Mexico. It soon became the paramount issue, and resulted in wide-spread divisions in both political parties. In consequence of this the Liberty party in 1848 was merged in the new Free-Soil party, formed

---

[1] Whittier wrote much for the "Emancipator," from 1837 to 1842. Some of his well-known anti-slavery lyrics appeared in it. After his return from Philadelphia in 1839–40, he aided Mr. Leavitt almost constantly. A letter from Elizabeth Whittier, preserved by a friend, and dated January 4, 1842, has this sentence : "Greenleaf is still in Boston. . . . He has the care of the 'Emancipator' while Joshua Leavitt is in Washington. . . . Greenleaf will be in Boston perhaps a month longer."

at Buffalo, when Martin Van Buren was nominated for President and Charles Francis Adams for Vice-President. Nearly 300,000 votes were cast for this ticket. The Free-Soil party had its candidates also in the elections of 1852 and 1856 ; but in 1860 it was absorbed in a newly formed Republican party, which carried the country in the election of Abraham Lincoln.

We have seen that Garrison and his friends stoutly opposed political action. After a time they went further, and declared that they could not conscientiously vote in national elections for any party ; for the reason that the guarantees given to slavery in the United States Constitution made it in Scripture phrase, "an agreement with death and a covenant with hell." There was not any marked personal contention between the two divisions of the anti-slavery forces, but each adhered to its own methods and raised its own funds.

Theodore Parker likened the divergence to the difference in the management of a sailing vessel and of a steamship. The latter, as long as the power lasts, pushes on to its destination in a straight line, regardless of wind and tide. The former tacks and trims sails to take advantage of every wind that blows. When the sailing ship stands off on a tack, the captain of the steamer

shouts, " Aha! you are off the course." But the
sailing master was content to be derided, if meanwhile his manœuvres brought him nearer his destination.

Whittier was from the first in favor of political
action, and bore his part in the various contests
before enumerated. He felt obliged by his view
of expediency to differ from his early friend, but
their personal relations were never strained. In
Oliver Johnson's " Life of Garrison" there is a
statement by Whittier of his position that should
have a place here.

" During the long and hard struggle in which the
abolitionists were engaged, and amidst the new and difficult questions and side issues which presented themselves,
it could scarcely be otherwise than that differences of
opinion and action should arise among them. The leader
and his disciples could not always see alike. My friend,
the author of this book, I think, generally found himself in full accord with him, while I often decidedly
dissented. I felt it my duty to use my right of citizenship at the ballot-box in the cause of liberty, while
Garrison, with equal sincerity, judged and counselled
otherwise. Each acted under a sense of individual duty
and responsibility, and our personal relations were un-
disturbed. If, at times, the great anti-slavery leader
failed to do justice to the motives of those who, while
in hearty sympathy with his hatred of slavery, did not
agree with some of his opinions and methods, it was but

the pardonable and not **unnatural result of** his **intensity**
of purpose, and his self-identification with **the cause he**
advocated; and, while compelled to dissent, in some **par-**
ticulars, from his judgment **of** men **and** measures, **the**
great mass of the anti-slavery people recognized his **moral**
leadership. The controversies of Old and New organiza-
tion, Non-Resistance and Political action, may now be
looked upon by the parties to them, who still survive,
with the philosophic calmness which follows **the subsi-**
dence of prejudice and passion. We were **but fallible**
men, **and** doubtless often **erred in feeling, speech, and**
action. Ours was but the common experience of Reformers in all ages —

> ' **Never in custom**'s oiled grooves
> The world to a higher level moves,
> But grates and grinds with friction hard
> On granite boulder and flinty shard.
>
> .　　.　　.　　.　　.
>
> The active Virtues blush to find
> The Vices wearing their badge behind,
> And Graces and Charities **feel the fire**
> Wherein the sins of the age expire.' [1]

"**It is too** late now to dwell on these differences. **I**
choose rather, with a feeling **of** gratitude **to God, to**
recall **the** great happiness of laboring with **the** noble
company **of whom** Garrison was the central **figure. I**
love to think of him as he seemed to me, when **in the**
fresh dawn of manhood he sat with me in the old Haverhill farm-house, revolving even then **schemes of** benevolence; or, with cheery **smile,** welcoming **me** to his frugal

---

[1] **From** Whittier's poem **upon** Whitefield, " The Preacher."

meal of bread and milk in the dingy Boston printing-room; or, as I found him in the gray December morning in the small attic of a colored man, in Philadelphia, finishing his night-long task of drafting his immortal ' Declaration of Sentiments ' of the American Anti-slavery Society ; or, as I saw him in the jail of Leverett Street, after his almost miraculous escape from the mob, playfully inviting me to share the safe lodgings which the State had provided for him ; and in all the varied scenes and situations where we acted together our parts in the great endeavor and success of Freedom."

Since the election of Abraham Lincoln, Whittier has been a steadfast supporter of the Republican party.

The Rev. S. J. May, in his " Reminiscences," [1] pays a warm tribute to the genius and services of Whittier, which we copy, although in some sentences there are repetitions of parts of our own narrative.

" But of all our American poets, John G. Whittier has from first to last done most for the abolition of slavery. All my anti-slavery brethren, I doubt not, will unite with me to crown him our laureate. From 1832 to the close of our dreadful war in 1865 his harp of liberty was never hung up. Not an important occasion escaped him. Every significant incident drew from his heart some pertinent and often very impressive or rousing verses. His name appears in the first volume of the

1 Page 263.

' Liberator,' with high commendations of his poetry and his character. As early as 1831 he was attracted to Mr. Garrison by sympathy with his avowed purpose to abolish slavery. Their acquaintance ripened into a heart-felt friendship, as he declared in the lines, written in 1833 [' To W. L. G.'] : —

> ' Champion of those who groan beneath
> Oppression's iron hand,' &c.[1]

"Mr. Whittier proved the sincerity of these professions. He joined the first anti-slavery society and became an active official. Notwithstanding his dislike of public speaking, he sometimes lectured at that early day, when so few were found willing to avow and advocate the right of the enslaved to immediate liberation from bondage, without the condition of removal to Liberia.

"Mr. Whittier attended the convention at Philadelphia (December, 1833) that formed the American Anti-slavery Society. He was one of the secretaries of that body, and a member, with Mr. Garrison, of the committee appointed to prepare the ' Declaration of our Sentiments and Purposes.' Although . . . Mr. Garrison wrote almost every sentence of that admirable document, just as it now stands, yet I well remember the intense interest with which Mr. Whittier scrutinized it, and how heartily he indorsed it.

" In 1834, by his invitation, I visited Haverhill, where he then resided. I was his guest, and lectured under his auspices in explanation and defence of our abolition doctrines and plans. Again, the next year, after the mob

[1] This was published in the " Emancipator," December 6, 1838.

spirit had broken out, I went to Haverhill by his invitation, and he shared with me in the perils which I have described. . . .

"In January, 1836, Mr. Whittier attended the annual meeting of the Massachusetts Anti-slavery Society, and boarded the while in the house where I was living. He heard Dr. Follen's great speech on that occasion, and came home so much affected by it that, either that night or the next morning, he wrote those 'Stanzas for the Times,' which are among the best of his productions : —

'Is this the land our fathers loved?'[1]

"I can hardly refrain from giving my readers the whole of these stanzas ; but I hope they all are, or will at once make themselves, familiar with them. As I read them now, they revive in my bosom not the memory only, but the glow they kindled there when I first pored over them. Then his lines entitled 'Massachusetts to Virginia,' and those he wrote on the adoption of Pinckney's Resolution, and the passage of Calhoun's bill, excluding anti-slavery newspapers, pamphlets, and letters from the United States mails, — indeed all his anti-slavery poetry, helped mightily to keep us alive to our high duties, and fired us with holy resolution. Let our laureate's verses still be said and sung throughout the land ; for if the portents of the day be true, our conflict with the enemies of liberty, the oppressors of humanity, is not yet ended."

[1] Mr. May's recollection is here at fault. No doubt Whittier wrote a poem on the occasion referred to, but the poem beginning, " Is this the land our fathers loved ? " was printed in the " Boston Courier," September 22, 1835, and was signed, " A FARMER."

CHAPTER IX.

TRIED BY FIRE.

A MAN in public life is fortunate who has an independent fortune. In the United States an official salary counts for nothing, being seldom sufficient for actual needs; and a man in public station who must be solicitous about resources, and who has a wholesome dread of debt, will never be able to hold a creditable position in society, nor to do justice to his own abilities. A reformer is under similar conditions. Wendell Phillips, Edmund Quincy, and Francis Jackson, as well as the Mays, Lorings, and Shaws, were possessed of wealth, and could give time and money to the cause. Garrison was poor, avowedly and honorably poor; but he was put forward and sustained by those who had the means, and he was never

in the least affected by the usual vices that adhere
to men in dependent positions. A chronic office-
holder, or a dependant upon subscriptions or
"passing the hat" at public meetings, generally
ends, if he does not begin, with being a Harold
Skimpole.

The sense of personal independence was as natural to Whittier as his Quaker garb and dialect.
He had the desire of Agar, neither poverty nor
riches, but to maintain himself he was bound to
a life of labor and to habits of rigid economy.
Not in the least avaricious, he gave his time when
he could be of service, and he wrote effective prose
and inspiring verse freely and without a thought
of profit. Poetry, as we have seen, was not a mer-
chantable commodity in 1836, and the productions
of an abolitionist were scorned by all but the few
illuminated souls. It is not probable that any
literary periodical out of New England would have
admitted a poem with his name, — at least after
the struggle began. The ties of honor and self-
respect held him to the farm, and no matter if he
had written with an angel's pen, his hands must
still be browned and hardened by toil. From the
death of his father in 1832 up to 1837 he managed
the farm, hiring some help, but working faithfully
himself. The results were as meagre as ever.

Every product had to be utilized. He used to drive his team in the autumn to Rocks Bridge, which is at the head of tide-water in the Merrimac, where the coasting vessels from Maine then came, carrying apples and vegetables to exchange for salt fish to eke out the winter stores. There are no hardships in a life of toil to a resolute and contented mind.

After the exciting experiences of 1835, Whittier remained at home, engaged in his daily work and in frequent correspondence. A poet always finds an odd hour in which to jot down his flashes of inspiration. Thoughts spring up even when the hands are busy; and lines will shape themselves in order and metre by the sweep of scythes, the strokes of flails, or the rhythm of a spinning-wheel. During these two years, and in fact for several years afterwards, there were no publications, and little to engage the attention of a literary biographer; but we know from subsequent results that the time was filled with rich and varied accomplishment.

In May, 1836, he was again engaged as editor of the "Gazette" in Haverhill, but the connection lasted only until the middle of December.

In the summer of 1837, having been chosen one of the secretaries of the National Anti-slavery Society, he went to New York and remained three months. His associates in the office were Henry B. Stanton and Theodore D. Weld.

Late in 1837 he went to Philadelphia to write for the " Pennsylvania Freeman." As has been stated already, Mr. A. W. Thayer, who had left Haverhill, was then conducting a newspaper in Philadelphia, and Whittier was once more a boarder in his family. Mrs. Thayer says that the anti-slavery people were isolated, shut out from general society, but were fortunately numerous enough to make a pleasant society of their own. As in Boston, the interests of merchants, bankers, and professional men were all on one side. Many of the Quakers, even, having grown rich and worldly, had caught the prevailing infection, and there was a sharp line of division between them and the unsophisticated believers in the primitive doctrines of Fox. Whittier remained faithful no less to his religious convictions than to his anti-slavery principles, and he was not to be turned aside from either. Mrs. Thayer remembers that *once* he was induced to attend a religious service at other than a Friends' meeting-house ; and that was when the Rev. Dr. Todd of Massachusetts was announced to preach in a Presbyterian church.

Whittier was formally announced as editor of the " Freeman " in the issue for March 15, 1838, but he

had written for **the** paper before; he resigned **his** charge February 20, 1840, and left Philadelphia **in May** following. But **his** residence in that city was not continuous; **he** made several long visits **to** Massachusetts in the period, and sent his editorial work by mail. He wrote from New York and Boston in June, 1838; and letters from him dated at Amesbury appeared between November, 1838, and March, **1839.** In July **and** again in September **of** 1839 he made **tours in the western part of Pennsylvania**, in the interests **of the society.**

A small collection of his **poems (180 pages, of** which 91 are devoted **to** phases of the question **of** slavery) was issued by the society on November 1, 1838, bearing the **name** of Joseph Healey as publisher. Mr. Healey **was** the society's financial agent, **and** the collection was put forth **as a** kind **of anti-**slavery tract.

The anti-slavery people of Philadelphia and other friends of free discussion had erected a large building, with business rooms in the basement and **on** the ground floor, and a spacious hall above. It was finished early **in May, 1838,** and the office of Whittier's paper was at **once** established in it. It was named Pennsylvania **Hall, and the** audience-room was opened to the public on **May** 15th, with appropriate exercises. **The** leading abolitionists of the country were present, and there were meetings for three days. The principal feature in the first day's proceedings was the long and elaborate oration of David Paul Brown. In the evening there were addresses by Arnold Buffum, of Philadelphia, and Thomas P. Hunt, of North Carolina. On the second day Charles C. Burleigh read a poetical address, written for the occasion by Whittier. This poem is included in the volume published in 1849 by B. B. Mussey & Co., but not in the complete edition of 1857. It contains about one hundred and fifty lines of ten-syllabled heroics. It is animated, full of vigorous thought, and has some striking passages ; but it is generally declamatory rather than poetical, and is better adapted to stir a sympathetic audience than to command unqualified admiration in the closet. Addresses followed during the day and evening, prominent among them being those of Garrison, Burleigh, and Angelina Grimké of South Carolina. The discussion was not monopolized by the abolitionists ; the platform was occupied partly by colonizationists and other opponents of immediate emancipation. Free speech prevailed, each speaker being solely responsible for his own opinions.

During the first evening there were indications of a disorderly spirit, and a pane of glass was

broken by a stone. On the second day a number
of people came to hiss and otherwise to interrupt
the proceedings. In the evening the disorder increased ; many windows were broken, and the con-
gregation was annoyed by the hooting and yelling
of the mob that had collected around and in the
building. On the morning of the 17th the president
of the Pennsylvania Hall Association formally invoked the protection of the mayor and of the sheriff.
The turmoil continued at intervals during the day,
and it is certain that nothing was done by the
authorities to check the mob. About sunset the
mayor told the president that if the building were
vacated and given into his possession he would
cause the rioters to disperse. The keys were there-
upon delivered to him, and he proceeded to address
his " Fellow Citizens." After a few words, depre-
cating disorder, he said : " There will be no meeting
here this evening. The house has been given up to
me. The managers had the right to hold the meeting, but as good citizens they have, at my request,
suspended their meeting for this evening. *We never
call out the military* here *!* We do not need such
measures. Indeed, I would, fellow-citizens, look
upon you as *my police !* I trust you will abide by
the laws and keep order. I now bid you farewell
for the night."

Upon this plain intimation the mob gave three cheers for the mayor, and soon after commenced a systematic attack. They forced the doors, ransacked the bookstore, carried papers and other combustible materials to the speakers' platform, where they set fire to them, and then, turning on the gas to add fury to the flames, they retired to enjoy the spectacle. The building was almost wholly consumed in a few hours.

A Southerner who witnessed the scene wrote an account of it for a New Orleans paper, from which the following paragraphs are copied; the italics are ours.

" At half-past seven, P. M., the people, *feeling themselves able and willing to do their duty*, burst open the doors of the house, entered their abolition bookstore, and made complete havoc of all within. They then beat out all the windows, and, gathering a pile of window blinds and a pile of abolition books together, they placed them under the pulpit and set fire to them and the building in general. . . . The multitude without, as soon as they perceived the building on fire, gave a loud shout of joy. A large number of splendid fire engines were immediately on the spot, many of which could throw water more than a hundred feet high; but *the noble firemen*, to a man, of all the numerous companies present, refused to throw one drop of water on the consuming building. All they did was to direct their engines to play upon the private buildings in the immediate vicinity of the blazing hall, some of which were in **great** danger, as they were nearly joining the hall. . . . Such conduct in the Philadelphia fire companies deserves the highest praise and gratitude of all friends of the Union, and **of all Southerners in** particular; and I hope **and** trust **the fire companies of New** Orleans **will** hold a meeting, **and** testify in some suitable manner **to the** Philadelphia fire companies their sincere approbation of their *noble conduct* on this occasion."

Another Southerner **wrote** an **account of the** affair **to a** paper **in Augusta, Ga. He and a friend** enjoyed **the spectacle. He says:** —

"**We lent our feeble efforts to effect the demolition** of this castle **of** iniquity. . . . The **fire** companies **repaired** tardily to the scene **of** action, **and not a drop** of water did they **pour upon** that accursed Moloch until **it was a** heap of ruins. **Sir, it** would have gladdened your heart to have beheld that lofty tower of mischief enveloped in flames. The devouring **element . . .** seemed **to** wear, combined with its terrible majesty, *beauty* **and** *delight.* To witness those beautiful spires of flame **gave** undoubted assurance to the heart **of the** Southron that in his brethren of the North he has friends who appreciate him, and who will defend **him,** though absent, at any and at every hazard."

In reading these letters **we cannot but regret** that the Rev. Petroleum V. **Nasby** had **not then** arisen ; for he only **could do justice to them.**

The vindictive spirit **of the** mob **was** far from being satisfied. **The** excitement continued during the next day, and in the evening a charitable institution called " Shelter for Colored Orphans " was burned. A church belonging to colored people was attacked the day after and somewhat damaged. After the tumults had subsided, which was six days later, the mayor offered a reward for the arrest and conviction of any of the rioters, but of course to no purpose. The day before the outrage the Pennsylvania Anti-slavery Society had given notice that a meeting would be held at the hall the next morning for the choice of officers. The members met together by the still smoking ruins, and, with the vast mob still howling around them, calmly transacted their business. A scene for a grand historical picture !

The office of Whittier's paper was in the basement of Pennsylvania Hall, and it was sacked as well as burned, involving a total destruction of his property therein. The publication was continued, however, with but little delay, and he remained in Philadelphia somewhat more than a year, when, on account of failing health, he gave up the enterprise and returned to Massachusetts.

An account of the dedicatory services, with most of the speeches in full, and of the destruction of the hall, with the futile " investigation " that followed, has been preserved in a book. The address of the Pennsylvania Anti-slavery Society upon the subject was written by Whittier and Charles C. Burleigh, and published in the "Pennsylvania Freeman."

Among the poems of this time preserved in the complete edition are the "New Year's Address" to the subscribers of the paper, "The Farewell of the Slave Mother," and the one entitled "A Relic," written on receiving a cane made from a piece of wood saved from the flames.

In 1840, the farm in East Haverhill having been sold, and Whittier's mother, sister, and aunt having removed to Amesbury (partly for the sake of being near their meeting-house), he joined them on his return from Philadelphia, and there is still his legal residence. For the last few years, however, he has spent most of his time at Oak Knoll, in Danvers, Mass., the attractive country-home of relatives.

The house in Amesbury is a plain, comfortable structure of two stories, standing on the main street, and its appearance is familiar to the public by means of engravings. In Amesbury, Whittier was nearer to many scenes he has drawn with such loving lines. The "swift Powow" is not far, nor the lovely river Artichoke (flowing under continuous green arches). Lake Attitash is but a few miles distant, and the unrivalled beauty of "The Laurels" is to be seen across the Merrimac, a little farther down.

It will be remembered that at the time of the change of residence the family consisted of four persons only. The farm having passed out of his hands, Whittier thenceforth depended on his pen for support.

CHAPTER X.

Whittier edits the "Middlesex Standard." — "The Stranger in
Lowell." — Intense Feeling shown in the "Voices." — "The
Pastoral Letter." — Poetical Merits of the "Voices."

THE four or five years following Whittier's removal to Amesbury were filled with earnest,
self-denying labor for the anti-slavery cause, done
with no reward and in straitened circumstances,
in addition to constant writing for the periodicals,
as will hereafter be seen. The time had not come
for any general appreciation of his poems; with
most readers it was sufficient that he was an abolitionist, and that fact put him without the pale
of sympathy. In addition to his purely literary
work, he wrote constantly for the newspapers
whenever he could gain admission for his unpopular views; and he often went from town to town,
endeavoring to create anti-slavery sentiment, and
to organize voters for effective service at the polls.
At this period his most intimate friend and co-
laborer was Henry B. Stanton, now a resident of

New York. They were great lobby workers in the State legislature, and Whittier, strange as it may appear, was "a superb hand at it."[1] With all his exterior calm he was a shrewd judge of men, and knew how to appeal to what was best in them. This steady, persistent work in politics, solely for moral ends, has never been intermitted.

In 1844 he resided in Lowell for six months, writing for the "Middlesex Standard," a Liberty party paper. This was a congenial labor, if poorly paid. One series of papers which he wrote for the "Standard" was afterwards reprinted in Boston, called "The Stranger in Lowell." Most of these articles will be found in the second volume of Whittier's prose works.

The election of 1844 was the precursor of the Mexican War, which was waged solely to extend the area of slavery, and thereby perpetuate its ascendency in the government. To Whittier, an opponent of war and slavery both, this was an unspeakable outrage, — a crime against a nation which had only too much reason for its jealousy of the United States, — a crime against all humanity. His poems written at this period are remarkable for their vigor and intensity of feeling. It would be difficult now to assign dates for many of them,

---

[1] From a letter of Wendell Phillips.

as they appeared in many different newspapers, and their order in the collected edition is not chronological.

It is well, perhaps, here to glance briefly at the "Voices of Freedom. From 1833 to 1848."[1] We must remember that Whittier has regarded poetry as a means and not an end. His aim has been to reach the hearts of men, and poetic diction has been only the feathering of his arrows. Had he lived in a time when there were no oppressed to be set free, no wrongs to be redressed, no evils to be overthrown, he might have sung hymns of pure beauty and joy; for no poet evinces a keener sense of the divine in man, or a more ecstatic pleasure in the divine manifestations in nature. Those who read poems for intellectual pleasure will not feel attracted by these strong utterances, so much as by the legends, ballads, and landscape pieces farther on. But to the elders, who were living in that dreary time when evil was good, injustice was honored, and God was mocked, these poems appear

---

[1] Published by Lindsay & Blakiston, Philadelphia, 1849. These poems were gathered from newspapers for which they were originally written. The most of them may be found in the files of the Liberator, Emancipator, Anti-slavery Standard, Haverhill Gazette, and National Era. Whittier's contributions to the "Era" began in 1847, and afterwards reached a very large number. But the sources of some of these "Voices" have not been found, although diligent search has been made.

to embody all their thoughts, their labors and sufferings, and their aspirations. More than this: they renew in mind the glow with which they were first read, as stanza succeeds stanza of impassioned eloquence, paralleled only by the majestic burdens of the prophets of old. Read now in the light of freedom, some of these poems have a sublime prophetic tone. That one entitled simply "Stanzas" (from the "Liberator," September, 1834) has an almost terrible force; and we can only wonder that the heart and conscience of the nation could have resisted its appeal. Evidently written in a white heat, the language is at once terse and vehement, and the sound of the lines is like the clashing of swords. The thoughts and emotions are sublimed, as happens only in the most exalted state of the creative soul. Such a poem could never have been *composed*. It is as difficult to quote from it, as to give a segment of a moving wave of lava; one familiar stanza may be given to recall the general character: —

> "Go — let us ask of Constantine
>   To loose his grasp on Poland's throat;
> And beg the lord of Mahmoud's line
>   To spare the struggling Suliote; —
> Will not the scorching answer come
>   From turbaned Turk and scornful Russ:
> 'Go, loose your fettered slaves at home,
>   Then turn and ask the like of us!'"

It was by the influence of lines like these, more, perhaps, than by the eloquence of the great anti-slavery orators, that the hearts of men were changed. For it was not so much right thinking that was needed as right action. The poetry of the world was all on one side, and could not have been otherwise. Read in country newspapers, and recited in schools, these humane and generous sentiments were infused into the minds of youth. The boys of 1844, with ideas of freedom in mind, grew up into the iron men of 1860; and no further triumph of slavery was possible, whether the civil war had come or had not come.

Perhaps the most brilliant and most aggressive of these poems is the one entitled "The Pastoral Letter," first printed in the "Liberator," October, 1837. A council of Congregational clergymen at Brookfield, Mass., had taken occasion to discourage the agitation of the question of slavery, and they censured especially the employment of female anti-slavery speakers, — quoting Paul, after the old fashion. This was directed mainly against the accomplished sisters, Sarah and Angelina Grimké, "Carolina's high-souled daughters," who had been slave-owners, and who now as advocates of freedom were making trouble for the quietist preachers by awakening the consciences of their hearers.

The reply of Whittier is filled with grim sarcasm and indignant invective. The blood of his Quaker ancestors was in a ferment. The lines hit like rapier thrusts. The memory of clerical oppression and of the wrongs inflicted upon his people in Puritanic times would not be restrained : —

> " Now, shame upon ye, parish Popes!
>   Was it thus with those, your predecessors,
> Who sealed with racks, and fire, and ropes
>   Their loving-kindness to transgressors ?
>
>   .   .   .   .   .
>
> Then, wholesome laws relieved the Church
>   Of heretic and mischief-maker,
> And priest and bailiff joined in search,
>   By turns, of Papist, witch, and Quaker!
> The stocks were at each church's door,
>   The gallows stood on Boston Common,
> A Papist's ears the pillory bore, —
>   The gallows-rope, a Quaker woman !
>
>   .   .   .   .   .
>
> Your fathers dealt not as ye deal
>   With ' non-professing ' frantic teachers ;
> They bored the tongue with red-hot steel,
>   And flayed the backs of ' female preachers.'
> Old Newbury, had her fields a tongue,
>   And Salem's streets could tell their story,
> Of fainting woman dragged along,
>   Gashed by the whip, accursed and gory ! "

Tenderer strains follow, as after a time sorrow takes up the burden of wrath ; but throughout the poem there is the same resistless movement, in which argument and expostulation are blended, while the apt rhymes give a series of epigrammatic as well as sonorous blows.

As a piece of literary workmanship (if such a phrase can be used in reference to an evident impromptu) this is not surpassed by any of the author's poems. What a pleasure — and what a surprise — it would be to see such vigorous strokes in any magazine to-day! Whatever Whittier has done or has failed to do, it is a matter of thankfulness that there is no "uncertain sound" in his verse. Now-a-days the muse appears "sicklied o'er with the pale cast" of philosophy, and it is considered fatal if a poem can be understood by the unlearned without exegesis.

The stated meetings of the anti-slavery societies were almost always enlivened by some new poem by Whittier, as well as by the magnificent and incomparable oratory of Wendell Phillips. Many of the "Voices" were first uttered on these occasions, as their titles and dates indicate. The reader will find them uniformly strong, religious, and hopeful.

It is too soon by many years to attempt to give a just and dispassionate view of these anti-slavery poems. The generation just coming to maturity cannot understand their fiery vehemence. On the other hand, there are men past middle age who have certain associations, arising partly from old party ties, and partly tinged by social and religious conservatism, which, though they are without any logical relation to the accepted doctrines and the natural feelings of to-day, continue unconsciously to sway their judgment and to nourish the old antipathy. The "Webster Whigs," as the leading men of Boston delighted to call themselves, who had spent the best years of their manhood in contending against anti-slavery agitation, and to whom every glowing lyric was only a new firebrand to imperil the national edifice, could not bring themselves to consider "Voices of Freedom" as poetry at all. They might admit the force of expression and the sure and effective rhythm, but who could expect the subjects of such terrible castigation to admire the skill with which it was administered? The truth is, that much of the old party prejudice still lingers, though unacknowledged, in many minds. The political leaders who were on what we may now fairly term the wrong side have quite generally remained aloof to this day, — not as justifying human slavery or approving the course of the South, but still reprobating the methods of the victors, and convinced that if *they* had been intrusted with the direction of affairs, the earthquake would have been put down, or would have done its upheaval more gently.[1]

If the conservative is still unable to appreciate the merits of the " Voices," the anti-slavery man who bore his part in the long and often desperate conflict is perhaps equally disqualified to form an impartial opinion. We may say once more that in his mind and memory the " Voices" are associated with all his toils and his triumphs; they represent his inmost feelings at the time when they were profoundly moved. They accord with his deepest convictions of right and duty; and their high, solemn phrases seem to come with a divine authority. For

[1] A prominent gentleman in Boston, seeing an advertisement of the proposed celebration of Lincoln's edict of freedom to the slave, January 1, 1863, expressed his surprise and regret to the author of this book, who was one of the committee, adding that such an act might be a millstone upon his neck in future times, and that for his own part he would not for ten thousand dollars have allowed his name to be coupled with an abolition jubilee. This was the general feeling among conservatives. It was with great difficulty that a meagre chorus — mostly of women — was gathered to perform the musical part of the services. Letters of invitation to singers were, many of them, sent back to the committee with indignant and often abusive comments. So far was Boston from being a liberty-loving city at the time when the shackles fell from three millions of men ! It may be mentioned that the celebration was eminently successful, excepting the unbalanced effects of the chorus, and it was rendered forever memorable by the rugged grandeur of Emerson's " Boston Hymn," read by the illustrious author.

an abolitionist to assume a critical attitude in regard to the "Voices" would be as hard as for a Hebrew to find fault with "The horse and his rider" or "By the rivers of Babylon." It will be for neither of the parties that were engaged in the long and momentous struggle to decide upon the purely poetical merits of these lyrics. If the prime test of poetry were to be its power to move the heart, there could be but one opinion; but we must remember that impassioned eloquence (which is not necessarily poetical) does the same thing. There are many of Whittier's ringing stanzas which are scarcely more than rhymed eloquence; but, judged by the same rule, some of the most stirring passages of Byron and Dryden, and nearly all the heroic verses of Pope, come into the same category.

As has been intimated, the remarkable trait in the "Voices" is the free, powerful, and melodious movement. The lines are not only strongly accented, but are alive with rhythmical feeling. Evidently there was no searching for words, no labor in finding assonances. The creative faculty combined and fused all the poet's logic, wit, and moral purpose, and poured out the result in stanzas that might seem to have been spoken into being as by miracle. They are whole, perfect, entire, and as incapable of change as if the members were endowed with life. Or, to vary the simile, the stream of song, though in constant flow, has the changeless beauty of a waterfall.

With one more observation we leave this part of our task. In certain of the most outspoken of the "Voices," such as "The Pine-Tree," "Massachusetts to Virginia," "Texas," and "The Branded Hand," there seems to prevail a spirit which is not only intense but fierce. But those who understand the reality of the danger then impending, which was the entire subjection of the government to the Slave Power, will not only pardon but applaud the energy with which the momentous issue was met. It was felt by all far-seeing men to be a question of life and death; and in such a terrible crisis courtesy would have been folly, and compliment crime. It was a *combat à l'outrance.*

Criticism is usually vague to every one but the critic, and the lightest suggestion of shortcomings is apt to be taken as meaning more than is seen at the first glance. Particularly is it so in these days of finical refinement in style, when it is thought witty and "knowing" to let a subtle undercurrent be perceived, quite at variance with the superficial sense of the words employed. The result is to damn in the most honeyed phrases, or to praise in a way to leave a sting.

That it may be clear what is intended, it is best to observe that pure poetry is the rarest of products; that many popular poets have no conception of what poetry is, and have never by accident created a poetical phrase; that absolute poetry is generally like veins of gold in quartz, — seldom if ever seen without some kind of admixture; that in the works of the greatest poets the specimens of pure poetry form but a very small part of their bulk,— probably never a fifth, often less than a tenth. With this limitation in view, we should say that the "Voices" are less purely poetic than the best contemplative and descriptive pieces of Whittier. They will be read with varied feelings; they will be fervently admired and warmly deprecated; but all will admit that in "The Last Walk in Autumn," "Evening by the Lakeside," "Amy Wentworth," and many others that might be named, there is a higher and purer poetic inspiration.

Still, we cannot desire that even one of the "Voices" should be silenced. They were uttered at the call of duty and encouraged by the heavenly influences. The "burden" was upon the poet as upon the prophets of the Jews. Whittier never faltered in his mission. His part in the great revolution is now historical, and after its triumphal success he can look back with more than satisfaction upon the results he aided in bringing about.

CHAPTER XI

FOUNDATIONS OF FAME.

"Moll Pitcher." — Nahant. — Buckingham's "New England Magazine." — The "Democratic Review." — "Songs of Labor." — "The Bridal of Pennacook." — The Ticknor Edition of 1843. — "Supernaturalism in New England." — "Memories" and their Significance. — The Merrimac River and its Scenery. — "Cassandra Southwick."

HAVING devoted as much space as could be given to Whittier's early anti-slavery labors, it is necessary to return to his purely literary work, beginning with the year 1832. Either in Hartford or shortly after his return to Haverhill he wrote a poem entitled "Moll Pitcher." As has been mentioned, some passages of this work had appeared in his newspaper; but the main portions of the story were new. Moll Pitcher was a fortune-teller, famous in the last century, who lived near High Rock in Lynn, Mass. She professed to derive her auguries from the appearance of tea-grounds. The story is told of a country maiden and her sailor lover, and covers twenty-seven pages octavo in

pamphlet form.[1] It is dedicated to Dr. Eli Todd
of Hartford. In the prefatory note Whittier says
it was " written during a few weeks of such leisure
as is afforded by indisposition, and is given to the
world in all its original negligence." The copy
lent to the author bears the name of a lifelong
friend of Whittier, written in a delicately beautiful hand. The poem was not reprinted, and is very
scarce.

The " New England Magazine " for May, 1832,
contains a notice of this poem, including admired
specimens of its versification ; but the tone of comment is not generally complimentary. In one paragraph the critic reproves Whittier for publishing a
poem " in its original negligence ; " saying, " Why
does a writer who is competent to the production
of elegant and perfect verses, &c. ? " The censure
is welcome on account of the admission that at this
early period, before any of Whittier's poems had
been gathered from a fugitive existence, he was
recognized as a maker of " elegant and perfect
verses." We give a short descriptive passage to
show the style : —

> " Nahant, thy beach is beautiful ! —
>   A dim line through the tossing waves,
>   Along whose verge the spectre gull
>   Her thin and snowy plumage laves,

[1] Carter & Hendee, Boston, 1832.

"What time the summer's greenness lingers
  Within thy sunned and sheltered nooks,
And the green vine with twining fingers
  Creeps up and **down** thy hanging rocks.
Around, **the** blue **and** level **main,**
  Above, **a** sunshine rich as fell,
Brightening of old with golden rain,
  The isle Apollo loved so well; —
And far off, dim and beautiful
The snow-white sail and graceful hull,
  Slow dipping to the billow's swell."

It may be best here to say something of this magazine and of Whittier's contributions to it. Its first appearance was in July, 1831, and it was continued to December, 1835, comprising nine octavo volumes. Joseph T. Buckingham and his son Edwin (afterwards lost at sea) were the first editors. The elder Buckingham, afterwards editor of the "Boston Courier," was the one to whom Lowell's first series of "Biglow Papers" was addressed. John O. Sargent, a noted journalist, and Dr. S. G. Howe, the philanthropist and educator of the blind, succeeded Mr. Buckingham at the beginning of the eighth volume; but they soon relinquished the charge to Park Benjamin, a writer of both prose and verse, brother-in-law of the historian Motley. At the end of the year 1835 the periodical came to an end, — having been "merged" in the "American Monthly Magazine," of New York.

As compensation to writers was out of the question, the contents of the magazine were in strange contrast. Many of the articles read like themes of undergraduates and the moral essays of budding clergymen. But in the midst of this dulness there were auroral gleams, — hints of future possibilities. About a dozen of Holmes's beautiful early poems — comic, tender, and graceful — appeared during the first two years. Longfellow was represented by his " Coplas de Manrique." Whittier furnished four prose articles and seven short poems, besides the whole of " Mogg Megone." There were also poems by Mrs. Sigourney, Miss Hannah F. Gould, James G. Percival, Dr. F. H. Hedge, Grenville Mellen, John Neal, Isaac McClellan, Jr., and Park Benjamin. Alexander H. Everett wrote on the French Revolution, and Judge Story gave a fine sketch of Daniel Webster. But most interesting of all are the exquisite early stories and sketches of Hawthorne. Readers of the " Twice Told Tales " know them by heart: the most original and subtile productions in the literature of America. It makes one sad to remember that those labors brought to the author less than a respectable copyist now earns.

The magazine was printed upon dingy paper with dull, small type, and was " illustrated " by the worst (lithographic) portraits ever seen. The portraits

are interesting — in fact priceless — on account of
their associations; but the **"art"** gives one a humiliating **sensation.**[1]

No intelligent view of Whittier's **life and** labors
can be gained from a minute and diaristic account,
but rather **by** grouping events **and** productions as
they are related to each other. We have seen that
while he wrote for the **" New** England Magazine "
the years were prolific in results. The anti-slavery

---

[1] **As the volumes** of this magazine are extremely **scarce, an enu-**
meration of Whittier's contributions **is given : —**

Powow Hill, **a prose sketch, vol. ii. p.** 416, **May, 1832 ;** Passa-
conaway, a **prose** story, **vol. iv. p. 121** (1833) ; **The** Opium Eater,
a prose disquisition, vol. **iv. p. 217** (1833) ; The Female Martyr, a
poem, vol. iv. p. 322, May, **1833 ; New England** Superstitions,
prose, with a poem included, **vol. v.,** July, 1833 ; Stanzas, an ama-
tory poem, vol. **v. p.** 141, July, 1833 ; Toussaint l'Ouverture, with
prefatory note, **vol. v. p.** 368 ; **A Lament, " The circle is** broken,
one seat is forsaken," vol. vi. p. 238 (1834) ; Suicide **Pond, vol. vi.
p. 419** (1834) ; The Demon **of the Study, a** humorous **poem, vol.**
viii., January, 1835 ; To Governor McDuffie (on the secessionist
sentiments in his inaugural address), vol. viii. **p.** 138, February,
1835 ; **Mogg** Megone, first part, vol. viii., March, 1835 ; the **same,**
second part, vol. viii., April, 1835.

The review of " Moll Pitcher," before mentioned, **is in vol. ii.**
p. 441. **There is a** notice of " The Literary Remains of John **G. C.**
Brainerd, **with a Sketch** of his **Life,** by John G. Whittier," **in vol.**
iii., September, **1832.**

The prose articles above named **are** all **extremely** interesting ;
they are not included in his late collected works. Of the poems,
" The Female Martyr," **" Toussaint l'Ouverture," " A** Lament,"
" The Demon of the Study," **and "** Mogg Megone " **have been**
preserved.

poems, " Voices of Freedom," make a group by
themselves. We have now to notice his writings
in the " Democratic Review." [1] It will be seen, by
referring to the list, that this was an important
series of poems. He was evidently a highly valued
contributor, being always assigned a prominent
place, and mentioned always with respect and affection. In the number for August, 1845, there is a
review of his " Stranger in Lowell," garnished with
quotations of great length. Much as he was admired as a poet, very high praise is given him for
his excellent and readable prose. A further proof
of the esteem in which he was held was furnished
by the printing of the " Bridal of Pennacook " en-

[1] The reader may be pleased to see the list, covering a period of
nearly five years : —

Palestine, October, 1837 ; The Familist's Hymn, January, 1838 ;
Pentucket, April, 1838 ; Democracy, December, 1841 ; Follen, September, 1842 ; Poems on Capital Punishment, October, 1842 ;
Raphael, December, 1842 ; To the Reformers of England, January,
1843 ; Cassandra Southwick, March, 1843 ; The Human Sacrifice,
May, 1843 ; Hampton Beach, August, 1843 ; New England Supernaturalism, September, October, and November, 1843 ; The New
Wife and the Old, October, 1843 ; Channing, January, 1844 ; Ezekiel, May, 1844 ; The Bridal of Pennacook, complete, June, 1845
(a part had been printed in September, 1844); Gone ("Another
hand," &c.), March, 1845 ; Songs of Labor : The Shoemaker, July,
1845 ; The Fisherman, October, 1845 ; The Lumberman, December, 1845 ; The Ship-Builder, April, 1846 (the other Songs of
Labor appeared in the " National Era "); To Ronge, March, 1846 ;
James Naylor (prose sketch), March, 1846.

tire in June, 1845, when half of it had already appeared in September, 1844. The second part was lost for nine months in the United States mail, and it is not believed that the poet had kept a copy. The series of papers on "The Supernaturalism of New England" was published in a volume in New York and London in 1847. If we are not in error, every prominent work of Whittier, whether in poetry or prose, was republished by some one, with or without permission, as being of permanent value.

It may be said here, once for all, that to trace *all* of Whittier's poems to their original publication is utterly impossible. There was a collection of anti-slavery poems, including a number by Whittier, published in Philadelphia in a volume entitled the "North Star." "The Prisoner for Debt" appeared in the "Boston Pearl" (either an annual or a literary magazine, edited by Isaac C. Pray, Jr.). "The Fountain" appeared in the "New York Mirror;" "Massachusetts," in the "Emancipator;" and a large number of the "Voices," and other poems, in the "Liberator." Many more were published in the "Gazette" of Haverhill, as has been already stated. The most that could be done was to examine files of periodicals to which it is known he was a contributor; but a large number remain concerning whose origin nothing can be known at present.

A small collection was made in 1843, embracing some of the poems written for the magazine and the review mentioned, and was published under the title of " Lays of my Home, and other Poems," by W. D. Ticknor. This little volume is now scarce, and its very existence has been doubted. The dedication is to John Pierpont, the brilliant and eccentric preacher and poet, and is preserved in the later complete edition. The reader will be surprised to find what a number of established favorites belong to this comparatively early period.[1] Some of them are remarkable for their poetic insight, and all bear the immortal *imprimatur*, which neither king nor chancellor could bestow. Some have a certain autobiographic tone,—the "leaves of memory" making " a mournful rustle in the dark."

[1] Lays of my Home, and other Poems : W. D. Ticknor, 1843. Dedicated to John Pierpont : " Not as a poor requital of the joy," &c., dated at Amesbury, May 10, 1843.

CONTENTS. — The Merrimac ; The Norsemen ; Cassandra Southwick ; Funeral Tree of the Sokokis ; St. John ; Lines written in the Book of a Friend ; Lucy Hooper ; Follen ; To a Friend on her Return from Europe ; Raphael ; Democracy ; Poems on Capital Punishment ; The Human Sacrifice ; The Cypress-Tree of Ceylon ; Chalkley Hall ; To the Reformers of England ; Massachusetts to Virginia ; Leggett's Monument ; To —— with Woolman's Journal ; Memories ; The Demon of the Study ; The Relic ; Extract from a New England Legend.

The poem called "Memories" is one that shows a certain unspeakable tenderness, belonging only to the time of glowing youth. It would not be difficult, perhaps, to frame a *scholium* on the implied propositions; but such things are better unsaid, — laid away in old receptacles with the dried rosebuds. We may imagine, however, that a touching romance is buried beneath the sweet and sad inscription.

> "How thrills once more the lengthening chain
>   Of memory, at the thought of thee!
>   Old hopes which long in dust have lain,
>   Old dreams come thronging back again,
>   And boyhood lives again in me;
>   I feel its glow upon my cheek,
>   Its fulness of the heart is mine,
>   As when I leaned to hear thee speak,
>   Or raised my doubtful eye to thine.
>
> "I hear again thy low replies,
>   I feel thine arm within my own,
>   And timidly again uprise
>   The fringéd lids of hazel eyes,
>   With soft brown tresses overblown.
>   Ah, memories of sweet summer eves,
>   Of moonlit wave and willowy way,
>   Of stars and flowers, and dewy leaves,
>   And smiles and tones more dear than they!
>
> "Ere this, thy quiet eye hath smiled
>   My picture of thy youth to see,
>   When, half a woman, half a child,
>   Thy very artlessness beguiled,
>   And folly's self seemed wise in thee;

> I too can smile when o'er that hour
> 　　The lights of memory backward stream,
> Yet feel the while that manhood's power
> 　　Is vainer than my boyhood's dream.
> 　　　.　　.　　.　　.　　.
>
> "Yet hath thy spirit left on me
> 　　An impress Time hath worn not out,
> A something of myself in thee,
> A shadow from the past, I see,
> 　　Lingering even yet thy way about;
> Not wholly can the heart unlearn
> 　　That lesson of its better hours,
> Nor yet has Time's dull footstep worn
> 　　To common dust that path of flowers.
>
> Thus while at times before our eyes
> 　　The shadows melt, and fall apart,
> And, smiling through them, round us lies
> The warm light of our morning skies, —
> 　　The Indian Summer of the heart, —
> In secret sympathies of mind,
> 　　In founts of feeling which retain
> Their pure, fresh flow, we yet may find
> 　　Our early dreams not wholly vain!"

The pictures which this charming poem conjures up are sacred; but if in all Whittier's verse there had been no expression of the pure and holy love of woman, such as we see here, how dreary would have been his life! Who has not truly loved has not truly lived. Whittier's *Dr. Singletary* perhaps means more than he utters in his remarks on Horace : —

"**Ah,** Elder Staples, there was a time when the Lyces and Glyceras of the poet **were** no fiction **to us.** They played blind-man's-buff with **us in** the **farmer's** kitchen, sang with us in **the** meeting-house, **and** romped **and** laughed **with** us at huskings and quilting parties."

"**The** Merrimac," in this early edition, is the precursor of many poems upon the scenery and the historic associations of the noble river. **Readers** will remember "The Bridal of Pennacook," "**The Laurels,**" "**Sewall's Prophecy,**" "**The Exiles,**" "Pentucket," "**The Swan Song of Parson Avery,**" and **many others.**

Burns and Scott have made the **Ayr** and **the** Tweed and the Scotch mountains **as classic as the** Ilissus, Olympus, and Ida; Wordsworth's spirit **still** haunts the lakes and hills **of Cumberland;** Bryant rejoiced in the Berkshire Hills; **but no poet has more** fully identified **himself** with **the** beauty **of** nature in the region of his birth than Whittier.

The Merrimac is **a** worthy subject for **song. It** receives **the** flow **of** springs **and** the melting **of** mountain **snows in the** middle district **of New** Hampshire, including the overflow from **its** chief lake, Winnepesaukee, **and from the streams** of the Pemigewasset valley; it traverses **the deep grassy** meadows near Concord, studded **with native elms,** that **stand** like slender, flaring Etruscan **vases; it** is perplexed for a time in the rapids of Suncook and Hookset, until it comes in view of the rounded loveliness of the twin Unacanoonucs, — " woman's breasts," in the Indian tongue, — and then dashes down the wild rocky cascades of Amoskeag, where now are the enormous factory piles of Manchester. From this point its course is through scenes of tranquil beauty, always in green meadows and under green trees, until it successively falls at Nashua, Lowell, and Lawrence, turning laborious wheels, and thence flows without hindrance, except for an occasional island, past Haverhill, Newbury, and Amesbury, and separates Newburyport and Salisbury as it reaches Ipswich Bay.

Geologists term it a mountain trough; and at the outset, before the current becomes polluted by the dyes and refuse of mills, the water is pure crystal. Above Lowell the water-bed is comparatively narrow, and the immediate banks are but little raised ; although elevations (often of sand and gravel) on either side testify to the force of the waters in remote periods. But below the last falls the river-bed is wider and the banks stretch out on either hand. The tourist, whether he follows the road on the north or the south side, will find himself on a high ridge, with a wide valley between him and the actual bank of the river; and, looking

across to the corresponding elevation, he will see
that the whole basin is frequently more than a
mile in width. It is ample for the scene of a new
Vision of Mirza.

The unusual breadth of the valley is due to the
action of glaciers, moving seaward in remote times,
blocking the waters and grinding their way. The
entire lower part of the river-bed and valley, from
Pentucket Falls, is full of the wreckage of the
ancient rocks torn from their beds during the
glacial period. But Nature has been repairing
the ravages, and covering the abraded surfaces of
the hills with beautiful trees and soft, turfy coats,
—forming the *roches moutonnées*, as the hills
rounded in the glacial period are termed.

These were in Whittier's mind when he wrote
" The Prophecy of Samuel Sewall : " —

> " The hills of Newbury rolling away,
>   With the many tints of the season gay,
>   Dreamily blending in autumn mist
>   Crimson, and gold, and amethyst.
>
> .   .   .   .   .
>
>   Inland, as far as the eye can go,
>   The hills curve round like a bended bow;
>   A silver arrow from out them sprung,
>   I see the shine of the Quasycung." [1]

[1] " Quascacunquen is allowed by the Court to be a plantation "
(Colonial Records of Massachusetts, May 6, 1635). Quascacunquen
was the Indian name of the river Parker, which empties into the

Further references will be made to the tributary streams and the scenery of the river valley in the course of the work.

Mention should be made of a few of the other poems in the edition of 1843. "To a Friend on her Return from Europe," written in a gay, lilting measure, and full of bright images, has long been a favorite. "Follen" commemorates the author's friend, Charles Follen, an eminent theologian and scholar, for a time professor at Harvard College, lost in the burning of the steamboat "Lexington," in 1840. The absorbing interest of the poem is, however, less in the portrait of the friend than in the keen and steady view of his immortal existence. The lines bring us face to face with the last and deepest problem of life, so that we seem looking with our own eyes into

> " The sphere that keeps
> The disembodied spirits of the dead."

The words are earnest and solemn, poured out from a full heart, and with the simplicity that befits the theme. Justly, this must be regarded as among Whittier's noblest poems, — an evidence of his spiritual convictions and his generous sympa-

Merrimac. The plantation was established under the name of Newbury, where lived the ancestors of the poets Longfellow and Lowell.

thy, and of his art of making readers **think** themselves sharers **in his** creative power.

There is a poem by Bryant entitled **" The Future Life,"** which resembles **this of** Whittier's. **It has the** same quality **of** leading **us to** look into the **dread** beyond ; and it is often cited **as a** proof of Bryant's sensibility and capacity for affection.

" Cassandra Southwick," a ballad founded on the persecution **of the early** Quakers, is widely **known** and **deservedly** admired.[1]

It is full of heart-beats, because **full of that** imagination **which puts the reader at once in the** place of the brave Quaker **girl.** We feel " the damp earth-floor" of her cell and look through the **grated** casement white with **frost.** We recall with her the beautiful past, **and shrink from the** coming shame. We walk with **her through the** streets, a prisoner, — feeling, rather **than** seeing, **all eyes**

---

[1] The story is given in the Mussey edition of 1847, substantially as follows : **A son and** daughter of Lawrence Southwick **of Salem,** Mass., who had himself been imprisoned and deprived of his property for having entertained two Quakers **in** his house, were fined **£10** each for non-attendance at church, a sum which they were unable to pay. The General Court issued an order signed by Edward Rawson, secretary, by which the **treasurer was " fully empowered to** sell the said persons to any of the English nation at Virginia or Barbadoes, **to** answer said fines." An attempt was **made to carry** into execution this barbarous order, but no shipmaster was found willing to convey them to **the** West Indies.

upon her.   Coming to the water's edge, we look with her at the shipping.

> "The merchant-ships lay idly there, in hard clear lines on
>   high,
>   Tracing with rope and slender spar their network on the
>   sky."

We behold the "dark and haughty Endicott," and note the "wine-empurpled cheek" of Rawson, the clerk.   Her sudden rebuke of the priest startles us, but with a sympathetic glow.

> "The Lord rebuke thee, thou smiter of the meek,
>   Thou robber of the righteous, thou trampler of the weak!"

Then the captains hesitate and are silent; no one offers to buy or to transport her.   We listen to the gentle words of the manly spokesman: —

> "God bless thee, and preserve thee, my gentle girl and dear!"

Then comes his thundering answer to the magistrates (and he is to be pardoned for the high swelling words which his tumultuous wrath dictates): —

> "Pile my ship with bars of silver, — pack with coins of Span-
>   ish gold,
>   From keel-piece up to deck-plank, the roomage of her hold;
>   By the living God who made me! — I would sooner in your
>   bay
>   Sink ship and crew and cargo, than bear this child away!"

Can we wonder, after this release, that all nature sympathizes in her joy and gratitude!

"Oh, at that hour the very earth seemed changed beneath my
    eye,
  A holier wonder round me rose the blue walls of the sky,
  A lovelier light on rock and hill, and stream and woodland
    lay,
  And softer lapsed on sunnier sands the waters of the bay."

Those who have pondered over the letters and journals of Quakers under bonds and stripes and in exile will feel how perfectly Whittier has reproduced the simple yet heroic trust in God which was the glory of so many sufferers and martyrs.

The regions personally known to Whittier, at least those particularly referred to in his verse, include the eastern portions of Massachusetts and Rhode Island, the southeastern part of New Hampshire, and the coast of Maine. We can see that his feet have trodden the fields he describes. Two of the poems in the edition of 1843 show us that the knowledge of Maine especially was gained in early life. The first, the ballad of "St. John," recalls the strife for mastery of the coast between the Protestants under La Tour and the Catholics under D'Aulney, two French noblemen, whose names are frequently to be met with in the colonial records of Massachusetts. This ballad forms one of the most striking pictures of the far distant time when Huguenot and Royalist waged war for existence. Its martial character is the more remarkable on account of its paternity ; the phrases ring as if the maker had himself heard the clang of steel. It is bright with points of local allusion, swift in energetic movement, and teeming with fire.

The other poem with strong local coloring is "The Funeral Tree of the Sokokis." In many poems one feels as if the descriptions were done as those in guide-books are, by a mere enumeration of details. It is only a true poet that vitalizes adjectives and epithets, and forms pictures that are imperishable. It is not the number of productions that are needed to establish the right of the poet : a single stanza is enough. The scenery of the Saco, which is often grand and always impressive even now, in spite of the ravages of lumbermen, becomes solemn and magnificent in Whittier's verse, wherein we see it restored to its primitive loneliness. Such stanzas as these carry their own weight : —

> " The sun looks o'er, with hazy eye,
> The snowy mountain-tops which lie
> Piled coldly up against the sky.
>
> .   .   .   .   .
>
> " Yet green are Saco's banks below,
> And belts of spruce and cedar show,
> Dark fringing round those cones of snow.
>
> .   .   .   .   .
>
> " Fresh grasses fringe the meadow-brooks,
> And mildly from its sunny nooks
> The blue eye of the violet looks.
>
> .   .   .   .   .

> " Deem ye that mother loveth **less**
> These bronzed forms of the wilderness
> She foldeth in **her long** caress ?

> " As sweet **o'er them her** wild flowers blow,
> **As** if with fairer **hair** and brow
> The blue-eyed Saxon slept below."

It will be seen that Whittier has **not** limited his sympathies **to** oppressed Africans nor **even to** his **own** persecuted people : his generous spirit takes in the whole **of suffering humanity.** The **wrongs of the** Indians are often **dwelt upon by him;** the prisoner for debt has a **share of his pity, and with** all his energy he has protested against capital punishment for crime. These traits have been exhibited from the first until **now.** The anti-slavery poems in the edition **of 1843** are few, **but in** fair proportion to the **whole.** Surely **this little book** was one full of promise, had **there** been unprejudiced eyes to read. **If** our **later** time has witnessed such a beginning, — has heard such free, melodious, natural, and fresh **verse from** any **of** the advancing generation, — we **do not remember it.**

CHAPTER XII.

THE " National Era " was established at the seat of government in 1847, and became one of the leading organs of the anti-slavery party. Dr. Gamaliel Bailey, the editor, was a man of literary predilections and good taste, and wise enough to understand the importance of securing for himself and the cause the aid of the best writers. Whittier was engaged as assistant or corresponding editor, and the connection lasted until the end of the year 1859. " Uncle Tom's Cabin " appeared in this paper as a serial in 1850. The sisters Alice and Phœbe Cary, and Lucy Larcom, contributed many poems ; Grace Greenwood wrote many bright and witty articles, and, later, the brilliant Gail Hamilton gave her aid. Altogether, the files of this paper are exceedingly interesting, and will reward the student of our humanitarian literature. In the first number (January **7, 1847**) appeared " Randolph of Roanoke," one of the finest and most *feeling* of all Whittier's political poems. Admiration and regret are seen struggling for mastery, and the result is a powerful portrait of a most remarkable man. Above eighty of Whittier's poems are contained in the files of this paper (from 1847 to **1859), and in** number, power, variety, **and** interest **they** exceed any series, except, perhaps, that contributed **to the** " Atlantic Monthly." Readers will remember " Barclay of Ury," " The Angels of Buena Vista," **" The** Curse of the Charter Breakers," " Summer by the Lakeside," " Burns," " Ichabod," " The Hermit of the Thebaid," " Mary Garvin," " Maud Muller," " The Garrison of **Cape Ann,"** " Tauler," " Our State," " The Kansas Emigrants," **and** " The Witch's Daughter." A list of these poems (reasonably complete) will be found in the Appendix.

The reader should bear in mind that neither the political nor the purely literary works **of** Whittier are capable of separation into periods. He always had many irons in the fire. His contributions to the magazines, already noticed, were parallel with his anti-slavery labors, and his poems as well as prose articles were widely distributed. The " Liberator," the " Emancipator," and the " Anti-slavery Standard " contain his original poems, written during the same period with those in the " Era ; " and as he and his seem to have been " common property," his poems frequently appear in more than one paper without acknowledgment, rendering it doubtful for which it was originally written. Whatever he wrote was sure to appear in each of the papers named, at one time or another. But from the time he began to write for the " Era " his contributions were less scattered ; the other anti-slavery papers generally copied them as " from the ' Era.' " For several years he may be said to have written almost exclusively for that paper ; although it will be seen hereafter that after the establishment of the " Atlantic," in 1857, a larger number of his poems went to that magazine.

Numerous as are his poems in the " Era," the bulk of his labor was done in prose. The series of biographical sketches entitled " Old Portraits," and a number of the papers in " Literary Recreations," appeared first in the " Era." But beyond question his most able and fortunate prose work during that connection was " Margaret Smith's Journal," reprinted by Ticknor, Reed, & Fields in 1849.

This is properly an historical novel, and belongs to the class of which " The Household of Sir Thomas

More," " The Maiden and Married Life of Mary Powell, afterwards Mistress Milton," and " The Artist's Married Life, being that of Albert Dürer," are eminent examples. The novel has been considerably developed since the time of Boccaccio, and the name has come to mean a something far more complex and exciting. To the modern reader, " Margaret Smith's Journal " is hardly a novel at all, but only a series of sketches of character, manners, and scenery, done in an antique style. The real excellence of the work will not be perceived by readers of Gaboriau, Dumas, and Victor Hugo; palates burned by peppery condiments do not welcome simple flavors. But for those who know well the early history of the Colony, the personages that figure in it, and the prevailing ideas and customs, this unpretending Journal will have a singular and enduring charm. The history of this or of any other colony is not to be gained alone from formal annals; it comes from personal knowledge of the scenes, from a study of institutions and laws, from familiarity with actual letters, journals, and memoirs, and from the traditions told at ancient firesides. There are students of history who could swear to the genuineness of the signatures of any of the fathers of the Colony; who could mark out the daily routine of the preacher or magistrate, or of his spouse; who could dress an historical figure, from his peaked hat to his stout shoes; who could spread his board in imagination, could repeat or sing his psalms, and number all the books in his scanty library. To a man who has a smack of the tastes of an antiquary, there is no more delightful book than " Margaret Smith's Journal." It is not oppressively learned nor archaic ; the fair journalist is not a Quaker nor other sectary, but a good Church-of-England woman, so that it is a view *from without*,— free and uncircumscribed. There is a slender thread of story, enough for the sense of continuity. The style is perfect for the intended purpose, though it is far less rigid or crabbed than the usual specimens of the time. Secretary Rawson, Sir Christopher Gardiner, Judge Samuel Sewall, Robert Pike, Richard Saltonstall, Rev. Mr. Ward, " the Simple Cobler of Aggawam," Eliot the apostle, Cotton Mather, Simon Bradstreet, and many others are seen in the narrative by turns, and are transfigured by the light of genius. Their conversation is separately, vitally characteristic ; and every detail is in such perfect keeping that the illusion grows and time and distance are forgotten. There is surely no parallel to this book in our prose literature of the United States; but to enjoy it one must be prepared by some knowledge, and must own the

kindred taste for a chastened view of life, and for
the beauty to be seen in humble and familiar
things ; to such a reader the enjoyment is unspeakable.

It should be added that the religious questions in
which the Colonists were so deeply interested are
treated with candor, and yet with an almost touching delicacy. Margaret herself cannot sympathize
greatly with the exalted feeling and the strained de-
meanor of those who were, according to the point
of view, fanatics or martyrs ; but she manifests a
sweet courtesy, not to say pity, for those who incurred ecclesiastic and secular penalties for following the dictates of conscience.

Numerous poems are interspersed, some of them
in imitation of the labored and pedantic style of
Wigglesworth and Mrs. Anne Bradstreet, others
modern and beautiful. Two of them are in the
complete volume, — "Autumn Thoughts" and the
ballad "Kathleen."

There was a collection of Whittier's poems made
in 1849, and published by B. B. Mussey & Co. in a
large and handsome octavo volume, with illustrations on steel by H. Billings. Mr. Mussey was a
prominent Free-Soiler, had presided at a State convention of the party, and took pride in the reputation of the poet of freedom. It was the first time

that Whittier's poems had been clothed in a manner suitable to their intrinsic worth. This appeared to be a step in advance, but the connection did not last many years. Mr. Mussey died about the year 1855, and the plates were purchased and transferred to Messrs. Ticknor & Fields. The Mussey edition contained a few poems which have since been dropped; but the bulk of them are now in the standard edition, unchanged. It may be observed, however, that in regard to historical and topographical notes the Mussey edition was more satisfactory. It must be an error of judgment to leave such poems as " St. John " without a note to guide the reader. How many persons, even among the educated, know enough of the contest between La Tour and D'Aulncy in 1647 on the eastern coast, to feel the significance of this stirring ballad? Very few, we imagine. And how many readers of poetry know what a " Familist " was, or that Samuel Gorton of the Massachusetts Colony was the man intended? And even as to later events it should be remembered that the beginning of the anti-slavery struggle is back of the memory of the younger generation, and it will not be many years before all the political poems of Whittier will need annotation. It is to be hoped that at no distant day there will be an ampler edition of the poems, with full explanatory notes; and if, further, it could be graced with artistic pictures of the various scenes described, it would be a treasure to all lovers of poetry.

As we have seen, four of the " Songs of Labor" were published in the "Democratic Review" in 1845–46. "The Drovers," "The Huskers," the "Corn Song," and the fine Dedication were written subsequently for the "National Era," and the whole issued in a volume by Ticknor & Fields in 1850. These are bright and cheerful poems, such as accord with the hopeful and energetic character of the laboring classes in a free country. There is seldom any occasion for depressing sympathy, least of all of pity, in contemplating the lot of the intelligent and skilful artisans of New England. They command at least living wages, and for every man the future has unnamed possibilities. Meanwhile there are comfortable homes, sufficient food and clothing, schools for the children, and newspapers and libraries for all.

But our minds are generally tinged with English thought, which has arisen from observation of quite other and less favorable circumstances. The word " labor" prepares us for suffering and deprivation, and for the stunting of mind and body in unwholesome work done in caverns, forges, and mills. Carlyle well shows the feelings that are associated with the condition of laborers : —

"Venerable to me is the hard Hand; crooked, coarse; wherein notwithstanding lies a cunning virtue, indefeasibly royal, as of the Sceptre of this Planet. Venerable too is the rugged face, all weather-tanned, besoiled, with its rude intelligence; for it is the face of a Man living manlike. O, but the more venerable for thy rudeness, and even because we must pity as well as love thee! Hardly entreated Brother! For us was thy back so bent, for us were thy straight limbs and fingers so deformed: thou wert our Conscript, on whom the lot fell, and fighting our battles wert so marred. For in thee too lay a god-created Form, but it was not to be unfolded; encrusted must it stand with the thick adhesions and defacements of Labour: and thy body, like thy soul, was not to know freedom."

Laments like this are largely out of place at present, however they may be inspired hereafter. In Essex County, where were the laborers that Whittier knew, labor was subject to none of the unimaginable sorrows. The ploughmen and mowers were as cheery as the thrushes and bobolinks in the meadows; the fishermen could troll with stout hearts of the "wet sheet and flowing sea" and all the glories of blue water; and the hearts and voices of smiths and ship-builders kept time to the rhythmic hammers and mallets.

In the same year (1850) a volume of biographical articles, reprinted from the "Era," was issued by the same publishers, with the title "Old Portraits."

In 1852 a volume containing a selection from his poems was published in London by George Routledge & Co. In 1853 was published "The Chapel of the Hermits," copied also from the "Era." In the year following appeared "Literary Recreations," the last of his prose works. "The Panorama" appeared in 1856. The reader knows, of course, that a large number of miscellaneous poems were published in each volume above named, so that in 1857, when the so-called "complete" edition was issued, there was a large and rich collection.

CHAPTER XIII.

Whittier's Home Life. — His Sister Elizabeth as a Poet. — Mercy
Hussey and her Romantic Story. — Dr. S. G. Howe. — Calef and
Cotton Mather. — Charles Sumner. — " Ichabod." — Relenting
toward Webster. — A Grand Portrait of the Orator. — The Fugi-
tive Slave Law. — Friends sketched in " The Last Walk in
Autumn." — Lake Winnepesaukee. — The Poet's Sketch of
Himself.

THE life of Whittier from the time he took up
his residence in Amesbury was uneventful.
He lived in Lowell, as has been stated, for six
months in the year 1845, but there was no other
change in his quiet life. He had become known to
many circles of readers, and he found employment
for his pen in many ways; but there were no
epochs except the publication of successive volumes.
Of his literary friendships something will be said
hereafter. He never lived, however, as many
authors have done, in a hall of glass; he was sincerely and wholly attached to his home, and found
all his pleasures and consolations in the society of

his mother, sisters, and aunt. Those were joys into which a stranger could not enter. His sister Elizabeth, as we saw, was writing verses at fifteen, and she remained through life his nearest literary companion. She was not robust, and could not cope with her brother in power or accomplishment; but her poems show that she had a spiritual nature, full of tender feeling as well as of sterling common sense. In "Hazel Blossoms" Whittier has printed a few of her poems, and in the selection has been guided by the same severity of judgment which he used in regard to his own. The number could have been greatly increased; since many of high merit may be found in the various periodicals that have been consulted in the preparation of this volume.

The family circle was soon to be broken, and one by one the beloved ones were to pass away. The elder sister, Mary, had been married some years before to Mr. Jacob Caldwell, at one time publisher of the "Gazette," of Haverhill. The maiden aunt, Mercy Hussey, whose charming picture in "Snow Bound" readers will remember, died April 14, 1846: —

> "The sweetest woman ever Fate
> Perverse denied a household mate."

There is a story related of her, illustrative of this couplet, which is said to have come from Whittier's lips, and which may interest susceptible readers.[1]

"She was betrothed in her youth to a young man every way worthy of her. She was then living with her sister in the old Whittier mansion at East Haverhill, and her lover was away on business in New York. She was about to marry 'out of society,' but love which laughs at locksmiths pays little heed to the little fences built about religious sects. Late one evening, while her lover was away, she sat musing by the fire, after all the rest of the family had retired. Some mysterious influence led her to the window.

> ' The moon above the eastern wood
> Shone at its full ; the hill range stood
> Transfigured in its silver flood.'

The road was then, as now, lined with shade trees, and in a moonlit space she saw a horse and its rider coming down the hill toward the house, and she clearly recognized her lover. While wondering at his unexpected return, and his call at an unseasonable hour, she noticed that he drew rein as he approached the house, and she went quickly to receive him at the door of the porch, the little porch next the road. There is a window in this porch which looks out upon the road, and as she stood unbolting the door she saw her lover ride by it, and turn as if to stop at the

---

[1] From an article in the " Portland Transcript," written by S. T. Pickard, whose wife is Whittier's niece. This gentleman has published a series of descriptions of Whittier's birthplace and early surroundings, at once minute and picturesque, — sufficient in bulk and in interest to form an attractive volume.

door she was opening, which was at the other side of the porch. The next instant the door was open, but Mercy saw no trace of man or horse! The poor girl was over-whelmed with astonishment, and bursting into tears called upon her sister, who had retired. Mrs. Whittier heard her story and tried to efface the powerful impression it had evidently made. 'Thee had better go to bed, Mercy; thee has been asleep and dreaming by the fire,' said she. But Mercy was quite sure she had not been asleep, and what she had seen was as real to her as any waking expe-rience of her life. In recalling the circumstances of her vision, one by one, she at length took notice that she *had heard no* **sound of hoofs!** It may be imagined what was the ghostly effect of all this upon the sensitive girl. She, at least, was not surprised, when, after a weary waiting of many days, a letter came to her in a strange hand, and from a distant city, stating that her lover was dead, — that he died on the very hour of her vision! In her grief she did not shut herself away from the world, but lived a life of cheerful charity. She did not forget her first love, and gave no encouragement to other suitors. This is the story of Aunt Mercy, as it is told in the family where her memory is cherished as that of a household saint."

Whittier's venerable mother lived until the end of the year 1857, and so had seen the fruition of her hopes in his wide-spread fame and in the devel-opment of his noble character. The filial attitude and feeling were never changed from boyhood to maturity, and the sacred bond was never loosened, as it is in so many households. Of all the sources of heartache there is none so common as the gradual *growing apart* of parent and child. The mother too often finds that as years go by her boy is changed, distant, impenetrable, although all the forms of respect and affection are preserved. The son, engrossed with his own thoughts and pursuits, fancies that the sympathy which surrounded him in childhood has no relevancy to his changed condition, and no place in his larger circle. It is almost pathetic to think of such meetings as can be remembered. Then it is seen that the affections reach forward with unuttered longing from the parent to the child, but are rarely reciprocated with any equal fervor. But Whittier's mother was spared this pain. The simplicity, truth, and trust of the early days remained to the last.

Elizabeth Whittier, like her brother, was an active worker in the anti-slavery cause. We saw her, after the meeting in Haverhill was broken up, walking through the mob with the speaker, the Rev. Samuel J. May. We remember that she was one of the courageous band of women who met in Boston, in spite of the advice of the mayor, and who bore with serene patience the insults .of rioters. But her nature was retiring, and she did not take any part in public exercises. The picture that is preserved of her shows clearly her moral and intellectual character. The brows are broad, and the head massive for a woman ; the eyes are large and earnest, yet tender and appealing ; the lower part of . the face is delicate and characteristically womanly. Mrs. Child has a brief and pleasant reference to her in a letter (1860), which shows also some of Whittier's minor trials.[1]

"Whittier made piteous complaints of time wasted and strength exhausted by the numerous loafers who came to see him out of mere idle curiosity, or to put up with him to save a penny. I was amused to hear his sister describe some of these irruptions in her slow, Quakerly fashion. 'Thee has no idea,' said she, 'how much time Greenleaf spends in trying to *lose* these people in the streets. Sometimes he comes home and says, "Well, sister, I had hard work to lose him, but I have lost him."' 'But I can never lose a *her*,' said Whittier. 'The women are more pertinacious than the men ; don't thee find them so, Maria?' I told him I did. 'How does thee manage to get time to do anything?' said he. I told him I took care to live away from the railroad, and kept a bulldog and a pitchfork, and advised him to do the same."

Of the poems of Elizabeth, the one which will most interest readers is entitled "The Wedding Veil," as it discloses a tender reminiscence. The poem addressed to Dr. Kane, the Arctic explorer,

[1] Letters, p. 142.

was read to him not long before he died, and he expressed to friends the deepest gratitude for the tribute.

THE WEDDING VEIL.

Dear Anna, when I brought her veil,
　Her white veil on her wedding night,
Threw o'er my thin brown hair its folds,
　And, laughing, turned me to the light.

"See, Bessie, see! you wear at last
　The bridal veil, forsworn for years!"
She saw my face — her laugh was hushed,
　Her happy eyes were filled with tears.

With kindly haste and trembling hand
　She drew away the gauzy mist;
"Forgive, dear heart!" her sweet voice said;
　Her loving lips my forehead kissed.

We passed from out the searching light;
　The summer night was calm and fair;
I did not see her pitying eyes,
　I felt her soft hand smooth my hair.

Her tender love unlocked my heart;
　'Mid falling tears, at last I said,
"Forsworn indeed to me that veil,
　Because I only love the dead!"

She stood one moment statue-still,
　And, musing, spoke in undertone:
"The living love may colder grow;
　The dead is safe with God alone!"

Elizabeth died in the autumn of 1864.

This may be a favorable time to look at some poems, written after the publication of the small volume of 1843, that need comment, or that refer to persons or events. Whittier has seldom taken pains to give explanations either of scenes or portraits. For example, take the poem "The Hero" (written for the "National Era," April, 1853). Readers in New England, and others acquainted with the public men and institutions of Boston, after seeing that the hero had served as a soldier in the Greek war for independence, had been imprisoned in Germany, and had afterwards been an instructor of the blind, and foremost in all philanthropic movements, would have no difficulty in deciding that the hero was Dr. Samuel G. Howe. Still, it is to be feared that many reasonably well-informed people, especially in England or in the West, might find the poem obscure, and so fail to appreciate its force and beauty. When the explanation is given, showing the brilliant phases of the "hero's" character and of his eventful life, the poem will begin to glow in the reader's mind and memory. Then will the opening stanza have its due significance : —

> "O for a knight like Bayard,
>   Without reproach or fear;
> My light glove on his casque of steel,
>   My love-knot on his spear!"

And who in foreign lands, or even of American birth, unless of the elders, will feel the significance of the noble tribute to Rantoul (copied from the "National Era," July, 1853)? The contemporaries of Whittier well remember Robert Rantoul, the young senator from Massachusetts, a native of Essex County, the great Webster's successor, who, though reared as a Democrat, had thoughts of liberty for all men, — not liberty for whites alone. They remember his face, lighted by genius and giving the sure signs of character and leadership. They remember how the hopes of the Free-Soilers were centred upon this able and accomplished man, and how soon those hopes were dashed by his sudden death.   And those who thus remember will never be able to read Whittier's ardent lines without a thrill of emotion.

Let the reader turn now to " Calef in Boston " (from the " National Era," September, 1849), and remember, if he will, that these comments are not for historians and antiquaries.   Every one has read of the terrible scenes in Massachusetts when witches were tried and executed; and most persons know that the Rev. Cotton Mather was the leading spirit in those trials, ministering to the popular superstition by accounts of demoniac possession, and spurring on judges to exterminate the wretched beings on whom suspicion fell. His book, "Wonders of the Invisible World Displayed," is known to all students of our early annals. But the general reader may not know that Robert Calef, a Boston merchant, wrote a common-sense reply, entitled "More Wonders of the Invisible World" (1700), which had a powerful influence in quelling the excitement against witchcraft. This book was naturally denounced by the clergy, and had the honor of being publicly burned in the yard of Harvard College by order of the president, Increase Mather. The Mathers and Calef, as intimated in the poem, are interred in Copp's Hill Burying-ground, in the North End of Boston.

"The Branded Hand" refers to the punishment of Captain Jonathan Walker, a shipmaster of Harwich, Mass., who for the crime of aiding a negro to escape from a Southern port was branded in the hand with the letters "S. S." (slave-stealer).

The appeals "To Faneuil Hall" and "To Massachusetts" were written upon the near approach of the war with Mexico; and "The Pine-Tree," in a still more passionate strain, called on the public to unite against the schemes for the extension of slavery which followed that unjust war. Remembering that the first national anti-slavery party was formed at Buffalo, in 1848, under the leadership of

Van Buren and Adams, we shall understand the significance of "The Pæan." The poem "To a Southern Statesman" is addressed to John C. Calhoun. "Leggett's Monument" is a tribute to an intrepid man, once an associate with the poet Bryant in his editorial labors, whose tomb was built by those who had contemned and resisted his efforts in the cause of freedom.

Continually we see that in choice of subjects Whittier is governed by the influences of his Quaker training, and by his deep convictions upon moral subjects. He has not sought out the world's heroes and favorites for eulogy, but has given his tributes of affection and sympathy to those whom the world neglected or despised. "Barclay of Ury" is an example of Whittier's brave championship of an unpopular cause, — a singularly perfect and touching poem. Readers will see also lines to Joseph Sturge, to William Forster, Daniel Wheeler, and Daniel Neall, — also to the abolitionists Storrs and Torrey. There are few, if any, adulatory verses addressed to the great, unless we except Charles Sumner, who was a co-worker and life-long friend. The poem "To C. S." (from the "National Era," December, 1854), though not in the least like a sonnet, has but one impulsive thought, which, gathering slowly, bursts like a great wave at the end. Perhaps Whittier has written poems more impeccable in diction, but none that is pervaded by a more single, intense motive, and none that culminates in more grandeur. This was before the brutal assault by Preston S. Brooks, and before any differences had occurred to separate Sumner from any of the loving hearts of the North.

There is an elaborate eulogy upon Sumner in a later volume, which in tone recalls Dryden's verses to the Lord Protector Cromwell.

This period must not be passed over without mention of a poem from the " National Era," May 2, 1850, which in a certain light exhibits Whittier's genius in its noblest form: that is " Ichabod," which signifies, as Biblical readers know, " the glory has departed." When in 1850, on the 7th of March, Webster made the great conciliatory speech, as conservatives thought it, — or gave the sign of apostasy, as abolitionists felt he had done, — Whittier expressed the almost unutterable regret of Northern men in stanzas of painful significance. They are burned into the memory of the admirers of Webster as he stood in his early days : —

> " O, dumb be passion's stormy rage,
> When he who might
> Have lighted up and led his age,
> Falls back in night.

> " All else is gone; from those great eyes
>   The soul has fled:
> When faith is lost, when honor dies,
>   The man is dead!
>
> " Then pay the reverence of old days
>   To his dead fame;
> Walk backward with averted gaze,
>   And hide the shame! "

At the public breakfast given to Whittier in 1877 Mr. Emerson read " Ichabod " as his tribute to the poet. It contains more storage of electric energy than anything we remember in our time. Although Whittier's judgment of the senator was irrevocable, yet his feelings afterwards softened towards the man. This is seen in one of his later poems, " The Lost Occasion." The picture of the great statesman is done with strong and masterly lines.

> " Whom the rich heavens did so endow
>   With eyes of power and Jove's own brow,
>   .   .   .   .   .
> New England's stateliest type of man,
> In port and speech Olympian;
> Whom no one met, at first, but took
> A second awed and wondering look,
>   .   .   .   .   .
> Whose words in simplest homespun clad
> The Saxon strength of Cædmon's had,
> With power reserved at need to reach
> The Roman forum's loftiest speech.
>   .   .   .   .   .

Thou, foiled in aim and hope, bereaved
Of old friends, by the new deceived,
Too soon for us, too soon for thee,
Beside thy lonely Northern sea,
Where long and low the marsh-lands spread,
Lay wearily down thy august head.

Thou shouldst have lived to feel below
Thy feet Disunion's fierce upthrow, —
The late-sprung mine that underlaid
Thy sad concessions vainly made.

  .   .   .   .   .

No stronger voice than thine had then
Called out the utmost might of men.

  .   .   .   .   .

Ah, cruel fate, that closed to thee,
O sleeper by the Northern sea,
The gates of opportunity !

  .   .   .   .   .

But, where thy native mountains bare
Their foreheads to diviner air,
Fit emblem of enduring fame,
One lofty summit keeps thy name.

  .   .   .   .   .

And evermore that mountain mass
Seems climbing from the shadowy pass
To light, as if to manifest
Thy nobler self, thy life at best ! "

To connect the anti-slavery poems of this period (before 1860), it is necessary to remember but a few events. The Fugitive Slave Law was enacted in 1850 as a part of the compromise assented to by Webster; and though the number of persons returned to slavery was very small, the enforcement of the law was carried out in an odious manner, with the design of humiliating the North. From these occasions came the poems, " Moloch in State Street" (in Boston), "The Rendition," "The Voices," "Lines" ("A pious magistrate," &c.), "Stanzas for the Times" ("The evil days have come," &c.), "A Sabbath Scene," and others.

Very soon came the candidacy of Fremont and the struggle between Northern and Southern emigrants for the possession of Kansas and Nebraska. In this sharp competition the North won, although Fremont was defeated; and meanwhile Whittier cheered on the friends of freedom with his most spirited lyrics, such as "To Pennsylvania," "The Pass of the Sierra," "The Kansas Emigrants," "The New Exodus," &c. The freedom of these new States was not established without bloodshed, as guerillas from Missouri made constant raids upon the " Yankee" settlements, and butchered men and women by scores. One of these massacres is the subject of a poem, " Le Marais du Cygne," published in 1858. " The Burial of Barbour" is another poem suggested by the murders of pro-slavery partisans.

We must find room for a characteristic poem written during the Fremont campaign for the

" National Era," and not included in the collections
hitherto : —

A SONG FOR THE TIME.

Up, laggards of Freedom ! — our free flag is cast
To the blaze of the sun and the wings of the blast ;
Will ye turn from a struggle so bravely begun, —
From a foe that is breaking, a field that 's half won ?

Whoso loves not his kind, and who fears not the Lord,
Let him join that foe's service, accursed and abhorred !
Let him do his base will, as the slave only can, —
Let him put on the bloodhound, and put off the Man !

Let him go where the cold blood that creeps in his veins
Shall stiffen the slave-whip, and rust on his chains ;
Where the black slave shall laugh in his bonds, to behold
The White Slave beside him, self-fettered and sold !

But ye, who still boast of hearts beating and warm,
Rise, from lake shore and ocean's, like waves in a storm !
Come, throng round our banner in Liberty's name,
Like winds from your mountains, like prairies aflame !

Our foe, hidden long in his ambush of night,
Now, forced from his covert, stands black in the light.
Oh, the cruel to Man, and the hateful to God,
Smite him down to the earth, that is cursed where he trod !

For deeper than thunder of summer's loud shower,
On the dome of the sky God is striking the hour !
Shall we falter before what we 've prayed for so long,
When the Wrong is so weak, and the Right is so strong ?

Come forth all together ! — come old and come young, —
Freedom's vote in each hand, and her song on each tongue ;

> Truth naked is stronger than Falsehood in mail —
> The Wrong cannot prosper, the Right cannot fail!
>
> Like leaves of the summer once numbered the foe,
> But the hoar-frost is falling, the northern winds blow;
> Like leaves of November ere long shall they fall,
> For earth wearies of them, and God 's over all!

What other conflict for human rights was ever enlivened by such thrilling odes, such glowing appeals to conscience, honor, and valor? Longfellow and Bryant had given their timely efforts and the weight of their great names to the cause of freedom; Lowell had employed all the resources of wit and sarcasm, and made the heads of the North keep time to his Yankee lyrics; but Whittier appeared to live for no other purpose than to sound the solemn call to duty at each new juncture. What an ease and affluence of melody in these swiftly moving verses! Never a thought maimed by its measure nor jostled out of place by a rhyme! The shuttle flies and returns, and the growing lines close up, — even, uniform, firm, and imperishable.

The immortal "Marseillaise" stands almost alone in the time of trial in France, and no similar crisis has called out the poets of England since the Restoration. The poetry of the anti-slavery movement in the United States exceeds in bulk, **as** it does in inspiration, power, **and** beauty, all the poems written on subjects of great national importance in the latter centuries. **The** change **of** ministers or of dynasties, wars foreign or domestic, tariffs, franchises, land tenures, could **never inspire** the lofty **thoughts or lead** to the exaltation of feeling such as have characterized **the poets** and orators of this era. It is wonderful, **too,** that natures perhaps far **from** poetic in grain became fired **with the general** enthusiasm **and broke out into song. "All the air was flame." Garrison** himself **at** times **wrote noble lines; Pierpont's** great heart beat audibly **; and Wendell Phillips by** the splendor of his genius **made every** audience a partaker of **the** spirit **that** moves **the** solid **world.**

We look back **as if** through smoke **and flame to** that eventful period ; **and we cannot but be grateful to** have lived **when great** thoughts, **eternal** principles, **and** sublime ideals actuated **men. From** these days **of** prosperity, greed, and **corruption,** back **to** the times when men were ready **to die for** the faith that **was in** them — can **it be that it is** only twenty **years ?**

Although our present task is chiefly to furnish necessary interpretation, **yet** we must pause to call attention to one poem every line of which is **full of** meaning. It is very simple and straightforward, and is not marked by the higher poetical qualities; but it is wholly without alloy, a solid piece of work,—a perfect poem of its kind. It is entitled "Our State," and its final stanzas are often quoted : —

> "For well she keeps her ancient stock,
>   The stubborn strength of Plymouth Rock ;
>   And still maintains, with milder laws
>   And clearer light, the Good Old Cause !
>
> " Nor heeds the sceptic's puny hands
>   While near her school the church-spire stands ;
>   Nor fears the blinded bigot's rule,
>   While near her church-spire stands the school."

Lines " To A. K." were addressed to Avis Keene, a minister of the Society of Friends ("National Era," August 22, 1850). She is the person referred to in the poem "The Meeting" ("Atlantic," vol. xxi. p. 221) : —

> " Whose eighty years but added grace
>   And saintlier meaning to her face —
>   The look of one who bore away
>   Glad tidings from the hills of day,
>   While all our hearts went forth to meet
>   The coming of her beautiful feet."

No one can doubt the genuine warmth of Whittier's heart in reading his many beautiful tributes to near friends, whether among the living or the dead. But these, **in** most instances, **are** discreetly anonymous, and the reader must **be content with** the expression of feeling without looking for names. The **poet is** exceedingly averse **to giving** publicity to names of private persons, **or to** making **to the** world any " confidential " relations whatever ; and it is far from the desire of the author to contravene his reasonable wishes.

Not infrequently **Whittier has sketched his** friends for **us.** In the fourteenth, **fifteenth, and** sixteenth stanzas **of " The Last Walk in Autumn "** **we find** clear outlines **of** Emerson, **Bayard** Taylor, and Charles Sumner : —

> " He who might Plato's banquet grace
>   Have I not seen before me sit,
> And watched his puritanic face
>   With more **than Eastern** wisdom **lit?**
>   .   .   .   .   .
> " Here too, of answering love secure,
>   Have I not welcomed to my hearth
> **The** gentle pilgrim troubadour,
>   Whose songs have girdled half the earth ?
>   .   .   .   .   .
> " And **he, who** to the lettered wealth
>   **Of** ages adds the lore unpriced,
> The wisdom and the moral health,
>   The **ethics of the school of Christ ;**
> The statesman to his **holy trust,**
>   As the Athenian archon, just,
> Struck down, exiled like him for truth alone,
> Has he not graced my home with beauty all his **own ?"**

Within this period (before 1857) are three ballads, much quoted : " Mary Garvin " (" National Era," January, 1856), " Maud Muller " (" National Era," December, 1854), and " The Ranger," which has not been traced to its original source.

One can see that in the last generation the region of romance was in Canada and the northern woods. It appears that the main incident in " Mary Garvin," the return of a daughter who had become a Catholic, was not an unlikely circumstance. In Chase's " History of Haverhill " there is preserved a letter from one Mary Wainwright, whose daughter had been carried away by the Indians and French, in which the mother asks that means be taken to get her child back before she should be perverted.[1]

In several poems Whittier has given pictures of the lake scenery of New Hampshire; the most widely read, and probably the most beautiful, is " Summer by the Lakeside."   In the present

[1] "HAVERHILL, 29th April, 1710.

" To his Excellency, Joseph Dudley, Captain-General and Governor in Chief, &c., &c., to the Honorable council and General Assembly now mett ; the petition of Mary Wainwright sheweth that, whereas my daughter hath been for a long time in captivity with the French of Canada, and I have late reason to fear that her soul is in great danger if not already captivated and she brought to their way ; therefore I humbly intreate your Excellency, that some care may be taken for her redemption before Canada be so endeared to her that I shall never have my daughter more."

chapter it is intended only to furnish necessary information ; an estimate of values may be given hereafter. The lake is Winnipiseogee, or, as it is now more commonly spelled, Winnepesaukee, situated in Central New Hampshire, where it receives the brooks and melted snows of the White Mountains. Tourists well know it, as it lies in the usual route of summer travel to the mountain region. It is irregular in form, and, having numerous islands as well as projecting headlands, there is seldom any distant prospect on the water level ; but at every turn new vistas are disclosed with new groupings of form and color, and behind every northward view the pale blue masses of hills form a background. No very large mountains are near its shores, — the chief being Red Hill towards the northwest, and the Ossipee Mountains towards the northeast ; therefore it lacks the elements of grandeur seen in the Swiss lakes, but it has perhaps an equal fascination in its unending phases of beauty.

Another equally celebrated poem, "The Last Walk in Autumn," referred to above, belongs to this period, and claims mention here only for the sake of saying that the scene is in the valley of the Merrimac, within sight of the river, among the beautiful rounded hills before described. Those who are familiar with the region will find some beauty in every line, hidden from eyes of strangers. This poem and the one just named, "Summer by the Lakeside," are perfect specimens of landscape painting.

It remains only to notice the poem, "My Namesake," which is addressed to Francis Greenleaf Allinson, of Burlington, N. J. It is a curious, truthful, quaint expression of impressions, feelings, and fancies, and may be taken as a piece of faithful spiritual self-delineation. It is wholly characteristic, — unlike any autobiography or "confession" or confidence ever penned. Some stanzas from it may be quoted hereafter. At present we copy only a few stanzas that come to the heart of a biographer with a force like that of an unlooked-for blow. The sensation is much like that one feels when reading Shakespeare's homely epitaph for the first time : —

> " Good frend for Iesvs sake forbeare
> To digg the dust encloased heare."

> " Let Love's and Friendship's tender debt
> Be paid by those I love in life ;
> Why should the unborn critic whet
> For me his scalping-knife ?

> " Why should the stranger peer and pry
> One's vacant house of life about,
> And drag for curious ear and eye
> His faults and follies out ?—

"Why stuff, for fools to gaze upon,
    With chaff of words, the garb he wore,
  As corn-husks when the car is gone
    Are rustled all the more?

"Let kindly Silence close again,
    The picture vanish from the eye,
  And on the dim and misty main
    Let the small ripple die."

CHAPTER XIV.

The Ticknor & Fields Edition. — Whittier at Maturity. — His
Place in Letters acknowledged. — The " Atlantic Monthly." —
Dissolution of Parties. — Reform no longer Unfashionable. —
Letters from Whittier amending Poems. — "Home Ballads."
— John Brown. — Letter of Whittier to Mrs. Child.

IN 1857, when the complete edition of poems
was published by Ticknor & Fields, Whittier,
then in his fiftieth year, had reached a position
which, if not the highest, was one of universally
recognized eminence. He had become famous by
natural causes, springing from the development of
his faculties, and without the aid of learned schools
or coteries, of travel, friendly reviews, political or
social influences. He had been simply, unpreten-
tiously independent, neither using arts to gain
favor, nor holding himself aloof to receive homage. He was distinctly eminent as a man, and
not admired solely because he was a poet. It was
at this period that the writer first met him, and
the impression made by his presence, and his few

but well-chosen words, will not be forgotten. His gravity was serene rather than forbidding, and his very reserve more attractive than the profuse speech of many others. He was invited to take part in organizing the " Atlantic Monthly," and he cordially gave the aid of his advice and his name. The attempt to combine the power of all the leading writers of the North in behalf of the cause to which he had devoted his life could not be otherwise than a matter of the highest moment in his view.

Whatever other agencies had been employed to make freedom national and universal, it is but truth to say that the " Atlantic" was the first periodical of high rank in which letters and art, — fiction, poetry, essays, and criticism, — the Muses and Graces, — all did homage to the great moral question of that day. From the time when Garrison and Knapp were found by Boston's fastidious and apologetic mayor " working in an obscure hole, with a negro for an assistant," to the establishment of this strong and splendid magazine, there was a change ! The publishers, Phillips, Sampson, & Co., had handsome quarters on Winter Street, and abolitionists, who gathered there, — Whittier, Emerson, Mrs. Stowe, Edmund Quincy, Professor Lowell, Theodore Parker, and others, as well as

the more purely literary contributors, such as Longfellow, Holmes, Prescott, Motley, Norton, Cabot,
and Trowbridge, — made the place an attractive
centre. The pay of writers was liberal for the
times ; and this fact, together with the prestige
that attended the enterprise from the first, drew
abundant contributions from every part of the
Union and from England.

The " Atlantic " became the fashion ; and as it
was the only literary periodical in America that
discussed moral and political questions with freedom, it undoubtedly gave tone and direction to the
thinking of young people of both sexes. The name
of " abolitionist " came to be less opprobrious than
" traitor " or " incendiary," — nay, even to acquire
a certain distinction. It is a great matter for a
writer to be *inside* the palings of society when he
would exert an influence in high quarters. An
unfashionable man might reason like Hume or
write like De Quincey, and might not be recognized
until he had finished his work and was in God's
peace.

The little senate which formed this magazine
fortunately comprised not only the highest names
in American literature, but men who had claims to
social distinction. Prejudices, original and inherited, as well as party ties, melted away. It was a

time of general solution, to be followed by crystallization around new centres of thought and activity. The names of Democrat and Whig no longer had any special significance, nor any power over free and liberal minds. The Whig party was expiring; its progressive members were becoming Republicans, and the residue not long after went over to the Democrats. The Democratic mass, too, was largely disintegrated,—a process begun by the coalition with Free-Soilers in electing Charles Sumner to the United States Senate, and hastened afterwards by the feeling of national loyalty during the War of the Rebellion,— so that many original Democrats became prominent Republicans, contending against malcontent Whigs who had turned Democrats by a kind of acetous fermentation. It was an instance of "changing partners" in the political figure. This movement of cross purposes, begun in 1851, continued in the presidential election of 1856, was greatly accelerated by literary and social influences, as well as by the aid of powerful newspapers in New York and other centres of opinion, and it culminated in 1860 in the election of Abraham Lincoln. There was an entirely new party classification thenceforward.

The "Atlantic" was mainly devoted to *belles*

lettres, and was intended, first of all, to be entertaining; but every number contained a political article by Parke Godwin or by Lowell, and the public understood and felt that this was the point of the ploughshare that was to break up the old fields. A plethora of discussion, of invective, or of passionate appeal, such as had been employed in the anti-slavery journals, would have swamped the magazine, or destroyed its influence with the classes to be reached. All the contributors, including the old abolitionists, were content to leave questions of politics to the editor. Whittier's poems for the first three years were upon general subjects, with the single exception of "Le Marais du Cygne," written upon a massacre by pro-slavery ruffians in Kansas. It was the peculiar good fortune of the magazine, as conducted, that all its sails drew; and whether it was Holmes discoursing at his immortal breakfast-table, Prescott giving a foretaste of his history of Philip II., Norton expounding ideas of art, Emerson astonishing readers with a touch of the mysticism of the Orient and much sublimity of his own, Dorsheimer (of New York) judging works of political biography, Longfellow singing his high and serene lyrics, Mitchell with his bright sea-songs, Dr. Palmer showing pictures of life in the ancient cradle of mankind, O'Brien flashing his Diamond Lens, Mrs. Rose Terry Cooke exhibiting the traits of the primitive Yankee, or Mrs. Stowe, fresh from her great triumph, telling of the Minister's Wooing, — each and all were giving an impulse to the cause of freedom such as the noblest efforts of previous advocates had never been able to accomplish.

It was an assault upon a more practicable level, — reaching the conscience of the nation through the pleasures of cultivated taste, and making the cause of sound morals and humane institutions accord with the highest literary art. Then it was seen that "the stars in their courses fought against Sisera." The notion of "vested rights" in man grew absurd. The clergy lost their conservatism or timidity. Party spirit had declined. The North had the lead in Kansas and Nebraska, — thanks to emigration societies, and to the wholesome respect for Sharpe's rifles in the hands of brave settlers. The long supremacy of Slavery was coming to an end, and every thinking man felt that great events were in the air.

The leading writers of the "Atlantic" were social, and were accustomed to dine together once a month; but Whittier, who was abstemious from necessity and habit, seldom came to the dinners. On account of delicate health he had accustomed

himself to simple fare, and he never tasted wine
or used tobacco; so that the meeting, so attractive
to others, had few charms for him beyond social
converse. In fact he seldom came to Boston, but
sent his poems and received proofs by mail. His
care over the productions of his brain never ceased,
and it was seldom that a poem was printed as
originally written. The poem upon laying the
Atlantic cable had been received, and was in type,
when a letter came from him, dated September 10,
1858, addressed to the author of this sketch, in
which are the following sentences : —

DEAR FRIEND, — In my haste, yesterday, I omitted
an idea which seems to me necessary to my little poem
on the Great Wire. After the fifth verse add the following : —

> " Through Orient seas, o'er Afric's plain
>   And Asian mountains borne,
> The vigor of the Northern brain
>   Shall nerve the world outworn.
>
> " From clime to clime, from shore to shore,
>   Shall thrill the magic thread;
> The new Prometheus steals once more
>   The fire that wakes the dead."

On another occasion (May 4, 1858) he wrote : —

MY DEAR FRIEND, — I am heartily obliged to thee
for thy kind suggestions. But see what has been the result of them ! Is the piece better or worse ? Who knows !

My sister thinks *she* does, and that I have altered for the better. I hope it will strike thee and Lowell in the same way. The sweep and rhythm please me, but I have had hard work to keep down my indignation. I feel a good deal more like a wild Bersark than like a carpet minstrel " with his singing robes about him," when recording atrocities like that of " The Swan's Marsh." . . . There is not a dull page in the last " Atlantic." If it could only be kept up to that point, it would take the precedence, by right, of all magazines on either side of the water.

February **12, 1858,** he wrote : —

" **Dr.** Holmes's ' Autocrat ' **is thrice** excellent ; **the** little poem **at the close** is booked for immortality."

The poem referred **to is " The** Chambered **Nautilus."**

January 20, 1858, he wrote : —

DEAR FRIEND, — Some **days ago I sent** my friend Lowell a copy **of** some lines, — " The Pipes **at** Lucknow." . . . If he submitted them to thee, **and** there **is** any probability of their appearance in the " Monthly," I would like to make an alteration in the last four lines of the first stanza, substituting these : —

> " **Not the braes of broom** and heather,
> Nor the mountains dark with rain,
> Nor strath, nor lake, nor frith-side
> Have heard their **sweetest strain."**

And I would like, also, to add the following stanza after the one closing with

> " Dinna ye hear it ? — 'T is the slogan !
> Will ye no believe it noo ?" —

> "Like the march of soundless music
>   Through the vision of the seer,
>   More of feeling than of hearing,
>   Of the heart than of the ear,
>   She knew the droning pibroch,
>   She knew the Campbell's call :
>   Hark ! hear ye no MacGregor's, —
>   The grandest o' them all !"

In the very striking poem entitled " Skipper Ireson's Ride," the refrain was originally written without use of the odd Marblehead dialect. His attention was called to this, and he adopted the phrases which the people of the old time would have used : —

> " Here 's Flud Oirson, fur his horrd horrt
>   Torred an' futherr'd an' corr'd in a corrt
>   By the women o' Morble'ead ! "

He wrote, December 6, 1857 : —

" I thank thee for sending the proof, with thy suggestions. I adopt them, as thou wilt see, mainly. It is an improvement. As it stands now, I like the thing well, — ' hugely,' as Captain Shandy would say."

There was a peaceful breathing-time before the war. In 1860 appeared a volume of " Home Ballads, Poems, and Lyrics." The volume is prefaced by a beautiful dedicatory poem to some unnamed friend of the poet's youth. " The Witch's Daughter " has the first place. This is founded upon a tradition of the neighborhood, and it is believed that the story is substantially true. The house of the heroine's father, in Amesbury, was standing not many years ago, and the site is still to be seen. This is one of the most charming of Whittier's pastorals, set with an intuitive sense of fitness in bright landscapes, full of masterly natural touches, and breathing through all a noble and humane spirit. At a later period the same poem, somewhat lengthened, was published as a holiday book, entitled "Mabel Martin," with numerous pictures of scenes in the neighborhood where the events took place.

"The Prophecy of Samuel Sewall" is rich in historic allusion, and in traits of the early times; and as the Diary of this celebrated judge has now been printed entire, the picturesque poem will be read with renewed interest and under a new light.

"The Sycamores," the "Occidental plane-trees," of which only a few are now remaining, were planted on the highway opposite the old Saltonstall mansion, a short distance from Haverhill.

"Kenoza Lake" lies near Haverhill, enclosed in a public park. In Chase's History it is mentioned that a meeting of citizens was held August 31, 1859, in favor of the improvement and re-naming of the "Fish House Lot." Trees were set out to the number of two hundred and fifty, and a fence was erected. Whittier gave the name Kenoza, which, in the Indian tongue, signifies "pickerel." The park was opened with appropriate ceremonies, and the poem was read on the occasion.

The poem "To G. B. C." is a tribute to the celebrated preacher and editor, Rev. George B. Cheever.

"The Preacher" is an account of the famous revivalist, Whitefield, who, after his labors in Georgia, came to Massachusetts and finished his work in Newburyport, where his remains lie beneath the church that bears his name.

"Brown of Ossawatomie" relates a touching anecdote of John Brown when on his way to execution. Some mention is made of him, and of his ill-judged attempt to free the slaves, in the present chapter.

In the very striking poem, "From Perugia," as well as in others preceding, such as "The Peace of Europe" and "The Prisoners of Naples," we see the deep interest which Whittier took in the uprisings in Europe in 1848. We know that his feelings could not be so stirred against the Catholic Church on any religious ground, for he is of all men most tolerant in the matter of religious beliefs; but the tremendous heat in which he wrought these lines was excited by sympathy **for the** victims of despotic government. The sentiment of justice in him has not been confined to any country nor race of men. A democrat pure and simple, he has advocated the equality of men everywhere before the law ; a believer in the primitive Christianity of the Sermon on **the** Mount, he has striven to recognize in all men his brothers. When the Pope (Pius **IX.)** joined with Russian Emperor, Austrian Kaiser, " Bomba " of Naples, **and the** " crowned **scandal** " **Louis** Napoleon, — " barnacle on the dead renown " of his uncle, — to put down **the** hopes of liberty-loving men, raised momen**tarily** by the successes of 1848, and to inflict the bloody and remorseless punishments that everywhere followed the reactionary movement, the head of the Church could not shelter himself by any ecclesiastical subterfuges. He and Cardinal Antonelli were as distinctly responsible for the " retributions " in the Papal States as was the **in**famous Napoleon III. for the daily massacres **in** the doomed Faubourg **of** Saint-Antoine that followed his treacherous *coup d'état.*

We have seen before **that whenever** the lives and liberties of **men** were concerned, Whittier never hesitated. He was always **to** be found on the **side of** the oppressed. And **though hitherto** the voices of the wise and humane have availed little with the masters of armies, yet we must believe that an equipoise will some time be reached, — a time when despots cannot control the ever increasing number of free spirits in the nations.

At this point it may be well to attend to some historical events.

A most profound impression was produced in both hemispheres by the attempt of John Brown to incite an insurrection of slaves at Harper's Ferry. He belonged to a plain Massachusetts family that traced its origin to one of the Pilgrims of the " Mayflower." He was a simple, hard-working, God-fearing man, abhorring war and slavery; and in peaceful times would probably have lived and died in some village in New England or Ohio, known only as a self-reliant, just, and blameless citizen. But he had long meditated upon the radical injustice of slavery, especially in the lonely home he had established on the borders of the wild Adirondack region. His mind took a fixed direction, and everything with him became secondary to the one purpose for which he lived. This purpose grew and dominated all his actions, so that it might be called by calmer men a symptom of insanity. But it was far from the madness which prevails in asylums. It was rather a singleness of

aim such as inspired **Joan of Arc,** George Fox, and
other immortal **visionaries. The** time **was** full **of**
thrilling **events.** Northern **men, pushing into Kan-**
sas, were murdered by bands **of guerillas.** These,
in turn, were pursued and shot, and still the re-
lentless warfare **went** on. Brown's four sons were
in these frays, **and on** several occasions he appeared with them, and by his intrepidity and masterly conduct **he** inflicted terrible **loss on** bodies **of**
armed men far larger **than his own. Once, with**
only thirty **men,** at **Ossawatomie, he held at bay a**
force of **five** hundred, until **he** made **a** retreat in
safety. This gave him **the** name **of** Ossawatomie
Brown. A full account **of his doings in** those
years would fill **a** volume.

A deeper scheme was **in** his mind. **He had be-**
come interested in many escaped slaves, **who were**
naturally the most courageous **of** their **class, and**
he conceived the idea **of** arming the colored people
of the South, and leading them to establish their
freedom. **For this end** he visited Boston **and** other
places in **New** England, and devoted his efforts **to**
raising money. **His** real aim was **known** only **to**
himself; those **who** aided him **with** money sup-
posed they were contributing **for the** defence of
free settlers in Kansas.

The writer of these pages well remembers seeing

him in Boston. He went little abroad, but received a great many visits from anti-slavery men. He was below the middle size, lean and sinewy. His long hair, nearly gray, was combed back in a smooth mass, leaving a clear, high forehead, and below it a pair of wonderful gray eyes. His manner had a singular deliberation, under which the surging of a fiery soul was apparent. He related some of his exploits, and calmly told of the retribution that had fallen upon the slayers of his sons. In describing the pitiful massacres he had witnessed, and the sufferings of his sons' families, his voice never faltered, no tears dimmed his steady eyes. There was an inward fire, however, of which his measured words gave no sign. He was a remarkable man, with every trait that goes to make up a hero, except for the lack of sound judgment.

He recruited and drilled a little force in Kansas, — less than twenty men, — and when they were ready he informed them, for the first time, that the field of operations was to be in Virginia, at Harper's Ferry, where was a large and well-stocked armory.

The attempt was made, as all readers of our history know, and it was unsuccessful. The negroes had none of the qualities necessary for carrying on a war of insurrection. The small band gathered no recruits of any consequence, and, after fighting like heroes, the survivors surrendered and met their fate.   The attack was made October 16, 1859; on the 19th Brown was placed in the jail at Charlestown, desperately wounded, and having lost both of his sons in the conflict.

Mrs. Child wrote to Governor Wise asking permission to visit Brown in prison, and to minister to his wants; to which the Governor replied in a caustic letter which he evidently supposed would leave nothing for her to say.   But she returned to the contest with an unexpected ardor, and by her logic, wit, and great-hearted eloquence completely vanquished her opponent.   These letters were printed in a pamphlet, of which more than three hundred thousand copies were sold.

At this time Whittier was deeply exercised in mind.   Much as he hated slavery, he was equally opposed to war, and the method of John Brown could not be countenanced by a consistent Friend. He wrote Mrs. Child as follows:—

OCTOBER 21, 1859.

MY DEAR FRIEND,— I was glad to get a line from thee, and glad of the opportunity it affords me and my sister to express our admiration of thy generous sympathy with the brave, but, we think, sadly misguided Captain Brown. We feel deeply (who does not?) for the noble-hearted, self-sacrificing old man.   But, as friends of peace as well as freedom, as believers in the Sermon on the Mount, we dare not lend *any* countenance to such attempts as that at Harper's Ferry.

I hope in our admiration of the noble traits of John Brown's character we shall be careful how we encourage a repetition of his rash and ill-judged movement. Thou and I believe in "a more excellent way." I have just been looking at one of the *pikes* sent here by a friend in Baltimore. It is not a Christian weapon; it looks too much like murder.

God is now putting our non-resistance principles to a severe test. I hope we shall not give the lie to our life-long professions. I quite agree with thee that we must judge of Brown by *his* standard; but at the same time we must be true to our own settled convictions, and to the duty we owe to humanity.

Thou wilt see how difficult it is for me to write as thee request. My heart is too heavy and sorrowful. I cannot write now, and can only *wait* with fervent prayer that the cause we love may receive no detriment.

CHAPTER XV.

IN WAR TIME.

THE breaking out of the civil war in 1861 absorbed all thoughts and feelings, and made everything subordinate to the central idea of patriotism. It was in its time of peril that the greatness of the Republic was revealed. The ideal nation, one and indivisible, was an object of uncalculating loyalty, of an almost passionate pride, and even of reverence. "God and our country," combined in equipoise, was no mere figure of speech. The occasion lifted common men into heroes. The great souls whose lineaments are preserved in Plutarch's Lives might have been paralleled in many a shop or forge or farmhouse. Life and treasure were of no value but for the country's sake. The lover left his mistress, the husband his wife and children. Delicately nurtured men endured the fatigues, privations, and squalor of camps without murmur. Wounds, maiming, prisons, and hospitals were encountered as gayly as if they had been incidents of a holiday fête.

The lurid splendor of that war! See it in verses of poets, that seem struggling between pity, horror, and heroic resolve! When did the world behold such a spectacle? The vast masses arrayed, the enormous energy developed, the great principles in issue, and the momentous results depending, all combined to make this the most tremendous and probably the most important of all wars in history. For this was not a question of national boundaries, of dispute between rival dynasties, nor of the subjugation of alien States to an imperial will; it was the establishment of the central idea of the Republic, — of the supremacy of democracy ; it was the overthrow of a privileged and dominant class, and leaving to all men equality of rights and duties. It was the necessary corollary of the Declaration of Independence, the vindication of the Golden Rule, making ethics the practical basis of constitution and law.

We can see now that this bloody arbitrament was inevitable. The fathers had temporized ; later, their sons compromised; but to no purpose. Freedom and slavery were not to coexist; one must destroy the other. Forty years ago, in speculating upon the future of America, the opponents of slavery used to imagine that centuries would pass before the legal distinctions as to color and race would be removed. It was supposed that slavery might imperceptibly fade away, as villanage slowly faded in England, — as the distinction between Norman lords and Saxon churls died out. It was thought that long before political equality could be established in the South the bulk of its population would be a bronzed mass, like the progeny of Spaniards, natives, and negroes in Mexico.

The habits of the Southern people fitted them for war. They lived in the open air, rode like Persians or Indians, were familiar with weapons both in hunting and in private quarrels; and their free spirits, grown turbulent from mastership, were moved at will by the fiery party leaders, whose impromptu utterances in groves and wayside places have given us the descriptive epithet of "stump-speaking." Such a people, fierce for constitutional and prescriptive rights, were naturally first to take up arms.

The Northern men, living in sight of schoolhouses and within sound of church bells, accustomed to

no sharper encounters than were afforded by the
annual " town-meeting," unused to arms since the
War of 1812, — with their " May training " turned
into a good-natured burlesque, their muskets of
antique pattern, and their habits wholly bucolic and
unwarlike, — were taken with a dazed surprise.
A concerted, vigorous, aggressive movement on the
part of a few improvised Southern armies at the
beginning might have taken the great Northern
cities, and enabled their generals to dictate terms
to the Government at Washington.

But the Rebels fortunately resisted the Government on their own ground, thereby drawing upon
themselves all the horrors they had prepared for
their foes, and, what was more, giving time for the
unarmed North to equip, drill, and forward its endless regiments.   The courage on both sides was
equal, when blood was up; and that being the case,
the North, with its vastly superior numbers and
resources, was sure to win in the end, — even if in
the terrible game man for man were to be sternly
sacrificed.

How abhorrent all this was to the soul of a sincere Quaker need not be said.   War to him was
only murder.   As the preparations were made and
the regiments departed, the feeling became intense
and agonizing.   He knew that only a solemn sense

of duty could **change the** peaceful farmers and
artisans of the **North into** crusaders **for** liberty.
But he could not favor the coercion of the South **by**
war. This will **be seen in the poem, " A Word for**
the Hour," written **in January, 1861. The feel-**
ing is shown more **fully** in the letter following,
addressed **to** the author : —

Amesbury, 7th 2d mo. 1861.

My dear Friend, — I wish I *could* answer thy letter
in the affirmative : **I** should only **be too glad to** join **with**
thee and **others** at this **time in aid of our " good old cause."**
But I am really very ill, — so much so that the writing of
a brief note like **this causes me a great deal of pain. . . .**

For myself, **I** would like **to maintain the Union if it**
could be *the* Union of our fathers. But **if it** is to be in
name only ; if the sacrifices and concessions upon which
it lives must all be made by **the Free States to the Slave**
States ; if the peaceful victories **of the ballot-box are to**
be turned into defeats by threats of secession ; **if** rebellion
and treason are to be encouraged into a standing **menace,**
a power above law and constitution, demanding perpetual
sacrifices, — **I, for one,** shall not lift a hand against its
dissolution. **As** for fighting, in any event, **to** *force back*
the seceders, **I** see no sense **in it.** Let them go on with
their mad experiment, — the Government simply holding
its own, and enforcing its revenue laws until this whole
matter can be fairly submitted to the people **for** their final
adjudication.

In a letter to Mrs. Child, dated April **1, 1861,** he
wrote : —

"I cannot but hope that in spite of the efforts of politicians and compromisers, the Great Nuisance is to fall off from us, and we are to be a free people."

The poem to John C. Fremont —

> "Thy error, Fremont, simply was to act
> A brave man's part without the statesman's tact" —

recalls an incident in the early part of the war, when Fremont was in command of the department of the West. Numbers of escaped slaves came into his lines, and he issued a proclamation, August 31, 1861, declaring all such to be free. President Lincoln, who had then much to learn about the objects of the war, annulled Fremont's proclamation, and three months afterwards relieved him from the command.

The poem was evidently written about the date of the following letter to Mrs. Child : —

AMESBURY, 10th of 9th mo. [1861].

I fully agree with thee as to the duty of the Government, and so far as I can I shall try to urge that duty. If this war is not for emancipation, it is both wicked and ridiculous. The war of the Fronde in France was wise in comparison. I am afraid the Government will tie up the hands of Fremont. I was just thinking of trying to thank him for his noble word "free," when lo! the papers this morning bring us Lincoln's letter to him, repudiating the grand utterance. Well, if the confiscated slaves are *not* free, then the Government has turned slaveholder, that is all.

I am sick of politicians. I know and appreciate the great difficulties in the way of the administration, but I see neither honesty nor worldly wisdom in attempting *to ignore the cause of the trouble.*

They tell us we must trust, and have patience: and I do not like to find fault with the administration, as in so doing I *seem* to take sides with the secession sympathizers of the North.

I thank thee for thy anecdotes of the "contrabands." If I can do anything in prose or verse to aid the cause, I shall be glad.

I wish somebody would write a song worthy of the people and the cause ; I am not able to do it.

Nevertheless, the suggestion made by Mrs. Child seems to have had its influence. After the taking of Port Royal, and the occupation of the sea-islands between Charleston and Savannah, the slaves of the coast were practically freed without proclamation. The intercourse among the islands was almost wholly by boats, and the negroes were expert oarsmen. It is true, also, that they habitually sung, keeping time with the strokes. But though there might be occasional gleams of humor in their rude verses, an actual copy in print of what they sung would be insipid and tedious. The author of " Uncle Remus " would imitate the real negro minstrelsy far better than Whittier has done. For

Whittier has filled the lines with good sense and point, and with the suggestions that belong to aspiring minds, while in fact the mental horizon hangs low over these black anachronisms, and very few of them could be made to understand the song, to say nothing of composing or singing it.

But Whittier is right. A song in imitation of the boatmen's solos, with their monotonous refrains, would be vapid. This is what the boatmen should have sung, if they had possessed the intelligence. In a similar way we approve of speeches at certain critical points in the action of a play, while we know that if such a scene were actually to happen, not a word beyond a monosyllable would have been uttered. No art is ever wholly free from the conventional.

Mrs. Child was greatly fascinated by the song, and sat down to write Whittier, we should imagine, on the very day it appeared in the " Atlantic " (February, 1862). At all events, her letter is dated January 21.

" But that Negro Boat Song at Port Royal! How I have chuckled over it and sighed over it! I keep repeating it morning, noon, and night; and, I believe, with almost as much satisfaction as the slaves themselves would do. It is a complete embodiment of African humor, and expressed as they would express it, if they were learned in the mysteries of rhyme and rhythm. . . . .

What a glorious, blessed gift is this of song, with which you are so lavishly endowed! Who can calculate its influence, which you always exert for good! My David, who always rejoices over your writings, was especially pleased with the Boat Song, which he prophesies will be sung ere long by thousands of darkies. . . ."

The war poems are not numerous. The position of an advocate of peace must have been particularly trying, even with the glorious object of freedom in view: —

> " Wherever Freedom's vanguard goes,
>   Where stand or fall her friends or foes,
>   *I know the place that should* be mine.
>
> .   .   .   .   .   .
>
> " O brothers! blest by partial Fate
>   With power to match the will and deed,
>   To him your summons comes too late
>   Who sinks beneath his armor's weight,
>   And has no answer but God-speed! "

During this terrible time of suspense Whittier is seen at his best in poems which show his reliance upon the Divine Providence, as in " Thy Will be Done," " The Battle Autumn of 1862," " Ein feste Burg ist unser Gott," and " The Watchers." The solemn appeals to God, and the sublime trust in the final triumph of right, affect the reader with a sense of exaltation. While the great thoughts are in mind, heroism appears to be the simple and natural attribute of man.

The miscellaneous poems in the volume "In War Time" are nearly all affected by the prevailing sadness and anxiety. Some line or couplet, or, it may be, an epithet, shows the drift of the poet's mind.

Thus in the prelude to the ballad "Amy Wentworth," dedicated to William Bradford, the marine painter, the author apologizes for having the heart to write of anything but the nation's trial:—

> "Let none upbraid us that the waves entice
> Thy sea-dipped pencil, — or some quaint device,
> Rhythmic and sweet, beguiles my pen away
> From the sharp strifes and sorrows of to-day."

So, in "Mountain Pictures," after sketching the grandeur of Franconia in a storm, he exclaims:—

> "So, let me hope, the battle-storm that beats
> The land with hail and fire may pass away
> With its spent thunders at the break of day,
> Like last night's clouds, and leave, as it retreats,
> A greener earth and fairer sky behind,
> Blown crystal-clear by Freedom's Northern wind!"

At the summer festival at "The Laurels" he remembers that

> "The drum rolls loud, — the bugle fills
> The summer air with clangor;
> The war-storm shakes the solid hills
> Beneath its tread of anger."

And after his aspiration for the freedom of Italy comes the calm expression of faith:—

> " Yet, surely as He lives, the day
> Of peace He promised shall be ours,
> To fold the flags of war, and **lay**
> Its sword and spear to rust away,
> **And sow its** ghastly fields with flowers ! "

" Barbara Frietchie " **is the only romantic** ballad suggested by the war, **in** this collection. **The** clear-cut lines, terse descriptions, and **heroic** tone made the poem universally popular ; and the name **of** the **brave old** German woman will be remembered while **the** country lasts. Some doubt **was** thrown upon the truth of the story, **but its substantial** correctness has been established.

Of the departure of regiments — the **pomp and** pride and circumstance of war — we see nothing in Whittier's poems. **His** abhorrence of slaughter was innate, and the splendor of the movement of **vast** masses had no charms for a devotee of peace. But when the Fifty-fourth Massachusetts regiment of colored troops marched away, headed by Colonel Robert G. Shaw (afterwards killed at the assault on Fort Wagner), he **wrote** to Mrs. Child : —

" I shall never forget the scene. **As** [Colonel **Shaw**] rode at the head **of** his troops, the flower of grace and chivalry, he seemed **to me** beautiful and awful as an angel of God come down to lead the hosts **of** freedom to victory. **I** have longed to speak the emotions of that hour, but **I** dared not, lest I should give a new impulse to war."

Before leaving the subject of the war, we quote from a letter written by Whittier to Mrs. Child, dated May 31, 1865, in which, after commending her work, "The Progress of Religious Ideas," he mentions the Vice-President, Andrew Johnson, as having the old Jacksonian strength of will. He says : —

"There is no fear that slavery is not to be utterly annihilated and ground into powder under his heel. What I fear is that he is not quite democratic enough to give the black man the suffrage. . . . But the safety of the negro is in the fact, more and more apparent, that there is no possibility of a safe reconstruction of the States without his vote. This will be perceived; and we shall be compelled, as a matter of self-interest, to do justice to the loyal black man."

The humane spirit has been always in the ascendant in the mind of Whittier. In the letter before quoted, doubtless referring to the prospective trials of Rebels for treason, he says : —

"I am glad to know thy views about capital punishment. I almost feared that, as in the case of others of my friends, the events of the last few years had changed thy views. I hope we shall have no unnecessary hangings to gratify an evil desire of revenge."

Some personal references in the poems under consideration remain to be noticed. "The Countess" is inscribed to "E. W.," — namely, to Dr.

Elias Weld, of Haverhill, the physician of the Whittier family, who **was very kind and** useful **to** the poet in his youth by lending him **books. There** is a grave of a titled lady in the old burying-ground above Rocks Bridge, and the inscription upon the ancient headstone is the foundation of this poem.

" A Memorial. M. A. C." was written upon the death of Moses A. Cartland, of Lee, N. II. His grandmother, Phœbe Hussey Austin, was sister **to** Whittier's maternal grandfather, Joseph **Hussey.** The Cartlands are among **the " hospitable cousins "** mentioned in Whittier's prose **sketch, " Yankee** Gypsies." " The River Path " is that leading from Haverhill to Amesbury.

During this period, " In **War** Time," there oc- curred a memorable celebration, **the** thirtieth an- niversary of the foundation **of the American Anti-** slavery Society, at Philadelphia, December **3 and** 4, 1863. There was a large attendance **of the** honored friends **of** the cause, and the proceedings were marked **by a** dignity **and** solemnity **seldom** witnessed. **The** address **of** the presiding **officer,** Mr. Garrison, **was** wonderfully impressive, leading **all to** see the signs **of** approaching **triumph.** One paragraph should perhaps **be** quoted.

" **It is no** longer a question confined to a few humble individuals **as** against a mighty nation ; but it **is** a nation rocking as by an earthquake, in travail with this tremendous issue. And now, instead of words, the question is debated on the battle-field at the cannon's mouth ; and undoubtedly, through this war of judgment, God means to vouchsafe deliverance to all in bondage.

" Welcome and benediction, upon this thrilling and joyous occasion, to those who entered earliest into the field of labor; who have gone through with all its toils, its sufferings, its sacrifices, and its perils ; and who have been graciously permitted to live to see this gladsome day ! "

Mr. Whittier was unable to attend, on account of ill health, but sent a letter. Before reading it, Mr. Garrison mentioned the poet as one " known and honored throughout the civilized world." He continued : —

" I have no words to express my sense of the value of his services. There are few living who have done so much to operate upon the public mind and conscience and heart of our country for the abolition of slavery as John Greenleaf Whittier."

The letter is substantially as follows, omitting only the regrets for not being able to be present : —

" . . . I look back over thirty years, and call to mind all the circumstances of my journey to Philadelphia in company with thyself and the excellent Dr. Thurston, of Maine, even then, as we thought, an old man, but still living, and true as ever to the good cause. I recall the early gray morning when, with Samuel J. May, our colleague on the committee to prepare a Declaration of Sentiments for the Convention, I climbed to the small 'upper chamber' of a colored friend to hear thee read the first draft of a paper which will live as long as our national history. I see the members of the Convention, solemnized by the responsibility, rise, one by one, and silently affix their names to that stern pledge of fidelity to freedom. Of the signers, many have passed away from earth, a few have faltered and turned back, but I believe the majority still live to rejoice over the great triumphs of truth and justice, and to devote what remains of time and strength to the cause to which they consecrated their youth and manhood thirty years ago. For while we may well thank God, and congratulate one another on the prospect of the speedy emancipation of the slaves of the United States, we must not for a moment forget that from this hour new and mighty responsibilities devolve upon us to aid, direct, and educate these millions, left free indeed, but bewildered, ignorant, naked, and foodless, in the wild chaos of civil war. We have to undo the accumulated wrongs of two centuries ; to remake the manhood that slavery has well-nigh unmade ; to see to it that the long-oppressed colored man has a fair field for development and improvement, and to tread under our feet the last vestige of that hateful prejudice which has been the strongest external support of Southern slavery. We must lift ourselves at once to the true Christian altitude where all distinctions of black and white are overlooked in the heart-felt recognition of the brotherhood of man.

"I must not close this letter without confessing that I cannot be sufficiently thankful to the Divine Providence which, in a great measure through thy instrumentality, turned me so early away from what Roger Williams calls 'the world's great trinity, pleasure, profit, and honor,' to take side with the poor and oppressed. I am not insensible to literary reputation ; I love, perhaps, too well the praise and good will of my fellow-men ; *but I set a higher value on my name as appended to the Anti-slavery Declaration of 1833 than on the titlepage of any book.*

" Looking over a life marked by many errors and shortcomings, I rejoice that I have been able to maintain the pledge of that signature, and that in the long intervening years

> ' My voice, though not the loudest, has been heard
> Wherever Freedom raised her cry of pain.'

" Let me, through thee, extend a warm greeting to the friends, whether of our own or the new generation, who may assemble on the occasion of commemoration. For thyself, I need not say that the love and esteem of early boyhood have lost nothing by the test of time."

It is a matter of history that on the New Year immediately following, the President's proclamation put an end to slavery ; and if there were any doubts as to his power to do this, the question was forever settled at the close of the war by the amendments to the Constitution.

CHAPTER XVI.

"Snow Bound" the Clearest Expression of Whittier's Genius. — "The Tent on the Beach." — Sketches of Fields and Bayard Taylor. — Pictures of Sea from Shore. — "The Grave by the Lake."—The Atlantic Cable.—The Duke of Argyll. — "National Lyrics." — Intense Religious Feeling. — "The Vanishers." — Bryant. — Thomas Starr King.

"SNOW BOUND," the most vivid and characteristic picture of country life in that older New England now far retreating with its forest lines, was published in 1866. The fame of the author had been steadily growing to continental proportions. The war had made freedom national, and had shown in a new and ennobling light the ante-bellum " fanatics " and " abolition-bards." Perhaps it would be more just to say that the liberation of men's minds from the bondage to Southern opinion — so long dominant in American letters as well as in trade and politics — served to quicken their perception and judgment so as to let the genius of poets like Whittier and Lowell, of novelists like Mrs. Stowe and Mrs. Child, and of orators like Phillips and Garrison, appear in their own proper splendor. Before the triumph of moral ideas, any writer identified with Abolitionists or Free-Soilers was regarded with feelings that wavered between pity and contempt. That time passed forever, and our literature was delivered from a subserviency that had dwarfed and demoralized it.

"Snow Bound" is perhaps the clearest expression of Whittier's genius. In a former chapter large parts of the poem were quoted to illustrate "A Quaker Home," and it will not be necessary to comment further upon it at present. It is only necessary to say that after the publication of this beautiful idyl Whittier became one of the most famous of modern poets, and probably the best beloved of any. Its success in every way was enormous, and its popularity continues without any intimation of decline.

"The Tent on the Beach" appeared in 1867. The framework is simple and natural. The poet and his two friends, Bayard Taylor and James T. Fields, are encamped on Salisbury beach; and, in sight of the broad bay, with the mouth of the Merrimac on the one hand and the Isles of Shoals and Boar's Head on the other, they tell tales of old times; meanwhile they watch the white specks of sails, or see the *lift* of the dim horizon, or wonder at the mirage that suspends the far rocky isles as if their pinnacles were about to plunge downward into the main.

The proem is saddened by the memory of recent griefs, and bids us think of the poet's "enforced leisure of slow pain," and the dear

> " Memory of one who might have tuned his song
> To sweeter music by her delicate ear."

The friends (Whittier, Bayard Taylor, and James T. Fields) are pleasantly sketched.[1] We see Fields, " with his beard scarce silvered," " a lettered magnate,"

> " In whom brain-currents, near and far,
> Converged as in a Leyden jar ; "

[1] Bayard Taylor, an editor, traveller, poet, and translator, — one of the most able, industrious, and accomplished literary men of our day, was a frequent visitor of the Whittier family, and was greatly beloved by them, as the references in this poem testify. He died in Berlin, December 19, 1878, while Minister of the United States to the Court of the German Empire.

James T. Fields, a prominent and successful publisher, also an author of merit, was well known on both sides of the Atlantic, and had probably a larger acquaintance with literary celebrities than any person in this century. His position between the usually jealous or hostile camps of authors and publishers was unprecedented ; and he had the rare honor of being heartily esteemed in both. His death (April 24, 1881), when he had scarcely passed his prime, and when so many reminiscences were yet to be expected from his pen, was greatly lamented. Both Taylor and Fields were far younger than Whittier, and both had fair prospects of higher accomplishment and lengthened life.

and we recognize the unequalled opportunities for
literary fellowship he had enjoyed : —

> " Pleasant it was to roam about
> The lettered world as he had done,
> And see the lords of song without
> Their singing robes and garlands on.
> With Wordsworth paddle Rydal mere,
> Taste rugged Elliott's home-brewed beer,
> And with the ears of Rogers, at fourscore,
> Hear Garrick's buskined tread and Walpole's wit once more."

Of himself Whittier writes : —

> " And one there was, a dreamer born,
> Who, with a mission to fulfil,
> Had left the Muses' haunts to turn
> The crank of an opinion-mill,
> Making his rustic reed of song
> A weapon in the war with wrong.
> .   .   .   .   .
> " The common air was thick with dreams, —
> He told them to the toiling crowd;
> Such music as the woods and streams
> Sang in his ear he sang aloud;
> In still, shut bays, on windy capes,
> He heard the call of beckoning shapes,
> And, as the gray old shadows prompted him,
> To homely moulds of rhyme he shaped their legends grim."

The picture of Taylor,

> " Whose Arab face was tanned
> By tropic sun and boreal frost,"

is striking and just : —

> " The very waves that washed the sand
> Below him, he had seen before

> Whitening the Scandinavian strand
>   And sultry Mauritanian shore.
> From ice-rimmed isles, from summer seas
> Palm-fringed, they bore him messages;
> He heard the plaintive Nubian songs again,   *
> And mule-bells tinkling down the mountain-paths of Spain."

> "His memory round the ransacked earth
>   On Puck's air-girdle slid at ease;
>   .   .   .   .   .
> Yet loved the while, that free cosmopolite,
> Old friends, old ways, and kept his boyhood's dreams in sight."

The descriptions of the immense gray beach and of the neighboring people are done with sharp, decisive strokes. If they fished, we see them

> " With an old Triton at the oar,
> Salt as the sea-wind, tough and dried
>   As a lean cusk from Labrador."

> " And there, on breezy morns, they saw
>   The fishing-schooners outward run,
> Their low-bent sails, in tack and flaw,
>   Turned white or dark to shade and sun.
>   .   .   .   t   .
> " Sometimes a cloud, with thunder black,
>   Stooped low upon the darkening main,
> Piercing the waves along its track
>   With the slant javelins of rain."

And " when the sunset splendors died," they saw

> " In lines outreaching far and wide
>   The white-maned billows sweep to land,
> Dim seen across the gathering shade,
>   A vast and ghostly cavalcade."

Luminous lines are these, gleaming with the light of genius, and destined to arrest the eyes of coming generations. Throughout this whole series of poems, so artlessly grouped together, are innumerable touches of a true poet's plastic hand.

Most of the pieces appeared separately, and at wide intervals, in the "Atlantic Monthly." Thus the poem upon the ocean cable was printed in the second volume, the "Wreck of Rivermouth" in the thirteenth, "The Grave by the Lake" in the fifteenth, "The Brother of Mercy" in the thirteenth, "The Changeling" in the sixteenth, "The Palatine" in the nineteenth.

"The Grave by the Lake" is founded upon the tradition that on the bank of Winnepesaukee, near Melvin stream, under a mound surrounded by a circle of huge stones, were found the bones of an Indian who when living must have been seven feet in height.

> "Who that Titan cromlech fills?
> Forest-kaiser, lord o' the hills?
> Knight who on the birchen tree
> Carved his savage heraldry?
> Priest o' the pine-wood temples dim,
> Prophet, sage, or wizard grim?"

The measure binds the poet to utter his thought in briefest and most pungent phrase; and many of the stanzas have a condensation of energy, as if

proverbs and Orphic responses had put themselves
in swift marching order at his call. So many stanzas, in fact, give these electric thrills as we read,
that a selection is difficult. We must venture : —

> " **Part** thy blue lips, Northern lake !
> Moss-grown rocks, your silence break !
> Tell the tale, thou ancient tree !
> Thou, too, slide-worn Ossipee !
> Speak, and tell us how and when
> **Lived and** died this king of men !
>
> " **Wordless moans the ancient pine ;**
> Lake and mountain **give no sign ;**
> **Vain to trace** this ring **of** stones ;
> **Vain the search of** crumbling bones :
> **Deepest of** all mysteries,
> And the saddest, silence **is.**
>
> " Nameless, noteless, clay with clay
> Mingles slowly day by day ;
> But somewhere, for **good** or ill,
> That dark soul is living still ;
> Somewhere yet that **atom's force**
> Moves the light-poised universe.
>   .   .   .   .   .
>
> " **Is** the Unseen with sight **at odds ?**
> Nature's pity more than God's ?
>   .   .   .   .   .
>
> " O the generations old
> Over whom no church-bells tolled,
> Christless, lifting up blind eyes
> To the silence of the skies !
> For the innumerable dead
> Is my soul disquieted.

> " Where be now these silent hosts ?
> Where the camping-ground of ghosts ?
> Where the spectral conscripts led
> To the white tents of the dead ?
> What strange shore or chartless sea
> Holds the awful mystery ?
>
> .   .   .   .   .
>
> " What is whispered by the trees ?
> 'Cast on God thy care for these.
>
> .   .   .   .   .
>
> " ' Not with hatred's undertow
> Doth the Love Eternal flow.'
>
> .   .   .   .   .
>
> "Therefore well may Nature keep
> Equal faith with all who sleep."

This is the concluding stanza : —

> " Keep, O pleasant Melvin stream,
> Thy sweet laugh in shade and gleam !
> On the Indian's grassy tomb
> Swing, O flowers, your bells of bloom !
> Deep below, as high above,
> Sweeps the circle of God's love."

It is only a sober statement, that this poem is one of which the greatest living man might be proud. The impressive scene, the far-reaching thoughts suggested, the deep yearning of humanity, and the unfaltering faith, are characteristic of the high regions to which genius leads us ; and as we read we feel as if we are made free in an immortal realm.

" The Maids of Attitash " is a poem containing a double love-story. Attitash, which in the Indian tongue signifies " whortleberry," is the name of a large and beautiful lake in the northern part of Amesbury. The maids were berrying, and exchanging maidenly confidences. Near by was a farmer mowing, and there was also a sportsman throwing his line for fish.

> " The supreme hours unnoted come;
> Unfelt the turning tides of doom :
> And so the maids laughed on,
> Nor dreamed what Fate had done, —
>
> " Nor knew the step was Destiny's
> That rustled in the birchen trees,
> As, with their lives forecast,
> Fisher and mower passed."

The poem upon the Atlantic cable has been often quoted, and is familiar to all readers. It is a noble strain of prophecy of peace on earth and good will to men.

Mr. George B. Prescott copied this poem from the " Atlantic " in his " History of the Electric Telegraph ; " and when Mr. Whittier's volume appeared, some years later, the poet was charged with plagiarism ! The matter, however, was easily explained.

At a banquet given in London, in 1868, to Cyrus W. Field, the chief American promoter of the undertaking, the Duke of Argyll, who presided, read this poem, introducing it as follows : —

"I trust you will allow me to read to you some striking and beautiful lines in which this expedition has been commemorated and these feelings expressed by that eminent Quaker poet of America, Mr. Whittier. . . . They are very noble lines, and express finely and solemnly the great hopes then entertained, and which I rejoice to think have now been fulfilled." [1]

The recitation of the poem was followed by cheers from the eminent guests assembled on the occasion from all parts of the United Kingdom.

The "National Lyrics" that follow in this volume suggest the absorbing interest felt in the issues of the civil war. "The Mantle of St. John de Matha," by which his vessel is carried to a Christian shore, has the colors of red, white, and blue. "What the Birds said" is the report from the South of fields of slaughter : —

> " They sang, ' The land we leave behind
>   Has swords for corn-blades, blood for dew.'
>   .   .   .   .   .
>
> " ' In shrouds of moss, in cypress swamps,
>   We saw your dead uncoffined lie.'
>   .   .   .   .   .
>
> " ' We heard,' they sang, ' the freedman's song,
>   The crash of Slavery's broken locks ! '
>   .   .   .   .   .

[1] Boston Daily Advertiser, November 4, 1874.

> " So to me, in a doubtful day
>   **Of** chill and slowly greening spring,
> **Low** stooping **from** the cloudy gray,
>   The wild birds sang or seemed **to sing.**

> " They vanished in the misty air ;
>   The song went with them in their flight ;
> **But lo** ! they left the sunset fair,
>   And in the evening there was light."

" Laus **Deo** ! " is the voice of gratitude and exultation at the passage of the constitutional amendment abolishing slavery. It is a Miriam's song of praise and thanksgiving, and is clad, as is proper, largely in scriptural phrases.

" The Peace Autumn " (1865) is full of the same glad thankfulness. The poem addressed to the Thirty-Ninth Congress is an appeal for wise and liberal legislation, — **for** equal laws for black and white, and for amnesty to the conquered.

To the Southern leaders he says : —

> " **Alas** ! no victor's pride is ours ;
>   We bend above our triumphs **won**
> Like David o'er his rebel son.

> " Be men, not beggars. Cancel all
>   By one brave, generous action ; **trust**
>   Your better instincts, and be **just** !

> " Make all men peers before the law ;
>   Take hands from off the negro's throat ;
>   Give black and white an equal vote."

This will recall Whittier's letter to Mrs. Child, quoted in a preceding chapter.

The "Occasional Poems," which follow, are characterized by an intense religious feeling which melts the heart of any man who has lived among primitive Christians and known what simple and natural piety is. "The Eternal Goodness" and "Our Master," — what can we say of such poems that will reveal the secret of their power? The gentler portions of the Psalms, the plaintive call upon God heard in the hymns of Cowper and Wesley and Madame Guyon, and all the deep and soul-moving utterances of the saints of all ages, such as Thomas à Kempis, seem to be blent in these exquisite verses. In an age of doubt and intellectual pride on the one hand, and of formalism or bigotry on the other, they seem to come as a new litany, a new confession of sublime faith, a new aspiration for the union of all created souls in the Divine. The thought and feeling are one; there is no seeking for effect, no parade of epithets, no conscious moulding of verse into stately form; but the movement from stanza to stanza is as natural as the outflow of an inspired voice. The extreme simplicity seems bald and prosaic to worldly men, — the simplicity which is of the very essence of an emotional mind in its highest state, wrought upon by the spirit of God.

Comparing these **sweet and holy** utterances **of** the soul with most **of** the **logical** quatrains which prosaic verse-makers **have** jointed and **framed together for** the service **of** song **is** like turning **from** the fresh and dewy lilies of the field **to** their muslin counterfeits. Such piety is as rare in our time as **is such** poetry; but it is an essential part of the life, as it is of the writings, of Whittier.

His work in this world, the **reader cannot fail to see, has been inspired always by God and human**ity. Justice **and reverence first, love and sym**pathy attending, and conscience keeping **guard over** thought and **act. And his poetry has come** from **the same** impulse that **led** him **to labor for the** slave, and to desire the light **of God's countenance as** his sole reward. Well may **he say** : —

> " And so beside the Silent Sea
>   I wait the muffled oar;
> No harm from Him can come to me
>   On ocean or on shore.
>
> " I know not where His islands lift
>   **Their** fronded palms in air;
> **I only** know **I cannot drift**
>   Beyond His love and care.
>
> " O brothers ! if **my** faith is vain,
>   If hopes like these betray,
> Pray for me that my feet may gain
>   The sure and safer way.

> " And Thou, O Lord ! by whom are seen
>   Thy creatures as they be,
> Forgive me if too close I lean
>   My human heart on Thee ! "

" The Vanishers " is the title of a poem founded on an Indian legend, full of touching suggestions, but elusive, and leading into the unknown realm beyond. It resembles somewhat — but only in a similar lightness of touch — the remarkable poem by Emerson, called " The Forerunners." The thought of separation from those who had preceded him in the way to the Silent Land is apparent in every line.

" Revisited " is a poem read at the annual gathering at " The Laurels " (before mentioned), on the south bank of the Merrimac, not far from Newburyport. It is an apostrophe to the noble river, joyous in spirit, bounding in musical rhythm, and brilliant with landscapes that a painter might copy. It is one of the most cheerful and inspiring of the later poems, and sets the blood in motion with its jubilant dactyls, and images of living beauty : —

> " Bring us the airs of hills and forests,
>   The sweet aroma of birch and pine ;
> Give us a waft of the north-wind, laden
>   With sweet-brier odors and breath of kine !
>
> " Bring us the purple of mountain sunsets,
>   Shadows of clouds that rake the hills,

> The green repose of thy Plymouth meadows,
>   The gleam and ripple of Campton rills.
>
> .   .   .   .   .
>
> "Shatter in sunshine **over thy ledges**,
>   Laugh in thy plunges from fall **to fall**;
> Play with thy fringes of elms, **and darken**
>   Under the shade of the mountain **wall.**
>
> "The cradle-song of thy hillside fountains
>   Here in thy glory and strength repeat;
> Give us a taste of thy upland music,
>   **Show us the** dance **of thy silver feet.**"

"**To Bryant on his Birthday,**" originally published in the New York "Independent," November 24, 1864, is a rare tribute to a poet, because it recognizes his manhood, and his long service in the cause of freedom, as giving higher renown than even his noble verses : —

> "We praise not **now** the poet's art,
>   The rounded beauty of his song;
> Who weighs him from his life apart
>   Must do his nobler nature wrong."

He compares him with Wordsworth in his love of nature, and characterizes his "**rapt hymn**" and "**woodland lay**" as

> "Too grave for **smiles, too sweet for tears.**"

This was in 1864, while the war still raged, and while patriotism was the only stop in the poet's instrument never shut. Therefore he exclaims : —

> " When Peace brings Freedom in her train,
>   Let happy lips his songs rehearse ;
>   His life is now his noblest strain,
>   His manhood better than his verse."

The last poems in this series relate to the Rev.
Thomas Starr King, a man of unusual power and
fervor, a devoted friend of our poet, and, like him,
a lover of natural scenery.   While a resident of
Boston he had given much time to the exploration
of the White Mountains of New Hampshire, and
had written the best descriptions of that picturesque
region.   He was, at the time the poem was first
published (January 21, 1864), minister of a church
in California.   His ardent patriotism and glowing
eloquence had full employment outside of his
pulpit; for California was full of Southern emis-
saries, and there was a vehement effort to turn the
State over to the Rebel side.   The vast distance
from the Atlantic States had stretched her ties of
interest and of sympathy with the Union almost to
the point of breaking.   Other ambitious politicians
were urging that this was the time to establish
a new and independent confederation of Pacific
States.   Meanwhile the central Government at
Washington had its hands already full, and could
not make its power felt in any effective way across
the Rocky Mountains.   Mr. King labored inces-
santly, and held audiences everywhere by his mar-

vellous power of speech, and by the magnetism of
his presence. To his efforts, and to the completion
of the transcontinental railway, through the energy of Oakes Ames of Massachusetts, the United
States owe the preservation of this important part
of their wide domain.

Few men in their capacity as simple citizens have
ever had the opportunity to do such service.

With this introduction, readers at a distance will
better perceive the significance of Whittier's poems.
Readers in New England and in California who are
old enough to remember the war will need no introduction to Thomas Starr King.

Thus it was that Whittier's invocation began : —

> " Amidst these glorious works of thine,
> The solemn minarets of the pine
> And awful Shasta's icy shrine."

The closing lines of the lament for the death of
the patriot preacher present a fine summary of his
great service : —

> " O East and West ! O morn and sunset, twain
> No more forever ! — has he lived in vain
> Who, priest of Freedom, made ye one, and told
> Your bridal service from his lips of gold ? "

CHAPTER XVII.

" AMONG THE HILLS."

" AMONG the Hills," published in 1868, is a pretty and melodious love-story, with a strongly realistic prelude. The romantic or pictorial side of rural life is contrasted with its reverse of narrow ways, prosaic discomfort, and unlovely personal traits. The poet shows himself

> " A farmer's son
> Proud of field-lore and harvest craft, and feeling
> All their fine possibilities."

He calls to mind

> " Old homesteads, where no flower
> Told that the spring had come, but evil weeds,
> Nightshade and rough-leaved burdock in the place
> Of the sweet doorway greeting of the rose ; "

> " The curtainless windows from whose panes
> Fluttered the signal rags of shiftlessness ; "

also the " best room," " bookless, pictureless,"

> " Save the inevitable sampler hung
>   Over the fireplace.
>
>   .   .   .   .   .
>
> " And, **in** sad keeping with all things about them,
>   Shrill, querulous women, sour and sullen men,
>   Untidy, loveless, old before their time,
>
>   .   .   .   .   .
>
>   Blind to the beauty everywhere revealed,
>   Treading the May-flowers with regardless feet;
>
>   .   .   .   .   .
>
>   Church-goers, **fearful of the unseen Powers,**
>   But grumbling over pulpit-tax **and pew-rent,**
>   **Saving, as shrewd economists, their souls**
>   **And** winter pork **with the least possible outlay**
>   Of salt and sanctity."

Rightly he claims

> " Our yeoman should be equal to his home
>   Set in the fair, green valleys, purple walled,
>   A man to match his mountains, not **to creep**
>   Dwarfed and abased below them."

And so the prelude concludes **with aspirations for** a higher and nobler life, — for " **home** loves **and the** beatitudes," " **all the** old virtues " **and for a** percep- tion of the **beauty in nature, as an outward type**

> " Of the eternal beauty which fulfils
>   The one great **purpose of creation, Love,**
>   The sole necessity **of Earth and Heaven !** "

As was intimated, the **story itself is** melodious and tender. It is wonderfully rich in suggestive lines

which bring remembered landscapes into brightness.
Dozens of stanzas succeed, each one of which might
serve as the motto of a picture. But the chief
interest invests the human figures. A farmer's
daughter is thus described : —

> " The sun-brown farmer in his frock
>   Shook hands, and called to Mary :
> Bare-armed, as Juno might, she came
>   White-aproned from her dairy.

> " Her air, her smile, her motions, told
>   Of womanly completeness ;
> A music, as of household songs,
>   Was in her voice of sweetness.

> " Not beautiful in curve and line
>   But something more and better,
> The secret charm eluding art,
>   Its spirit, not its letter."

The story is of a delicate lady of city birth and
culture, and her manly farmer lover, showing how
the grace of the one and the firm poise of the other
blended in an ideal union. Nothing more simply
beautiful is to be found in Whittier's volumes.
Summary and quotation are alike inadequate when
considering a picture so complete. It is to be
received as it is, the heart, rather than the brain,
keeping time with the rhythmic movement. It is
an instance of how high above all effort and artifice
is the unaffected simplicity of genius.

The scene of the poem is near Bearcamp River, close under the shadow of Mount Ossipee, but affording a magnificent view of the Chocorua range. The river, fringed with elms and maples,—here broad and quiet, reflecting sky, mountains, and trees, and there brawling among boulders, winds through the valley, often doubling upon itself, and receives the overflow of many ponds. Just below, it is joined by the Chocorua stream, and together they flow into Ossipee Lake, which finds its outlet by Ossipee River into the Saco. The maple thrives in this region, and some of these trees grow to enormous size. The majestic tree known as the " Whittier Maple " is perfectly symmetrical in form, and nearly one hundred feet in height.

Here only can the savage peak and rough shoulders of Chocorua be seen to advantage. The valley is so broad that the mountain and its fellows are at the right distance for scenic effect. There is an atmospheric bloom over all the jagged ridge which is to the eye like the softness of velvet, but which hides no outline, and does not obliterate the distinction between rock and forest. The colors change from hour to hour: rich blues and dark purples alternate through the day, varied with cloud shadows and gray-winged mists.

A drive along the Bearcamp River to the village

of Sandwich is especially beautiful. The river, with its fringes of trees, is almost always in sight; great orchards are loaded with fruit; the tinkle of cow-bells is heard on the mountain slopes. The way-side fences are festooned with clematis in bloom. The golden-rod and purple aster fill the spaces beside the road. Woodbine twines among the trees, its leaves already aflame with the autumn colors.

Meanwhile the mountains move slowly among themselves, changing their relative positions. Mount Whittier, at the left, assumes new dignity and grace as it emerges from behind the shoulder of Ossipee. Chocorua, heretofore the dominant figure in the group at the right, yields precedence to loftier Whiteface.[1]

Whittier's own view of this wonderful landscape may be seen in his poem, published later, entitled "Sunset on the Bearcamp." One stanza may be quoted : —

> "Touched by a light that hath no name,
>   A glory never sung,
>   Aloft on sky and mountain wall
>   Are God's great pictures hung.
>   How changed the summits vast and old!
>   No longer granite browed,

[1] The description of this picturesque mountain region is abridged from a letter in the "Portland Transcript" by S. T. Pickard, Esq.

> They melt in **rosy mist ; the rock**
> Is softer than the **cloud.**
> The **valley** holds its breath ; **no leaf**
> **Of** all its **elms is twirled :**
> The silence of eternity
> Seems falling on the **world."**

The lines headed **" G. L. S."** are a tribute to George **L. Stearns,** one of the **most** energetic and unselfish of the anti-slavery leaders. He was not a writer, nor had he the **gift** of impressive speech ; but he was brave, generous, and full of sympathy, and his sterling character and efficient service brought him into close relations with the more famous men of the party, such as Sumner, Theodore Parker, and Dr. Howe.

The **" Lines on a Fly-Leaf "** furnish an instance of Whittier's clear insight and felicitous portraiture, — a picture of mind and character rather than of personal and superficial traits. When we read, —

> **" Yet, spite of all** the critics tell,
> **I frankly own** I like **her** well.
> It may **be that** she **wields a pen**
> Too sharply nibbed **for** thin-skinned **men,**
> That her keen **arrows search and try**
> The armor joints **of** dignity," —

we have no hesitation in naming the brilliant Gail Hamilton as the subject of the verse. The

feeling is hearty and buoyant, and the praise richly
deserved: —

> " Give me the wine of thought whose bead
> Sparkles along the page I read ;
> Electric words in which I find
> The tonic of the northwest wind, —
> The wisdom which itself allies
> To sweet and pure humanities,
>
> .   .   .   .   .
>
> The genial play of mirth that lights
> Grave themes of thought."

The allusions, near the close, to Mrs. Child, to
Grace Greenwood, and to Mrs. Stowe will be easily
recognized.

" The Meeting," a touching description of a gathering of Friends for worship, containing a sketch
of Avis Keene, a beloved minister of that body, has
been already referred to in a preceding chapter.

The dedication of this volume, " Among the
Hills," is to Mrs. Annie Fields, wife of the late
James T. Fields, author and publisher, of whom
mention has been made.

" Miriam and other Poems," which appeared two
years later, was dedicated to Frederic A. P. Bar-
nard, President of Columbia College, a gentleman
who has been distinguished in the cause of education, and who in his youth wrote for the " New
England Review," of Hartford, Conn., at the time

when Whittier was editor. Miriam is the name
of a Christian slave, a favorite wife of an Oriental
monarch, the Shah Akbar, and one who kept alive
(as best she could) something of the pure faith in
which she had been reared. At the command of
her lord she told him what she knew of Christ.
Her character prepared him to give some credence,
and he quoted Mohammed's testimony : —

> " Our Prophet saith:
> ' He was a true apostle, yea, a Word
> And Spirit sent before me from the Lord.'
> Thus the Book witnesseth ; and well I know
> By what thou art, O dearest, it is so.
> As the lute's tone the maker's hand betrays,
> The sweet disciple speaks her Master's praise."

Afterwards, when the Shah had doomed to death
one of the women of his harem for suspected in-
fidelity, his wrath was turned to mercy by the
persuasion of Miriam. The story is told with exceeding grace, and the scenery and surroundings
are fitly colored by the gorgeous atmosphere of the
East.

The proem is filled with weighty thoughts concerning the dealings of God with men born outside the pale of Christianity, and the measure of
spiritual truth attained by the seers and prophets
of elder races. The course of the argument (if
the word is admissible) is not unlike that fol-

lowed in the admired poem, " The Grave by the
Lake : " —

> " Wherever through the ages rise
> The altars of self-sacrifice,
> Where love its arms has opened wide,
> Or man for man has calmly died,
> I see the same white wings outspread
> That hovered o'er the Master's head.
>
> .   .   .   .   .
>
> I trace His presence in the blind
> Pathetic gropings of my kind, —
> In prayers from sin and sorrow wrung,
> In cradle-hymns of life they sung.
>
> .   .   .   .   .
>
> Since everywhere the Spirit walks
> The garden of the heart, and talks
> With man, as under Eden's trees,
> In all his varied languages."

The " Occasional Poems " in this volume are
of varied character, but all noteworthy for some
feature of excellence. " Norembega " is a pathetic
ballad of an unknown explorer of the wild forests
of Maine. " Nauhaught, the Deacon " is an interesting legend of a " praying Indian " of Cape Cod.
" In School Days " is in its artless way a most exquisite reminiscence. It has the quick and change-
ful feeling and the sweet touches of nature, which
are the charm of the ancient ballad, — a production
perhaps rare in any age, but especially in our own.
It is the directness and the simplicity of phrase

which **go to** the heart.   Most writers of verse
would have tried to refine the language **and** attempted to *describe* the feeling which **Whittier**
dramatically thrusts at the reader **in a line.**

It is not yet time for this bit of school-girl **sentiment to** have become needlessly familiar, and a few
stanzas are quoted.   The little heroine was sorrowful, and she lingered after the scholars had gone, —
save one : —

> **" For near her stood** the little boy
>   **Her** childish favor singled ;
> His cap pulled low upon **a face**
>   Where pride and shame were **mingled.**
>
> " Pushing with restless feet the snow
>   To right **and** left, he lingered ; —
> As restlessly her tiny hands
>   The blue-checked apron **fingered.**
>
> " He saw her lift her eyes ; he felt
>   The soft hand's light caressing,
> And heard the tremble of her voice,
>   **As if a** fault confessing.
>
> " ' I 'm sorry that I spelt the word ;
>   **I hate to** go above you,
> Because,' — the brown eyes lower **fell,** —
>   ' Because, **you see, I love you ! ' "**

Among the purely **personal poems few** are read
with **more profound feeling than** " My Triumph."
It rises to **a noble and** prophetic strain as it con-

nects the life and work of the poet with the future possibilities of our race. Careless of fame and indifferent to praise, he thinks only of what good has been wrought, and how vast is the unattained : —

> "Sweeter than any sung
> My songs that found no tongue ;
> Nobler than any fact
> My wish that failed of act."

Others, he exclaims, are to sing the songs, and to right the wrongs. A vision of the future beauty and holiness rises, — a vision of a new heaven upon earth, — and he salutes it in memorable lines : —

> " Ring, bells in unreared steeples,
> The joy of unborn peoples !
> Sound, trumpets far off blown,
> Your triumph is my own ! "

In the poem, " To Lydia Maria Child," the allusion is to the death of Ellis Gray Loring, of Boston, — a lawyer, a man of wealth and position, who was an abolitionist in the early days, when the avowal required some courage.

The reader of Whittier frequently makes a discovery ; or rather it might be said that he comes upon something at times which has the force of novelty and the brilliancy of the unexpected, because it had been before overlooked. Such a " discovery " the writer made in " A Spiritual Mani-

festation." Roger Williams, the wise and tolerant
founder of Rhode Island, is represented as recount-
ing his experiences with the various sectaries and
malcontents driven from the Massachusetts Colony
to seek shelter in his little realm. There is a serious purpose, of course, but the tone is gay and the
rhymes are now and then *jinglish*. The verses,
as to form, may be likened to a *Toccata* in music,
—a kind of "touch-and-go" style of composition.
They are sufficiently correct for the purpose, and
the occasional imperfection of the assonances, as in
"Hudibras," gives a comic twist to the expression.
It is an amusing category of heretics and "cranks"
that he gives,—an historic and versified list of
Puritanic aversions. But there are strong and
solid lines, as, for example : —

> "For Truth's worst foe is he who claims
> To act as God's avenger,
> And deems, beyond his sentry beat,
> The crystal walls in danger ; —

> "Who sets for heresy his traps
> Of verbal quirk and quibble,
> And weeds the garden of the Lord
> With Satan's borrowed dibble."

Then the tone shifts imperceptibly, and at the close
are some memorable stanzas : —

> "Forgive, dear saint, the playful tone,
> Too light for thy deserving ;

> Thanks for thy generous faith in man,
> Thy trust in God unswerving.
>
> .　.　.　.　.
>
> "The pilgrim needs a pass no more
> From Roman or Genevan ;
> Thought-free, no ghostly tollman keeps
> Henceforth the road to heaven ! "

"The Pennsylvania Pilgrim " (1872) is pitched upon a lower key than most of its predecessors. As the poet says, " The colors of my sketch are all very sober, — toned down to the quiet and dreamy atmosphere through which its subject is visible." It is a pleasant account of the German jurist and scholar, Pastorius, who at the invitation of Penn led a colony of his countrymen to settle near Philadelphia, and founded Germantown. The prefatory note is full, attractive, and at times eloquent. Judging rightly that the influence of the Puritans has been celebrated with enough eulogy, the poet claims the meed of praise as well for the Quaker settlers of Pennsylvania. " The two principal currents of American civilization," he says, " had their sources in the entirely opposite directions of the Puritan and the Quaker colonies." Pastorius and his beautiful wife, their charming home, gardens, and vineyard, and their fine old-time manners are depicted in tender if sober colors. The quiet of the scene becomes contagious, and the reader, harassed by the bustle and worry of modern life, slips back in imagination into those pastoral times, and gains rest and refreshment of soul. It is a story to be read under apple-blossoms, while bees are filling the air with a drowsy hum, and the landscape lies in dream-like repose. The Friends alone among moderns appear to know the blessedness of calm souls.

"The Singer" is the title of a beautiful descriptive poem commemorating the sisters Alice and Phœbe Cary, of Cincinnati, Ohio. Both were intuitive observers of nature, and they were equally fresh in feeling. Both were writers of verse, but the productions of Alice quite surpass those of her sister. Their beautiful characters and gentle manners endeared them to a wide circle of friends. Both, it will be remembered, wrote for the "National Era" while Whittier was connected with it, and were valued contributors to other periodicals. Horace Greeley, founder of the "New York Tribune," was their stanch friend, and it is to him that Whittier alludes in this stanza : —

> "When last I saw her, full of peace,
> She waited for her great release ;
> And that old friend, so sage and bland,
> Our later Franklin, held her hand."

The sweet and pensive tone of the poem is characteristic of the poet in his tenderest mood.

Among other fine poems in this volume, — such as " Marguerite " and " King Volmer and Elsie," — " The Sisters " may be instanced as one with a strong dramatic element, and containing a startling surprise for the reader.

Two years later (1874) appeared " Mabel Martin," with illustrations taken from scenes in the Merrimac valley. This poem is an amplification of "The Witch's Daughter," which has been previously noticed.

CHAPTER XVIII.

THE letters of Mrs. Child contain many references to Whittier, and throw light upon his character as well as upon their relations. Whittier's letters to her are equally touching and significant. A few of them, furnished by the representative of Mrs. Child,[1] are now printed for the first time. Unlike the studied letters of many famous people, which show the marks of labor and the refinements of rhetoric, these are evidently written without a thought of publication or of effect. The charm of real letters is unmistakable; although polished epistles may be more brilliant and epigrammatic, they fail to touch the heart. In the first we seem to see the quick mantling color and the hearty grasp of hands; in the other, the guarded manner of self-possessed and worldly people.

[1] Mrs. Sarah Parsons, of New York.

Mrs. Child we have seen renouncing a literary career at the time she was the most famous and probably the ablest woman in America. Her husband, David Lee Child, a studious, not to say scholarly man, had devoted himself to every good work, especially to the cause of the slave. They both lived to a good old age, and have passed into the eternal state, leaving behind them the memory that is blessed.

DECEMBER 6, 1856.

God forbid that I should forget or neglect an early and much loved friend! When we have reached middle years, and begin to tread the sunset declivities of life, it is not easy to make new friends or give up old ones. Long before I knew thee I had loved thy writings, and honored thee for thy noble efforts in the cause of freedom. I have had no occasion to qualify my respect and admiration, or to regard thy friendship as anything less than one of the blessings which the Divine Providence has bestowed upon me in more than compensation for whatever trifling sacrifice I may have made for the welfare of my fellow-men.

NOVEMBER 15, 1864.

It was an exceedingly happy thought of thine to send these words of cheer to those of us who are beginning to pass down life's sunset declivities. I do not like, however, to have thee call thyself old. I never think of thee as such. While the heart and fancy are still young, why should we recur to family registers?

I am thinking how much my sister would have liked

thy book.[1] How strange and terrible are these separations! — this utter silence! — this dumb agony of mystery! — this reaching out for the love which we feel *must* be ever-living, but which gives us no sign! Ah, my friend, what is there for us but to hold faster and firmer our faith in the goodness of God? — that all which he allots to us or our friends is for the best! — best for them, for us, for all! Let theology, hate, and bigotry talk as they will, I for one will hold fast to this: God *is* good; he is our Father! He knows what love is, — what our hearts, sore and bereaved, long for, and he will not leave us comfortless; for is he not Love?

19th 12th mo., 1869.

I thank thee from my heart for thy very kind notice of me and mine in the [Boston] "Journal" of this morning. I know very well I don't deserve it, but I am grateful for it, notwithstanding. What gives it the greater value in my eyes is that it comes from thee. If I were younger, and did not wear a plain coat, I might be tempted to exclaim with Burns, when similarly favored: —

> "Now diel-ma-care about their jaw, —
> The senseless, gawky million;
> I'll cock my nose aboon them a' —
> I'm roosed [2] by Craigengillan."

I am always glad to see thy name in print. I read anything thee may write, — not only for its literary qualities,

---

[1] She had died about a month before the date of this letter. The book is entitled "Looking towards Sunset."

[2] Praised.

but because I know a true and noble woman stands behind it.

God's blessing be with thee, my dear friend.

AUGUST 3, 1870.

My deepest sympathies are with Prussia in the impending contest. What a monster Napoleon is! — Was he born without moral sense? Has he no conscience, no remorse? There is something weird and dreadful about him. The prayers of all the priests of Rome are with him; but the cry of innocent blood, rising to heaven, will drown them. I think he is rushing upon his fate.

In the same letter he says of the Vice-President, Henry Wilson: —

"He is in the main a very true and noble man, when the politician allows the *man* to act freely; and he has done great service to the cause of freedom. I shall do what I can to secure his re-election." [1]

JUNE 29, 1874.

I was reading D. L. C.'s [David Lee Child] speech at the first annual meeting of the N. E. A. S. Society, a few days ago, and the old, old days seemed to be fresh in my memory. I see that the second annual report of the Society in 1834 gives the following list of the 'works' on slavery which had been circulated by the Society: Paxton's Letters, Wright's Sin of Slavery, Mr. Child's Speech, Whittier's Justice and Expediency, and Mrs.

---

[1] Wilson on his death-bed said : " If I had to do, — to think, to act, and to vote just as I was directed by one man, I would choose Whittier. I believe him the purest man living on earth." — *From a letter by S. A. Boyden.*

Child's **Appeal.** So we were early found working together.

I have been looking over **Wilson's second volume of the "** Rise and Fall of the Slave **Power."** It is highly creditable to his ability, impartiality, and discrimination. It entitles him **to** higher honor **than** the Vice-Presidency.

Give my kindest regards **to** Mr. Child, and **may** the **dear** Lord and Father bless you both!

The following letter **from Whittier is indorsed in** the handwriting **of Mrs. Child, as follows : —**

"**Sent to me in answer to a letter enclosing a stereo**scopic view **of Charles** Sumner's portrait, seen through a **grotto of** white phantom **leaves."**

20th 9th mo., 1874.

I am always **glad to** see thy handwriting **on an en**velope. I make many new friends, **but my heart, as I grow older,** turns longingly **to** the surviving **friends of my** early years, who **have shared in the struggles and** triumphs of **a** great cause.

The picture of our great **and** good **friend in its ad**mirably fitting **setting I shall value** highly **for its own** sake, but also for that of **the friend** who **sent it.**

I shall **have a little book of mine to send thee next** month.

I hope thy husband **is by this time more** comfortable. We are all growing old, and nearing **the unknown shore.** I am in my sixty-sixth **year, and yet** it seems but a little **space** of time since I was a boy.

My health has been feeble all summer, but a visit to the **New** Hampshire hills **at** North **Conway** and West

Ossipee has done me good.   But a few hours of reading or writing entirely prostrates me.   Indeed, for a long time I have only been able to write from half an hour to an hour at a time, — often only a few minutes.

Amesbury, 9th mo. 23d [year wanting].

Since sending thee my note in reply to thine, I learn that my old friend, thy honored husband, has passed from this life.   It must have been very sudden to thee.   Indeed, death is always a surprise.

A brave, true, and strong man has gone from us.   He was one of the very first to throw himself with unselfish devotion into the anti-slavery cause; and I well remember his exceedingly able speech at the first annual meeting of the N. E. A. S. [New England Anti-slavery Society], — a speech which was published by thousands in pamphlet form, and which was at the time the best and fullest exposition of our principles and objects.

Dear friend of many years, all who know and love thee will draw near to thee at this time in tender sympathy.   May the dear God and Father keep and comfort thee!   Always and affectionately thy friend.

25th 3d mo., 1876.

Thy confession as respects thy services in the cause of emancipation does not "shock" me at all.   The emancipation that came by military necessity and was enforced by bayonets was not the emancipation for which we worked and prayed.   But, like the Apostle, I am glad that the Gospel of Freedom was preached. even if by strife and contention.   It cannot be said that *we* did it; we, indeed, had no triumph.

But the work itself was **a** success. It made us stronger and better men and women. Some **had** little to sacrifice, but I always felt that thee had made the costliest offering **to** the cause ; for thee, alone, of all of **us** had **won a** literary reputation which any one might have **been** proud **of.** I read all thy early works with enthusiastic interest, **as** I have all the later. Some time ago I searched Boston and **New** York for thy "Hobomok," and succeeded in finding a defaced copy. How few American books can compare **with** thy "Philothea" ! Why, my friend, thy reputation, in spite of the anti-slavery surrender **of it for** so many years, **is still a** living **and** beautiful **reality.** And, after all, **good as thy books are, we know thee to be** better than **any** book. **I wish thee could know how proudly** and tenderly thee **are loved and honored by the best and** wisest of **the** land. **God bless thee always !**

28th 6th mo., 1879.

I did not see thee at our dear **Garrison's funeral. Was** thee there ? **It** was a most impressive **occasion.** Phillips outdid himself ; and Theodore Weld, under **the** stress **of** powerful emotion, renewed **that** marvellous eloquence which in the early days of anti-slavery shamed **the church** and silenced **the mob. I never heard** anything more beautiful **and** more moving.

Garrison's faith in **the** continuity of life was **very** positive. He trusted more **to the phenomena of** spiritualism than I can, however. *My* faith is **not helped by** them. **I do** believe, apart from all outward signs, in **the** future **life ; and** that the happiness of that life, as **in** this, will consist in labor and self-sacrifice. **In** this sense, as thee say, " there is no death."

I trust, with thee, that the wretched Pocasset horror [1] will teach all honest expounders the folly and danger of going back to the Stone Age for models of right living. I am shocked by the barbarism and superstition of our popular faith. There needs another George Fox, with broader vision, to call men from the death of the letter to the life of the spirit, and to tread under foot the ghastly and bloody materialism among us.

I hope these pure days find thee well, and able to enjoy them. It seems to me they were never so lovely as now. Do our friends who have left us see them? I think so, or something akin to them, but fairer. Thanks for the translation of George Sand. It is full of suggestive beauty. Perhaps I may some time add rhyme to the melody.

Among the friends of Whittier mention should be made of Mary Grew, of Philadelphia, a woman of eminent ability and well known for her philanthropic labors. She attended a meeting of the Radical Club in Boston on one occasion, and read an essay entitled "Essential Christianity." Mr. Whittier, who was unable to be present, sent a poem. It is purely personal, but as it has been printed in Mrs. Sargent's volume which gives an account of the Club, its reproduction may be pardoned.

---

[1] One Freeman, in Pocasset, Mass., in a fit of religious frenzy killed his child under the belief that he was commanded to make the sacrifice in imitation of Abraham. He was treated as a lunatic and shut up in an asylum, but is now said to have become sane.

HOW MARY GREW.

With wisdom far beyond her years,
And graver than her wondering peers,
So strong, so mild, combining still
The tender heart and queenly will,
To conscience and to duty true,
So, up from childhood, Mary Grew!

Then in her gracious womanhood
She gave her days to doing good.
She dared the scornful laugh of men,
The hounding mob, the slanderer's pen.
She did the work she found to do, —
A Christian heroine, Mary Grew!

The freed slave thanks her; blessing comes
To her from women's weary homes;
The wronged and erring find in her
Their censor mild and comforter.
The world were safe if but a few
Could grow in grace as Mary Grew!

So, New Year's Eve, I sit and say,
By this low wood-fire, ashen gray;
Just wishing, as the night shuts down,
That I could hear in Boston town,
In pleasant Chestnut Avenue,
From her own lips, how Mary Grew!

And hear her graceful hostess tell
The silver-voicèd oracle
Who lately through her parlors spoke
As through Dodona's sacred oak,
A wiser truth than any told
By Sappho's lips of ruddy gold, —
The way to make the world anew,
Is just to grow—as Mary Grew!

In Mrs. Sargent's "Recollections of the Radical Club" there is an account of the meeting of Whittier with Dom Pedro, the Emperor of Brazil, at her house. The Emperor, it is stated, had been an admirer of Whittier, and had corresponded with him both in regard to poetry and the emancipation of slaves. He had translated the poem of Whittier entitled "The Cry of a Lost Soul," beginning : —

> "In that black forest, where, when day is done,
> With a snake's stillness glides the Amazon."

As the poet stepped forward it appeared to all that the Emperor was about to embrace him, after the warm-hearted manner of the Latin races. But Whittier, somewhat abashed at the demonstration, gave his imperial admirer a cordial grasp of the hand and led him to a sofa, where they indulged in friendly conversation.

On retiring from the room, the Emperor placed his arm around his brother poet's waist and gently drew him down the staircase. Over their farewell we can properly drop the curtain.

Grace Greenwood, an eminent writer, and a deserved favorite with all readers, became an abolitionist in that elder day when the confession was suicidal. Her stories and sketches, full of wit and good humor, had been the chief attraction in many magazines ; but when she was proclaimed an agitator, a certain publisher, alarmed for his Southern circulation, not only dropped her name from his list of contributors, **but made** an offensive parade of his action, **with the view of strengthening** his position **among** slaveholders **and** conservatives. **By some** coincidence his portrait **was issued** about **the same** time. Whittier was always a chivalrous friend, and above all things he despised subserviency. He published in the " National Era " a stinging satire, which **we** copy. **It is not** necessary **to** say that **in literary merit this is not equal to his** best; **but it is** worth **preserving as a specimen of** what we may **call** righteous indignation, as **well as** a part of the history **of** the time : —

[April 4, 1850.]

LINES ON THE PORTRAIT OF **A** CELEBRATED **PUBLISHER.**

A moony breadth of virgin **face,**
  By thought unviolated ;
A patient mouth, to take from scorn
  The hook with bank-notes baited !
Its self-complacent sleekness shows
  How thrift goes with the fawner —
An unctuous unconcern of all
  Which nice folks call dishonor !

A pleasant print **to** peddle **out**
  In lands of rice and cotton ;
The model of that face in dough
  Would make the artist's fortune.

For Fame to thee has come unsought,
  While others vainly woo her,
In proof how mean a thing can make
  A great man of its doer.

To whom shall men thyself compare,
  Since common models fail 'em,
Save classic goose of ancient Rome,
  Or sacred ass of Balaam?
The gabble of that wakeful goose
  Saved Rome from sack of Brennus;
The braying of the prophet's ass
  Betrayed the angel's menace!

So when Guy Fawkes, with silken skirt
  And azure-tinted hose on,
Was twisting from thy love-lorn sheets
  The slow-match of explosion —
An earthquake blast that would have tossed
  The Union as a feather,
Thy instinct saved a perilled land
  And perilled purse together.

Just think of Carolina's sage
  Sent whirling like a Dervish,
Of Quettlebum in middle air
  Performing strange drill-service!
Doomed like Assyria's lord of old,
  Who fell before the Jewess,
Or sad Abimelech, to sigh,
  "Alas! a woman slew us!"

Thou saw'st beneath a fair disguise
  The danger darkly working,

In flowing locks and laughing eyes
  The cunning mischief lurking.
How keen to scent the hidden plot !
  How prompt wert thou to balk it,
With patriot zeal and pedler thrift,
  For country and for pocket !

Thy likeness here is doubtless well,
  But higher honor 's due it ;
On auction-block and negro-jail
  Admiring eyes should view it.
Or, hung aloft, it well might grace
  The nation's senate-chamber —
A greedy Northern bottle-fly
  Preserved in Slavery's amber !

Another friend may be named, Miss Lucy Larcom, of Beverly, Mass., well known by a poem full of homely fidelity and pathos, entitled " Hannah at the Window," and by others of perhaps equal merit. Mr. Pickard, from whose letters quotations have been made in this volume, writing from the Bearcamp River, says : —

" Mr. Whittier is not alone among the poets who have been inspired by this scenery. At this place, and in the neighboring town of Sandwich, in the same valley, Lucy Larcom has spent some part of every summer for many years. She has thoroughly explored the region, and ascended all the principal summits. As will be observed, her name is given to one of the Ossipee hills [Lucy's Peak].

"It has been my good fortune to meet both of the poets in this visit. Each of them was accompanied by relatives and friends, and the group almost filled this ancient and comfortable inn. The grave and reverend poet who wrote the 'Centennial Hymn' has smiled benignantly upon them, and even written witty nonsense verses which have capped the climax of their fun. The author of 'Hannah at the Window' enlivened the festivities of one rainy evening by reading with an irresistibly comic effect a very amusing poem composed for the occasion. I wish it were allowable to give some specimens of the work, or rather play, of both these poets, but, of course, it is out of the question."

Whittier has been the most prolific of letter-writers. From the beginning of the anti-slavery movement his pen was in constant use. His letters, if collected, would fill volumes. How much it is to be regretted that they could not be collected under his own supervision! He has kept no copies, but it is to be hoped his correspondents have preserved them. They are in possession of the most eminent men in public and in literary life both in the United States and in England.

His friendships have been faithful and lasting. Readers will remember the warm-hearted references to Sumner, Dr. Howe, Stearns, Garrison, Samuel E. Sewall, Theodore D. Weld, Fields, and Taylor, as well as to the humbler laborers among

Friends, and to the women mentioned in these pages. But there are many unnamed in this work ; such as John P. Hale, the poet Lowell, Salmon P. Chase, Joshua R. Giddings, E. P. Whipple, Anson Burlingame, William H. Seward, Henry Wilson, N. P. Rogers, Dr. Henry I. Bowditch, Samuel Fessenden, Governor William Claflin, Myron Holley, and others, who enjoyed his friendship and received his frequent letters. When the time shall come there may be a large collection, from which the history of our era will be more fully illustrated.

It should be added that with the leading American poets his relations have always been cordial. Between him and Emerson there was a pleasant interchange of visits and letters. With Holmes he enjoyed a warm and generous communion. Longfellow he saw less frequently, though they were on the best terms, and always ready to do mutual kind offices. With Bryant he had an acquaintance, but they seldom met.

But for the full appreciation of Whittier we must go among the people of Amesbury and of his native Haverhill. Though they may not all be able to gauge his merits as a poet, they love him as a man and neighbor. He has always been democratic in his feelings (if a political term may be allowed), and the reputation he has won as a man of letters has not in the least impaired his kindly interest in, or his natural familiarity with, all classes of his townsmen.

It was largely due to his efforts that Essex County became the early home of the anti-slavery movement. His poems have celebrated its scenery and historical events with a fidelity and beauty elsewhere unparalleled; and his fame is felt to be a part of the inheritance of every one who traces his descent from the colonists of the river towns. The feeling is universal and intense. Other poets may be admired on the Merrimac, but it is only Whittier who is regarded with love and reverence.

Perhaps a paragraph of another sort should be added by way of antidote, or, at least, of caution. It is a pity that those who compile accounts of public men by the use of scissors, should not have some way to test the accuracy of their clippings. Unfortunately not all the stories in newspapers are true.

Here is a story from a Western periodical, purporting to have been written by its well-informed correspondent in New York. It is sufficiently worthless in itself, but it may serve one good purpose.

HOW THACKERAY HUGGED WHITTIER.

Now that I am talking of literary men, I want to repeat a good story which was told me the other day of the little quarrel which **John G. Whittier** had **with** Thackeray, the great English novelist. Whittier, **as you** know, is **very** reserved, **and the story comes** through a friend of his brother **for the first time to the** public. When **Mr.** Whittier was in London **many years ago,** he **was** made a lion by the literary people of **the** metropolis. The father of Pendennis and Becky Sharp was prominent among his entertainers, and among other things he honored him by a dinner at his club. Whittier and Thackeray went together in Thackeray's carriage to the club rooms. **At the** dinner much wine **was** drunk, **as is the custom at** all **such feasts in England.** Thackeray seemed **to have no** limit **in his capacity in this direction, and** drank **bottle** after bottle apparently without **being in the** least affected by **it. He was as** witty and clear-headed as though he had **been** taking nothing but soda. Whittier **was** temperate, and drank but little. **As** morning crept **on,** however, and the feast ended, Thackeray succumbed, **and, on** leaving, his valet had **to carry him to** the carriage. On the way home he became maudlin, and threw his **arms** around Whittier's neck, vowing **eternal** friendship. **In** short, he acted **so** that Whittier grew thoroughly disgusted and left, resolving to have nothing more to do with Thackeray.

It is sad **to think** of Thackeray as **such a** toper; but what has **the** ordinary reader **to say** concerning a circumstantial **account** like this,—and by one with **such** an evident knowledge **of** the customs **of** London clubs? It is **"from a** friend of Whittier's brother," **too, and so is authentic.** If Thackeray had been helped into his carriage by his " valet," that, of course, was proof positive. And to be hugged by a great strapping Englishman in a maudlin and slobbery way! No wonder the staid Quaker resolved to have nothing more to do with him. The more, because Whittier drinks no wine, and never did, having been all his life a total abstainer. He is also averse to late hours and club dinners, and eats (sparingly) at mid-day as his ancestors did. One is quite sure he was never out of his bed " when morning crept on." He has always been averse, likewise, to playing the lion, even in our small city of Boston ; and has generally fled from any public demonstration. There is a further difficulty. He could not well have dined at a swell club in London with Thackeray, because he was never in that city, and never crossed the Atlantic. Finally, he lately assured the present writer that he had never " met " Thackeray any- where, and had never even seen him. So the story vanishes like a guilty ghost. Of such trust- worthy materials are many biographies composed.

The Witch-Hazel. — Charles Sumner ; an Estimate. — Whittier's Grand Elegy. — The Atmosphere of the Later Poems. — Agassiz. — The *Sea Dream.* — Poems of Elizabeth.

THIS little volume was published in 1875, when Whittier was in his sixty-eighth year. The blossoms are not those of the sturdy and full-leaved hazel-bush, whose clustered nuts — resembling filberts — are so eagerly sought by boys in autumn, but of the witch-hazel (originally *wych*-hazel), a shrub that is found in damp forests throughout the United States. Its name is *Hamamelis Virginica*, and it is renowned for its (supposed) medicinal virtues, also for its reputed occult power (in certain hands!) of discovering water in subterranean springs. The use of its essential quality in the form of a lotion for the cure of diseases is almost universal. The other and mysterious use of its twigs as divining-rods is confined to the uneducated and credulous; but, within the memory of many now living, the aid of the fork of witch-hazel was very commonly invoked by those about to dig wells, or to find springs for the supply of aqueducts. The flowers of the witch-hazel, developed from buds formed in summer, open in October or November just as all the forest leaves are falling. They are bright yellow, — " twisted gold," — and are therefore conspicuous among the bare shrubbery. Brilliant as they are, they are not joyous emblems, although they belong to New England's most beautiful and exhilarating season, because they remind us that the procession of flowers has passed, — that the hectic bloom of the doomed forest leaves has been succeeded by eager frosts and brisk north winds, and that in the woodland paths and openings we must trample the faded glories of summer.

The principal poem in the collection is an elegy upon Charles Sumner, who died in March, 1874. It is a work of some importance, containing over fifty stanzas; and though its conception was due to feelings of grateful admiration and sincere friendship, yet it is evident that its composition was the result of careful study. It is vigorous, but stately in movement; it is warm and generous in what it suggests, but the language is academic and the feeling under command. There are no impassioned utterances, no apostrophes that make the nerves tingle; but all **is strong, steady, and decorous, like** the subject of the verse. For Sumner, intellectual, spotless, faithful, persistent, and brave **as he was,** had little personal magnetism, and **no** winning gayety or grace.

> "**No** sense of humor dropped its oil
> On the hard ways his purpose went;
> Small play of fancy lightened toil;
> He spake alone the thing he meant."

His emotions were limited **to the great cause he served, and his sympathies mainly to his fellow-**workers. **He was** fortunate in having **a** reading and thinking constituency, **who at** first appreciated and supported him as a representative **of** their convictions. **Had he lived** in a Western State he would have been at most **an** essayist, **a judge, or a court** reporter; **any** cross-roads **orator, not to mention such** adroit politicians as **Clay,** Corwin, **and Crittenden,** would have easily discomfited him.

As time went on, his intellectual view broadened, and his knowledge and experience culminated **in** statesmanship; **so that he reached a** height where he was unmoved by the passions **or** clamors of **the** hour, and was often exposed **to** ill-considered **censure. In** his denunciation **of the** seizure **of the rebel** envoys by Commodore Wilkes, **he** incurred great odium; **and** still **more by** his magnanimous proposition that the colors of the national regiments should not bear the names of battles of the civil war in which they had been carried. For his advocacy of this most wise and just measure the legislature of Massachusetts, in 1873, passed upon him a vote of censure. It was, however, reversed and expunged at the next session, a very short time before the senator's death.[1] To this Whittier refers in two suggestive stanzas : —

> " If for one moment turned thy face,
>   O mother, from thy son, not long
> He waited calmly in his place
>   The sure remorse which follows wrong.

> " Forgiven be the State he loved
>   The one brief lapse, the single blot;
> Forgotten be the stain removed,
>   Her righted record shows it not."

So, throughout this long procession of stanzas, moving to the time of a funeral march, we see that Sumner is honored and even revered, but scarcely

---

[1] The injustice of this censure stirred Whittier to the depths of his nature. He at once drew up and signed a memorial to the legislature, asking that it be rescinded. Mr. Sewall gave his signature gladly, and the paper was then sent to Longfellow, who signed it, and got other signatures from Harvard professors. It was duly presented, but the prayer was not successful until the next year, 1874. The recall of Massachusetts to an honorable position towards its great senator was due solely to Whittier's prompt and generous efforts.

loved ; albeit the poet **would not** perhaps admit
so much. **He was the** steel point **of** the ploughshare, the very *acies* at the **front of** the battle.
He addressed **the** higher intellectual faculties, **and**
the absolute sense **of** right. That **he** did this in
latinized sentences, heavy with ornament, was due
to the training he had received and **to the** usage **of**
the classical circle in which he moved.

Of his style Whittier says : —

> " **The sea** rolled **chorus** to his speech
> Three-banked **like** Latium's tall **trireme,**
> With laboring **oars ;** the grove and beach
> **Were Forum and** the Academe."

As to his **rather** distant manner, **the** poet inti-
mates that it was due to his pride in his **native**
State : —

> " **If than Rome's tribunes** statelier
> He wore his senatorial robe,
> His lofty port was all for her,
> **The** one dear spot in all the globe."

There are many reasons why Whittier followed
the course of Sumner — excepting **in his defection**
from the Republican party in 1872 — with **intense**
admiration. **As a Quaker, an** advocate of peace, he
was naturally impressed **by the** oration upon **the**
" True Grandeur **of** Nations." **As a** believer in
equal rights, his thanks were due **to** the man who

first formulated the sentiment that " Freedom is
national and Slavery is sectional." His sympathy
went out for the victim of a brutal assault by an
infuriated slaveholder ; and upon Sumner's return
to his seat, the abolitionist could but rejoice at the
terrible presentation of the Barbarism of Slavery.

Whittier was moved, too, by the calm grandeur
of Sumner's view of a reunited Republic. We have
seen in his own letters how strongly he felt upon
the subject of punishing the leaders of a conquered
people. He was anxious that the triumph of freedom should be sullied by no bloodshed ; therefore
he exulted in Sumner's clemency : —

> " The first to smite, the first to spare ;
>   When once the hostile ensigns fell,
>   He stretched out hands of generous care
>   To lift the foe he fought so well."

As a whole, the career of Sumner, as a scholar,
jurist, orator, senator, and diplomatist, is doubtless
the noblest and most complete in our history. That
he was irritated at times into unwise deflections,
and that he had not *all* the gifts and graces of a
perfect man, may be admitted without any impair-
ment of the claims made for him. Phillips was a
more brilliant and impassioned orator, but he has
remained in private station. Webster's was a
grander and broader mind, and fuller of varied

resources, but his life was darkened **by** a fatal compromise with wrong. There were **greater** lawyers than Sumner, **both as members of our courts and** as exponents of the laws of nations; **there** were abolitionists whose life-long services antedate and surpass his own; there were scholars **and** poets whose perception of beauty and knowledge of letters, and whose command of pure idiomatic English, were quite beyond his. But to make up the **sum** of his capacity **and** accomplishment we must **take the best** parts **and** rarest achievements **of** many picked **men.**

The extended **view of** Sumner in this poem is in every way admirable. **Some** truisms **are** inevitable in the eulogy of a friend, but **the successive** stanzas generally **have** something important to add, **and** are not merely cumulative. **It is a** fitting tribute to the **most** representative **of** Northern statesmen from the most intensely American poet.

> " The marble image of **her** son
>   Her loving hands shall yearly crown,
> And from her pictured Pantheon
>   His grand, majestic face look down.

> "**O** State, so passing rich before,
>   Who now shall doubt thy highest claim?
> The world that counts thy jewels **o'er**
>   Shall longest pause at SUMNER's name!"

There is a charm in **these** later poems quite beyond analysis. They **are not** simply beautiful;

they have an atmosphere which subdues us, while the nobility of thought inspires, and the sense of holiness descends upon our souls. It seems as if the voice were from the heights, and the singer far away, climbing towards the transfiguration.

"The Prayer of Agassiz" has this quality, — lifting contemplation "from nature up to nature's God." In "John Underhill" we see the serene pity of a humane soul for human frailty, — the spirit of Jesus shown in the sentence, "Neither do I condemn thee : go, and sin no more." In "The Friend's Burial" — that of a woman beloved of the poet's mother — is seen the most exquisite tenderness of feeling revealed by the most sympathetic touches of art. It is in its *tone* that the unobtrusive power of the poet is felt. The air is pervaded as by undulations of sorrow, and inanimate nature seems to throb with the general grief : —

> "No sound should break the quietude
>   Alike of earth and sky ; —
> O wandering wind in Seabrook [1] wood
>   Breathe but a half-heard sigh !

> "Sing softly, spring bird, for her sake ;
>   And thou not distant sea,
> Lapse lightly as if Jesus spake,
>   And thou wert Galilee ! "

---

[1] Seabrook is a town in New Hampshire, not far from the border of Massachusetts.

Quoting from a poem like this is like cutting a square from a landscape of Corot. The beauty is entire, and enwraps the whole as in a luminous veil.

In the " Sea Dream " there is an attraction of a different nature. The sea and its shore are sketched with free and masterly strokes, and then appears a singer with the memory of a lasting sorrow, and we hear his voice of melody apostrophizing his beloved : —

> " Thou art not here, thou art not there,
>   Thy place I cannot see ;
> I only know that where thou art
>   The blessed angels be,
> And heaven is glad for thee.
>
> " Forgive me if the evil years
>   Have left on me their sign ;
> Wash out, O soul so beautiful,
>   The many stains of mine
>   In tears of love divine !
>
> " I could not look on thee and live
>   If thou wert by my side ;
> The vision of a shining one,
>   The white and heavenly bride,
>   Is well to me denied.
>
> " But turn to me thy dear girl-face
>   Without the angel's crown,
> The wedded roses of thy lips,
>   Thy loose hair rippling down
>   In waves of golden brown.

> "Look forth once more through space and time,
> And let thy sweet shade fall
> In tenderest grace of soul and form
> On memory's frescoed wall,
> A shadow, and yet all!"

It is perhaps a frequent experience with imaginative men, when traversing some hitherto unknown region, to find the perceptions and memory playing at cross-purposes, and making new landscapes wear familiar looks. The startled faculties spring up as if they would say, "All this has been visited before." Upon this *quasi* delusion is built the poem entitled "A Mystery." The illusory nature of the vision is intimated, while each view is brought into sharp relief. This is a poem for poets, and its subtile elements will linger in memory long after its images and details of description have been lost in the haze of the past. It is not Whittier's greatest, nor among his greatest, but it is a poem which no art could compass, and at which the merely cultivated framers of verse must stop short. It is of the very essence of poetry, and an attestation of the poet's right divine.

"Child Songs" is pervaded with a benignant spirit, and will touch the hearts of those who realize the force of the Master's words, "Of such is the kingdom of heaven."

"The Golden Wedding of Longwood" was written

for the fiftieth anniversary of the marriage of John and Hannah Cox, of Kennett, Penn., members of the Society of Friends. John Cox, says the poet, was one of

> " The fire-tried men of Thirty-eight who saw with me the fall,
>   **Midst** roaring flames and shouting mob, **of** Pennsylvania
>   Hall."

Cox was a neighbor and friend of Bayard Taylor, who lived at Cedarcroft, near **by, and** had often entertained him **with** Whittier. **The estate of** Longwood, **and the** whole region **as well, has an air** of quiet beauty, **with** evident plenty **and prosperity.** Whittier's recollections of this rich farming country, **and** of the hospitality of its people, are exceedingly pleasant.[1] The bounty of nature and the mild climate were in strong contrast **with the** sterile soil and bitter winds of Massachusetts.

> " Again before me, with your names, fair Chester's landscape
>   comes,
>   Its meadows, **woods, and** ample **barns,** and quaint **stone-**
>   builded **homes.**

> " The smooth-shorn **vales, the** wheaten slopes, **the boscage**
>   green and soft,
>   Of which their poet sings so well from towered Cedarcroft."

The poems of Elizabeth H. Whittier, **or** rather a limited number of **them, are contained in** " Hazel

[1] **It seems** probable that this is **the scene in which** " Maud Muller " **is** located.

Blossoms." The collection is all too brief, and could have been greatly extended. In the introduction Whittier says that his sister was distrustful of her powers, without ambition, and inclined to shun publicity. "Yet it has always seemed to me," he adds, "that had her health, sense of duty and fitness, and her extreme self-distrust permitted, she might have taken a high place among lyrical singers." These poems attest the correctness of his judgment. "Dr. Kane in Cuba " is always read with warm appreciation, both of its spirit and of its rounded art. As much can be said also of " The Wedding Veil," quoted in a preceding chapter.

The repeated references to this beloved sister throughout Whittier's later poems show how close were the ties that bound them, and what a sense of desolation came upon him after her departure. Many poems, such, for instance, as "The Vanishers," were inspired in whole or in part by the memory of this rooted sorrow.

CHAPTER XX.

Dinner given by the Publishers of the "Atlantic." — Whittier's Response. — Longfellow. — Emerson. — Holmes. — Warner. — Howells. — Norton. — The "Literary World's" Symposium. — Tributes. — Bryant (in prose). — Mrs. Stowe. — President Eliot. — "Deer Island's Mistress."

THE publishers of the "Atlantic Monthly" gave a dinner in honor of Whittier on his seventieth birthday (December 17, 1877), at Hotel Brunswick, in Boston. Invitations had been sent to the leading poets and writers of New England and New York, and between sixty and seventy guests were present. Mr. Houghton, the senior publisher, presided, and at the head of the table on one side were Whittier, Emerson, and Longfellow, and on the other Holmes, Howells, and Charles Dudley Warner. Mr. Houghton, in a felicitous speech, introduced the guest of the evening, who, upon rising, was heartily cheered. Mr. Whittier excused himself from speaking, but stated that he had written "a little bit of verse" which his friend Longfellow would read.   The following is the

RESPONSE.

> Beside that milestone where the level sun,
> Nigh unto setting, sheds his last, low rays
> On word and work irrevocably done,
> Life's blending threads of good and ill outspun,
> I hear, O friends! your words of cheer and praise,
> Half doubtful if myself or otherwise,
> Like him in the old Arabian joke,
> A beggar slept and crownèd Caliph woke.
> Thanks not the less.   With not unglad surprise
> I see my life-work through your partial eyes;
> Assured, in giving to my home-taught songs
> A higher value than of right belongs,
> You do but read between the written lines
> The finer grace of unfulfilled designs.

Mr. Emerson was next introduced, and in place of a contribution of his own read Whittier's poem "Ichabod."

Mr. Howells came next, with a brilliant retrospect of the "Atlantic" and its corps of writers, mentioning with especial praise Holmes and Lowell. It was a most fortunate effort, generous and hearty as it was graceful.

Professor Norton responded for Lowell, who at that time was our Minister in Spain.

Dr. Holmes followed with one of his indescribable poems, in which he characterized the works of

Longfellow, Emerson, **Lowell, and** Whittier. The ease of the measure, and the occasional banter that relieved and **set off the** serious passages, might lead **some to consider this** only a clever **piece of** society verse. **But** beneath **the** playfulness **there is a** power **of** sharp portraiture which no prosaic critic could approach. **We copy the portion that** refers to Whittier : —

> " And the wood-thrush **of Essex,** — you know **whom I mean,**
> Whose song echoes **round us** while he sits unseen,
> Whose heart-throbs of **verse through our** memories thrill
> **Like a breath from the wood,** like **a breeze from the hill,**
> So fervid, so simple, **so loving, so pure,**
> **We** hear but one strain, and our verdict is sure, —
> **Thee** cannot elude us, — **no** further we search, —
> 'T is holy George Herbert cut loose from the church !
> **We** think it the **voice of** a seraph that sings, —
> **Alas,** we remember that angels have wings : —
> **What** story is this of the day of his birth ?
> **Let** him live to a hundred ! we want him on earth !
> One life has been paid him (in gold) by the sun ;
> One account has been squared and another begun ;
> But he never will die if he lingers below
> Till **we 've paid** him in love half the balance we owe."

Letters of regret were read from the venerable poet Bryant, from **George** William Curtis, **T. B.** Aldrich, Bayard Taylor, **Dr.** William Everett, **John Hay, Dr.** J. G. Holland, Clarence **Cook.** Poems **were** contributed by R. H. Stoddard, **John** James Piatt, **the Rev.** John Weiss, and others. **As the** tables were filled with men of eminence, the speaking was unusually interesting. One feature in the entertainment was wholly unique, — as it was unexpected. Mr. Clemens, known by the pseudonym of " Mark Twain," read a sketch in which Emerson, Longfellow, Holmes, and Whittier were made to figure as masqueraders in the guise of California roughs. It was audacious, and perhaps in questionable taste; but nothing more comic was ever conceived. The manner in which the poets were supposed to have pelted each other with quotations was wholly irresistible.

The celebration of the birthday was not confined to the " Atlantic " coterie. The " Literary World," of Boston, issued a special Whittier number, with contributions from leading authors. It contained poems by Longfellow, Holmes, Bayard Taylor, Stedman, Celia Thaxter, Mrs. Child, Dr. J. F. Clarke, Elizabeth Stuart Phelps, and others ; also brief tributes in prose from many eminent writers. We find room for a few only.

THE THREE SILENCES.

BY HENRY W. LONGFELLOW.

Three Silences there are ; the first of speech,
The second of desire, the third of thought ;
This is the lore a Spanish monk, distraught
With dreams and visions, was the first to teach.
These silences, commingling each with each,

Made up the perfect Silence that he sought
And prayed for, **and wherein** at times **he** caught
Mysterious sounds from realms beyond our **reach.**
O thou, whose daily life anticipates
The life to come, and in whose thought and word
The spiritual world preponderates,
Hermit **of** Amesbury! thou too hast heard
Voices and melodies from beyond **the gates,**
And speakest only when thy soul is stirred!

THE GOLDEN CALENDAR.

BY OLIVER WENDELL HOLMES.

Count **not the years that hoarding time has told,**
Save by the starry memories in their **train;**
Not by the vacant **moons that wax and wane,**
Nor all the seasons' changing robes enfold;
Look on the life whose record is unrolled!
Bid thought, word, action, breathe, burn, strive **again,**
Old altars **flame** whose ashes **scarce are cold,**
Bid the freed captive clank his broken chain!
So will we count thy years **and months** and **days,**
Poet whose heart-strings thrill upon thy lyre,
Whose kindling spirit lent like Hecla's fire
Its heat to Freedom's faint auroral blaze,
But waste no words the loving soul to tire
That finds its **life in duty, not in** praise!

[From W. C. Bryant.]

I should be glad **to celebrate in verse the** seventieth
return of John Greenleaf **Whittier's** birthday, if the
thoughts and words fitting for such an occasion would
come at call, to be arranged **in** some poetic form, but I
find that **I must content myself** with humble prose. Let

me say, then, that I rejoice at the dispensation which has so long spared to the world a poet whose life is as beautiful as his verse, who has occupied himself only with noble themes, and treated them nobly and grandly, and whose songs in the evening of life are as sweet and thrilling as those of his vigorous meridian. If the prayers of those who delight in his poems shall be heard, that life will be prolonged in all its beauty and serenity for the sake of a world which is the better for his having lived; and far will be the day when all that we have of him will be his writings and his memory.

[From Francis Parkman, the historian.]

John G. Whittier, the poet of New England: his genius drew its nourishment from her soil; his pages are the mirror of her outward nature, and the strong utterance of her inward life.

[From Mrs. H. B. Stowe.]

I am glad that there is to be a tribute of affectionate remembrance on the seventieth birthday of our friend Mr. Whittier. He is the true poet whose *life* is a poem, and our friend has received grace of the Father to live such a life. His life has been a consecration, his songs an inspiration, to all that is highest and best. It has been his chief glory, not that he could speak inspired words, but that he spoke them for the despised, the helpless, and the dumb; for those too ignorant to honor, too poor to reward him. Grace was given him to know his Lord in the lowest disguise, even that of the poor hunted slave, and to follow him in heart into prison and unto

death. He had words **of** pity **for all** — words of severity for none but the cruel and hard-hearted. Though the land beyond this world be more beautiful and more worthy of him, let **us** pray the Father to spare him **to us yet more** years, and to fill those years with blessing.

[Signed **"H."**]

When Whittier's biography shall **be written**, — distant **be** the day! — the world will know something more of the helpful and affectionate companionship between him and the **sister** whose beautiful life is already commemorated **in** his **verse.** She **was his** critic, **counsellor, and best** friend. She **had a wonderful imagination, and excelled as a** story-teller. Elizabeth Whittier must **have been a** delightful woman, whose **very presence** brought gladness. **One who** knew **her** says: "**She sometimes** visited **at** my father's house, and all **of us** children used **to** climb upon **the** bed **of** an invalid sister, and listen, rapt, **to** Elizabeth, who, sitting **at** the foot, **told us** stories by **the hour."**

[From President Eliot, of Harvard **College.**]

A great multitude will **gladly join in celebrating Mr.** Whittier's seventieth birthday. They **who love** their country will **thank** him for **the** verses, sometimes **pa-** thetic, sometimes stirring, which helped to redeem that country from a **great** sin **and shame; they who rejoice** in natural beauty will thank him that he has delight- fully opened their eyes to **the** varied charms **of the** rough New England landscape, by highway, river, moun- **tain, and** sea-shore; they who **love** God will thank him from their hearts for the tenderness and simple trust with which he has sung of the Infinite Goodness.

The celebration in Boston was noticed throughout the United States and in England. The number of poems and prose tributes was enormous. There is a scrap-book on the author's table containing over seventy pages of articles, — mostly newspaper clippings in triple columns of compact type. The occasion showed that the noble life and labors of the venerable poet were held by all men in honor and affectionate remembrance. Many of the articles are marked by high literary qualities, and some are seen to be throbbing with tender recollections. The scrap-book contains also several poems in manuscript, written by life-long friends, which were not intended for publication.

We copy an article from the "New York Evening Post," believed to have been written by the poet Bryant, as a fair specimen of the general comment.

WHITTIER.

What words of ours can add one touch of green to the bays with which the poet Whittier is crowned on this the seventieth anniversary of his birth? His fame is securely rooted in the hearts of the great English-speaking race of men, and his praise is not a chorus which needs swelling by loudly attuned voices. His simple ballads, breathing the very life-breath of truth and nature, are in the hands, the memories, the hearts, of men and women and children all over the land. He is canonized already of the people,

and his place in the poetic calendar is too firmly fixed to
be altered by any critical examination of his works; and
yet it seems to us that critical examination is still necessary, if for no other reason, because there is a popular
misapprehension, as we think, of the nature and source
of Whittier's power. Even critics are misled sometimes
by the notion that the Quaker poet owes much of his
fame to his early championship of the anti-slavery cause.
The fact is that when Whittier first undertook to do
battle for the slave, the sentiments as well as the opinions of men in this country were hostile to the cause in
which he enlisted; and his course in declaring himself an
abolitionist and proving his faith abundantly in his works
hindered rather than helped his efforts to gain the ear
and the heart of the people. There are men and women
certainly whose road to literary success, or to popularity
of other kinds, has been made smooth by anti-slavery
opinions; but these came later. They wrote when to
utter sentiments of hostility to slavery was to give expression to that which the great heart of the people felt and
ached to utter; and the literary worth of their work was
magnified because it was seen through the lens of a deep,
earnest, passionate public sentiment. In Whittier's case,
however, the reverse of this was true. He made himself
the champion of the slave when hostility to slavery was
understood, by the general mind of the country, to mean
black treason, when to say aught against the national
curse was to draw upon one's self the bitterest hatred,
loathing, and contempt of the great majority of men
throughout the land.

He won his way to fame as a poet, notwithstanding his

anti-slavery earnestness, rather than by reason of it. He marched straight up hill, with a heavy load upon his shoulders; and to call that a help which was in fact a sore hindrance, however much it might have helped at a later day, is to lose sight of the fact which most strongly attests the genuineness of Whittier's genius.

For ourselves, we find the chief source of his poetic power where it is pleasantest to find it, in the intense truthfulness, naturalness, and simplicity of his poetry. He is a bard of human nature, and he has helped human nature in honoring it. As truthful and as candid as Wordsworth, he is less metaphysical — simpler. Underneath the calm exterior of the Quaker he has the enthusiasm of the warmest poetic nature, and he has known how to make hearts throb violently in contemplation of noble deeds in common life. He has interpreted the thought of a rural maiden and made us share her day dreaming. He has uttered for us the deep admiration which chokes us when we see in common life the heroism of such men as Conductor Bradley. In a word, Whittier has been and is the truthful voice of the every-day life of this time; he is the poet of our work-a-day world. Let us hope that the years of his healthful old age may be lengthened, and that they may bring with them only the peace which belongs to the evening of a well-used day.

In Whittier's poem, "June on the Merrimac," occurs this stanza : —

> "The Hawkswood oaks, the storm-torn plumes
>   Of old pine-forest kings,
>   Beneath whose century-woven shade
>   Deer Island's mistress sings."

Hawkswood is the name of a beautiful residence on the river, not far above Newburyport, built in a remnant of an aboriginal forest by the Rev. J. C. Fletcher, the well-known traveller. Just below it is Deer Island, a beautiful and grassy but irregular ellipse, covered in part with ancient trees, mostly sombre and venerable pines, and resting on foundations of granite in the midst of the powerful current. On one side there is a sheer wall of rock forty feet above the water. A chain bridge crosses the river over the island. Near as the trees are to the travelled road, they shelter hawks, crows, and kingfishers, with now and then eagles and herons; and in stormy weather are heard the cries of sea-fowl winging along the river. Broad apple-trees and familiar shrubs relieve the level about the roomy and comfortable old house; and around the margin, and far down in the crevices of the blackened and lichened rocks, in graceful disorder, are bushes of lilac and sumac, draperies of clematis, and lonely wild flowers. The western outlook along the river, as seen from under the stately trees, is something to remember. It is one of the most picturesque spots in New England. The singular beauty, the quiet, and the sense of seclusion wrap one around as with the silken folds of a dream.

"Deer Island's mistress" is Harriet Prescott Spofford, an author of deserved renown both in prose and verse. She contributed to one of the early numbers of the "Atlantic" a story of remarkable merit, "In a Cellar"; and since that time she has been a prolific writer of fiction. She has the clear sight, the *vivida vis*, and the brilliant expression, which mark imaginative minds.

We copy a poem by her in honor of Whittier, entitled "Our Neighbor;" also one by her husband, Richard S. Spofford, a lawyer by profession, with literary tastes, and a devoted friend of our poet. Mr. Whittier has expressed peculiar satisfaction with these friendly tributes from neighbors, and admired especially the free movement and crystal brightness of the poem from the less practised hands of a busy man.

OUR NEIGHBOR.

BY HARRIET PRESCOTT SPOFFORD.

Old neighbor, for how many a year
The same horizon, stretching here,
Has held us in its happy bound
From Rivermouth to Ipswich Sound!
How many a wave-washed day we 've seen
Above that low horizon lean,
And marked within the Merrimac
The self-same sunset reddening back,
Or in the Powow's shining stream,
That silent river of a dream!

Where Craneneck o'er the woodly gloom
Lifts her steep mile of apple-bloom;
Where Salisbury Sands, in yellow length,
With the great breaker measure strength;
Where Artichoke in shadow slides,
The lily on her painted tides, —
There 's naught in the enchanted view
That does not seem a part of you;
Your legends hang on every hill,
Your songs have made it dearer still.

Yours is the river-road; and yours
Are all the mighty meadow floors
Where the long Hampton levels lie
Alone between the sea and sky.
Fresher in Follymill shall blow
The May-flowers, that you loved them so;
Prouder Deer Island's ancient pines
Toss to their measure in your lines;
And purpler gleam old Appledore,
Because your foot has trod her shore.

Still shall the great Cape wade to meet
The storms that fawn about her feet,
The summer evening linger late
In many-rivered Stackyard Gate,
When we, when all your people here,
Have fled; but like the atmosphere
You still the region shall surround,
The spirit of the sacred ground,
Though you have risen, as mounts the star,
Into horizons vaster far!

MERRIMAC RIVER AND POET.

BY RICHARD S. SPOFFORD.

Long as thy pebbly shores shall keep
  Their tides, O gallant river,
Thy mountain heights to ocean's deep
  Their crystal streams deliver, —

Long as her bugle on thy hills
  The hosts of Freedom rallies,
And Labor's choral anthem fills
  Thy loveliest of valleys, —

So long thy poet's praise and thine
  Shall live, the years descending,
Thy ripple and his flowing line
  Like song with music blending !

As widens to the waiting sea
  Thy course, by hill and meadow,
So flows his sweet humanity
  Through circling sun and shadow.

While hallowed thus, no mortal ban
  Unpitying Time imposes,
His life who loves his fellow-man
  Wins Heaven before it closes !

CHAPTER XXI.

WE are accustomed to make distinctions in regard to poetry which are more apparent than real. We hear of the poetry of the senses and passions, — of the heart or the affections, — of the intellectual nature, and of the moral or spiritual nature ; but while these distinctions are based on clearly perceived differences in the productions of poets, there is at bottom the fallacious assumption of the existence of more than *one* thinking, feeling, will-ing principle in man. The Ego is subtile and many-visaged. When we assign to perception, judgment, emotion, and conscience a coordinate existence, we are only vaguely accounting for the swift and dazzling changes in the modes of mental action. The mysterious Being within is simultaneously witness, expert, advocate, recorder, judge, and executant.

Poetry written in youth naturally shows an exuberance of feeling, a vivid perception of external beauty, an excess of sensuous joy or pain; written in manhood, nerved by great purposes and called to high duties, it has an energy corresponding with the maturity of power and the depth and wisdom that come with experience; written in later years, when the demands of the bodily nature are less exigent and dominating, it is occupied with more purely intellectual and moral perceptions and thoughts, as well as with discursive retrospections and memories.

It is in this last stage that the poet is subjected to the extreme test. Many ardent natures in the first flush of youth give us glowing impressions both of the beauty of nature and of their own fresh and exquisite sensations. At the acme of physical and mental power they are less effusive of sentiment, more sparing of images and epithets, and they learn to put their conceptions in compact lines with the potency of proverbs.

In few instances does the poetic power retain its vitality and spring beyond this stage. After a poet has once laid bare his virgin sensibilities, and then has addressed himself to the highest work to which he is called, and done his part, he has generally exhausted his capabilities; and if he continues, we are apt to recognize mainly echoes of early song, with a tendency towards moralizing and exhortation.

The poetry that is born of passion must languish early; that which is concerned with external nature must have its limits, for landscapes will not satisfy the soul forever; that which is aroused by the call of duty, or by the stress of a great occasion, will exhaust itself in the triumph or in the hopelessness of the cause; that which is evolved from spiritual perceptions and longings, which is supplied from the Fountain of all ideas and analogies, and sustained by sure relation to the great Poet or Maker, — that alone is immortal and unfading.

Now comes the application of the ancient saying that " Memory is the mother of the Muses," — not the memory merely of scenes and events, but the power to recall *with* *them* the thrilling emotions they originally excited. This is the continuing source and the conservation of poetic power in the later years of life : to be able to renew at pleasure all the keen sensations of the days of young blood, to keep command of the vital experiences of manhood, and to bring these, unimpaired, into the serener atmosphere of age. That would be an ideally perfect condition for a creative soul, if its accumulated *negatives* of past experiences, thoughts, feelings, and visions were ready for the projection of images in their original brightness, and if the faculties, after being refined and spiritualized by long converse with high and holy things, could still be reinforced through the " Mother of the Muses " by all the deftness, grace, and tenderness, all the imaginative force and quenchless spirit, and all the power of perceiving analogies that had ever characterized them. Such a creative soul would be a microcosm, an epitome of all powers and perfections.

But such to a considerable degree is the soul of a poet. By his imagination he is enabled in youth to anticipate the calm wisdom of age, — in age to recreate the ecstatic sensations of youth.

We have seen Whittier as a barefoot boy, first stirred by the lyrics of Burns, — as a novice in poetic art striving to set his fancies in verse, — as a reformer forcing his coy muse to the hard service he had undertaken, — as a sedate man of middle age, gaining yearly in affluence of poetic similitudes and in unborrowed splendor of expression. At this point we see him crossing the allotted line of threescore years and ten;—but not old; nor is anything of the past dead; for, reversing the order of the Chinese concentric ivory spheres, **each** previous **mental** condition and experience **is** still contained one within another, all clearly visible **to him, and all** ready **to** be lived over at will.

Is it doubted that a man of seventy may write of love like a youthful lover? We shall for answer insert " The Henchman," and ask readers to observe the deathless feeling **that animates it, the lightness of touch, which few besides Tennyson have equalled, and the** perfect **tone, such as the** most **courtly of King** Charles's cavalier **poets would have pro**nounced incomparable.

THE HENCHMAN.

My lady walks her morning round,
My lady's page her fleet grey hound,
My lady's hair the fond winds stir,
And all the birds make songs for her.

Her thrushes sing in Rathburn bowers,
And Rathburn side is gay with flowers;
But ne'er like hers, in flower or bird,
Was beauty seen or music heard.

The distance of the stars is hers;
The least of all her worshippers,
The dust beneath her dainty heel,
She knows not that I see or feel.

Oh proud and calm! — she cannot know
Where'er she goes with her I go;
Oh cold and fair! — she cannot guess
I kneel to share her hound's caress!

Gay knights beside her hunt and hawk,
I rob their ears of her sweet talk;
Her suitors come from east and west,
I steal her smiles from every guest.

Unheard of her, in loving words,
I greet her with the song of birds;
I reach her with her green-armed bowers,
I kiss her with the lips of flowers.

The hound and I are on her trail,
The wind and I uplift her veil;
As if the calm, cold moon she were,
And I the tide, I follow her.

As unrebuked as they, I share
The license of the sun and air,
And in a common homage hide
My worship from her scorn and pride.

World-wide apart, and yet so near,
I breathe her charmèd atmosphere,
Wherein to her my service brings
The reverence due to holy things.

Her maiden pride, her haughty name,
My dumb devotion shall not shame;
The love that no return doth crave
To knightly levels lifts the slave.

> No lance have I, in joust or fight,
> To splinter in my lady's sight;
> But, at her feet, how blest were I
> For any need of hers to die!

Many love poems are fanciful merely, — mere playing at sentiment with pretty words. In this there is audible an undertone of tragedy; the Henchman is as truly a hero as any who ever went to death for love. Observe, too, the strokes of imagination.

> "I rob their ears of her sweet talk;"
> "I steal her smiles from every guest;"
> "I greet her with the songs of birds."

The title poem, "The Vision of Echard," concerns a Benedictine monk of Marsberg, who had a vision and heard the voice of God respecting the traditional forms of worship and the true service of the heart. It is an excellent homily upon spiritual things, conceived in an exalted mood and expressed with the poet's usual vigor. Every stanza, and almost every line, is quotable for power or for nobility of sentiment.

"The Witch of Wenham" is a spirited ballad based on an ancient colonial tradition. The scene is near Salem, anciently called Naumkeag, by a lake since famed both in New and Old England for its pure crystalline ice. The directness of phrase, and the many dramatic points in the story, remind us of the inimitable old ballads that have come down to us from the times of English Henrys and Edwards.

"Sunset on the Bearcamp" is a magnificent landscape in verse, one of the finest of the many which Whittier has given us. Details enough there are, but one does not observe them as if they were separate bits of mosaic. The picture is broad and entire, and the impression is like that left by the grandeur of nature itself. A passage from this poem was quoted in a previous chapter.

Of a kindred nature is "The Seeking of the Waterfall," a series of beautiful scenes wherein rocks and gurgling brooks, wild woods, granite ledges, and purple peaks allure us on towards the sublime and inaccessible.

> "So, always baffled, not misled,
>   We follow where before us runs
>   The vision of the shining ones.
>
> "Not where they seem their signals fly,
>   Their voices while we listen die;
>   We cannot keep, however fleet,
>   The quick time of their wingèd feet."

"June on the Merrimac" was written for the annual meeting at the Laurels,—a festival which has been mentioned before. The tone of the poem

is sweet and tender, and full of memories of the
departed : —

> " You know full well these banks of bloom,
>   The upland's wavy line,
> And how the sunshine tips with fire
>   The needles of the pine.

> " Yet like some old remembered psalm,
>   Or sweet, familiar face,
> Not less because of commonness
>   You love the day and place.

> . . . . .

> " A sacred presence overbroods
>   The earth whereon we meet;
> These winding forest-paths are trod
>   By more than mortal feet."

The scenery around Curzon's Mill at the conflu-
ence of the " pictured Artichoke " with the Merrimac is exceedingly beautiful. Mr. J. Appleton
Brown and other eminent artists have found there
congenial subjects.

Almost every writer, certainly every one who
owns to the sway of moods, has been conscious of
being *led* in regard to his subjects and their treatment. Poets, doubtless, are influenced by airs that
never blow upon duller mortals; and we can believe that when waiting for inspiration they may
not be sure in what form it will come. Burns has
expressed this with his usual offhand vigor : —

> " But how the subject theme may gang
>   Let time and chance determine;
>   Perhaps it may turn out a sang,
>   Perhaps turn out a sermon."

Whittier has gone deeper than this, and in a rather solemn strain has shown the subordination of the soul to influences seen and unseen. Two stanzas from the poem " Overruled " will show its drift and its remarkable power : —

> " Ah ! small the choice of him who sings
>   What sound shall leave the smitten strings;
>   Fate holds and guides the hand of art ;
>   The singer's is the servant's part.

> " The wind-harp chooses not the tone
>   That through its trembling threads is blown;
>   The patient organ cannot guess
>   What hand its passive keys shall press."

In one poem Whittier has given us what preachers might call " a realizing sense " of what was meant by a Quaker woman's " bearing her testimony." Those who have read the accounts of the preaching by the first disciples of Fox, and especially the letters and diaries of those earnest and single-minded people, will not need to be told that there were no improprieties in their dress or behavior, and that their speech, though bold and unsparing, was no more so than were the common utterances of Puritans in regard to Episcopalians and others from whom *they* differed. The few remains of the intellectual and spiritual life of those self-devoted missionaries show them to have been possessed of the very spirit of Christ. It was after they had been forbidden to hold meetings or exhort, — after they had been scourged from town to town, and flung in jail without so much care as would have been bestowed upon a wounded dog, or banished into the wilderness, or disfigured by loss of ears, — after modest women had been stripped to be examined for witch marks, and after the menace of the gallows was forever present in the consciousness of them all, — it was then that the minds of some were shaken and a religious delusion but little removed from insanity took possession of them; and then ensued the spectacles which have so variously affected mankind. The Puritans paraded these isolated cases of apparent immodesty as an excuse for persecution. Others have reflected upon these strange cases with an overwhelming pity for the sufferings and mental strain which led the victims to such deplorable conduct. The poem is entitled " In the Old South, 1677." Three stanzas afford a vivid picture of the enthusiast who was called upon, as she believed, to denounce the unchristian conduct of the oppressors of the Friends : —

> " She came and stood in the Old South Church,
>   A wonder and a sign,
>   With a look the old-time sibyls wore,
>   Half crazed and half divine.
>
> " Save the mournful sackcloth about her wound,
>   Unclothed as the primal mother,
>   With limbs that trembled and eyes that blazed
>   With a fire she dared not smother.
>
> " Loose on her shoulders fell her hair
>   With sprinkled ashes gray,
>   She stood in the broad aisle strange and weird
>   As a soul at the judgment day."

It is not necessary here to quote her solemn words of warning, nor to dwell upon the poet's natural exultation in view of the fact that the principle of religious freedom has at last been acknowledged.

" The Library " was written for the opening of a free public library in Haverhill. It is a very strong production, tracing the slow progress of recording ideas from the time of pictures and symbols up to the invention of writing and printing. This is the final stanza : —

> " As if some Pantheon's marbles broke
>   Their stormy trance, and lived and spoke,
>   Life thrills along the alcoved hall;
>   The lords of thought await our call."

" King Solomon and the Ants " is a lesson in humanity towards the lower orders of creation, showing how the great king turned his cavalcade aside so as not to crush an ant-hill in his way. " Red Riding Hood " has a similar burden of compassion towards the birds and squirrels, representing a sensitive and generous child feeding them in winter weather.

We may mention, in passing, the well-known " Centennial Hymn," two fine sonnets upon Thiers, the pleasant tribute to Fitz-Greene Halleck (who was one of the prominent poets when Whittier began to write), " The Pressed Gentian," and the feeling eulogy upon General Bartlett, one of the heroes of the civil war, and who was descended from an Essex County family. " At Eventide " is a charming retrospect, and in a certain way is an epitome of Whittier's life.

> " Poor and inadequate the shadow-play
> Of gain and loss, of waking and of dream,
> Against life's solemn background needs must seem
> At this late hour ; yet not unthankfully
> I call to mind the fountains by the way,
> The breath of flowers, the bird-song on the spray,
> Dear friends, sweet human loves, the joy of giving
> And of receiving, the great boon of living
> In grand historic years when liberty
> Had need of word and work, quick sympathies
> For all who fail and suffer, song's relief,
> Nature's uncloying loveliness, and chief,
> The kind restraining hand of Providence,
> The inward witness, the assuring sense

> Of an Eternal Good which overlies
> The sorrow of the world, Love which outlives
> All sin and wrong, Compassion which forgives
> To the uttermost, and Justice whose clear eyes
> Through lapse and failure look to the intent,
> And judge our frailty by the life we meant."

"The King's Missive" renewed the discussion between the friends of the Puritan and those of the Quaker. The Rev. Dr. Ellis attempted to show that the poem was without historical foundation, and Mr. Whittier replied in an earnest defence of the position he had taken. The main point made by Dr. Ellis is that no record exists in the books showing that an order of release was passed by the council. In reply to which it may be urged that if the council had desired to retire silently from an untenable position, it would have been an easy and natural way to release the prisoners by a verbal order. Thus much is certain: the royal missive came, and the imprisoned Quakers were set at liberty. Whether, according to the old maxim, it was *post hoc* or *propter hoc* is not very important — in the case of a poem.

In this volume is found the magnificent poem "The Lost Occasion," referring to the career of Daniel Webster, which has been considered in a previous chapter.

"The Emancipation Group" (Lincoln looking

down upon a kneeling negro, whose manacles have fallen) stands in Park Square, Boston. It is the work of Thomas Ball, cast in bronze, and was presented to the city by the Hon. Moses Kimball.

"Abram Morrison" is a poem which it is difficult to characterize. Had Burns been a Quaker and a New Englander, we should have expected from him a similar combination of homely truth, solid good sense, tender recollection, and sly humor. The staple of the verse is not wholly poetic in any high sense. It is rather a literal portraiture of a man and of an age which have passed away. But the tone is hearty and natural, and it will be read with delight by all who are able to comprehend the essential goodness with the droll external traits of a simple, bucolic man. It is not a poem to be rated among Whittier's nobler and more imaginative productions, but it is one that endears the poet to every reader who appreciates humor and enjoys the quaint delineation of character. "Po Hill" may puzzle the reader who does not know that the people of the neighborhood thus shorten the old Indian name of Powow.

It is the fate of age to be saddened by the departure of friends. As the long day draws near its close the blithe companions of morning and the stout-hearted workers of mid-day begin to fall by the way. The man of seventy years might almost pass his time at funerals of his comrades. Poems at this period are mostly elegies, tributes, and sorrowful memories. "Within the Gate" testifies to the life-long and devoted friendship of the poet for Mrs. Child; Bayard Taylor, still in his prime, had closed his brilliant career; and in the poem the reader will see the familiar and affectionate relation he sustained to the poet's household; Garrison had died at a ripe age, in the fruition of his great hope for universal liberty and in the fulness of conviction of an immortal life. Into these poems Whittier has put his whole heart.

So we may say of his verses in honor of "Our Autocrat."

To thinking minds perhaps the most significant of the poems in this last volume is "The Minister's Daughter." The just and compassionate nature of Whittier had been moved by the consideration of the dogma of election; and instead of resorting to argument he touches the intellect through the natural feelings. The child of the grave Calvinist, ignorant of proof-texts and helpless in logic, is made to find the way to her father's heart; and by the silent force of love — the same in creature as in Creator — his system topples down. The narration is exquisitely done.

" A Name " is addressed to Greenleaf Whittier
Pickard, son of the daughter of Whittier's brother
Matthew. The first Greenleaf in the Colony came
from St. Malo, and bore the name Feuillevert.
Like the poem written for the young Allison, this
is singularly interesting from what it shows of the
poet's life and character : —

A NAME.

The name the Gallie exile bore,
  St. Malo ! from thy ancient mart,
Became upon our Western shore
  Greenleaf for Feuillevert.

A name to hear in soft accord
  Of leaves by light winds overrun,
Or read, upon the greening sward
  Of June, in shade and sun.

That name my infant ear first heard
  Breathed softly with a mother's kiss ;
His mother's own, no tenderer word
  My father spake than this.

No child have I to bear it on ;
  Be thou its keeper ; let it take
From gifts well used and duty done
  New beauty for thy sake.

The fair ideals that outran
  My halting footsteps seek and find —
The flawless symmetry of man,
  The poise of heart and mind.

Stand firmly where I felt the sway
  Of every wing that fancy flew,
See clearly where I groped my way,
  Nor real from seeming knew.

And wisely choose, and bravely hold
  Thy faith unswerved by cross or crown,
Like the stout Huguenot of old
  Whose name to thee comes down.

As Marot's songs made glad the heart
  Of that lone exile, haply mine
May, in life's heavy hours, impart
  Some strength and hope to thine.

Yet when did Age transfer to Youth
  The hard-gained lessons of its day?
Each lip must learn the taste of truth,
  Each foot must feel its way.

We cannot hold the hands of choice
  That touch or shun life's fateful keys;
The whisper of the inward voice
  Is more than homilies.

Dear boy! for whom the flowers are born,
  Stars shine, and happy song-birds sing,
What can my evening give to morn,
  My winter to thy spring!

A life not void of pure intent,
  With small desert of praise or blame,
The love I felt, the good I meant,
  I leave thee with my name.

CHAPTER XXII.

IN considering the sources of a poet's power, our analysis is at fault when identical qualities are seen in distinct and opposing combinations. Shakespeare and Bacon, greatest among men, were divided by a narrow line, — narrow but impassable.

We may know a poet as a man, but it is not until he sings that we know he is a poet. An examination of his faculties no more discloses the secret of poetic creation than the dissection of the brain reveals soul. Has he keen perception and reason? So have the philosopher and logician. Has he enthusiasm, feeling, and grace? So have the orator and actor. Has he love of beauty? So has the artist. Can he create characters and lay bare the secrets of the soul? Great novelists do the same. Can he restore the dead past? The great historian does this. Has he sense of melody and rhythmic form? So has the composer. In truth, unless we consider the ability to mould poetic thought in living verse as a distinct and incommunicable faculty, there is no single mental power which the poet does not share with others. How near were Webster and Hawthorne to being poets! There was often a Miltonic grandeur in Webster's periods; the elevation of thought and the stately diction separated them from ordinary prose utterances; and in the perorations his ideas and feelings, kindled to white heat, were poured out in molten sentences, incandescent poetry. The delicate and spiritual conceptions of Hawthorne were illumined by poetic lights, and are fully seen and comprehended only by those to whom the secret of poetry has been revealed. Visions of grandeur filled the soul of the orator, and a radiance of celestial beauty hovered over the creations of the novelist, but neither of them was a maker of verse; neither possessed the " faculty divine."

Of the writers of verse, how few appear to have been led by a native, spontaneous influence! The greater number, so far as we can judge, have rather sought laboriously for inspiration, and toiled for what should be the natural outflow of melody. A visible effort is fatal; if there is no exuberance of thought, no natural beat of measure, no predestination of rhyme, the attempt only awakens commiseration. Equally fatal is the want of genuine feeling, or sincerity : no art can deceive us when this quality is absent.

Carlyle says (in characteristic phrase) :—

"Much has been written; but the perennial Scriptures of Mankind have had small accession : from all English Books, in rhyme or prose, in leather binding or in paper wrappage, how many verses have been added to these? Our most melodious Singers have sung as from the throat outwards : from the inner Heart of Man, from the great Heart of Nature, through no Pope or Philips, has there come any tone. The Oracles have been dumb."

It is from " the inner heart " that the poems of Whittier have come; never " from the throat outwards." This is attested by the answering hearts of the vast multitudes of readers. The strains he has sung have always found their echoes; merely as music they have been sure of responsive chords ; and then (as Emerson said of oratory), it is a great matter that there is a *man* behind them.

In the nice distribution of hereditary faculties, impulses, and tendencies, there had come to his share joy in the presence of nature, a divine sense of beauty, a perception of the swift shuttle-play of analogy, a reverence for what is pure and noble, an aspiration towards spiritual life, and, with all, the subtile, unnamed power of commanding and arraying his thoughts and feelings, clothing them in apt, symbolic phrases, subordinating a full and glowing diction to melody, and so conveying to receptive minds impressions in accord with universal experience, yet vitally new. The order of thought and the sequences of feeling may vary ; processes may differ, or may be beyond the sharpest analysis ; but the results of genius in some way include all modes of mental action ; they are creations. "Labor and learning," in Webster's phrase, "may toil for them in vain."

As we have seen, the early life of Whittier was not of a nature to have fostered the growth of the poetic faculty. The hard necessity of constant labor, the lack of schooling and of books, the want of literary companionship, advice, and encouragement, the practical, plodding ideas of the time and the neighborhood, and the austerity which prevailed among the Friends, were all calculated to depress the feelings of an ardent boy, and to turn him, if anything could turn him, into a prosaic and contented delver of the soil. That the fountain of bright imaginings kept bubbling in its hidden recess, when every surrounding influence tended to choke its natural flow, is proof enough of its origin. In the light of his after development we see how truly it was a dual life that he led. The silent valley was vocal to him. The day brimmed **it with beauty,** and the night **arched it over as** with a dome of magnificence. The songs **of** birds, their capricious motion and their rhythmic flight, **filled his** mind with struggling sensations. Every flower looked at him with soul-full eyes. The flocks and herds were expressions of the general joy as well as of the bounty of the universe. The little brook below the garden went on with its garrulous soliloquy among the stones. **The** broad **velvety** backs **of** the hills, near **and far,** and the skirts **of forests,** whether in **the** glory of summer or **in the** miraculous colors **of autumn, filled the eyes of the boy** with uncloying delight. **All** these sights and sounds were in an interior **world, with** which ploughs and hoes, carts and **crops,** had nothing **to** do.

But all was a kind of dumb pleasure until by the electrical contact **of Burns** his soul **was** awakened to perceive the relation **of** the natural world **to the** world of poetic thought. The effect of **this kindling** touch of genius we **can see in our poet's own** artless narration. Then began the struggle **for** expression, the pursuit of knowledge, the study **of** models, and the long apprenticeship in gaining the mastery of English and in fashioning it into forms of power and **grace. It is a** signal proof **of the** strength and versatility of Whittier's native faculties, that with such a meagre outfit and such inadequate mental training he has been able to reach his present position among men of renown. A college-bred youth has been grounded in reason by exercises in mathematics, logic, and philosophy; the sciences have enlarged his ideas of the universe; by the study of languages he has been taught precision, finesse, and delicacy in choice of words. In place of all these priceless advantages Whittier was obliged to cultivate his reasoning powers by dealing with actual, momentous questions; his knowledge came from wide but unmethodical reading, and his command of language from his own unassisted efforts in verse. Truly, the apprenticeship was long, and in some respects there were elements to be desired; but upon the whole the results were surprising.

The question frequently arises when we are looking at the development of a self-taught man, What would have been the effect of a full and thorough training under competent instructors? There can never be a wholly satisfactory answer. "College training," it has been said, "polishes bricks and dulls diamonds." Jeffrey in his article upon Burns makes some valuable suggestions on this point: —

"**We** cannot conceive any one less likely **to be added** to the short list of original poets, **than a** young man **of** fine fancy and delicate **taste,** who has acquired **a high** relish for poetry by perusing the most celebrated writers and conversing with the most intelligent judges. **The head** of such a person is filled, **of** course, with all **the** splendid passages of modern **authors, and with the fine** and fastidious remarks which have been made even on those passages. When he turns his eyes, therefore, on his own conceptions and designs, they can scarcely fail to appear rude and contemptible. He is perpetually **haunted** by the ideal **presence** of **those great masters and their** exacting **critics. . . .**

"**But the** natural tendency **of** their studies, **and by far** their most common effect, is to repress originality and discourage enterprise ; and either to **change** those whom nature meant for poets into mere readers of poetry, or to bring them out in **the form of** witty **parodists or** ingenious imitators. . . .

"**A** solitary and uninstructed man, with lively feelings and an inflammable imagination, will often be irresistibly led to exercise those gifts, and **to** occupy and relieve his **mind in** poetical composition ; but **if** his education, his reading, **and his** society supply him **with an abundant** store of images and emotions, he **will** probably think **but** little of those internal resources, and feed his mind **con**tentedly with what has been provided by **the** industry **of** others. . . .

"**A** youth of quick parts and creative fancy, — **with just so** much reading as to guide his ambition and roughhew his notions of excellence, — if his lot be thrown in humble retirement where he has no reputation to lose, and where he can easily hope to excel all that he sees around him, is much more likely, we think, to give himself up to poetry, and to train himself to habits of invention, than if he had been encumbered by the pretended helps of extended study and literary society."

On the other hand, it must be admitted that certain elements are wanting in the verse of self-taught men, — not vital qualities, because those are presupposed by the poet's inspiration, but the stores of allusion, the exterior finish, the perfection of metre, and the silent exclusion of the superfluous. The laws of English verse are elastic and lax, and a good ear is generally a sufficient guide; but the last refinements in measure, accent, assonance, and form are known only to the patient students of the great masters in many tongues. Undoubtedly, scholars lay too much stress upon pharisaic attention to externals. For them the neglect of any minor canon is almost as fatal as the want of creative force. Nothing less than the perfection of art satisfies them. But the current poetry of our time is far more distinguished for verbal nicety than genuine inspiration. Verse in which the elaborate finish is apparent is apt to give an impression of tameness; so much so, that those who know the real power of poetry are willing to forgive slight defects in works that show their high origin. The most brilliant passages of Burns, or of Shakespeare, even, would scarcely get through the hands of our fastidious editors without being shorn of their characteristic phrases and epithets. We are too silken-fine to tolerate homespun and natural style, or words with blood in them. Every word that would give the pleasing shock of originality, of hitherto unsuggested force, or the complex surprises of humor, is marked *dele*. Writers go through the manual and drill at the editorial command, and their great successes are in composing by stratagem, as Pope's fine ladies drank tea. The reign of rhetoricians and purists is the sure indication of decadence. " It is against rule," said the critics to Beethoven. " Who made the rule ? " " The masters before us." " Well, I am a master ; *I* make the rule." He made the rule, and the critics were referred to the next generation.

In letters, as in music and art, great men originate ideas and forms ; then come critics with the apparatus of their craft, and would fain have us believe themselves superior to the men of genius whom they attempt to measure and weigh.

The estimate by Lowell in the " Fable for Critics," thirty-five years ago, is a blending of generous praise and acute criticism. The tribute to

Whittier's character and works has great force, coming from a poet of high rank, and all the more that the *per contra* of the account is so rigidly stated. No one has since added much to the eulogy, and the keenest critic has found all his objections anticipated. No passage in that brilliant satire has been more frequently quoted; most readers of poetry know it by heart; but it appears necessary here to reproduce the more important points of the judgment: —

  "There is Whittier, whose swelling and vehement heart
    Strains the strait-breasted drab of the Quaker apart,
    And reveals the live Man, still supreme and erect,
    Underneath the bemummying wrappers of sect;
    There was ne'er a man born who had more of the swing
    Of the true lyric bard and all that kind of thing;
    And his failures arise (though perhaps he don't know it)
    From the very same cause that has made him a poet, —
    A fervor of mind which knows no separation
    'Twixt simple excitement and pure inspiration.

    .   .   .   .   .

    Let his mind once get head in its favorite direction,
    And the torrent of verse bursts the dams of reflection,
    While, borne with the rush of the metre along,
    The poet may chance to go right or go wrong,
    Content with the whirl and delirium of song;
    Then his grammar 's not always correct, nor his rhymes,
    And he 's prone to repeat his own lyrics sometimes, —
    Not his best, though, for those are struck off at white-heats,
    When the heart in his breast like a trip-hammer beats,
    And can ne'er be repeated again any more
    Than they could have been carefully plotted before."

Another paragraph has a bold, prophetic tone, which at the time it was written was wonderful to some, and absurd to most:—

> "I need not to name them, already for each
> I see History preparing the statue and niche."

Sumner's stately form is already represented in bronze; the statues of Theodore Parker and Garrison are soon to be set up; and no one can doubt that in due time similar memorials of Whittier, Phillips, and Harriet Beecher Stowe are to follow.

When Lowell's "Fable" was published, neither he, nor any of the great abolitionists whom he celebrated, could have addressed a public meeting without risk of insult or violence. The tardy popular reparation is like that foretold in another grand poem of Lowell's, wherein we see

> "The hooting mob of yesterday in silent awe return
> To gather up the scattered ashes into History's golden urn."

We must return to the critical objections, but shall not consider them in any formal order.

It is proper to state that no critic has a clearer sense of limitations in these poems than has Whittier himself. In fact, his estimate of their value is quite below that of careful judges among his friends. He would not dispute the *per contra* of Lowell's statement, but admit the charge of false rhymes, repeated lyrics, and mistaken inspiration. He has been known to indulge in sarcasms upon his own early works, such as friends would hesitate to repeat. For instance, he has stigmatized "Mogg Megone" as a "big Injun strutting about in Walter Scott's plaid," which is the fact in a nut-shell.

But in general it may be said that the verse of Whittier satisfies all reasonable demands as to measure and melody. His nature is buoyant and his diction is copious; and the exuberant feeling and natural energy give his lines an elastic movement that carries the reader on, as upon waves that swell and never submerge. The nicest results of art we find less frequently; although some poems may be named, so near perfection that higher finish could scarcely be desired.

His rhymes are never a clog to his thought; they never lead him astray; they are generally facile and lucky, without being always correct. In this respect he resembles Burns, who was indifferent to the perfect wedding of terminations provided he could make an effective stroke.

> "Whene'er my Muse does on me glance,
>   I jingle at her."

We cannot but regret the occasional imperfect rhymes and accents of Whittier, but they are not numerous enough to impair the general effect. There is no poet without faults ; and, if it must be so, it is better that they should exist in details, rather than detract from the spirit and sense of completeness.

It was believed that in the ancient sacrifices the gods had the supreme pleasure of the odors, while the enjoyment of the substantial viands was left to mortals. In certain poems of a high order there is a similar distinction between the force and beauty open to every reader and the spiritual essence appreciated by few. This essence consists of subtile suggestions, and the aroma of allusion and learning. To elucidate this point would require more time than can be given in a work of this kind. The poets especially distinguished for learning are not numerous, and, excepting Milton and Tennyson, they are not among the great. In a song, which is an outburst of feeling, there is no room for a classic reminiscence ; the least hint of scholasticism would be fatal. In a ballad, simplicity is the one unalterable quality. But in an epic, like "Paradise Lost," the utmost wealth of historical allusion is not too much. The lines of Milton, as has been often said, are rich with the spoils of every language and time.

To the character of a learned poet Whittier

would make no claim. His reading has been extensive and varied, and a collection of topics from his poems would be found large and interesting; but we do not often see in his verse the fusion of rare or recondite elements. One Book alone he has profoundly studied, and his references to its sublime lessons are always apposite and often powerful.

In the subtile quality of suggestion Whittier shows his birthright as poet. This is the quality which forever separates poetry from prose. As in harmonies a delicate ear catches sympathetic octaves and over-tones, so in true poetry the unexpressed suggestion is quite beyond the actual words. Hints are in the air of something finer than language can depict. Tones linger and tremble long after the first and strong vibration has ceased.

In Whittier's youth the accepted American poets were prone to the choice of Scriptural scenes and subjects. The early poems of Willis will be remembered; also Lowell's stinging couplet in reference to them : —

  "And he ought to let Scripture alone ; 't is self-slaughter,
    For nobody likes inspiration-and-water."

Hillhouse, Brainard, Mrs. Sigourney, Pierpont with his "Airs of Palestine," Eliza Townsend, and others had set the example which Whittier followed. His first printed poem is a versification of a passage from the Old Testament. For years afterward he toiled over similar scenes, as the reader has observed. Most of them have been quietly dropped, but there remain a number, — such as " The Crucifixion," " The Cities of the Plain," " The Wife of Manoah," " The Star of Bethlehem," — which show the original influence and tendency.

This direction, strengthened by his religious training, resulted in his giving a formal moral to the ending of poems which did not especially require one. This has been a fault from which few poets have been free. Many of Longfellow's most noted poems would be improved by the omission of their final stanzas. It has been the common but erroneous opinion that, as the aim of all poetry should be to elevate the moral nature, a poem could not be complete without a tag, like the conclusion of a sermon. Religious readers may find it hard to accept the canon, and devout poets even may rebel and disregard it, but it is none the less true that the only effective lesson of a poem is in its spirit and suggestion, and that the most epigrammatic ethical application, at the close, is an artistic mistake. Nothing is sounder than the advice of a poet often quoted : —

> " Put all your beauty in your rhymes,
>   Your morals in your living."

We have mentioned " the exclusion of the superfluous" as one of the necessities of art. The couplets of Story will be recalled to the reader : —

> " Strive not to say the whole! the Poet in his art
>   Must intimate the whole, and say the smallest part.

> " The young moon's silver arc her perfect circle tells,
>   The limitless within Art's bounded outline dwells.

> " Of every noble work the silent part is best,
>   Of all expression that which cannot be expressed."

Nothing tests the poet's self-discipline like an adherence to this Spartan rule. In the heat of composition there is a fulness of thought and emotion, and in the struggle to express all the thronging conceptions the molten stream overruns the mould. There is even a tendency to repetition in slightly varying phrases, — or perhaps to ill-judged discursions, leading away from the strict line of thought, — or, more rarely, the temptation to plunge into metaphysics, from which no poet ever emerged without mental asphyxia.

If the poems of Whittier, meaning those now recognized and collected in his volumes, could be seen as originally written with a view to comparison with their present forms, readers would recognize with astonishment the sharp and resolute pruning to which they have been subjected. Some poets, believing in the plenary inspiration of their own works, have scrupulously printed every line. A stern self-examination and a rigid self-criticism on the part of Wordsworth would have eliminated two fifths of his lines, with manifest advantage to the remainder, and with a great heightening of his fame. Look at the wretched shreds and patches of verse gathered by ill-judging editors of Herrick, Swift, Byron, and many others. Far better is the wise exclusion of the superfluous as it has been understood and practised by Whittier.

There is, however, a noted exception in his anti-slavery poems, which we must consider. If Garrison, when he first announced the moral basis of his enterprise, had stopped there and never repeated it, the South might have been under the black shadow to this day. Garrison knew that the mere statement of eternal principles was not enough ; it was necessary to reason, to re-state, to enforce by analogy, to illustrate by historical examples, to arouse feelings and sympathies, to appeal to Divine authority, — in short, to use the whole armory of argument and pursuasion in order to arouse the conscience and enlighten the moral perceptions of his countrymen. Whittier, as the poet of the same great cause, felt it necessary to turn every form of cogency into verse. The limits were narrow; he had simply to say all men are born free, and slavery is an unjust, unwise, and dangerous infringement of an eternal law. There was nothing more. Within those narrow limits, for years, he pleaded for the slave and denounced his oppressor. Considering the burden upon his soul, we must admire the invincible spirit with which he attacked the great crime of the century, and still more wonder at the ever new forms in which his pleadings and denunciations were clothed.

Whittier "repeated his lyrics" not as a poet, but as an apostle,—as the first apostles repeated their messages. All his powers were devoted to the cause; and his reputation as a poet, and all his other belongings and advantages, were as nothing to him if he could win converts.

The reader will not fail to observe that it has not been the purpose of the writer in any part of this work to make what is termed a critical study. The first and chief object has been to present Whittier as a man, and to show his place and his work in the world; next to notice the origin and the progress of his literary labors, especially his poems; and then to give such illustrations of his writings as may help the general reader to a due comprehension of them. In carrying out this plan certain estimates or judgments of greater or less are inevitable. But it has been the desire chiefly to illuminate the separate works mentioned, calling attention to substantial merits and lively graces, rather than searching for defects. The observant reader will still see something of the limitations; for if the writer is fortunate in his choice of phrases, the terms of praise will at least indicate negatively what may appear to be wanting.

It may be doubted whether critical studies of living men, or of those recently deceased, can have any real value. What we call the spirit of the age enfolds and surrounds us all like an atmosphere, and no solid and enduring judgment of any poet can be made until such time as the age itself, with its complex ideas, feelings, and tendencies, can be calmly reviewed.

But there are not wanting in our time, as in the centuries before, the kind of critics to whom the pen is both scalpel and stiletto. Criticism, in their view, is first the search for moles and deformities; next, the merciless dissection of the structure; lastly, the exhibition of an analysis in the shape of a chemical formula. The result is something like that attained by younger analysts in crushing a butterfly to a paste; the beauty of motion and splendor of color are gone, and in place of a bright and airy being, hovering over flowers, there remains in the hand something shapeless and disgusting. Many a poem is served thus, and the triumphant "critic" exhibits the sorry remains as if he had done a great feat.

Lord Byron said : —

> " The lawyer and the critic but behold
> The baser sides of literature and life."

This is true of the destructive critic, and it should lead us to admire rather the canon of Carlyle, which is (in substance) to endeavor to place ourselves in sympathy with the subject and to point out first of all its merits.

In the course of the previous comments many poems have been transiently presented ; but it is desirable now, even at the risk of repetition, to mention some distinguishing features of Whittier's work, and cite a few examples.

First of all, he may be considered an artist in landscape. The forms and colors of nature have made vivid and lasting impressions upon his mind ; and the scenery, or background, of his compositions is always faithful, strong, and impressive. There could be selected a gallery of his pictures, of mountains, lakes, rivers, and sea, that would be remarkable among the best ever drawn. The limits are coequal with his personal experience, and they embrace all the phases to be met with in the White Mountain region, the Merrimac valley, the northern lakes, and the sea-coast from Newburyport to Casco Bay. But he has not dealt alone with the grander features : the smaller valleys and streams, the rounded hills, the various wild flowers, the green masses of summer foliage, and the gay colors of autumn have likewise employed his pencil ; so that the reader who is familiar with the subjects has a perpetual pleasure in his delineations. In giving instances, the difficulty lies in the abundance of materials.[1]

Without pausing to discriminate strictly between imagination and fancy, we may instance some passages in which the grandeur of nature is fitly imaged in the grandeur of phrase. Observe these stanzas from " Evening by the Lakeside : " —

> " Yon mountain's side is black with night,
>   While, broad-orbed, o'er its gleaming crown
> The moon, slow-rounding into sight,
>   On the hushed inland sea looks down.

.   .   .   .   .   .

[1] Mogg Megone, 1836 ; The Bridal of Pennacook, 1845 ; The Lakeside, 1849 ; The Hill-Top, 1850 ; Summer by the Lakeside, 1853 ; The Ranger (date unknown) ; The Last Walk in Autumn, 1857 ; Our River, 1861 ; Mountain Pictures, 1862 ; The Countess, 1863 ; The Grave by the Lake, 1865 ; The Tent on the Beach, 1867 ; Among the Hills, 1868 ; The Sea Dream, 1875. These are the chief in this class ; yet scattered through all the volumes are many exquisite pictures, subordinate to the leading themes.

> " How far and strange the mountains seem,
>   Dim-looming through the pale still light!
> The vague, vast grouping of a dream,
>   They stretch into the solemn night.
>   .   .   .   .   .
>
> " Fair scenes! whereto the Day and Night
>   Make rival love, I leave ye soon,
> What time before the eastern light
>   The pale ghost of the setting moon
>
> Shall hide behind yon rocky spines,
>   And the young archer, Morn, shall break
> His arrows on the mountain pines,
>   And, golden-sandalled, walk the lake !
>   .   .   .   .   .
>
> " O, watched by Silence and the Night,
>   And folded in the strong embrace
> Of the great mountains, with the light
>   Of the sweet heavens upon thy face,
>
> " Lake of the Northland! keep thy dower
>   Of beauty still, and while above
> Thy solemn mountains speak of power,
>   Be thou the mirror of God's love."

In " Tauler," a poem of remarkable spiritual insight, there is a picture of the cathedral of Strasburg, so vivid that the majestic structure seems visibly rising before us as we read : —

> " He saw, far down the street
> A mighty shadow break the light of noon,
> Which tracing backward till its airy lines
> Hardened to stony plinths, he raised his eyes

> O'er broad façade and lofty pediment,
> O'er architrave and frieze and sainted niche,
> Up the stone lace-work chiselled by the wise
> Erwin of Steinbach, dizzily up to where
> In the noon-brightness the great Minster's tower,
> Jewelled with sunbeams on its mural crown,
> Rose like a visible prayer."

We should quote a few stanzas from "The Last Walk in Autumn," — a poem equal in many respects to the best of our time. The scene is in Amesbury, partly from Powow Hill: —

> " O'er the bare woods, whose outstretched hands
>   Plead with the leaden heavens in vain,
>   I see, beyond the valley lands,
>   The sea's long level dim with rain.
>   .   .   .   .   .
>
> " Along the river's summer walk
>   The withered tufts of asters nod;
>   And trembles on its arid stalk
>   The hoar plume of the golden-rod.
>   And on a ground of sombre fir,
>   And azure-studded juniper,
> The silver birch its buds of purple shows,
> And scarlet berries tell where bloomed the sweet wild rose.
>   .   .   .   .   .
>
> " I know not how, in other lands,
>   The changing seasons come and go;
>   What splendors fall on Syrian sands,
>   What purple lights on Alpine snow !
>   Nor how the pomp of sunrise waits
>   On Venice at her watery gates;
> A dream alone to me is Arno's vale,
> And the Alhambra's halls are but a traveller's tale.

> " Yet, on life's current, he who drifts
> 　　Is one with him who rows or sails ;
> 　And he who wanders widest lifts
> 　　No more of beauty's jealous veils
> 　Than he who from his doorway sees
> 　The miracle of flowers and trees,
> Feels the warm Orient in the noonday air,
> And from cloud-minarets hears the sunset call to prayer !
>
> " The eye may well be glad that looks
> 　　Where Pharpar's fountains rise and fall,
> 　But he who sees his native brooks
> 　　Laugh in the sun, has seen them all.
> 　The marble palaces of Ind
> 　Rise round him in the snow and wind ;
> From his lone sweetbrier Persian Hafiz smiles,
> And Rome's cathedral awe is in his woodland aisles."

The temptation to continue is strong, for the interest is sustained ; the lines sparkle with light and are warm with feeling ; but enough has been quoted from this poem for the brief space allotted.

In the search for picturesque passages a great number could be gathered from " Snow Bound ; " but they are seldom separable without loss ; and, as that poem is better known, probably, than any in the collection, we shall quote only the delightful image with which it closes : —

> " And thanks untraced to lips unknown
> 　Shall greet me like the odors blown
> 　From unseen meadows newly mown,

> Or lilies floating in some pond,
> Wood-fringed, the wayside gaze beyond;
> The traveller owns the grateful sense
> Of sweetness near, **he knows not whence,**
> And, pausing, takes with forehead bare
> The benediction of the air."

In his tributes **to the** eminent men and women **of his** day, after making allowance for the friendly warmth of color, **we** observe **a** fine discrimination of character, and **the power of** placing mental **and** moral **traits in high relief.** The two poems upon Sumner are eminent **specimens of careful study and strong** portraiture. The same may be said **of the sketch** of Dr. Howe, of Mrs. Avis Keene, of John Randolph, **of Webster in " The Lost Occasion," —** of Fields **and Taylor, —** and still more **of the** touching **and** matchless eulogy of **Burns.** The concluding stanzas of the last-named **poem are so** full **of** tenderness, shadowed by inevitable **regret, —** so fervent in **the** appreciation **of** genius, **and so** throbbing **with** manly love, that **it is hard** for **a** man of sensibility to repeat them without tears.

All true poetry **is in a** sense autobiographic, **for** the poet must use his own feelings **and** experiences **as** the staple **of** his verse; **but there are many of** Whittier's **which have a peculiar** interest on account **of the utter** frankness **of** their confidences. **Who-ever** will read these personal poems with **attention**

and thought will have a better idea of the man
than the most elaborate biography could give.
Among the earliest is the one entitled " Lines
written in the Book of a Friend : " —

> " On page of thine I cannot trace
>   The cold and heartless commonplace."

This was written before 1843, when the anti-slavery
cause engaged his best efforts, and relates with
touching simplicity his call to duty and the consequences.

In the poem " My Namesake " (written in 1857),
from which a few stanzas have been already quoted,
he gives an account of himself, one that cannot be
abridged. The reader must summarize for himself,
but we will present one or two stanzas : —

> " In him the grave and playful mixed,
>   And wisdom held with folly truce,
> And Nature compromised betwixt
>   Good fellow and recluse.
>
>   .   .   .   .   .
>
> " Ill served his tides of feeling strong
>   To turn the common mills of use ;
> And, over restless wings of song
>   His birthright garb hung loose !
>
> " His eye was beauty's powerless slave,
>   And his the ear which discord pains ;
> Few guessed beneath his aspect grave
>   What passions strove in chains."

" My Psalm," written in 1859, is of a similar character, but its burden is more purely religious. "My Birthday," written in 1871, is tender and beautiful ; but worldly-minded readers will doubtless smile to observe that he fears his long-delayed but unsought popularity may weaken his moral fibre : —

> " The bark by tempest vainly tossed
> May founder in the calm,
> And he who braved the polar frost
> Faint by the isles of balm."

> " Better than self-indulgent years
> The outflung heart of youth,
> Than pleasant songs in idle ears
> The tumult of the truth."

The religious element in Whittier's poems is something vital and inseparable. The supremacy of moral ideas is indeed inculcated by almost all great poets, and at no time more than in the present. And in almost all modern verse the filial relation of man to his Creator, and the immanence of the Spirit in the human heart, are at least tacitly recognized. The leading poets of America are, one and all, reverent in feeling and tone. But it is quite evident that Whittier alone is religious in a high and inward sense.

The reader's attention was called to this in comments upon " The Eternal Goodness " and poems in a similar holy strain. We see that in such verses there is not simply the decorous homage of the lips, but the strong feeling of communion with God, deep as the sources of being, high as the aspirations of the soul, lasting as eternity. These are utterances which no art can simulate, which carry irresistible conviction, and are immortally classic in their sphere. Whatever gifts and graces belong by right to Whittier, it is by his expression of religious ideas that he has the place of honor.

It may appear unnecessary to add that the idea of God is never associated in his verse with images of terror; it is the God of Love, the Eternal Goodness, that he adores. Nor is there any hint of theologic dogmas, nor of stated observances; it is the idea of right living and holy thinking without the hedges of human codes, — of actual personal communion without rigid forms of words. Compare these soul-full poems with the icy edifice of Pope's Universal Prayer, — a temple without a humble worshipper, and with only the shadowy eidolon of a God!

A lover of nature, an artist in landscape, a chivalrous philanthropist, — pouring out his whole heart in lyrics for the poor and oppressed, — and a psalmist under a Divine call, — he who unites these qualities and functions has a right to the love and admiration of mankind. But there are other things to be considered, such as ideality, imagination in a high and restricted sense, and philosophy. The nature of Whittier's mind is primarily realistic ; — that is, his feet are planted on the ground, and he has sung mostly of what has been visible to his mortal eyes. "Snow Bound," one of the most popular of his poems, is a specimen of intense realism. And yet who has not felt in reading its simple lines strong suggestions of *the beyond?* Pictures arise in mind wholly above the level of the farm. To alter a line of Lowell, —

"He rings commonplace things with mystical hues."

The realism of Whittier does not generally bound and determine the treatment of his theme. We are conscious of an increasing glow, and as image succeeds image, the course of thought rises and tends more towards an ideal realm, until at length the actual landscape or story is left far below, and the poet and reader are in the midst of

"The light that never was, on sea or land."

Imagination is the highest attribute, as all admit. When we think of the stupendous edifice of "Paradise Lost," or of the scenes and ever-living characters of Shakespeare, the works of other poets seem puny; but the field of poetry is broad, and the elements of poetic power are many; and there are other and lesser poets from whom we receive intellectual pleasure as well as moral strength. No poet, however, can be considered great in whom the faculty of imagination is wanting or feeble. There are strokes in Byron as startling as in the masters. Coleridge had the faculty; so had Wordsworth, Keats, and Shelley. Tennyson, too, often shows it in some vigorous line. He sees an eagle poised at an airy height. A common observer would mention, perhaps, that the majestic bird seemed a mere dot in the ether; but Tennyson puts himself in the eagle's place, and he measures the height thus : —

> "The wrinkled sea beneath him crawls."

Whatever definitions may be ventured, we know this, that imagination is shown by putting one's self in the place; as Shakespeare *lived* in the persons he had created.

In the poems of Whittier there are many traces of this high quality. It is less condensed into adamantine phrases, but its presence is often strongly felt. The poems entitled "Follen," "Ezekiel," "My Triumph," and many others convey the impression of imaginative power. "The Henchman," though upon a hackneyed theme, is a pure piece of imagination; so are certain stanzas in "Evening by the Lakeside,"—as, for instance, where the sun is imaged as the far-darting Apollo:—

> " **And** the young archer, Morn, shall break
> **His** arrows on the mountain pines,
> And, golden-sandalled, walk the lake!"

The reader will see, of course, **that the new** image is in the last line.

The conclusion of "Snow Bound" is delicately imaginative, and certain stanzas **on Sumner are** strongly **so.**

On the other hand, as has been before intimated, **there** are prosaic places, especially **in** poems of a moral character,—fragments of excellent good sense and high purpose, but not distinguishable, except **in** form, from prose. Many of these the poet would have altered or cancelled **in later** days, except that they had become public property by lapse of time. That he has often chosen homely **themes** we cannot consider a serious fault. He has not **been a poet** for stately occasions only, but the celebrant of home affections and rural life.

Philosophy may **stand** in poetry for the consideration of the problems of being, mind, origin, and destiny. The fine-spun distinctions of metaphysics, the obscure phrases used **in** the so-called science, **and the** utter hopelessness of its aims, are too well known. The value of such discussions has been discredited by most intellectual men, from Goethe downward. That metaphysics, pure and simple, is wholly antipathetic to poetry, there can be no doubt; although certain rare geniuses, like Emerson, by drawing analogies from the sources of speculative ideas, give to unquestionably inspired poetry a philosophic tone. But such poems are as rare as are Emersons, and the intelligent admirers of them are very few.

In Wordsworth the philosophic pieces are often prosy, though sometimes (as in the " Ode on the Intimations of Immortality ") strongly attractive, and even magnificent. It does not appear that philosophy is so much the proper staple of poetry as it is material for the adornment of it ; or rather, it may be said that while philosophic observations give pleasure to all intelligent readers, the actual pursuit of a philosophic question in the guise of a poem is wholly foreign to the purpose of poetry and certain to result in dulness or disaster.

Of such philosophic reflections or remarks, by the way, there are enough in Whittier to justify his place among thinking men; but he is not, in the confined acceptation of the word, a philosophic poet. And we can easily see he could not be one, with his strong religious principles and feelings.

The author of "The Eternal Goodness" could never have originated the questioning, doubting, mocking lines that we find in "Faust." The soul that is "stayed on God" must dismiss most of the current philosophy without hesitation.

After all deductions there remain the solid and enduring qualities of genuine poetry. Few poets have had the opportunity to do such work for their fellow-men as Whittier has done; and few have exerted such an elevating influence, even upon readers for pleasure. From small beginnings his fame has risen until it has become the pride of all loyal Americans, and is cherished also by English-speaking people around the world.

CHAPTER XXIII.

CONCLUSION.

OUR narration has reached its natural close. The events of Whittier's later years are few, and the account of his works has been finished. The careful reader will have noticed that many poems printed in magazines and newspapers remain ungathered, and that abundant materials exist for additional volumes. Without doubt, if the poet's life is spared, these will appear in due time.

The poems and letters that have been referred to and the brief account of his labors show what manner of man he is. It is not necessary to make a catalogue of his mental or moral characteristics, still less to sketch for the curious his personal manners and habits. A discreet editor, having in mind the inborn modesty and delicacy of feeling of the poet, will choose to let his works and deeds stand in place of formal portrait and labored eulogy. No summary of his life-work is now possible even if its propriety were beyond question.

Many sketches of the man have been written, and multitudes of reviews exist, each with points of light and with flaws of error. There is not room to refer to them. This may be said, however, that the only thorough appreciation of Whittier, as man and poet, is shown by those who have studied him longest and known him best. The glib and facile critic can lay his finger on faults, and sum his excellences in familiar formulas, but Whittier is to be judged by men of heart as well as brain, and his genius will be felt through sympathy. After patient endeavor to arrive at the secret of his power, it is but just to say that the impression has been steadily cumulative; and that the casual reader, who has not been admitted, as it were, into the poet's confidence, can have but a slight conception of his place in the realm of letters, or of his firm hold upon the hearts of all natural men.

The idea of making a personal sketch of the poet was considered, but has been reluctantly abandoned. The minute traits as well as the strong lines of his character offer to a writer a fascinating subject; but it can be postponed;— and may the proper time for it be late!

The best and most affectionate study of him has been recently made by Miss Nora Perry. It is a charming article, and will repay a careful perusal.[1]

There may be a correct bibliography of Whittier, but the writer has never seen one that did not contain errors. In the Appendix may be found a list of his works, which has been made with care; but that it is complete and beyond criticism no one can say. Some alleged publications depend upon tradition rather than proof.

It has been mentioned before that a great number of Whittier's poems have never been collected from the newspapers and magazines in which they appeared. It is also probable that a very large number of his minor poems sent to neighbors and friends remain unpublished. There may be a time when these can be properly gathered and printed. His relations with his friends have been hearty and unconventional; and as he was always a natural and spontaneous rhymer, there will be found hereafter, in manuscript, beyond doubt, many charming off-hand verses. As a specimen, we present an impromptu, written on receiving a jar of butter from a lady living at Pond Hills in Amesbury : —

> "'Words butter no parsnips,' the old adage says,
>   And to fill up the trencher is better than praise;
>   So, trust me, dear friend, that, while eating thy butter,
>   The thanks that I feel are far more than I utter.

[1] See Appendix.

> " Kind Providence grant thee a life without ills;
>   May the cows never dry up that feed on Pond Hills.
>   May the cream never fail in thy cellar **so cold,**
>   Nor thy hand lose its cunning **to turn it to** gold.

> " **Thrice** welcome to him, who, unblest with a wife,
>   **Sits** and bungles alone at the ripped seams **of** life,
>   **Is** the womanly kindness that pities his fate,
>   And sews on his buttons, and fills up his plate ! "

Between these homely and realistic lines and the burning lyrics of the Abolition period, or **the splendors of** his lake **and mountain scenes, there is a wide** interval **; but we** have **a** peculiar **pleasure in** seeing that the poet is a man of simple and genuine feeling, that he shares the common joys and sympathies, and **that the** contemplation of **great** subjects **and the use of high** and imaginative phrases **do not isolate** him **from** humble and **faithful friends and** neighbors.

Recurring once more to the matter of character, it must **be** said that few men have presented such a tempting **and** such **a** baffling study. While he **is** neither " odd " nor " eccentric " **(in usual** parlance), his personality **is** marked, **and there** is **a** strongly individual flavor in **all** his utterances. Many great writers adopt **the** state **of** kings, **and** their only sincere worshippers are **those** who adore from a distance. Goethe came **to be** more royal than the Grand **Duke** whom **he** served. In the case of

Whittier, with his perception of the beautiful, his devotion to right, his hatred of falsity and oppression, there are found many endearing human traits, — generous sympathy, a well-spring of humor, a relish for native wit and for quaint phases of character. He is utterly free from the vanity, envy, and jealousy which belittle so many writers. Some imperfection clings to all souls, but few have been observed in our time so well poised, so pure, and so stainless as his.

APPENDIX.

A PERSONAL SKETCH OF WHITTIER.

BY NORA PERRY.

[From the Boston "Home Journal," June 2, 1883.]

IT is fifteen years ago that I first met Mr. Whittier. I was spending the latter half of the summer in one of the quaint old neighborhoods on the eastern shore of Massachusetts, not a great distance from Newburyport and Amesbury, and there formed the acquaintance of one of his warmest friends, who, surprised that I had never seen the Quaker poet, at once made hospitable arrangements for me to meet him at her house. It was a charming late summer afternoon that I was summoned to her parlor by the announcement that Mr. Whittier had arrived. I entered the room with the preconceived idea of the poet's *personale*, that I had gathered from the various portraits I had seen, and found myself face to face with a personality that differed very decidedly from these counterfeit presentments. Instead of the severe, almost ascetic countenance of somewhat exaggerated proportions which I had in my mind, I saw before me a gentle, cordial face, the features of which were finely and sharply cut, and the general contour of more than ordinary refinement and delicacy. The salient expression was that of earnest interest in and for the person before him. It was the poet's generous interest in a younger worker, which I found later was one of his chief characteristics. This interest was not that of patronage, but of sincere sympathy. The self-effacement which this sympathy produces has been called modesty on the part of Mr. Whittier. It is not so self-conscious a quality as that. Modesty presupposes some consciousness of self, in its retirement of the personality. Mr. Whittier is forgetful of this personality in his sympathetic interest in another and another's work. It was this self-forgetfulness and sympathy that at once made me feel entirely at ease, and at home with him; and it is this that at once puts every one at ease with him. I dwell upon this point, because it betokens the strongest qualities in Mr. Whittier's character, and is the key-note to the hold which his poems have upon the world. He is not indifferent to, nor does he underrate, personal recognition by any means, but he is not facing his own image all the time, as seems to be the unfortunate attitude of some whom fame has crowned. With a perfectly clear-headed estimate of the applause that has followed his work, he is not for a moment influenced or swayed by it.

"Be careful," he wrote to a young author about to publish her first book of verse, "not to make the book too large. Don't put *everything* into it, let who will advise it. Sit like Rhadamanthus in stern judgment upon all that claims admission. I speak out of the depths of a bitter experience." At another time to the same young author, who had sent him a magazine containing some warm words of admiration about him and his work, he writes: " Many thanks for thy letter and magazine. I am sorry I don't deserve the kind words of my too lenient reviewers. When I read such notices I sum up the account on the other side, — reckon all the little meannesses and selfish feelings and weaknesses I can think of, and bring myself sadly in debt."

This, of course, is in reference to the personal praise lavished upon his character. Upon the subject of appreciation and recognition by the world, he once expressed himself to me with that candor which characterizes his statements. I had been telling him of a conversation that I had had with a certain poetess, a friend of his, who had declared to me that she would be perfectly content to receive no personal recognition of her work if the work itself was recognized, — that her name, her authorship, might be entirely unknown to her readers and she be content. Not sympathizing precisely with this separation of one's individual self from one's work in this manner, I laid the matter before Mr. Whittier, asking him what *his* feeling was upon the subject. He replied: " I don't feel as our friend does. I don't like notoriety. I don't like that part of personal recognition which, when I get into a car, makes people nudge their neighbors, and whisper, 'That's Whittier!' But I like the interesting persons it has introduced to me, — the friends it has brought me."

With a natural New England reserve and shyness, strengthened by his Quaker education, Mr. Whittier doubtless felt that his best introduction to others was through his writings, and that the personal acquaintance that followed was on fuller and easier terms than if he had been denied that vehicle of expression. He would never have been one to seek others, however he might have been placed. When, however, others seek him, they find him always ready to respond to their advances, if those advances are from genuine emotions of sympathy and attraction. Never anything but kind in his treatment of any person, he discriminates at once between the curious celebrity hunter, the autograph bore, and the person who approaches him with that interest which is born of kindred thought. When he meets such a one, it is with that gladness that Emerson voices, when he says, " Every new person may be an event to me." With none of that self-consciousness of achievement which usually creates an atmosphere that invites personal remark, it is not an easy matter for a person of taste to abruptly introduce Mr. Whittier's work when in his presence. Most celebrated persons receive with equanimity the direct words of praise that are bestowed upon them. Mr. Whittier seems to *bear* them with a sort of resigned patience and composure that is sometimes very amusing. I recall an occasion of this kind. It was at rather a noted gathering, and a lady who was a great admirer of his poems sought an introduction to him. An impulsive and emotional person, she was so carried away by the unexpected delight of the moment, — the honor and pleasure of meeting and speaking with the poet whose books she had read and reverenced so long, that, at the first sentence, when giving way to her emotional tendencies she attempted to put this delight into words, she broke down completely, and wept. Mr. Whittier stood dumb, receiving the tearful words like a gentle martyr. He no doubt appreciated to the full the affectionate yet reverential admiration **that** drew forth this display of emotion, but he had **been made** the centre of a ***scene***, and this was embarrassing and painful to him. At the first note of agitation after the introduction, **I had basely** betaken myself **out** of the immediate **range of** this scene. **When it was over I** returned, to be **greeted with** a quizzical glance from Mr. Whittier's dark, **penetrating** eyes, and the remark, "*Thee* could run away, but *I* had to stay."

Yet, as **I have** said, he had no doubt appreciated **the feeling that** had **called forth all this emotion, for I have never** seen him insensible **to the *real*** feeling that lurked **under any** demonstration; but for the time **such** demonstrations embarrass him. They **are** not **in** accord with his reserved **nature, the** education that he **has** received, and **the** lifelong associations with the calm, self-repressed **Quakers. It is a significant** fact, however, that to the Quakers themselves **Mr.** Whittier does **not seem specially** self-repressed. **His** outspokenness upon **the anti-slavery question, his deeper interest in** the political affairs of the state and **the** nation, and his expression **by** his vote **and pen of** this interest, show **that** the external sign of quiet is more that of training **than of nature.** As some one once said of him, "He was born **a** soldier and made over into a Quaker, and the soldier knocks the Quaker down now and **then."** This was during the days **of** the **war,** when words and opinions **ran** high and the soldierly spirit came more prominently **to** the surface. All through this period, when the nation was being baptized in blood, we know how this Quaker soldier used both tongue and pen, — two weapons more than equal to any sword or musket he might have carried.

"I remember," said a gentleman to me the other day, when we were speaking of Mr. Whittier's life and character, "the effect that some of his war poems had upon the community. I specially recall now that stirring thing, beginning : —

> ' We wait beneath the furnace-blast
> The pangs of transformation ;
> Not painlessly doth God recast
> And mould anew the nation.'

There is one stanza that I cannot now recollect, which made the Copperheads rave ; it spoke of the broken oath of the men of the South."

The stanza alluded to is the following : —

> " What gives the wheat-field blades of steel ?
> What points the rebel cannon ?
> What sets the roaring rabble's heel
> On the old star-spangled pennon ?
> What breaks the oath
> Of the men o' the South ?
> What whets the knife
> For the Union's life ?
> Hark to the answer : Slavery !"

But it was not only during the war that these impassioned lyrics sprang forth ; — all along the years that led up to that war they rang out like bugle calls. His poem entitled " Slave Ships " glows like Turner's picture, with the accurate realism that Turner lacks. His " To Faneuil Hall," " Massachusetts," " To a Southern Statesman," " To William Lloyd Garrison," and indeed every poem in the collection styled " Voices of Freedom " burns and beats with the red-hot soldier fire. **All** this put him in the front ranks of the anti-slavery party, and ostracized him in the old days as it ostracized Garrison **and** Phillips and Sumner and the rest of the abolitionists. **But** history **was** making rapidly at that time, and those that **were ostracized** before **the war were** recognized as heroes **during** the latter part of the struggle and after it.

Looking back down the years, it is interesting to speculate as to the position, the place, that Whittier had held if he had lacked that peculiar moral impulse **toward** reform that made him join hands with **the** abolitionists. **It is** difficult to separate him from his **fiery,** protesting **spirit ;** still, a shade less **here, a shade** more there, and **we** might **yet** have had the poet attuned **to other** speech, for **he** must have been **a poet under** any condition. There **are always those who** will **cry** that opportunity **is** the great thing, and that **poet,** soldier, or statesman is the outgrowth of that. **This** is the petty tape measurement of spiritual things, which delights the small mind, alert with **jealousy** of superior gifts. If the young Quaker, brooding over his plough in those early days, and finding in every change of the landscape some **poetic** inspiration, **had** not been stirred in his moral nature **by the** anti-slavery agitation, or if there had been no anti-slavery agitation, somewhere he would have found **the** " subject made to his hand " which doubtless would have rendered his name as famous, but **scarcely** as beloved, as **it is now.** Fortunately for the great cause, however, of the country, he ranged himself at the outset with what was thought then to be the fanatical minority, and, from beginning to end fighting the good fight without thought of selfish reckoning, he has won for himself a triple crown of honor and glory.

It is interesting to hear sometimes from his lips pithy description of those old days of conflict. Once, not long ago, I remember in some conversation the topic of personal courage came up, and Mr. Whittier disclaimed for himself the possession of that quality.

"But," I said, "you always seemed to have the courage of your opinions under any trying circumstances."

"Oh, well," he returned, "a man, if he *is* a man, must face some things. I recollect a time when I came out of a meeting, in the old anti-slavery days, that some rough fellows threatened us, and I turned and faced them, and so holding their eyes went out. No other way would have done, you know. The thing for a man to do was to face 'em, not to turn his back on 'em, or run."

It was of no use to tell Mr. Whittier that this was the highest kind of courage. He might have recognized the fact as connected with another, but with himself, never. What would have called forth from him hearty appreciation and admiration if another had been the hero, only appeared in the most commonplace aspect as his own act. It is this quality of humility which sometimes diverges into self-deprecation that makes him so acceptable a neighbor to his townsmen. He is not counting his own honors, but on the contrary is sincerely interested in the welfare of those about him, and always a kind and hospitable host. He must weary of a great many of the travellers that seek him, and as the years go on he must find means to protect himself from the mere celebrity hunter. But in that old home at Amesbury very few, I fancy, have crossed the threshold who have not been made to feel **that** they were welcome. **The** host **is not only** hospitable **to** the visitor in the usual manner, but he **is** hospitable **to** the visitor's thoughts, opinions, and tastes, though **these** may differ materially from his own. Knowing something of his liberality and acceptance, I was **yet** taken by **sur**prise **on** one occasion. I **was** spending the day at Amesbury ; the other guest **was a** gentleman acquaintance of Mr. Whittier's, — one that the Quakers would very decidedly term " one of the world's people." As we rose from the table, Mr. Whittier **led** the **way** into his study. **It** was a lovely June **day, and the** door **that communicated** with the little side piazza **or porch was set** wide **open.** With a sudden, quick perception **of** his guest's afterdinner habit, Mr. Whittier turned and said, " Now if thee **wants** to smoke, don't hesitate — the porch **is** just the place."

The guest **very** politely uttered **his thanks — he** knew Mr. Whittier did n't smoke — he would **take** himself into the garden, etc., if Mr. Whittier would permit him. But Mr. Whittier would hear nothing **of the** kind. **To be** sure he did n't smoke, but he liked his friends the smokers, etc., and would n't hear of *this* friend going farther. **So** while the feminine portion of the company sat just within, the Quaker host sat without on the little porch while "one of the world's people" enjoyed his after-dinner **cigar to his** heart's content. But **one** might **go on** multiplying **these genial** stories to almost any **extent.** It is not necessary, however, **to** multiply such incidents **to** show the healthy equipoise of Mr. Whittier's character. A reformer, he is not a fanatic, and does not insist that there is but one road to righteousness. **In** reply to something that **I once** said to him in regard **to** "meeting **matters,"** he wrote thus succinctly and half humorously : —

"**I** quite agree with ———— ———— about meeting matters, but I don't make it a specialty. The world is wide, **and as the Moslem says, '** God is great.' Things will **worry** along somehow, as they **always have done ;** and **the end will be** well."

Of Mr. Whittier's social side less has been written than **of the reformatory and** literary. **He is generally spoken** of **as a shy man,** avoiding **all society. If** 'by society we mean large parties, dinners, and receptions, the general idea is a true one. But I think that no one enjoys the **society of a few** friends better than this accredited society **hater ; and with** these, his humor, **and** sometimes keen **wit, finds** ready **play. No** one relishes a good story more, **nor can relate one with better grace. The** sense of the **ludicrous is very vivid, and the absurdities** of life and its **situations strike** him never more forcibly **than when they** involve himself. Thus in the many instances **where the celebrity hunter,** the autograph tramp, has ferreted him **out, some** point of the ludicrous in the experience has **lighted it up,** and made a little comedy of what would otherwise have been an unmitigated bore. Like Mr. Longfellow, Mr. Whittier is more indulgent **to the auto**graph tramp than he ought to be, but he **can say "** No," on occasions, and turn his back upon **the** pursuer with commendable courage. But capable always of making clear distinctions, of separating the wheat from the tares, he recognizes the sincerity of true sympathy and appreciation, and responds **with** a courtesy **and kindness that is**

full of hearty friendliness. Some of his best thoughts have been tersely put in a verse or two that he has written for such occasions. One of these was penned at the request of a friend for an ancient sun-dial that stood in his — the friend's — garden. What could be better, more complete, than this? —

> " With warning hand I mark Time's rapid flight,
> From life's glad morning to its solemn night,
> Yet through the dear God's love I also show
> There 's light above me by the shade below." [1]

In the poet's published volumes, though we find now and then a grim humor, we do not see the lighter strain of wit and gayety that occasionally breaks out in his conversation. The brightness and lightness of this strain is very charmingly exemplified in the following stanza that he wrote in a young friend's album, and which I am permitted to copy : —

> " Ah, ladies, you love to levy a tax
> On my poor little paper parcel of fame ;
> Yet strange it seems that among you all
> No one is willing to take my name —
> To write and rewrite till the angels pity her,
> The weariful words,
>
> > Thine truly, Whittier."

Examples of equal sportiveness might be collected from various unpublished verses of this sort, and they would serve to show perhaps that, given less grave and serious associations, Mr. Whittier might have developed, or worked this lighter vein very successfully. But with these less serious conditions of life we might have missed

[1] Written for Dr. Henry I. Bowditch.

such burning poems as were inspired by the stormy times
in which he found himself; and as he himself has said in
his eloquent poem, "My Birthday,"

> "Better than self-indulgent years
> The outflung heart of youth,
> Than pleasant songs in idle years,
> The tumult of the truth."

True to the letter of this verse has been the poet's life,
yet in the very thick of the fight, in the very heart of
these tumultuous days, the friends that came to him never
found him set up upon any pinnacle of reformation, never
anxious to preach and hold forth upon these truths exclusively, as if no other topics existed.

Time and place are greatly regarded by the Quakers.
They wait for the spirit to move, and it generally moves
in an orderly manner. Sitting in the simple cosey study
at Amesbury, — that has been so accurately portrayed in
the "illustrated Whittier," — or upon the porch outside,
friends of varying beliefs and tastes have enjoyed themselves gayly or gravely as the mood prompted them.
Whatever the subject of the talk, it is always easy because never forced, and always interesting because Mr.
Whittier has that great essential for a host, sympathy,
and the appreciation that grows out of that companionable
quality.

MIDDLE–CENTURY POLITICS.

THE following humorous and satirical **verses were pub-lished in the** "Boston Chronotype" **in 1846. They refer to the contest in New Hampshire,** which resulted **in the defeat of** the pro-slavery Democracy, and in the election of John P. Hale to the United States Senate. Although their authorship was not acknowledged by Mr. Whittier at the time, **there** was a strong suspicion that they **were from** his pen. **They** furnish **a specimen of the way, on the** whole **rather good-natured, in which the liberty-lovers of** half a century **ago** answered **the social and political out-** lawry and mob violence to which they **were subjected.**

A LETTER

SUPPOSED TO BE WRITTEN BY THE CHAIRMAN OF THE "CENTRAL CLIQUE" AT CONCORD, N. H., TO THE HON. M. N., JR., AT WASHINGTON, GIVING THE RESULT OF THE ELECTION.

'T is over, Moses ! All is lost !
  I hear the bells a-ringing ;
Of Pharaoh and his Red Sea host
  I hear the Free-Wills singing.[1]
We 're routed, Moses, horse and foot,
  If there be truth in figures,
With federal Whigs in hot pursuit,
  And Hale, and all the " niggers."

Alack ! alas ! this month or more
  We 've felt a sad foreboding ;
Our very dreams the burden bore
  Of central cliques exploding ;

---

[1] **The book establishment of the Free-Will Baptists in Dover** was refused the act of incorporation by the New Hampshire Legislature, for the reason that the newspaper organ of that sect and its leading preachers favored abolition.

Before our eyes a **furnace shone,**
　Where heads of dough were roasting,
And one we took to be your own
　The traitor Hale was toasting !

Our Belknap brother [1] **heard** with awe
　The Congo minstrels playing ;
At Pittsfield Reuben **Leavitt** [2] **saw**
　The ghost of Storrs a-praying ;
And Carroll's woods were sad to see,
　With-black-winged crows a-darting ;
And Black **Snout looked on Ossipee,**
　New-glossed with Day and Martin.

We thought the " Old Man of the Notch "
　His face seemed changing wholly —
His lips seemed thick ; his nose seemed flat ;
　His misty hair looked woolly ;
And Coös teamsters, shrieking, fled
　From the metamorphosed figure.
"**Look there !" they said, "**the Old Stone Head
　Himself is turning nigger ! "

Gray Hubbard [3] **heard o' nights the sound**
　Of rail-cars onward faring ;
Right over Democratic ground
　The iron horse came tearing.
A flag waved o'er that spectral train,
　As high as Pittsfield steeple ;
Its emblem was a broken chain ;
　Its motto : " To the people ! "

I dreamed **that** Charley took his bed,
　With Hale **for** his physician ;

---

[1] **The senatorial editor of** the " Belknap Gazette " **has all along** manifested
a peculiar horror of " niggers " and " nigger parties."
　[2] **The justice before** whom Elder Storrs **was brought** for preaching abolition,
on a writ drawn by Hon. M. N., Jr., of Pittsfield. **The** sheriff served the writ
while the elder was praying.
　[3] Ex-Governor Hubbard's **peculiar notions of** the rights of individuals and
of corporations in respect of railroad routes are well known.

His daily dose an old "unread
  And unreferred" petition.[1]
There Hayes and Tuck as nurses sat,
  As near as near could be, man ;
They leeched him with the "Democrat;"
  They blistered with the "Freeman."

Ah ! grisly portents ! What avail
  Your terrors of forewarning ?
We wake to find the nightmare Halo
  Astride our breasts at morning !
From Portsmouth lights to Indian stream
  Our foes their throats are trying ;
The very factory-spindles **seem**
  To mock us while they 're **flying.**

The hills have bonfires ; **in** our streets
  Flags flout us in our faces ;
The newsboys, peddling off their sheets,
  Are hoarse with our disgraces.
In vain we turn, for gibing wit
  And shoutings follow after,
As if old Kearsarge had split
  His granite sides with laughter !

What boots it that we pelted out
  The anti-slavery women,[2]
And bravely strewed their hall about
  With tattered lace and trimming !
Was it for such a sad reverse
  Our mobs became peacemakers,
And kept their tar and wooden horse
  For Englishmen and Quakers ?[3]

[1] "Papers and memorials touching the subject of slavery shall be laid on the table without reading, debate, or reference." — *Atherton's Congressional Gag Law.*

[2] **The** Female Anti-slavery Society, at its first meeting in Concord, was assailed with stones and brickbats.

[3] The celebrated English abolitionist, George Thompson, and his Quaker friend, John G. Whittier. It is but fair to say that the honors of the great Concord mob of 1835 belong in a very equal degree to Whigs and Democrats.

For this did shifty Atherton
  Make gag rules for the Great House ?
Wiped we for this our feet upon
  Petitions in our State House ?
Plied we for **this our axe of doom,**
  No stubborn **traitor sparing,**
Who scoffed at our opinion **loom,**
  And took to homespun wearing ?

Ah, **Moses ! hard it is to scan**
  These crooked providences,
Deducing from the wisest plan
  The saddest **consequences !**
Strange that, in trampling **as was meet**
  The nigger-men's petition,
We sprung a mine beneath our feet
  Which opened up perdition.

The very thing we greatly feared
  At last has come upon us ;
Like autumn leaves the frost has **seared**
  Fall off our blushing **honors.**
The blow we dreaded most has come
  From **Hale, (the more's the pity !)**
Appealing to the people from
  The people's own committee !

How goodly, Moses, was the game
  In which we 've long been actors,
Supplying freedom with the name
  And slavery with the practice !
Our smooth words fed the people's mouth,
  Their ears our party rattle ;
We kept them headed to the South,
  As drovers do their cattle.

But now our game of politics
  The world at large is learning ;
And men grown gray in all our tricks
  State's evidence are turning.

Votes and preambles subtly spun
  They cram with meanings louder,
And load the Democratic gun
  With abolition powder.

The ides of June ! Woe worth the day
  When, turning all things over,
The traitor Hale shall make his **hay**
  From Democratic clover !
Who then **shall take** him in the law,
  Who punish crime so flagrant ?
Whose hand shall serve, whose pen shall **draw,**
  A writ against that " vagrant " ?[1]

Alas ! no hope is left us here,
  And one can only pine for
The envied place of overseer
  Of slaves in Carolina !
Pray, Moses, give Calhoun the wink,
  And see what pay he 's giving !
We 've practised long enough, we think,
  To know the art of driving.

And for the **faithful rank and file,**
  Who know their proper stations,
Perhaps it may be worth their while
  To try the rice plantations.
Let Hale exult, let Wilson scoff,
  To see us southward scamper ;
The slaves, we know, are " better off
  Than laborers in New Hampshire ! "

---

[1] **Elder Storrs** was described as a " vagrant " in **the Hon. M.** N.'s writ.

WOMAN SUFFRAGE.

LETTER TO THE NEWPORT CONVENTION.

AMESBURY, MASS., 12th 8th Month, 1869.

MY DEAR FRIEND, — I have received thy letter inviting me to attend the Convention in behalf of Woman's Suffrage, at Newport, R. I., on the 25th inst. I do not see how it is possible for me to accept the invitation; and, were I to do so, the state of my health would prevent me from taking such a part in the meeting as would relieve me from the responsibility of seeming to sanction anything in its action which might conflict with my own views of duty or policy. Yet I should do myself great injustice if I did not embrace this occasion to express my general sympathy with the movement. I have seen no good reason why mothers, wives, and daughters should not have the same right of person, property, and citizenship which fathers, husbands, and brothers have.

The sacred memory of mother and sister — the wisdom and dignity of women of my own religious communion who have been accustomed to something like equality in rights as well as duties — my experience as a co-worker with noble and self-sacrificing women, as graceful and helpful in their household duties as firm and courageous in their public advocacy of unpopular truth — the steady friendships which have inspired and strengthened me — and the reverence and respect which I feel for human nature, irrespective of sex, compel me to look with something more than acquiescence on the efforts you are making. I frankly confess that **I am not** able **to foresee all the** consequences of the great social **and** political change proposed, but of this I am, at least, sure, it **is always safe** to do right, and the truest expediency is simple justice. **I** can understand, **without** sharing, **the** misgivings of those who fear that, when the **vote** drops from woman's hand into the ballot-box, the beauty and sentiment, the bloom **and** sweetness, of womanhood will go with it. But in this matter it seems to me we can trust Nature. Stronger than statutes or conventions, she will be conservative of all that the true man loves and honors in woman. **Here** and there may be found an equivocal, unsexed **Chevalier** D'Eon, but the eternal order and fitness **of** things **will** remain. I have no fear that man will be less manly or woman less womanly when they meet on terms of equality before the law.

On the other hand, I **do** not see that the exercise of the ballot by woman will prove a remedy for all the evils of **which** she justly complains. **It** is her right as truly as mine, **and** when she asks for it, it **is** something less than manhood to withhold it. But, unsupported by **a more** practical education, higher aims, and a deeper sense **of the** responsibilities of life and duty, it is not likely to **prove** a blessing in her hands any more than in man's.

With great respect and hearty sympathy, **I am very** truly thy friend,

John G. Whittier.

THE DEITY.

[Believed to be the first poem of Whittier in print.]

THE Prophet stood
On the high mount, and saw the tempest cloud
Pour the fierce whirlwind from its reservoir
Of congregated gloom.   The mountain oak,
Torn from the earth, heaved high its roots where once
Its branches waved.   The fir-tree's shapely form,
Smote by the tempest, lashed the mountain's side.
Yet, calm in conscious purity, the Seer
Beheld the awful desolation, for
The Eternal Spirit moved not in the storm.

The tempest ceased.   The caverned earthquake burst
Forth from its prison, and the mountain rocked
Even to its base.   The topmost crags were thrown,
With fearful crashing, down its shuddering sides,
Unawed, the Prophet saw and heard ; he felt
Not in the earthquake moved the God of Heaven.

The murmur died away ; and from the height,
Torn by the storm and shattered by the shock,
Rose far and clear a pyramid of flame
Mighty and vast ; the startled mountain deer
Shrank from its glare, and cowered within the shade ;
The wild fowl shrieked — but even then the Seer
Untrembling stood and marked the fearful glow,
For Israel's God came not within the flame !

The fiery beacon sank.   A still, small voice,
Unlike to human sound, at once conveyed
Deep awe and reverence to his pious heart.
Then bowed the holy man ; his face he veiled
Within his mantle — and in meekness owned
The presence of his God, discerned not in
The storm, the earthquake, or the mighty flame.

LIST OF POEMS FIRST PRINTED IN THE "NATIONAL ERA."

On the Death of Thomas Clarkson	Jan.	1847.
Song of Slaves in the Desert	Jan.	1847.
Randolph of Roanoke	Jan.	1847.
A Dream of Summer	Jan.	1847.
Barclay of Ury	March,	1847.
Yorktown	April,	1847.
What the Voice said	April,	1847.
The Angel of Patience	May,	**1847.**
The Angels of Buena Vista	May,	**1847.**
Lines accompanying Manuscripts	**July,**	**1847.**
The Drovers	**Nov.**	1847.
The Huskers	**Dec.**	1847.
The Slaves of Martinique	**Jan.**	1848.
The Reward	**Feb.**	1848.
The Crisis	March,	**1848.**
The Holy Land	April,	**1848.**
The Curse of the Charter-Breakers	May,	1848.
Pæan	**Sept.**	1848.
The Wish of To-day	Nov.	**1848.**
The Peace Convention at Brussels	**Dec.**	**1848.**
Impromptu	Feb.	1849.
The Christian Tourists	March,	1849.
The Legend of St. Mark	May,	1849.
The Men **of Old**	June,	1849.
Lines by the Lakeside	July,	1849.
To Pius IX.	**Aug.**	1849.
Calef in Boston	**Sept.**	1849.
Our State	**Nov.**	**1849.**
To Fredrika Bremer	**Nov.**	1849.
Elliott	Jan.	1850.
Lines on a Portrait	April,	1850.
The Hill Top	May,	1850.
Ichabod	May,	1850.
A Sabbath Scene	June,	1850.

TWO EARLY POEMS.

THE poems which follow were written by **Mr.** Whittier between forty and fifty years ago, and have not been published in his collected works.

ISABELLA OF AUSTRIA.

[Isabella, Infanta of Parma, and consort of Joseph of Austria, predicted her own death, immediately after her marriage with the Emperor. **Amidst the gayety and** splendor of Vienna and Presburg, she was reserved and melancholy ; she **believed that** Heaven had given her a view of the future, and that her child, the namesake of the great Maria Theresa, would perish with her. Her prediction was fulfilled.]

Midst the palace bowers of Hungary, imperial Presburg's pride,
With the noble born and beautiful assembled **at** her side,
She stood beneath the summer heavens, the soft wind sighing on,
Stirring the green and arching boughs like dancers in the sun.

The beautiful pomegranate flower, the snowy orange bloom,
The lotus and the trailing vine, the rose's meek perfume,
The willow crossing with its green some statue's marble hair,
All that might charm the fresh young sense, or light the soul, was
      there !

But she, a monarch's treasured one, leaned gloomily apart,
With her dark eyes tearfully cast down, and a shadow on her
      heart.
Young, beautiful, and dearly loved, what sorrow hath she known ?
Are not the hearts and swords of all held sacred as her own ?
Is not her lord the kingliest in battle-field or tower ?
The wisest in the council-hall, the gayest in the bower ?
Is not his love as full and deep as his own Danube's tide ?
And wherefore in her princely home weeps Isabel his bride ?

She raised her jewelled hand, and flung her veiling tresses back,
Bathing its snowy tapering within their glossy black.
A tear fell on the orange leaves, rich gem and mimic blossom
And fringèd robe shook fearfully upon her sighing bosom.
" Smile on, smile on," she murmured low, " for all is joy around,
Shadow and sunshine, stainless sky, soft airs, and blossomed ground.
'T is meet the light of heart should smile, when nature's smile is
      fair,
And melody and fragrance meet, twin sisters of the air.

" But ask me not to share with you the beauty of the scene,
The fountain-fall, mosaic walk, and breadths of tender green ;
And point not to the mild blue sky, or glorious summer sun,
I know how very fair is all the hand of God has done.
The hills, the sky, the sunlit cloud, the waters leaping forth,
The swaying trees, the scented flowers, the dark green robes of
      earth, —
I love them well, but I have learned to turn aside from all,
And nevermore my heart must own their sweet but fatal thrall.

" And I could love the noble one whose mighty name I bear,
And closer to my breaking heart his princely image wear,
And I could love our sweet young flower, unfolding day by day,
And taste of that unearthly joy which mothers only may, —

But what am I to cling to these ? — A voice is in my ear,
A shadow lingers at my side, the death-wail and the bier !
The cold and starless night of Death where day may never beam,
The silence and forgetfulness, the sleep that hath no dream !

"O God, to **leave this** fair bright **world, and more than** all to
    know
The moment when the Spectral One shall strike his fearful blow ;
To **know the day, the** very hour, to feel the tide roll on,
To shudder at the gloom before and weep the sunshine gone,
To count the days, the few short days, of light and love and breath
Between me and the noisome grave, the voiceless home of death ! —
Alas ! — if feeling, knowing this, I murmur at my doom,
Let not thy frowning O my God ! lend darkness to the tomb.

" O, I have **borne my** spirit up, **and** smiled amidst the **chill**
Remembrance of my certain doom which lingers with me still ;
I would not cloud my fair child's brow, nor let a tear-drop dim
The eye that met my wedded lord's, lest it should sadden him ;
But there are moments when the strength of feeling must have way ;
That hidden tide of unnamed woe nor fear nor love can stay.
Smile on, smile on, light-hearted ones ! Your sun of joy is high :
Smile on, and leave the doomed of Heaven alone to weep and die !"

A funeral chant was wailing through Vienna's holy pile,
A coffin with its gorgeous pall **was** borne **along** the aisle ;
The drooping flags of many lands waved **slow above the** dead,
A mighty band of mourners came, **a king was at its** head, —
A youthful king, with mournful tread, and dim and tearful eye ;
He scarce had dreamed that one so pure as his fair bride could die.
And sad and long above the throng the funeral anthem rung :
" Mourn for the hope of Austria | Mourn for the loved and young !"

The wail went up from other **lands, the valleys of the Hun,**
Fair Parma with its orange bowers, and hills of vine and sun ;
The lilies of imperial France drooped as the sound **went by,**
The long lament of cloistered Spain was mingled with the cry.
The dwellers in Colorno's halls, the Slowak at his cave,
The bowed at the Escurial, the Magyar stoutly brave,
All wept the early stricken flower ; and still the anthem rung :
" Mourn for the pride of Austria ! Mourn for the loved and young !"

BOLIVAR: THE HERO OF COLOMBIA.

A dirge is wailing from the Gulf of storm-vexed Mexico,
To where through Pampas' solitudes the mighty rivers flow ;
The dark Sierras hear the sound, and from each mountain rift,
Where Andes and Cordilleras their awful summits lift,
Where Cotopaxi's fiery eye glares redly upon heaven,
And Chimborazo's shattered peak the upper sky has riven, —
From mount to mount, from wave to wave, a wild and long lament,
A sob that shakes like her earthquakes the startled continent !

A light dies out, a life is sped — the hero's at whose word
The nations started as from sleep, and girded on the sword.
The victor of a hundred fields where blood was poured like rain,
And Freedom's loosened avalanche hurled down the hosts of Spain,
The eagle soul on Junin's slope who showed his shouting men
A grander sight than Balboa saw from wave-washed Darien,
As from the snows with battle red died out the sinking sun,
And broad and vast beneath him lay a world for freedom won.

How died that victor ? In the field with banners o'er him thrown,
With trumpets in his failing ear, by charging squadrons blown,
With scattered foemen flying fast and fearfully before him,
With shouts of triumph swelling round and brave men bending o'er
        him ?
Not on his fields of victory, nor in his council hall
The worn and sorrowing leader heard the inevitable call.
Alone he perished in the land he saved from slavery's ban,
Maligned and doubted and denied, a broken-hearted man !

Now let the New World's banners droop above the fallen chief,
And let the mountaineer's dark eyes be wet with tears of grief !
For slander's sting, for envy's hiss, for friendship hatred grown,
Can funeral pomp, and tolling bell, and priestly mass atone ? —
Better to leave unmourned the dead than wrong men while they
        live ;
What if the strong man failed or erred, could not his own forgive ?
O people freed by him, repent above your hero's bier :
The sole resource of late remorse is now his tomb to rear !

WHAT OF THE DAY?

THIS poem, written in 1857, **four years before the** outbreak of the **Civil War,** seems to foreshadow **the** terrible **contest then** impending. Its powerful imagery and **its prophetic** tone attracted **general** attention ; and, now that its fulfilment has been witnessed, its repetition in this volume has been asked for by **many** of the **author's** friends.

A sound of tumult troubles **all the air,**
  Like the low thunders of a sultry sky
Far-rolling ere the downright lightnings glare ;
  The hills blaze red with warnings ; foes draw nigh,
  Treading the dark with challenge and reply.
Behold the burden of the prophet's vision, —
The gathering hosts, — the Valley of Decision,
  Dusk with the wings of eagles wheeling o'er.
Day of the Lord, of darkness and not light !
  It breaks in thunder and the whirlwind's roar !
Even so, Father ! Let thy will **be done,** —
Turn and o'erturn, end what thou hast begun
In judgment or in mercy : as for me,
If but the least and frailest, let me be
Evermore numbered with the truly free
Who find thy **service perfect liberty !**
I fain would thank thee that my mortal life
  Has reached the hour (albeit through care **and pain)**
When Good and Evil, as for final strife,
  Close dim and vast on Armageddon's plain ;
And Michael and his angels once again
  Drive howling back the Spirits of the Night.
O for the faith to read the signs aright
And, from the angle of thy perfect sight,
  See Truth's white banner floating on before ;

And the Good Cause, despite of venal friends,
  And base expedients, move to noble ends ;
See Peace with Freedom make the Time amends,
And, through its cloud of dust, to threshing-floor
  Flailed by the thunder, heaped with chaffless grain !

WHAT THE TRAVELLER SAID AT SUN

[From the " New York Independent," May 17, 1883.]

THE shadows grow and deepen round me ;
  I feel the dew-fall in the air ;
The muezzin of the darkening thicket
  I hear the night-thrush call to prayer.

The evening wind is sad with farewells,
  And loving hands unclasp from mine :
Alone I go to meet the darkness
  Across an awful boundary-line.

As from the lighted hearths behind me
  I pass with slow, reluctant feet,
What waits me in the land of strangeness ?
  What face shall smile, what voice shall greet ?

What space shall awe, what brightness blind me ?
  What thunder roll of music stun ?
What vast processions sweep before me
  Of shapes unknown beneath the sun ?

I shrink from unaccustomed glory,
  I dread the myriad-voicéd strain ;
Give me the unforgotten faces,
  And let my lost ones speak again.

He will not chide my mortal yearning
  Who is our Brother and our Friend,
In whose full life divine and human
  The heavenly and the earthly blend.

Mine be the joy of soul-communion,
  The sense of spiritual strength **renewed,**
The reverence for the pure and holy,
  The dear delight **of** doing good.

No fitting ear is mine to listen
  An endless anthem's rise and fall ;
No curious eye is mine to measure
  The pearl gate and the jasper wall.

For love must needs be more than knowledge :
  What matter if I never know
Why Aldebaran's star is ruddy
  And warmer Sirius white as snow !

Forgive my human words, O Father !
  I go Thy larger truth to prove ;
Thy mercy shall transcend my longing :
  I seek but love, and Thou art Love !

I go to find my lost and mourned for
  Safe in Thy sheltering goodness still,
And all that hope and faith foreshadow
  Made perfect in Thy holy will !

LIST OF WHITTIER'S WRITINGS.

INDEX.

www.ingramcontent.com/pod-product-compliance
Lightning Source LLC
Chambersburg PA
CBHW020859130726
47900CB00014B/1144